THE SCATHING

THE SCATHING

KING'S BANE

C. R. MAY

COPYRIGHT

ISBN-10: 1547238518
ISBN-13: 978-1547238514

The Scathing is for Ioan
ychydig tywysog Cymreig

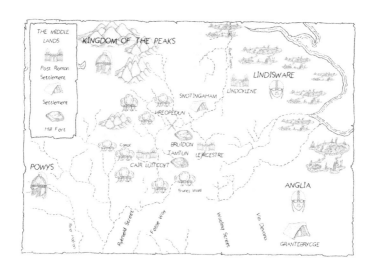

THE MIDDLE
LANDS

Post Roman
Settlement

Settlement

Hill Fort

KINGDOM OF THE PEAKS

SNOTINGAHAM

HREOPEDUN

LINDISWARE

LINDCYLENE

BRUIDON
IAMTUN   LEIRCESTRE
Conoc
CAIR LUITCOYT

Gumes Wald

POWYS

ANGLIA

River Hafren

Ryknield Street

Fosse Way

Watling Street

Via Devana

GRANTEBRYCGE

GLOSSARY

Cantrefs - A lord's personal bodyguard. The Brito-Welsh equivalent to the English hearth troop.

Duguth – Doughty men, veteran fighters.

Ealdorman – A provincial governor.

Eorle – A hero.

Fiend – The enemy.

Folctoga – A leader in war, the ancient English equivalent to a General or Field Marshal.

Gesith– The king's closest companions, a bodyguard.

Guda – A male priest/holy man.

Scegth – A light warship.

Scop – A poet/word smith, usually itinerant.

Snaca – Snake, a larger warship, forerunner of the later Viking period dragon ship, the *'Drakkar'*.

Thegn – A nobleman with military obligations.

Wyrd - Fate.

In this year pagans came from Germany and occupied East Anglia, that is the region which became known as the kingdom of England, some of whom invaded Mercia and fought many battles with the British; but, since their leaders were many, their names are missing.

Flores Historiarum. 527AD

1

'So, this is it then Huwel. Your last days of freedom.'

The rider shared a look and a smirk with his companions as the horses walked on. The harsh screech of a badger call floated across the lea, away to the east the moon had risen to sheen the southern hills. Owain added his voice to that of his friend. 'It sounds like even old Broch is telling you to keep riding, boy. Sensible animal the badger. Not given to hasty decisions.'

Huwel snorted, turning his head to flash them a grin. 'That must be why they live in a dampish hole and eat slugs and the like. Where is the sense in that?' He chuckled along with the rest as a ripple of laughter rolled around the group. Their hearts were as light as the mood as the long journey neared its end, the metallic thrum of horse shoes unnaturally loud in the still airs of the evening. The Briton shook his head in wonder, his voice trailing away as his thoughts turned to home. 'She's the one,' he said as his companions exchanged knowing smiles. 'Always has been: sturdy, she is. You know,' he continued with a dreamy smile. 'My Branwen can carry two sheep up the hillside, one under each arm, and come straight back down for more.'

'I seen that,' a voice piped up from the gloom. 'So, you are telling me now that all that hair I saw sprouting from her armpits was not her own?'

Huwel ignored the jibe. The men were his friends and neighbours, they knew the bond between the pair was stronger than iron, always had been, ever since the days not so long ago when they had all romped together defending the old hill fort atop Mam Tor from imaginary invaders. The carefree days of childhood were behind them now and the spearmen of Powys were pressing down on the little kingdom of The Peaks for real. Now they had the bodies of men and the responsibilities which went with them. Still they had been heady days, the best he now realised, and the memory caused a flutter of happiness within him as his mind drifted back over the years.

Ahead the long grey line of irregular sets, polished smooth by the footfalls of centuries, rose slightly as it neared the dark outline of the earthwork they had sweated to repair last summer as the first attacks had harrowed the land. The moon had risen enough now to pick out the place where the old Roman roadway, storm grey and arrow straight, cut through the dyke on its way to the head of the valley and the fort which was to be their home for the next few weeks. Huwel allowed himself a smile of satisfaction as the good natured banter swirled around him. Handfast men were excused from militia duties unless the kingdom came under serious attack. The raids of late, both here in the south and in the north along the border with the kingdom of Elmet were little more than pinpricks. Let the others freeze their balls off staring into the dark, night after night. Be the last man to laugh and you laugh the longest, his old da used to say.

The column passed through the great earthwork, and spirits lifted as they entered the final few miles of their journey. Within the hour the walls of the fort came into view, the lime washed ramparts shining in their nighttime brilliance.

Cair Luit Coyt stood perched on its bluff above the river, the brooding sentinel straddling Watling Street as it had ever since the walls had echoed to the hobnailed sandals of the Empire's legions, and conversations trailed away as thoughts turned to a hot meal and a warm bed. High above ragged clouds moved away to the east, the torn edges haloed silver as the moon cast its wan light upon the earth. The end of their trek in plain sight, the little war troop instinctively put back their heels and increased the pace.

The tumbledown walls of the old Roman town of Letocetum stood off to one side, the timeworn remains testament to the years of strife which had plagued the borderlands over the course of the previous centuries, and Huwel saw to his surprise that men were moving among them. At the head of the column Cadwr had seen it too, and Huwel snorted at his leader's caution as he raised an arm, slowing his mount to a walk as he ran his eyes over the strangers. A voice carried from the rear as the men there peered ahead to see the cause of the sudden drop in pace. 'The boys we are relieving are coming out to meet us, all friendly like, Cadwr. Anyone would think that they were eager to be away.'

To Huwel's surprise the big warrior, usually so jovial despite the militiamen's unsoldierly ways ignored the comment, and he sensed the first feelings of unease spreading through the group at the change in their leader's demeanour. As the horses slowed the riders instinctively bunched together, hands moving from rein to spear shaft as they exchanged worried glances. With a squeeze of his knees Huwel urged his mount alongside the tough veteran.

'Who do you think they are, Cadwr?'

The big man raised his chin and pointed along the valley. 'That may well be a welcoming party lad, but not the kind we were expecting.'

Huwel looked up ahead. Horsemen were beginning to emerge onto the roadway, the pale moonlight reflecting dully from helm and spear blade as they came. He cast a look at his leader as the others caught the mood and moved forward to fill the width of the track. 'Men of Powys?'

Cadwr gave a curt nod. 'That is my guess.' As shields were hefted and spears couched, he raised his voice to carry. 'It looks like we are going to have to fight our way through, boys. Keep together, hit them hard and keep riding. If you break through, don't stop. Take the road east and make your way back home as best you can.'

Owain looked along the line, all the earlier mirth driven from the shepherd as the seriousness of their situation became obvious. 'What about the men in the fort? They will see us approaching, won't they make a sally to help us through?'

Cadwr cast a look at Huwel as he answered for him. 'Dead men can't mount attacks, Owain.'

'What about moving back to the Grey Bank? We can hold them at the earthwork, that's what we laboured all last summer for. There's a ditch in front and a palisade on top. All we would have to do is throw a line of shields across and block the roadway.'

Cadwr shook his head sadly. 'It's too late for that, Owain. There are horsemen behind us already.'

The men in the group craned their necks as one, peering back along the ancient stones before turning back with sullen expressions as they saw that their leader was right.

'Remember,' he said as the Powys' horsemen began to fan out into a skirmish line to bar the road ahead. 'Go in full tilt.

Stick to the road if you can and form a wedge on me. Hit hard and ride hard.' He gave them a final smile of encouragement as the horses picked up the change in mood, tossing their heads and skittering excitedly.

'Time is against us boys,' he cried, 'and there will be none left over for rescues. If a man goes down, leave him; he will be as good as dead already. Hit them hard,' he smiled savagely, 'and you will live to see your loved ones again.'

Lupine howls cut the night air as the men of The Peaks dug in their heels, urged their mounts forward and hunkered down into their shields. Huwel kept pace with his leader as the group picked up speed, raising his eyes to search the gloom as the tide of horseflesh thundered on. A hundred yards to go and the Powys' horsemen were still hurrying to form their wall, and Huwel felt the first surge of hope build within him as he realised that Cadwr's plan could work. If they could hit the enemy before their defences were complete their own horses would find a way through, barging horsemen and spearmen aside in an irresistible tide. The enemy quickly grew to fill the youth's vision, and a heartbeat later the peace of the valley was shattered as men and animals came together in a bone jarring crash. Cadwr's horse was bred and trained for battle and it knew its work; snaking this way and that it carved a path through the Powys' barricade as Huwel clung on in its wake. Pale columns flashed by, as white as old bones in the moonlight, and Huwel knew that they had broken through to the ruined walls of the old Roman mansio and bath-houses.

Several spearmen were gathered at the entrance to the old stone bridge, craning their necks to see the cause of the commotion which had drawn them from their watch fires, but the pair were past them and clattering across before the guards had time to react. As they gained the eastern bank the

men of The Peaks could see for the first time that the meadow
on the far side of the stream was a field of light, a hundred
campfires mirroring the star speckled sky above. Made overconfident by their numbers the invaders had left the way
clear, and Cadwr led Huwel eastwards along the old stone
sets of Watling Street itself as they plunged back into
darkness.

Out beyond the campfires the dome of Oak Hill domi-
nated the skyline, the crown of trees which had lent the
mound its name painted white by the ascendant moon, and
soon they were leaving the ancient road behind them as
Cadwr took a dusty track towards the lower slopes. Within a
mile they had breasted a grassy knoll and Cadwr drew rein,
hauling his mount around as he peered back to the west.
Breathless after the ride Huwel came up, but all sense of
elation at their escape was driven from him as he saw the
concern still etched on the big man's face.

'What's wrong?'

Cadwr spat in disgust. 'There are riders following, that's
why we left the road. I had hoped to give them the slip but it
would seem that they are determined to nab us.'

Huwel's face lit up as a thought came to him. 'They could
be our boys? They may have got through!'

'No,' Cadwr replied with a sour look which crushed the
younger man's hopes, 'they are not. Come on lad,' he said
sadly. 'There is only one thing for it.'

Before Huwel could question him further Cadwr had
hauled the head of his mount back to the east, the big warrior
urging the horse onwards as the clatter of hoofbeats carried to
them on the wind. A mile further on a spur of land came
down to pinch the path and Cadwr raised a hand to slow his
friend as he slid to the ground. Huwel curbed his own mount,
looking across in surprise as the great ribcage of his horse

moved like bellows beneath him. The warrior recognised the militiaman's confusion and explained. 'We can't outrun them, our horses have been travelling all day, theirs are fresh. Our only hope was that they would prefer the delights of the fire-side to puncturing our sorry hides. Take yourself off,' he said with a jerk of his head as he unhooked his shield from the crupper. 'Follow the valley of the River Mease northwards and tell Sawyl Penuchel what you have seen. You saw the size of the army of Powys, the people in The Peaks need to know what is happening down here as soon as they can if they are to stand any chance of surviving the onslaught.'

Huwel made to argue, but the worries of the ride finally caught up with the man and Cadwr cut him dead. 'Get away boy and do as I say.' Huwel's face fell, and Cadwr regretted his tone instantly, throwing the youth a paternal smile as he explained his reasoning. 'God gave us all a task to perform in life and the means to do it. He made me a warrior, to bring light where before there was only darkness,' he said as a look of pride came into his features. 'And I was good at it, He will be pleased. He had other plans for you Huwel, plans involving a strong woman and a hut knee deep in little ones I am thinking. Now, get yourself away from here and let me do God's work. Powys' horsemen hold no fear for me, lovelorn shepherdesses scare me shitless!'

Huwel smiled despite the grimness of the moment, and a nod came as he saw the sense in the big man's decision. He hauled at his reins as the clatter of hooves grew louder in their ears, turning to fix the warrior's face in his memory. 'I will name a son in your honour, Cadwr,' he said proudly as the warrior bestrode the track and drew his sword. 'May the good Lord receive your soul.'

'GOOD HIT!' A covey of rooks rose into the cool spring air, the shrill clamour building as they gave voice to their outrage at the act. Wihta laughed, clapping his son on the shoulder as the dog bounded away. Swinna beamed at the praise as he fished inside the bag for another pebble. 'It's just a matter of practice, father,' he said with a self depreciating shrug. 'You could have done just as well.'

Withta laughed again. Modesty was the least of the boy's virtues. Fourteen winters had passed by in a flash, he would have to give more thought to a wife for the lad. 'You know full well that I would have been lucky to hit the tree from this distance. I never could master the sling. How many is that now: three?'

Swinna slid his foot across, lifting the edge of the leather sack with the toe of his boot to reveal the broken bodies within. 'Five, including that one.'

'That's enough, then. Take them back to your mother and sister when the dog gets back, I am going up to the top field to check on your brother. That ploughing needs to be completed today, one of Gwynfor's boys will be here in the morning to take the ox away.'

Giving his son an affectionate pat on the shoulder, the Engle started back up the slope as the air about him echoed to the cawing of angry birds. Wihta's mind wandered as he paced the hillside. The spring sunshine fell upon his face as he left the shadow of the trees, and he allowed himself a smile of contentment as he found that the warmth reflected his mood. Treading the dewy grass he considered his life and found that it was good. The gods had blessed him with two strong sons and a daughter of elfin beauty, a sturdy wife and a smallholding which served to fill their bellies more often than not. True, he mused, he had had to hack the fields from the ancient greenwood and build a hall where none had ever stood before, but he had been a young man then, newlywed, and his own father, neighbours and friends had pitched in to help set the couple on their way.

Wihta paused as he gained the track, turning back to survey his land. The wildwood still crowded in on all sides, but he had three fields now, enough to rotate the crops. Roots, swede and turnip in one, barley in the next and a third left fallow, perfect for the half dozen sheep which produced milk and cheese all year round with a gods-given bonus of woollen fleece each spring and dung to feed the soil. The surrounding woodland, oak, hazel and wych elm were perfect mast for the swine which he shared with his neighbour, the meadow yonder a short flight for the bees which filled his hive.

Gwynfor was more than a neighbour, he was a good friend, and it had been the Briton's idea that they pool their resources to invest in the shared ownership of an ox. Thræls, the more usual form of labour at plough time, were often more trouble than they were worth on the fringes of the English settlements, the slaves prone to make a break for freedom, stealing hard to replace items and sometimes killing their owners. He had seen with his own eyes what had happened to one family, down in the vale, and although a hue and cry had been quickly raised and the culprit tracked down and drowned in the mere like all murderers, with the trackless backwoods of Canoc and Brunes Wald within a few days walk it had still not put off the most determined among them.

He was about to turn away when another note carried to him on the breeze, higher in tone, and Wihta felt a kick of anxiety in his guts as he recognised the shrill war horn for what it was. His eyes were fixed now on the point where the track from the south exited the tree line and within moments a horse, its flanks heaving and foam lathered, clattered into view. Wihta was walking towards the red faced rider before he realised that he had moved, and the man he now recognised as Edwin from past musters hauled at the reins and brought the horse to a halt before him.

'There are raiders in the vale,' he blurted out as Wihta held out a hand to calm the mount. 'Everyone is to arm and gather at the oak as soon as they can.'

'How many are there?'

Edwin pulled a pained smile as he began to turn the head of his mount back towards the track. 'More than enough to spoil your day, Wihta. Join the fyrd at the thunder oak, but leave a few spears for your boys, they may have need of them soon.'

As the rider put back his heels and cantered away to spread the alarm Wihta started back to the hall, forcing down the almost overwhelming desire to run. The situation seemed bad, desperate maybe, but the eyes of his family would be upon him and he knew that he had to set an example to them.

Ebba was already at the doorway as he crossed the yard, the knife which she had been using held forgotten in her hand as she watched his approach. Wihta threw his wife what he hoped was a reassuring smile as he grew near, but he could see from her expression that she was not to be so easily fooled. Anyone who had spent their entire life on the frontier knew what the war horn signalled, and he allowed himself a snort of pride as he saw that his daughter was already fixing the bridle to Arthur. His share of the spoils from a previous raid and named after the old British warlord, everyone had thought that the choice was amusing at the time, and a small part of him hoped that they would still be laughing when the sun dipped that evening.

'The Powys' are in the vale,' he offered as he reached the doorway. 'Fetch my spears.'

Wihta ducked into the hall, throwing off his work clothes

as he began to rummage in the settle. Slipping into his best blue breeks, he was wriggling into his leather war shirt as Swinna reached the hall and held him with his gaze. 'I am coming too, father. I am ready and we will need all the spearmen we have.' His thoughts whirled as he used his busyness to mask his indecision. The boy had been training at the moot hall for a year or more now. Spear work, shield work, he had learnt quickly how to act in the wall and obey orders without question. He had a right to go, but who would protect the family with both men away?

The reply had left his mouth before he really had time to think, but the look on his son's face told him that it was the right one. 'Dress and arm, quickly.'

As the boy scurried away he looked up with a frown. 'Where are my winingas, the gold ones?'

Ebba was there, and she shook her head as she replied. 'They are in your hand. Here,' she said as she moved forward. 'Let me tie them.'

Wihta sat back and drew a breath, collecting his thoughts as she knelt before him and began to wind the leg ties around his calves. He watched her as she worked, crisscrossing the golden tapes before tying them off just below the knee. She was a good wife, strong and open handed, popular within the valley and a faultless mother. Her body had filled out a little since the children came, but the strands of silver which lined her hair matched his own and he realised that the shared triumphs and tragedies of the years had almost made them one. Of all the hard earned trappings of wealth which surrounded him, Ebba and the children were the most precious of all.

A shadow fell across him and he looked up to see that Swinna stood ready, spear and shield in hand, his chin raised proudly as his younger siblings looked on. Wihta stood and took his own great war board down from its place upon the wall. 'Ready?'

Without waiting for a reply, the Engle strode purposefully away, past the smouldering hearth which had witnessed so many happy moments and out into the weak spring sunshine. Arthur stood ready, and he hooked his toughened leather war cap and shield into place on the crupper as he hauled himself up into the saddle. Swinna was alongside him, and Wihta held out a hand to help the boy leap up onto the horse's rump.

Ebba had gained the yard and she led the younger children across as Wihta took up the reins and bent low. 'Take yourselves off into the woods until we return.' She made to argue but the words were stillborn as she saw the look on his face and it became plain that this was no ordinary raid, a few young hotheads out to drive away a handful of sheep and cows to prove their manhood and impress the girls back home. She placed a hand upon his thigh as the seriousness of the situation which faced them sunk in, and Wihta moved his own down to give it a small squeeze. The younger children had recognised the action for what it was, and Wihta flashed them a smile of reassurance, tousling the boy's hair and throwing his daughter a wink. 'Look after your mother,' he said. 'We will be back before you all know it.'

With a click of his tongue they were away, the horse quickly exiting the yard to clatter onto the roadway. Guiding the mount southwards the sunny clearing which contained all that he held dear was soon behind him, and the horse increased its pace to a canter as it plunged into the shadows. It was a little shy of three miles to the lightning ravaged oak, and he had already covered half the distance before the horse could break sweat.

Lost in his thoughts, the horsemen were almost upon him before he had time to react.

The red dragon of Powys snaked above the pair and he felt Swinna throw a steadying arm around him as he snatched at the reins and desperately turned back. All things being equal he still had enough of a head start to regain the farm before he was overtaken, but he soon realised to his consternation that things were far from that. His horse was bred for plough and cart, no war horse, and the chasing riders were gaining with every step taken.

They had only travelled half the distance back to the farm when he felt his son slide from the back of the horse as the foemen came up and he prepared to sell his life dearly. A moment of indecision and Wihta was at his side, father and son exchanging a last look as their shields came together with a clatter.

2

A flash of movement, flint grey and menacing, and it was gone. The men gripped their spears a little tighter as they sensed the death-spirits begin to seep forth from the shadows, gathering about the little group as they came to claim their prize. Hemming exhaled in wonder. 'There he is: big bastard too.' The duguth licked his thumb, running the pad along the edge of his spear blade as the corners of his mouth turned up into a wicked smile. 'Not too big to spit though, especially after the runaround he has given us all night.'

The early morning sun was slanting in from the east as the hunters moved into a skirmish line and fanned out to either side, the paling light from the brand each man carried throwing long shadows inland.

Eofer ran his eyes along the flanks of the headland to the north and was gratified to see that the others were already in position, a line of leather capped men moving down to close the trap beneath their own blooms of light. He looked to either side, motioning with the point of his spear that the wing men move around to complete the encirclement. The thegn shot his duguth a happy smile. Despite the weariness which came from a night in the saddle, hunting really was the finest of sports. 'Come on,' he said as he slipped from his mount with a hasty look seaward. 'Let's get this done. It will be fully light soon and I could use an early breakfast.'

Eofer scanned the rise ahead, unbuckling Gleaming from its baldric as he did so. The broken ground before him rose to a shield-like dome. Scrubby bushes of gorse and heather littered the lower slopes, while at its high point the crest was marked by a hoary old birch, the skeletal limbs stark outlines against a rapidly lightening sky. He handed the ancient blade to Finn for safekeeping. Despite the words which the scops and poets trilled as they gladdened the hall with flowery prose, sword work required room; there would be none in the scrub ahead, and the scabbard could very well upend him when he faced the cornered animal.

Hemming arrived at his side, rolling his shoulders for the spear work to come. 'Ready, lord?'

A curt nod and a wink. 'Let's finish it.'

Hemming drifted a spear length to the right as the pair set off. The sandy soil was loose and broken after the dry weather which had gone before, and they placed their feet with care as they ghosted the shadows. The apex of the hillock was small, almost barrow-like, little more than a hummock in the rolling landscape which folk called the Sandlings, and the men moved into a fighting crouch as the gorse began to thin.

The first rays of the sun broke free of the earth's rim at that moment, turning the outline of the tree before them into a fiery hand as they reached the foot of the final incline and halted, horror-struck at the sight which met them.

.   .   .

EOFER GATHERED the men around him and swept them with his gaze. 'Remember,' he said. 'Return to your villages and spread the word. The old wolf is not to be touched. Any man, woman or child who so much as denies the animal its cravings will pay with their life.'

The men shifted uncomfortably, but a murmur of agreement left them all the same. Most of the locals were Engles like himself, but Eofer knew that there was a fair smattering of other people added to the mix; Swæfe, Frisians, even a few who still counted themselves as Britons, despite their English speech and the passage of time since their own rulers had died out or been driven westwards by the new folk who had begun to pour into Anglia generations before. He knew that these men would find his order the hardest to accept, and he made a point of pinning them with a stare until they made eye contact and nodded their acceptance. Whether they clung to their mistaken beliefs or not, any Christ men would follow the ways of their new lords or pay the price.

As the men sought out kin and neighbours for the homeward trek, Eofer risked a light brush of the seat of his trews as his hearth warriors moved among the beaters with food for their journey. Hemming caught his eye and threw him a sympathetic look. 'Can you ride?'

Eofer shook his head, running his fingertips lightly across the bloody punctures which had lacerated his buttock as he stifled a laugh. The shock was beginning to wear off now and he was beginning to see the humour in the moment. The corners of his mouth turned upwards into a smile as he attempted to move the flap of material back to cover his nakedness. 'No, I am bloody walking!'

The reply finally broke the tension of the morning and the pair, thegn and duguth, chuckled like carefree young lads despite the weariness of a nightlong chase. Hemming ambled across, tugging at the reins of his mount as he did so. 'Well it looks like it's going to be a fine morning for a walk, Eofer,' he said with a smile. 'I think that I will join you.'

The pair set off back to the south as the hunting party dispersed hither and yon. As Eofer's hearth men took up their own reins and fell in behind the pair, Hemming spoke again. 'He may have been an old grey muzzle, but he could still move like lightning.' Eofer nodded agreement as the pathway dipped down into a grassy bowl and curved away towards home. The pair instinctively glanced across their shoulders, back towards the lonely rise with its crowning birch. Despite the distance, Hemming lowered his voice as he returned his gaze. 'You have looked into his eye before, Eofer, at the symbel back in Engeln. Do you think that it could have been him?'

'Who can say? Woden can appear in many guises. A one eyed wolf though?' Eofer gave a shrug. 'I wasn't about to take the chance.' He pursed his lips as another stab of pain shot through him. 'Besides, he didn't seem in the mood to talk whether he was the god or not. I know what he was not though,' he continued with a grimace. 'The ghost of some old British brigand.' He threw Hemming a look of amusement. 'What was the name were they muttering back there? They looked like they were in more pain than I was when we described it to them.'

'Blæcce shucca, the black demon. He was sacrificed by Engles at a place just south of here called the Haugh, a few years back. Before he died he cursed the English, and the ceorls say that soon after a monstrous dog-like troll appeared in Anglia, huge and shaggy, as black as pitch. He haunts the byways and heathland about the Sandlings and, although he howls and growls like a regular wolf, his footfall leaves no sound. You may scoff, lord,' he added as he saw Eofer's look of amusement. 'But I have met a man who has seen him and lived to tell the tale.' Eofer raised a brow and his eyes twinkled. 'It wouldn't be one of your drinking partners from Friston by any chance, would it?'

'No...well, yes,' he replied defensively. 'Sort of. He is Frisian but he lives over near Saimund's Ham. *And,* he said that Snarly yowl, which is what the Fris call him, only had one eye which shone like a fiery garnet.' Eofer winced as they scrambled up a short slope and gained the lip of the gully. 'Well next time you see your friend, you can tell him from me that Snarly yowl makes up for his lack of an eye with the sharpness of his fangs!'

'That's not all though, lord,' Hemming added earnestly. Eofer caught the concern in his old friend's voice and was surprised to see that he was fingering the hammer pendant at his neck. 'Well?' he said, 'spit it out. Whatever it is I doubt that it will feel as bad as having a wolf chew on your arse, so my day can only get better.' Hemming pursed his lips. 'The ceorls say that whenever shucca appears to someone, either they or a member of their close family dies that year.'

The land rose again as the pathway arced away towards Snæpe, and the pair paused as the tawny ridge-line of Eofer's hall came into view in the distance. Eofer gave his weorthman a look of pity. 'That was no fell-wraith, Thrush. You would know that if your arse had more holes than a straw whistle.' He raised his gaze and let out a weary sigh. 'It looks like we have company too, that's just what we needed today. Let us hope that it is nobody important.'

A smear of dust on the road told the pair that a rider was approaching, but they soon exchanged a smile as they recognised that the horse carried Osbeorn. Eofer's duguth had been left back at the hall along with the majority of Eofer's hearth men; there had been no sign of hostility from the

Wulfing lands just across the river but it always paid to be sure. If his man had left his duty of care the mystery visitors were sure to be friendly and in all likelihood carrying important news. Eofer felt the old familiar kick of excitement at the nearness of action. If the messengers *were* carrying the war-sword, the small wooden call to arms which English king's back beyond the time of Offa the Great had sent out to muster the army, it could not have come at a better time. Despite the fact that his backside felt as if it had been used as a pin cushion by a giantess, at least it would get him away from the more mundane duties of lordship. If he had to rule on whether a boundary marker had been moved a few feet or a sheep rustled one more time it would be once too many.

The dust cloud paled and cleared away to the south in the light airs as the horseman veered from the road. Within a short time Osbeorn was waving a greeting, and the party paused on the fore slope as they awaited his arrival.

The rider slowed to a halt, and Eofer exchanged a look with Hemming as he noticed the seriousness of his duguth's expression. Osbeorn dismounted and threw them a questioning look as Eofer twisted to show why they were all walking their mounts. 'I got bitten on the arse by a wolf. And yes,' he added as the big man's face creased into a grin, 'before you ask, it does hurt.'

Eofer nodded back towards the hall. At his back the sun was a hand's breadth above the horizon, the day already hot. A drowsy hum came from the grassland which led up to the coastal road as crickets, roaches and horsefly basked in the heat of a perfect spring morning. 'Go on,' he said. 'Tell me the worst.'

Osbeorn took a peek behind his lord and smirked. 'Apart from that you mean.' He made an o with his lips in mock sympathy as those following on shared a chuckle. 'Wealhtheow is here, lord, with a party of Wulfings.'

Eofer pulled a face as he sought to place the name. 'The Danish queen, old King Hygelac's wife?'

Osbeorn nodded. 'The very same, the mother of young Hrothmund, the Dane who we rescued from the clutches of his wicked uncle. King Hrothulf let her return to her own people with her daughter.' He gave a shrug. 'She did raise him as her own after his father was killed after all. Not that it did her a lot of good. Anyway, she has come bearing handsome gifts, although,' he said, with another look at his lord's shredded breeks, 'she probably could have timed it better, considering what they are.'

'Yes, well,' Eofer replied with a sigh of disappointment. 'If we have exalted guests to entertain, it's best that we get home as quickly as possible.' Osbeorn caught the meaning immediately and knelt beside his lord, making a cup with his hands. Eofer hauled himself up onto his mount and lowered himself gingerly into the saddle as the men of his troop exchanged sly smirks of amusement at his discomfort.

Hemming had noticed Eofer's despondency and shot him a sympathetic smile. 'No war-sword this time eh, lord?'

They shared a chuckle at the transparency of his emotions as Osbeorn fell back to question the others about the mad wolf, and Hemming continued as the rest of the hunting party mounted their own steeds and fell into line.

'Astrid will be loving that, lord,' he said. 'It's not everyday that a queen comes calling.'

Eofer rolled his eyes. 'Good for her.'

Hemming cleared his throat as Eofer squirmed in the saddle, desperately attempting to find a comfortable position as the horse picked its way down the slope. 'She's still a bit tetchy then?'

Eofer nodded.

'About the fact that you are still a thegn?'

'It's something which she will have to get used to,' he snapped as the discomfort shortened his temper. 'I am not ready to be tied to hearth and hall, I want to be free to carry my sword wherever I please.'

They shared a look, and Eofer snorted. Both men knew that it was enough of an apology for the ill tempered reply and the duguth ploughed on. 'You did tell her that king Eomær had pressed you to accept your father's old ealdormanship though?'

Eofer let out a bitter laugh. 'No, that would only make matters worse between us. At the moment Astrid is laying most of the blame for my lowly status on the king's shoulders. If she knew the truth…' He let the conclusion hang in the air as they gained the ridge top roadway and guided their mounts along the track which led to the hall.

Hemming probed again. If his lord was troubled it was his duty as both friend and weorthman to help in any way that he could. 'And this has all worsened since her brother became king of Geats?'

'Well yes,' Eofer sighed. 'But it was becoming a problem even earlier than that. You have to understand that Astrid never expected her immediate family to come so close to the king helm. At the time she was married off to me it must have seemed a good match to her father, Hygelac. Although his own father was king of Geats, he had two elder brothers who stood between him and the kingship when the old man eventually died. But the gods, as they say, are fickle. Suddenly, within a year they were all dead, Hygelac was king and Astrid was no longer content to be the wife of an English thegn. That was bad enough, but then her father goes off and gets himself killed in Frankland and Heardred, her brother, is now king.'

Hemming drew in a breath as the ramifications of Astrid's meteoric rise through the ranks of Geatish nobility began to dawn upon him. 'And with Heardred childless, for now at least, that makes her sons, your sons, the next in line to the Geatish king helm.'

Eofer flicked him a meaningful look as Hemming's mind worked through the ramifications. Hemming set his face into a scowl, and Eofer knew that his duguth had reached the same conclusion which he too had reached over the winter months, as the warmth between Astrid and himself had cooled with the season and he had set to thinking during the long nights. 'So you think that she is already plotting to have you replaced with a far loftier husband? The son of a lowly English thegn is unlikely to attract many swords to his banner.'

Eofer shrugged. 'Could be.'

'And the boys?' Hemming asked, fearful of the reply. 'Weohstan is already in the care of her brother.'

'Would be in her way if she intended to remarry after I meet with my unfortunate accident. You saw what happened in Dane Land last year. Young lads who get in the way of women who think they deserve better often meet with accidents of their own. It's not like her family find such a thing unthinkable. Hythcyn, the second brother 'accidentally' killed his older sibling during a hunt. Then their father, king Hrethel, died in his care. Following that of course,' he added with a look, 'he was hunted down himself by his younger brother Hygelac and his English allies. You will recall that of course Hemming,' he said. 'We were there.'

Hemming nodded. 'At Ravenswood. We got there too late and the king of Swedes had beaten us to it. Not that it did

King Ongentheow any good either,' he said, allowing himself a brief wolfish smile despite the gloomy conversation. 'He too fell beneath the sword of a certain Englishman the following morning, a man who earned himself the title king's bane by the killing. But,' he continued, 'surely you are getting carried away, Eofer? Heardred was brought up in your father's household when he was at foster. It's no exaggeration to say that without your family's support and protection, neither Hygelac nor Heardred would ever have become king. It was only a few years ago that we,' he paused and looked across to add emphasis to his words, 'by we I mean you, his kinsman, appeared from nowhere to save him from the vengeance of a Frankish fleet off Frisia. That must count for something?'

Eofer snorted and threw his weorthman a sympathetic look. 'You underestimate the power of the king helm old friend, it's a madness that creeps up on folk without them even realising. I have seen with my own eyes how it changes people. They start to look at the world as if peering down a dark tunnel, all they see is the glittering prize at the end, beckoning them onward, until nothing else matters but to have it for their own. You have to understand,' he said, 'the Geats are in a weak position at home. A large part of their army was destroyed along with King Hygelac in Frankland. Their greatest ally, us, has migrated across the sea, just as a bloodletting among their powerful neighbours, the Danes *and* the Swedes, has installed energetic new kings. Not only do such kings like to start off their reign with a handy victory or two, especially if they have usurped the king helm, but, thanks in part to us, the Geats have become host to renegade princes from both nations.'

Hemming pursed his lips and nodded sadly as the reality of the situation dawned upon him. 'So, even if the Geats give up these æthelings they will still need to form an alliance with one or other of their neighbours, if only to dissuade the other from attacking them.'

Eofer fixed him with a stare. 'Neither the Swedes nor the Danes happen to have a spare princess of the right age at the moment, so King Heardred can't sacrifice himself on the grisly alter of marriage on behalf of his kingdom. Which leaves Astrid as the only marriageable member of the Geatish royal house who could be used to forge an alliance.'

A cry of acclamation drew their eyes ahead, and both men saw to their surprise that they were almost home. Eofer hauled at his reins as the dusty pathway which led to the hall came abreast of the riders, and he was pleased to see that the men of his hearth troop were armed and alert. Friendly or not, foreign men were on his land and it paid to prepare for treachery, however unlikely that seemed.

Eofer dismounted as the women came through the doorway, lowering himself painfully to the ground at their approach. Tall, distinguished and handsomely dressed in a sable dress which set off the darkness of her hair, Wealhtheow beamed as she approached. 'Ealdorman Eofer,' she began brightly. 'I have brought gifts which I hope that you will find acceptable, however inadequately they express my gratitude at the saving of my son's life.'

Eofer caught a glimpse of Hemming wincing at his side at the mistake which the visitor had made in his rank. At Wealhtheow's side Astrid was flushing at the description, and it was all that Eofer could do to push down the laugh which built within him as her mouth puckered in anger. Eofer returned the smile as the queen came forward, oblivious to the tension which her innocent mistake had caused in those around her. Things were rapidly going from bad to worse between them, but Eofer pushed the cares aside. He would deal with the fall-out from the slip tomorrow, this night was made for drinking.

'Is the prince here?' Eofer replied as he led the women back towards the hall. He shot Hemming a wicked look. 'I know that my lads would love to match him cup for cup. Men who have stood shoulder to shoulder at the clash of shields share a unique brotherhood.' The trio had reached the doorway, and the women stepped aside to allow the lord of the hall to enter first as was right. A quick glance was all that was needed for Astrid to flush with embarrassment at the sight of her husband's bare arse on show for all to see, and she moved across to cover his nakedness as best she could. Wealhtheow averted her eyes, hiding her smile with a hand as Astrid hissed. 'We need to talk, tomorrow when they have gone.'

Eofer felt himself die a little inside at the words but, to his joy the chance never came. In the morning, as the Wulfings took their leave nursing sore heads and bearing fine gifts of their own back across the River Aldu and the first of the wandering birds returned to slash the blue sky above, the warsword finally arrived.

3

A heartfelt cheer broke the peace of the glade as the riders exchanged weary smiles. 'It looks like we have arrived then, lord.'

Eofer threw his weorthman a smile as Finn waited for them on the lip of the rise, the width of the youth's smile all the confirmation that they required. 'It's about time too,' he replied. 'I don't think that my teeth could have taken much more rye bread.'

Hemming gave a snort and rolled his eyes. 'That's because you grew up the privileged son of an ealdorman.' He pulled a face and shrugged as Eofer's eyes widened at his frankness. 'Well, it is true lord. Most of the lads here will have lived on the same, especially at this time of the year. Early summer can be the hardest time for the common folk. The grain bins contain little more than husks and dry stalks and the trees and hedgerows are empty of fruit, nuts and berries. Snaring a rabbit can get the family through a few more days.' He cast a look into the darkness of the forest which hemmed them in as he spoke. 'Especially out here in the borderlands where it might be unsafe to wander. The silver which you paid them for their hospitality will get the families through to the harvest with a bit left over. The gods smiled on them the day that a thegn of their nation and his hearth troop appeared out of the blue.'

Eofer nodded that he understood. 'Well, they will be seeing a lot more English warriors out here now the people are settled in Anglia. Now that Icel has moved out here with his own hearth troop, our settlers can begin to push further north and west. They can hunt deer in the greenwood and flash their perfect teeth in safety,' he quipped as they finally crested the rise. The pair reined in as they came alongside Finn, and they shared a grin as their eyes followed the line of the Via Devana, the old paved road which arrowed across the island of Britain from the Saxon settlements around Colnecestre to the South, to the distant city of Deva near the great seas to the West.

A week earlier they had picked up the ancient road at the English settlement of Grantebrycge. Hacked out of the great wood the Engle now called Brunes Wald and paved by the army of Rome centuries before the old route, though unkempt and failing in places, was still the swiftest way to reach the new settlements on the frontier.

The group ran their eyes over the town of Ratae for the first time as they waited for the column to close up. Nestling against the eastern bank of the River Leir, the town lay cloaked beneath a blanket of smoke as fires were lit and food prepared for the evening to come. The high stone walls which encompassed the town glowed pink in the light of the westering sun, and Eofer raised his gaze to take in the marshy valley floor and the distant tree line which marked the continuation of the great forest. On the high point the white dragon of Anglia snaked in the light airs alongside the raven battle banner of king Eomær's son, while capping it all a swirl of crows circled as they spied out easy pickings in the town below. 'Let's get down there,' he said as the men of his own hearth troop crested the rise, 'and find out why the ætheling has sent for us. I can't wait to see his face when we deliver our gift to him.'

Hemming twisted in the saddle and looked back along the column. 'Sure, he will be overjoyed to see them,' he said. 'It's a long walk to the western sea. Fifty of the finest geldings, true war horses,' he breathed. 'And to think that Eadward wanted to throw him off the *Hwælspere*.'

They shared a smile as their minds drifted back to that spring morning. The Danish prince, Hrothmund Hrothgarson, had sought sanctuary on the English ship but the forces of the new king of Daneland were chasing him down. They had had to abandon the warship in Scania to save the Dane from his cousin's huscarls but the young man's mother, Wealhtheow, was aware of the pressing need for war horses in the new Anglian kingdom and had repaid the debt and more besides.

All eyes in the column were upon him as they waited for the order to move down into the valley, and Eofer called his banner man across as he sought to put on a show. 'Grimwulf, raise my herebeacn. Let them know that we have arrived.' The youth unfastened the travel bindings, shaking out the battle flag before raising it into the evening air and falling into place behind his lord. The banner shone as the waning sunlight caught the scarlet and golden threads, and Eofer led them proudly into the vale as the rest of the column, their destination in sight, made a final effort to reach their goal after a hard day on the road.

Eofer flicked a look at Hemming as folk straightened their backs in the surrounding fields to watch the arrival of the famous eorle, the man who had slain a king on the field of battle, the same man who had burnt the hall of their greatest enemy on its mound. 'How do you think that Osbeorn and the lads have got on, eating dust all day?' Hemming's mouth widened into a grin, and he let out a chuckle as the first of the wagons waddled down the slope like a line of fat ducks. 'He'll be looking to wash that dust from his throat, lord, and eat whatever is going.'

Eofer snorted. 'And he won't be alone in that.'

They had begun to gather a tail of settlers as soon as they had passed through the fleama dyke and picked up the Via Devana. Once past Grantebrycge English settlements became as rare as hens teeth as the resurgent greenwood threatened to swallow up the work of men. It was perfect country for wolf heads, outlaws, lordless men who lived off the hard work of others, and Eofer had been happy to shepherd them to safety despite the delay it would cause. Britons were known to harry the English settlers, fast moving war bands coming up from the South and west to kill and burn, rustling the cattle and sheep on which the new territories depended. Warriors were here now in numbers, but, unable to carry horses across the sea they had been sacrificed wholesale to the gods before the people had left old Engeln. With Icel looking to build a kingdom for himself in the West he would need settlers to fill those lands and horse thegns to protect them. Besides, Eofer knew, the sight of playful children had lifted the spirits of his own men, something they needed after the death of Rand the previous autumn and Spearhafoc's painful banishment.

The light dimmed suddenly as the great gatehouse of the town obscured the sun, and Eofer was brought back from his thoughts as they came up on Ratae's burial ground. He shook his head in agreement as he saw Hemming instinctively touch his fingertips to the hammer which hung at his throat.

'What do they call these places?'

'A necropolis, lord.'

Eofer nodded, but could not suppress a slight shiver as he did so. He had seen many of these necropoleis, here in Britain and in Frankia, but he knew that he would never see them as anything other than an alien imposition on the northern lands, however long his life thread ran. The houses of the dead ran the length of the road, from the city gate almost to the foot of the hill down which they had just travelled. Small structures resembling the homes of the living, their grandeur reflecting the wealth and importance of the occupant in life. Large and small, some were colonnaded in the style of the Romans while others looked to have incorporated more native elements. Eofer held a grudging respect for the ones which had done so. To retain a sense of nationhood, a distinct other- ness, even through centuries of occupation was a thing of worth. Other grave markers, less elaborate than the ornate columns and inscribed markers nearer the road, marked the final resting place of Rome's less distinguished citizens; the graves becoming plainer, chased wood replacing chiselled stone, until they petered out completely.

Hemming spoke again, shaking his head as the horses plodded on. 'It's not decent, treating your dead as if they are still living. Folk should be buried away from settlements, lords and kings in their barrow, commoners cremated and interred in urns. All this,' he said with a sweep of his arm. 'It's all a bit, well, spooky.'

He was interrupted by a cry from above, and the pair raised their eyes to see the face of Icel grinning down at them from the gatehouse. 'Eofer's here,' he cried out as the men flanking him chuckled happily. 'And look what he has brought us. War can't be far away!' Eofer allowed himself a snort of his own at the sight of his prince. Known by the nickname of Haystack on account of his unruly blond mop, the king's son radiated good humour like heat from a winter hearth. The ætheling's mood was infectious, and Eofer sensed the cares of the journey and the lingering discomfort of a wolf-bitten arse melt away like smoke on the wind as those around him echoed the smiles.

Icel disappeared as Eofer passed smiling spearmen and crossed the threshold into the fortress, the sound of hooves echoing loudly in the space. Icel's outline appeared in a doorway and he cried out as he bounded across. 'Welcome to Leircestre. What took you so long?'

Eofer slipped from his saddle, pushing down the desire to kneed life and feeling into his aching buttocks as he dipped his head in supplication. 'We picked up a few waifs and strays along the way, lord. Farming folk eager for land.'

'Well, land is what we have and settlers are what we need.' He looked across to Eofer's weorthman and nodded a greeting: 'Thrush.'

Hemming beamed at the familiarity, as Octa led the first of Wealhtheow's gift horses through the gateway and into the city. Icel's eyes shone with delight at the sight, and the little group walked across as Octa corralled the herd in the shadow of the great stone wall. 'These are beautiful, Eofer,' the ætheling breathed. 'Where did you get them?'

'They were a gift from my neighbours, lord.'

Icel's eyes opened in surprise. 'The Wulfings send you war horses? Have they a death wish?'

Eofer and Hemming shared a chuckle. 'It's a long story, a debt handsomely repaid. I will explain later, lord. I thought that you could find a use for them so I brought them along.'

Icel whistled softly as he ran an appreciative hand down the flank of the nearest horse. 'This is just what we need, Eofer,' he replied. 'You have my thanks.' He turned back with a smile. 'I daresay that your lads could do with a drink or three to celebrate the end of the journey?' He indicated an oak framed building with a flick of his head. Like the majority of the buildings which Eofer could see, the squat building was well past its prime. Nestling against the foot of the city walls, the peeling plaster and moss covered thatch might have looked uninviting, but the sounds which drifted over from within caused a smile of recognition to play across his features.

'They have what the Romans called a taverna to greet weary travellers. Leave the rest of the troop there and I will show you two the English city of Leircestre.' The tail end of the column was just entering the archway as Hemming turned to spread the good news among his companions. Eofer threw Icel a look as the pair walked away from the harsh clatter of iron rimmed wheels on stone. 'That's the second time that you have called the town Leircestre. I thought that this place was called Ratae?' Icel shook his head. 'Not any more. This is English land and it deserves an English name. The river is called the Leir and this was a Roman army town, so it's a cestre to us. Everywhere I go I am going to sweep away the old and replace it with the new.' He gave Eofer a nudge as Hemming rejoined them. 'Here, like this.'

A pedlar was hawking his wares along the main thorough-fare which led into the centre of the settlement, and Icel called across to gain his attention. The man looked horrified to have been singled out by so exalted a person as the son of the king, but Icel smiled to ease his worries as they ambled across. 'How goes your day?' The man had the startled look of a thief caught in the act, but he whipped off his leather cap as he attempted to answer the unexpected question. Eofer suppressed a smile at the sight of the man's discomfort. Not everyone knew of the ætheling's good nature, and he could only begin to imagine the thoughts which were swirling around the pedlar's mind. The colour had drained from the unfortunate man's cheeks, but he answered his lord as well as he could manage. 'The day goes well, lord. I have made enough now to travel home on the morrow.'

Icel raised a brow. 'And where is this place that you call home?'

'On the far side of the River Trenta, lord.'

Icel beamed. 'You live on the far bank?'

'Yes, lord.'

'Then you are the type of man I need in my new kingdom, a man unafraid to push my borders outwards and settle new lands. And does this place have a name?'

'I don't know what the Romans called it, lord,' the man admitted with a shrug, 'but the local British call it Tigguocobauc.'

Icel pulled a face. 'Tigg what?'

'Tigguocobauc, lord. It means the place of caves.'

'You speak Welsh then?'

'Have to lord,' the man admitted as Icel's natural charm lowered his defences and he risked a wry smile. 'I would have to speak to myself most days if I didn't. If a man wants to trade, he has to be able to talk to all sorts. There's not many Engles to be found on the far bank of the Trenta.'

Icel nodded. 'We shall be seeing what we can do to change that situation very soon,' he smiled. 'At least you will have neighbours with pronounceable names. And what do folk call you, friend?'

'Snota, lord.'

Eofer and Hemming had a good idea of what Icel had in mind, and the pair exchanged a look of amusement as they watched the ætheling's shoulders sag. Icel cleared his throat as he attempted to hide his disappointment.

'Your name is Snota?'

'Yes, lord, Snota, that's me. Everyone around Tigguo-cobauc knows old Snota. I come from a long line of Snota's. There's always been a Snota in my family, always will be.'

Icel could sense the smiles forming on Eofer and Hemming as Snota rambled on about his lineage, and he dared not look their way as he forged ahead with his plan.

'Snota,' he said as the man looked at his lord expectantly. 'I am going to send spearmen back with you tomorrow. When you reach this Tigg...place, I want you to tell the inhabitants that they are the subjects of the Anglian ætheling, Icel, and that they now live in Snotingaham, Snota's home.'

Snota gaped in shock before gabbling his thanks, but Icel held up a hand to stop him. 'Snota, you are just the type of man I need in my new kingdom, think nothing of it. Travel safely and spread the word to everyman you meet that these are English lands now.'

Snota's face shone with pride as Icel moved away, Eofer and Thrush Hemming following on, stifling their own laughter as they passed the slack jawed pedlar. As the trio moved towards the centre of town the ætheling shook his head in wonder. 'Of all the men to pick. Still,' he consoled himself, 'I daresay that the thegn will change it to something a bit less snotty as soon as I appoint one.' He shot the pair a wicked smile. 'I can't imagine that anyone in their right mind would want to live in a place called Snotingaham.'

A short walk brought them to the central area of the newly renamed English town of Leircestre, and Icel paused as the central marketplace opened up before them. 'This used to be what the Romans called the forum, but as you can see it's looking a bit ramshackle. Most of the civic buildings were destroyed by fire years ago; it's been cleared and used as a marketplace ever since. Eofer looked at the open space. Cattle

34

were corralled at the far corner in a makeshift pen, sloshing about ankle deep in dung. The animals lowed mournfully as night came on, and several were eating from wide feed bins attached to a massive wall of dun coloured stones set within decorative brickwork. Tall arches built within the masonry hinted at a past magnificence. Folk were packing away their wares, and the first of the night watchmen were firing up their braziers in readiness for the long hours of darkness to come.

Icel motioned ahead as the flag of Anglia was lowered on its staff. 'The roads of the town cross here and lead to the four gates, one in the centre of each wall. The road which carried you here goes ahead to the river and the crossing place there. The other road which crosses the marketplace from north-east to south-west is the Fosse Way which runs from the country of the Lindisware down to the southern coast at a place called Isca.'

Eofer glanced across at the mention of the northern people. 'Have the Lindisware replied to King Eomær's demand for tribute yet?'

Icel pulled a pained smile. 'Unfortunately, yes. They have offered something in return for their fealty. Someone called Creoda is styling himself king up there.' He shrugged as if it was of little consequence. 'He can be a king if he wants, as long as he recognises the overlordship of the line of Offa and pays his dues.' He blew out as he worried at his beard. 'They want to bind our agreement with a marriage.'

Eofer let out a gasp of delight as he realised the price of the alliance. 'Icel Eomæring, great-grandson of Offa the Great, the hammer of the Myrgings. You are being traded for a herd of horses!'

Icel winced. 'Thank you for your concern, but yes, a cruel man could describe my immediate future thus.' He raised an eyebrow and Eofer laughed at the mischief he saw there.

'Still,' the ætheling added hopefully as he rediscovered his natural sense of optimism and wit. 'She could be a beauty!'

Eofer grinned. 'Or a bloater!'

They shared a laugh, and the ætheling shook his head. 'Thanks again for your kind words of support. I feel much better about the whole thing now.'

The pair walked on, prince and thegn at ease in each other's company. Icel shrugged his shoulders. 'It's of little consequence. An ætheling is raised to understand that wives are for alliance building and producing heirs, there are always other women available for fun.'

Eofer pulled a face as he realised with a start that Icel's explanation had perfectly described the way that his own wife's mind must now be working. He pushed down the feeling and changed the subject as he sought to keep the conversation lighthearted.

'So, you are pushing across the Trenta then?'

Icel shook his head. 'It's a bit more delicate than that, Eofer. This is not an unsettled island you know, other folk already claim those lands as their own.' He snorted and gave his thegn a look of amusement. 'At least they try to when you are not around! There have been folk drifting in from the west for a week or so claiming that an army from Powys has crossed the great belt of woodland called Canoc. I had best ensure that my flank is secure first.'

'So you want me to lead the men to the far bank?'

Icel gave a snort at the eorle's keenness. 'No, not yet,' he laughed. 'You are getting ahead of us king's bane, we need to consolidate our hold on the south bank before we move northwards. But,' he added as he walked, 'there is truth in your words. Those lands will fall to us in time.' He plucked at Eofer's sleeve as the accompanying spearmen cleared a path through the throng. 'There is someone who I would like you to meet, a Briton of high birth; tonight when we are at our cups. But first,' he said with an enigmatic smile, 'let me show you why I have led you this way. It is a thing which I stumbled across quite by accident, something which I know you have been looking for these past few months, without even realising that you were.'

4

Osbeorn puckered his mouth, kneading his belly as he pointed to the empty plate. Icel had caught the look, and he laughed along with his thegn as he tossed a bone to a waiting hound. Leaning forward he spoke across Eofer to the Briton at his side. 'That's not necessarily a good indication of the quality of food on offer, there's very little that Eofer's duguth will not eat and enjoy. But,' he said, as he struggled to make his voice heard over the hubbub in the hall, 'in this instance he has my support. That was some of the finest lamb which I have ever had the pleasure to eat.'

Ceretic ap Cynfawr, legate to Sawyl Penuchel, king of The Peaks, dipped his head in recognition of the compliment. 'It is very kind of you to say so ætheling,' he replied. 'But any thanks should be directed towards the cook. My kingdom produces the finest lamb in Britain, but it still takes a man with Urien's skill with herbs and sauces to produce a dish fit for the son of King Eomær.'

The Engles shared a look of amusement at the go-between's flowery praise as Icel rose and clapped Eofer on the shoulder. 'Ceretic you do your office well, you shall have your alliance. For now enjoy the entertainments of my hall as a small repayment for the magnificence of this meal while I walk with my thegn.'

The Briton beamed at the news that his mission to the barbarian prince had been successful. His king would be pleased, despite the disquiet felt among many of his ministers that English warriors could soon be moving among them. Where spearmen went settlers were never far behind, but the pressure bearing down on the little kingdom from its neighbours was becoming intolerable and the alliance was the only way to keep even a degree of independence before their naked ambition. The fortress of Cair Luit Coyt had fallen after a short siege, and the army of Powys were sweeping all before them as they advanced along the valley of the River Trenta. With the British kingdom of Elmet raiding her border to the north the hilly kingdom was desperate for allies: even pagan barbarians.

Although he had hidden the fact during the negotiations, Icel knew that the Engles themselves were little better placed to see out the onslaught. Survivors from the westernmost settlements had carried tales of slaughter and rapine to Leircestre, a life of slavery the best that any man, woman or child of English race could hope for once the army of Powys reached them. The stark truth was that the English settlers around the Trenta faced annihilation. If Icel could not find help, his dream of carving a kingdom from the middle lands would remain just that, a dream.

The pair hesitated at the door, chuckling to themselves as they watched the warriors torment a long-suffering entertainer. As jugglers went this one was not too bad, but the ale had worked its magic and the drinkers had their own entertainments in mind. As Eofer and Icel watched, a lamb bone spun through the air to neatly take out a spinning sword blade and, his concentration shot, the warriors roared with laughter as a shower of blades rained down about the juggler's head.

As the bone thrower rose to receive the acclamation of the hall, Icel shook his head sadly. 'Jugglers: throwing things up in the air and catching them. What possesses a man to spend his life doing such a thing?'

They ducked outside, and the ætheling held up a hand to let the spearmen guarding the doorway know that they wished to be alone. As Icel spoke with the men, Eofer raised his chin and ran his eyes across the night sky. The vault was clear, the air still as the ætheling ambled across, and Eofer marvelled for the thousandth time at the whiteness of the moon. 'It's funny to think,' he said as Icel came up. 'That the same moonlight bathes the old country, even as we walk here.'

Icel pursed his lips. 'Shining on the bones of our horses,' he replied with a sigh before lowering his eyes. 'And other bones, noble bones, the remains of the best of us.'

Eofer gave a slight nod in recognition of the compliment his family was being paid. It had been over a year now since he had left his father at the head of the ghost army, arrayed across the hillside outside the remains of Sleyswic. He shook his head in disbelief. 'There will be Danes there now,' he said, the pain still evident in his tone. 'Danes living in Engeln.'

As Eofer's voice trailed away, Icel laid a hand upon his shoulder. 'It was a noble end, a death fit for a *foltoga* of the Engles. For myself I will say to you now that I would live my life in happiness, if I but knew that such an end awaited me. But the old country is in the past, what's done is done. There is no going back for us now.' He looked at Eofer and set his expression as he glanced back across his shoulder. Satisfied that the guards were out of earshot he continued. 'That's part of why I wanted us to speak alone. I realise that we could not have carried our horses *and* people across the German Sea in our hulls, but if our new neighbours realise just how desperate for mounts we really are, we may very well find that we are back in Anglia defending the fleama dyke. You are one of my most trusted men, Eofer, and I want to share with you my plans for the coming campaigning season.'

Eofer widened his eyes in surprise. 'So, I am not going to The Peaks then?' Icel shook his head. 'Not yet, not this year anyway. I will send what few spearmen I can spare up there of course, just enough to keep the kingdom from falling, but I think that you will agree we have more pressing matters here in the south.'

The thegn's expression darkened. 'Cynlas Goch and the men of Powys? I have only heard snippets of information about what is happening in the west since I arrived here, and none of it seemed particularly good. How bad is it really?'

'Now that we have a few more horses we may be able to slow their progress on this side of the Trenta,' Icel replied. 'Hopefully long enough for us to organise a counterattack later in the summer. Otherwise...' He shrugged as he let the thegn draw his own conclusion.

Eofer nodded thoughtfully as the size of the fight ahead became obvious for the first time. 'How far away are they?'

Icel nodded to the west. 'The nearest are only twenty miles or so from the place where we are standing, beyond that wood. There is another valley on the other side which has been settled by Engles who call themselves the Tamsætan, the Tame Settlers, after the name of the river there. Whether they are already on their way to the west in chains or lie in their graves is anybody's guess.'

Eofer looked sidelong, keen to gauge the ætheling's reaction to his following statement. 'Ceretic seemed to think that this king of Powys fancies himself as the next Arthur, the Bear Man who unites the British kingdoms against us.'

Icel snorted. 'I doubt that will be the case, we are much stronger here now. They may yet frustrate our plans in the middle lands, but they will never recover Anglia itself. Fortunately for us it takes an exceptional leader to overcome the traditional rivalries and hatreds among the British kingdoms, not every generation supplies such a man.' He smiled triumphantly. 'Three Arthurs is enough for one island. Even the Saxons down south attempted to claim overlordship of Britain but it will never last longer than the warlord who creates it.'

'Aelle, you mean?'

Icel shrugged. 'He termed himself *Bretwalda*, wide ruler, but nobody north of the River Tamesas took much notice. It will be the same with this Cynlas Goch, the British don't take too kindly to being given orders by folk far away, especially when they demand tribute be sent abroad year after year.'

A wave of noise washed over the pair as a door opened, and a flash of honey coloured light gilded the ground at their feet. Icel plucked at his thegn's sleeve, guiding him to one side as they looked away to the west. The bone white line of the old Roman Road shone dully in the moonlight as it crossed the valley side and was swallowed by the darkness of the Wolds. Eofer was the first to break the silence.

'And that street leads there?'

Icel nodded. 'Indirectly: that's why I need to leave you and your men here while I head north.'

'Then you are leading us up the Trenta Valley to confront them when you return?'

'If I manage to get enough horses,' the ætheling replied with a frown. 'I am going to visit the Lindisware to see my lovely bride. Apparently the wolds there are ideal for horse breeding. If I can get more mounts than already promised to me, either as part of a dowry or tribute, I will. Thankfully you brought a few with you,' he joked, 'or I would be walking.' The ætheling turned to face the eorle, and Eofer was troubled to see concern come into his lord's features as he spoke again. 'If this king of Powys does attack us here at Leircestre before we are ready Eofer the town will fall, and the luckiest among the English settlers hereabouts will find themselves on the way to the slave market in Frankland. That's why I sent for you, I need a man that I can trust with such a responsibility.'

THE SHARP RAP of bare knuckles on wood told Eofer that it was time, and the eorle cast his eyes around the small room as his vision began to blur. Opposite him Osbeorn was leaning forward, clutching at air and laughing like a halfwit as he attempted to grasp the handle of the ladle and refill his cup. The strong mead had woven its spell, the little group more than merry, and the giddiness which indicated that the Allfather had entered their minds held them firmly in its grip. It was time for the next part of the ritual, and Eofer screwed up his face as he took in the details of the stone tablet set into the wall above his head.

They were seated within a mithraeum, a temple dedicated to the god Mithras. The deity had been avidly worshipped by the soldiers of Rome in days gone by, but it could only have been the fact that the tiny shrine had been concealed beneath a much larger building which had saved it from the cleansing zeal of the Christians who had taken over the Empire more than a century before. An old Welshman had described the details of the religion to Eofer at the start of the evening as Icel had thrashed out the terms of the deal with Ceretic ap Cynfawr, and he had agreed with the ætheling's view; the place was ideal for the ceremony which he knew he had delayed for far too long.

The image depicted the god tussling with a bull, and the Engle recalled the words of the aged Briton as his drink fuddled mind took in the details. Mithras had hunted the sacred bull until, exhausted, he had dragged it into a cave for slaughter. Gripping the bull by the nostrils, Mithras was tugging the animal's head back as he prepared to stab at its throat with a short dagger. Other details swam into focus, strange to him but powerful all the same as were all gods-images. A dog and a snake are licking at the blood which poured from the bull's wound, and a strange otherworldly creature with crab-like claws and a curved dagger for a tail is attacking the animal's genitals. Mithras looks at the sun as he strikes down the bull as if in sacrifice, and the moon is being drawn away on a cart in much the same way that it travelled the heavens in his own gods-tales.

The scene explained why the temple was built under-ground, it was obvious even to a man of the North that the room represented the cave in the image, the fading and time-worn blue paint which covered the ceiling a representation of the sky. The floor of the room was obscured by the debris and grime of a century of disuse, but the facing panels of the twin benches which lined the walls still carried images of naked spearmen and a winged man with a monstrous head.

Faces were turned his way, and the eorle swilled the last of the honeyed drink before he drained the dregs, tossing the cup to the floor as he slid from the bench. The others followed his actions, and the rowdiness drained away with the drink as Eofer's duguth composed themselves for the ritual to come.

The initiates, Finn and Horsa, mirrored the warriors on the temple reliefs, each man naked save from his wide belt and baldric, the empty scabbard a sign of the gift to come. The pair slipped their helms upon their heads as they approached the doorway, exchanging a look of determination as they tightened the straps and ascended the steps.

The cool of the evening was a balm to the mead-giddy men as they left the fug of the temple and climbed into the slanting light above. Ahead of them three of Icel's gesith were surrounding the dark outline of a bull, its heaving flanks blushed scarlet by the light of the returning sun. As Finn and Horsa walked forward the warriors hauled on ropes looped around the great neck of the beast, dragging it forward and down until its front legs gave way under the strain and the animal fell to its knees.

The third gesith stepped forward to offer a seax to the pair, and Finn took the short sword as Horsa lowered himself onto the bull's shoulder. As Eofer and his doughty men looked on Horsa reached forward, hooking his fingers into the animal's nostrils to haul the great head skywards with a grunt of effort. In an echo of the scene on the tablet in its underground vault, Finn stepped in to open the beast's throat in a hot rush of blood as the power of the moment crackled the air.

Finn exchanged a look with his fellow initiate, and Eofer recognised the moment they became of one mind. The younger man continued cutting, working the razor sharp blade back and forth as Horsa tightened his grip, and as the beast's eyes rolled back and its legs kicked out in its final moments, Horsa wrenched the great head from the neck in a torrent of blood. The bull's body spasmed as the severed head was held aloft to steam in the cool morning air, and Finn rose to stand beside his new brother as the gory trophy was turned towards the dawn.

A cry rolled around the ruins as the warriors hailed the

spirit of the sacrifice, and Finn moved down to open the chest of the bull, reaching inside to draw its great heart out into the light. As he held the bloody organ forward towards his lord, Eofer dipped his head, tearing a mouthful before they all moved in to take a bite of their own. The great heart was passed from man to man, reddening beards and chests as they retraced their steps for the culmination of the ceremony.

Back in the mithraeum Eofer took his place on the gift stool. At his place, beneath the watching eye of the Persian god, the thegn lowered his own grim helm onto his head as he prepared to add the pair to the ranks of his most trusted warriors.

Horsa came forward first, kneeling before his chosen lord as his brothers looked on. Thrush Hemming moved to his lord's side, holding out a silver chalice as Eofer drew Gleaming and made a cut. Octa and Osbeorn came forward to repeat the action with their own blades, each man making a fist to squeeze the lifeblood from his palm into the bowl before them.

Eofer turned his gaze back onto the figure kneeling before him.

'Horsa, I offer you a place at my hearth as a doughty man, a trusted duguth. Become a brother in blood to those around you, hold their lives dearer to your heart than your own as you step forward together to the place of slaughter, where file-hardened spears stab from fists, grim darts fly forth, bows sing and shields resound in the bitter clash of war. Pledge, here before us all, never to leave the field before your ring giver, whether he lives and fights on or lies fallen in grim battle-play. Is it in your heart to accept this offer?'

Horsa raised his head to look at his lord, the weight of the moment heavy in his expression.

'I so pledge, lord.'

Eofer took up a sword from his lap, holding it forward with both hands as Horsa moved his own up to grip the silvered blade. Despite the reverence of the moment, Eofer heard the soft intake of breath as the surprised duguth recognised the sword before him. He had heard the tale of Imma Gold's death, fighting heroically between the armies at the place in Juteland known as The Crossing. The duguth's sacrifice that day had bought the beleaguered English force enough time to withstand the Jutish onslaught, saving the lives of his lord and brothers until Icel's relieving army had arrived to win the day.

Eofer spoke again. 'Accept Fame-Bright, renowned blade: bear it forward with pride.'

Horsa took the blade and moved back. As he did so, Eofer slipped a golden arm ring from his forearm and slid the hoop onto Gleaming's wide blade. Horsa moved the tip of Fame-Bright forward until the sword points came together, and the hushed room echoed to the sound of gold grating on steel as the ring slid from thegn to duguth. Sheathing the sword Horsa moved forward to place his hands on Eofer's knee, laying his forehead there as his lord's hands came to rest upon them.

Horsa's part in the ceremony had reached its conclusion, and his new brothers boomed their acclamation, beating out a staccato thrum on the dusty floor with the heel of their spears. Finn moved forward to take the oath, and soon the ritual was completed.

Eofer drank deeply from the chalice containing the broth of bloody mead as backs were slapped and grins split beards all around. As the vessel was passed from man to man and the latest additions to his blood-brotherhood were acclaimed by their peers, Eofer settled back and watched the revelry with a look of satisfaction.

Imma Gold would be a tough act to follow, but Horsa's

amiable exterior hid a core of iron. Already an experienced warrior, the man had suffered the miseries of surviving his lord and hearth mates and would be in no hurry to repeat the sense of shame which accompanied it.

Finn had shown bravery, steadfastness and cunning during the fighting in Daneland and the chase through Scania. He had all the makings of a fine duguth, and Eofer was certain that he would blossom under the ongoing tutelage of his new brothers.

The chalice had been drained, the initiations completed as Eofer led his men back out into the bright light of dawn. A deep hole had been dug outside the doorway and the men clustered around as he took up the bull head by the horns and made the final dedication.

Tiw, the war god, would be pleased by the additions to his doughty men Eofer reflected as the thing was lowered into the earth.

After the conversations of the previous evening it seemed certain that they would be fighting again, and soon.

5

Leaning on the parapet of the city wall, the men watched as the column wound its way northwards, climbed the valley side and disappeared from view. Eofer and Hemming shared a grin. 'Thank the gods. I thought that they would never leave!'

The pair turned back, resting their backs against the ancient stonework as their eyes took in the town below them. An area had been cleared and a new settlement was rising from the ruins of the old, the thatch of the roofs a golden bronze against the darker background, smoke-blackened from the fire which had destroyed the area around the old forum in the days of their grandfather's grandfather. In the far corner a tumbledown tower showed the remains of a Christian church, stark against the lightening skyline like a giant hollow tooth, its worshippers long gone to heaven or hell. The first wagons were entering by the gate below them, and the thegn indicated that they take the stairway as bovine lowing and the smell of sweat and dung drifted up to them from the cattle on their way to slaughter in the town. 'Come on,' Eofer said with a flick of his head, 'let's go and meet this Briton of Osbeorn's. If he can help us, he is about to become a rich man.'

The pair descended the steps, the clack clack of their footsteps echoing back from the stone wall as they went. 'Do you think that we can do it, lord?'

Eofer nodded. 'The gods have always been with us before Thrush, and the guda says that the signs are clear. They crave disorder, if only for their entertainment. Icel said that he had men out shadowing the Powys army who would give us ample warning if they got too close to Leircestre.'

Hemming snorted and cocked a brow. 'That will not help much if we are not here to receive the message though.'

Eofer flashed a wicked grin. 'You must be getting old, Thrush. I can leave you here if you want.'

'Just you try!'

Eofer hopped across a puddle as they reached the ground level and looked back. 'Which way?'

'They will be in The Tewdwr, lord.'

'The ale house next to the main gate?'

Hemming nodded as he skirted the muddy pool. 'That's the one, the lads have got their own bench there. The food is hearty and plentiful and the ale is strong and dark.'

'Who found it?'

A twinkle entered Hemming's eye. 'Ozzy.'

'Pickled eggs?'

'They have now.'

They shared a laugh as they edged the town wall. Up ahead the cattle had cleared the archway and the spearmen were back at their station. Above them the early morning sun glinted on spearpoints as the guards in the tower, weary from the night watch, stared with red rimmed eyes back up the Via Devana, past the necropolis to the dark line of the woodlands beyond.

'So, tell me about this brigand. Can he be trusted?'

'Ioan?' Hemming shrugged. 'Probably not, but he's no fool. He knows that he would be the first to die if he led us into a trap.'

Eofer paused at the gate as Hemming crossed towards the taverna, exchanging a few lighthearted words with the guards before moving on. All fighting men whatever their rank had experienced the bone numbing boredom of the night watch, and the thegn knew that a few words from the king's bane, the new commander of the town now that the ætheling was away, would add a little pep to their stride as they awaited the longed for relief. Hemming was waiting at the entrance and Eofer shook his head in amusement as he came up. 'Sounds busy.'

The big duguth threw a reply over his shoulder as he pushed the door open. 'Always is on market day, lord. Once the livestock are safely in their pens the drovers hightail it over here to wash the road dust from their throats and fill their bellies. The men who have furthest to travel will not reach the town until midmorning. That gives the early birds the chance to grab the best tables.'

Eofer watched as Hemming took a pace inside the dimly lit room, his hand moving to the handle of the short seax at his waist as he scanned the room for any sign of danger. Satisfied that it was safe for his lord to enter he moved further in, stepping to one side with a smile and a flick of his head. 'There are our boys in the corner, lord.'

Eofer paused, sweeping the room with his gaze as he took in the scene before him. Wood scraped as his hearth men rose to their feet at the appearance of their ring giver, heads turning his way as men cut short their conversations to see the cause of the interruption. The room, Eofer could now see, was a large rectangle with a floor laid to flagstones surrounding a central hearth. Wispy sparks curled upwards as a log settled into the ash, the flames flaring before settling back to a dull red glow.

Along the far wall a heavy-set man with close-cropped crow-black hair above a clean shaven face paused just long enough to take in the new entrants. Recognising Eofer for who he was, the man left the girl to her duties and painted his face with a welcoming smile. Wiping his hands on a grimy cloth he bobbed his head as he came across. 'Welcome lord,' he beamed, 'your fame goes before you. You show me honour visiting my establishment.' He leaned in as close as his station in life allowed. 'Let myself or one of the girls know anything that you require,' he added, lowering his voice and thumbing his nose. 'If I don't have it here already, it's a fair bet that old Tewdwr knows a man who can get it in a trice.'

Eofer nodded his thanks as he made his way across. Osbeorn shuffled along the bench, clearing a space at the head of the table as they approached. 'Welcome, lord,' he said as a cup was produced and the first ale of the day flowed, 'to our favourite bolt-hole.'

The men grinned as Eofer took his place, sinking the ale with relish and holding out the cup for a refill. He ran his tongue across his lips, sucking in the froth from his moustache as he waited for the next cupful. 'So,' he asked as Osbeorn poured, 'where is this dodgy lad of yours?'

Osbeorn rolled his eyes upwards as the other members of Eofer's hearth troop exchanged knowing looks. A group of drinkers at the far end of the room were beating the table in time, and Eofer screwed up his face in question.

'You see those stairs built into the end wall, lord?'

Eofer looked across to a series of stone steps, the middle of their treads dished by the footfalls of men long since gone to the grave. Climbing upwards where his duguth had indicated the steps ended abruptly, to be replaced for the final few feet by roughly hewn blocks of wood which disappeared into the void of the roof above. Eofer saw for the first time that most of the upper level of the building had been removed at some time in the past and replaced by wattle and daub, the great roof beams blackened and scarred by fire long ago. They must, he decided, have been reused from the damaged buildings he had seen earlier with Icel in the central forum when the folk had begun to rebuild the city after the devastation. Osbeorn was continuing his explanation as Eofer's eyes were drawn upward. 'There is a room up there were the girls take their customers. It's right above that table, and the lads there think that it's great fun to bang the table in time with the drumming on the ceiling.' The rhythmic beat increased in speed and then finished with a final bang of fists against wood and the clatter of pewter drinking pots as the performance came to an abrupt end. As cheers and laughter filled the room, Osbeorn leaned in with a smirk. 'That will be our lad on his way now, lord.'

As if in confirmation, the heads of the drinkers turned upwards as a pair of tough leather boots appeared at the head of the staircase. Within moments the room was in uproar as the legs and body of the Welshman appeared, and Eofer studied the man as he acknowledged the cheers and catcalls with a wide smile. He had expected to find the rustler a gnarled old veteran, short and stocky and carrying the scars of a lifetime spent at his dangerous trade but, to his surprise, Eofer saw that the man before him was anything but. Not much older than his own new duguth, Finn, deep blue eyes peeked out beneath a mop of chestnut hair which contained just enough curl to attract the attention of the girls and keep it. His clothing, far from being the rough workaday greens and browns common in his line of work, were almost as fine as Eofer's own. Checked trews in the British style were topped by a shirt as blue as any midsummer sky, both items edged with golden braiding which sparkled in the gloom of the room. Eofer cursed. Far from blending in this Welshman was the life and soul of the place, he would have to bring his plans forward if they were to have any chance of success.

The men of Eofer's hearth troop picked up on the change in their lord's mood immediately, and Octa and Horsa rose from the table and led the others to the two tables nearest to their own. A quiet word with the drinkers there and Eofer's men were slipping into their places, both groups sent on their way with a pitcher of ale to compensate them for their trouble.

Safely out of earshot now, Osbeorn nodded in greeting as the newcomer dipped his head and Eofer indicated that the man join them at the table. 'This is Ioan, lord,' Osbeorn began. 'The man that I told Hemming about.'

If Eofer had been disappointed by the man's flamboyant entrance, he was pleased and thankful to see that the jovial look of moments earlier had been replaced by a more business-like mask as the Briton put away his public persona and got ready to talk. As Osbeorn slid a cup of ale across, Eofer came straight to the point. Only the gods knew what type of men were in the room, but he would be surprised if the army of Powys had not seeded the town with informants.

'Ozzy tells us that you can lead us to horses. Tell me where and how.'

Ioan sipped his drink and regarded them over the rim of the cup. Clearing his throat he replied with a nonchalant shrug. 'Sure, I can lead you to as fine a store of warhorses it has ever been my pleasure to see.' He took another sip of his ale, replacing the cup on the table with the confident air of a gambler who knew that he held the winning hand. 'But it will be dangerous,' he continued as he traced a pattern in the ale slops with a finger. 'Very dangerous. I value my life and that of my men, it would have to be worth my while.'

Eofer fought down a scowl. Haggling never came easy to him, but he needed the Welshman's help and the man knew it. 'I am not here to play games, Ioan. I want as many horses as I can get and I want them now.' He fixed the Briton with a stare. 'Tell me everything I need to know and you will receive a fair price for your information. Agree to lead us and I will treble that price.'

Ioan's gaze flicked from face to face as he pondered his answer. A quick look across his shoulder at the men of Eofer's hearth troop sat at the tables there finally convinced the Briton that these were as tough a group of men that he had ever had dealings with. 'I will tell you what I know using your English words for places where they exist to save any confusion. But I warn you now, I doubt that you will carry off more than a few of these horses. It would take an army to breach the walls which shelter them, and if you don't mind me saying lord I just watched a large part of your army head off over the ridge from Tewdwr's upper floor.'

Eofer had noticed Hemming struggling to contain his rising anger as the rustler negotiated, and he sympathised as his weorthman's patience finally snapped. 'Actually, he does mind you saying,' he growled, 'and so do I.' He flicked a look at Eofer and back again. 'This is the man who burned the king of Daneland's hall and cleaved the king of Swedeland's head in the clash of shields. Tell him what he needs to know and let him decide.'

Eofer held out a hand to calm his duguth as he pinned the Welshman with a look. 'Unless you describe this place to me I will not have the information which I need to make an informed decision. Which also means that you miss out, not only on a sackful of silver, but a tale which will keep you in ale for the rest of your days. And knowing my plans,' he added with a warning scowl, 'you would be very lucky if I only locked you up somewhere until the ætheling returned. It might just be easier to gut you now and have done with it.'

Ioan's features creased into a disarming smile. 'There will be no need for that lord, I think that we can do business. There is an old Roman fort a hard days ride from here known as Cair Luit Coyt, Fort Grey Wood in English. It stands at the junction of two Roman roads, the ones which the Engles and Saxons call Watling Street and Ryknield Street. Watling Street passes through the fortress before entering the forest of Canoc on its way to Cair Guricon, the main fortress in Powys itself. It is here that the army of Cynlas Goch have left the majority of their horses while they harry the valley of the Trenta.'

Eofer nodded. 'I have heard of this place. How many horses are we talking about?'

'I saw up to two hundred while I was there, but you will not take them all. They are corralled within the fort and the walls are high and stone built. But,' Ioan added, as the Englishmen exchanged looks of excitement and wonder at the numbers involved, 'the Powys' are relying on the strength of the defences to protect their mounts. Only a token force has been left to actually guard the place and that gives us a chance to dive in quick and cut a few out from the herd. War horses need to be exercised daily, and that needs an open space. Luckily for them, and us, there is such a space between the Cair and a stream which runs down to join the Trenta. I watched them while I was there,' he added wolfishly, 'and there were never more than half a dozen men guarding them.

A fast moving force of men such as your own would have no trouble driving a batch off.'

Ioan lowered his voice and levelled his speech to add weight to his next statement. 'Cynlas Goch is not here on a raid lord, he intends to stay.' He added a scowl of his own. 'You may think of we Britons as one people but we are many, just like the people that Hemming mentioned from your own past, the Danes and the Swedes. We may have once existed under the heel of Rome, but those days ended long ago. You should not expect the men of Powys to harbour anymore feelings of brotherliness with those of say, Dyfed, than *you* would towards any other Germans. Believe me,' he said, 'there is no love lost between this tyrant and his neighbours. All of what you would call the Welsh kingdoms which border Powys have suffered from his armies. I and most of my men are from Gwent in the south and a couple are from Cair Gloui, but the thing which unites us all is our shared hatred of Powys. We know what it is to have Powys as a neighbour, bitter experience tells us that they have an insatiable appetite for gold and land. The majority of Cynlas Goch's army is moving slowly forward on foot, accompanied by workmen and carts laden with building materials, refortifying the old strongpoints as they go. As I said, this is a war of conquest, lord, no lightning raid. Believe me when I say that they mean to stay.'

A rectangle of light cut the floor as the door was pushed inwards, and a babble of excited voices drew the thegn's attention away from their conversation as another group of thirsty drovers ducked into the taverna. He looked around the room once again. Ioan was a known rustler and the place was filling up fast as the morning advanced and men drifted in. Eofer realised that if this dream was to become reality, he would have to move as quickly as possible. Cynlas Goch's invasion had been well prepared and executed with care and precision. Men came and went from Leircestre every day, it was unthinkable that the Welsh prince would come so close without sending spies to warn him of the time when the English must respond to the threat he posed to their new lands. If those men reported that Icel had already led his own hearth troop away it could even provoke an attack on the town itself. He came to a decision and turned his gaze back on the Welshman. 'We go now. Each man carries his own food and there will be no remounts.' He looked across the table. 'Thrush, have a word with our friend Tewdwr and have him prepare a small sack of food and drink for each man.' Hemming nodded and left the table immediately. From the corner of his eye, Eofer noticed that his hearth men at the nearby tables had noticed the movement and were already draining their cups as they prepared to leave the place. He turned back to Ioan. 'I want to be there by sundown tonight. Leave now, gather your men and meet me at the western gate as quickly as you can. How long do you think that you will need?'

Ioan raised his chin, peering across the room at the raucous group of men who had earlier been banging the table in time with his actions in the upper room. A quick jerk of his head and the men were on their feet and halfway to the door. Eofer looked at the group and back to the Briton in surprise as Ioan flashed a grin. 'We are ready, lord. How long will your boys need?'

6

The men stood deep within the shadows of the greenwood as a westering sun drew a crimson line on the horizon. Shielding his eyes against the glare, Eofer chewed his lip as he studied the defences. 'There she is, lord,' Ioan said at his side. 'We made it, just in time.' Eofer nodded as his mind raced to form a plan of attack before the rapidly fading light left them altogether.

Cair Luit Coyt looked every bit as imposing as Ioan had said. The main gate straddled Watling Street itself, twin towers of creamy coloured stone rising to double the height of the main curtain wall with a crenellated walkway linking the two. Eofer saw to his disappointment that each corner of the fort had been protected by circular towers, the massive stone strongpoints projecting outward from the walls which ran into them. He indicated the one to the south with a jerk of his chin. 'You said that there are not many men here. Do you expect all of the towers to be manned?'

Ioan pulled a face. 'It's been a week since we were here, lord. As I said there were not many men here then, but I can't guarantee that others have not arrived. I will say though,' he volunteered as he recognised Eofer's concern, 'that unless they came during the last two or three days, I would have heard. There's not much that travels the roads within fifty miles of Tewdwr's ale house that's not the talk of the place within that time.'

Eofer took a final look back as the sun flared a copper red against the base of the clouds beyond. Low now, the last of the light played upon the brows of the ditches which encircled the walls of the fort. Three in number, Eofer clicked his tongue in frustration as the light revealed that the obstacles had been well maintained. Wide and steep sided, they would preclude any approach by horsemen to the fortress other than by way of the roadway itself. His knowledge of other Roman fortifications, gleaned from visits both here in Britain and in the lands of the Franks and Frisians, told him that a fort of this size would have four gates, each one protected by identical gatehouses midway along the outside walls; he had seen enough Roman forts now to know that they had been built to an identical pattern all over the empire. Watling Street would cross a smaller road which bisected the camp from north-east to south-west from these other gatehouses, quartering the area within the walls. If the corner towers did contain additional guards they could sweep the approaches and defensive ditches with enfilading shot; Cair Luit Coyt would be pretty much impregnable to his meagre force.

He had hoped to trick his way into the fort. The stables were always located near to the main gate, but he saw now that Ioan had been right to doubt his plan. If the guards at the gate saw through his ruse and failed to open them, it was difficult to see just how they could break into the fortress. The eorle's hand moved down to touch the pommel of Gleaming as he called on the gods to send him a sign that he was still doing their bidding, but as his eyes scanned the gathering gloom his heart sank at a world scoured of other living things. Suddenly the merest flicker of light caught his eye, and his head snapped around. 'What's that? There at the base of the wall?'

Ioan's gaze followed the Englishman's outstretched arm. A blood red eye had appeared among the heavy shadows; as they watched it blinked and slowly faded as the sun dipped beneath the earth's rim. Ioan threw him a sympathetic look. 'That's a culvert, lord,' he answered. 'It carries the shit and muck from the stables to the brook.'

Eofer's eyes widened and the corners of his mouth curled into a smile. Woden, the one-eyed father of the gods seemed to have shown him the way after all.

Ioan recognised the look for what it was and moved to crush the Englishman's hopes before they took root. 'You will never get in that way,' he said sadly, 'it's been tried before. Oh, you will get past the first grate no problem,' he spat. 'But then you will find that you are trapped against the inner bars with dogs and spearmen gathering for the kill. It's a trap, made to look easy so that they can lure anyone dumb enough to fall for it into a killing ground.'

Eofer raised a brow and the Welshman quickly backtracked. 'Not saying that you would have fallen for it lord,' he gabbled apologetically. 'Not once you got a proper look.'

Eofer rubbed his face wearily, suddenly overcome by the rigours and worries of the day. Maybe he was losing his touch? Not so long ago he would given a rousing speech and stormed the walls. Now he was considering the consequences of failure, worrying about the affect a defeat here would have on the wider war. Ioan looked at him in surprise as a thought came to Eofer, and he snorted in amusement: maybe Astrid was right after all. Like a snake ship, a big fifty oar Snaca, he had cleaved the sea, battered it to froth and foam in his wake;

but the waters ahead were smooth and calm and would remain so if he hauled on the steering oar of his life and set course on a different heading. Perhaps his best fighting years were behind him? Maybe he should become an ealdorman? As hard as he racked his mind he just could not understand why he had become so half-hearted about the attack.

Then, as the light finally left the western sky and the awkwardness of the moment began to stretch gossamer thin, a smile came to his face as he realised that he knew.

'So, what do you think, Thrush?'

Hemming placed his hands on his hips and looked out across the surrounding countryside. The moon was full and bright, painting the lands below them with a ghostly sheen. The river which the villagers had called the Anker hugged the base of the slope before clearing away to the north to merge with the silver ribbon which marked the course of the River Tame. Not so many miles further downstream the waters would join the River Trenta and continue its long journey northwards to the sea. Finally he nodded in agreement. 'Yes, lord,' he said. 'It's perfect. But where would you find a madman with the balls to cling on here until the ætheling can flush the Britons from the valley?'

Eofer placed a hand on his weorthman's shoulder and looked him in the eye. 'I was thinking that I had already found one,' he said. 'Right here.'

Hemming laughed in reply, but his look changed to one of incredulity as he realised that he was laughing alone. 'You mean it?'

Eofer nodded. 'Of course.' As Hemming struggled to come to terms with the importance of his lord's words, Eofer continued. 'King Eomær was impressed by the way you handled the boys in Scania after I was taken, he made a point of telling me so at the symbel in Theodford before we set old king Offa in his barrow. Icel mentioned you too. He is looking for experienced fighters to hold down the lands which we will conquer here in the valley of the Trenta and elsewhere. What do you think? Do you want to be a warlord?'

A fox barked in the near distance, drawing the men's gaze away. When Eofer looked back he could see that Hemming was already studying the land thereabouts with a practiced eye. It was a good sign, and the eorle spoke again to encourage the outcome he wanted. 'Don't worry about me,' he said. 'I have plenty of men to look after me now. Horsa is a good man and Finn could turn out to be one of the best. After all,' he said with a smile. 'He had a good example to follow.'

Hemming turned back, the moon highlighting the excitement writ large on his features. Eofer felt his own kick of excitement as he saw that his man had already reached his decision. 'He could be *one* of the best, I agree,' Hemming said as he flashed his lord a grin, 'but I am *the* best. A warlord in his glory.'

'Come on then,' Eofer replied with a snort. 'Let's put everyone to work. Even glorious warlords need a hall and a fence.'

EOFER'S HAND moved down to the scabbard of his sword. As he ran the pad of his forefinger around the gold and garnet raven there, he was aware that other hands to either side were moving up to finger gods-luck charms of their own. The silver hammer of Thunor would be most common he knew. Crusher, the great hammer of the thunder god hung at most

English throats, but there would be the odd figure of Ing among them to add to the Iesus crosses of Ioan's boys. He had made a gift of his own hammer pendant of course, to the Long Beard warrior Wulf shield breaker back in the old country, the day before they had boarded the *Skua* and left for good. His mind wondered for a heartbeat whether they were still together before a whoop cut the air and his mind snapped back to the matter at hand.

They had stood immobile, deep within the dappled shade for what had seemed like a lifetime before there had been any sign of movement from the great Cair to the south. Watching, biding their time as the shadow of the tree line crept slowly towards them as the morning advanced. This day was to be a balancing act, and the scales would be weighted with men's lives.

He had left Hemming and the fifty warriors who had joined his war band before leaving Leircestre at the hill, helping the villagers put the finishing touches to the defences at the hall there. Hemming had named the new fortress Tamtun after the stream which curled past its base. The small English settlement of Tamworthy had grown up on the floodplain opposite, its inhabitants so far overlooked by the Powys as they scoured the valley of the Trenta to the north. But they knew that it was only gods-luck, the vagaries of wyrd which had saved them so far from suffering the devastation which had visited so many others of their race. Promised protection within the new fort by Hemming in time of danger they were digging in furiously, keen to make the hill fort as strong as possible before their fiend became aware of this wildcat force which had been thrown into their midst.

Eofer turned to Ioan at his side as the Powys' stable hands drove the geldings past the hiding place in a thunder of hoofbeats. 'Whereabouts do they turn?'

The Welshman indicated a large willow at the head of the meadow, the branches sweeping down to brush the surface of the brook like a young lad's floppy fringe. Eofer nodded with satisfaction, the location was perfect for their plan. Far enough away from the walls of the Cair to put them out of range, even in the unlikely event that the defenders had bowmen stationed on the walls or towers on this peaceful, sunny morning, but also beyond help by any but horsemen, and horsemen already set in their saddles at that. Suddenly a realisation came to him, and he turned to Ioan with a gasp of surprise. 'You had this plan in mind all along. You had learnt that the Powys' had gathered their horses there and travelled to the Cair to spy out their defences.' The corners of Ioan's mouth curled into a sheepish smile and he shrugged his shoulders. 'I am always on the lookout for any opportunities which might present themselves, lord.' His smile widened into a grin as he saw the laughter dancing in Eofer's eyes at his cheekiness. 'I like nice things lord: and whores. Neither come cheap.' Eofer snorted at the man's honesty. 'You saw the strength of the defences and travelled to Leircestre to see if you could enlist some added muscle and had the luck to run into Ozzy. So now we do the fighting and you get a guaranteed pay day.' He shook his head. 'Well, it so happens that I think that it's a price worth paying. Maybe our gods have teamed up for the day? Come on,' he said. 'Let's find out.'

Eofer looked to his left and gave the sign. Leather creaked as the warriors hauled themselves into their saddles, took up spears and turned their heads his way. Eofer swept his gaze along the length of the water meadow a final time. Away to the left the Cair dozed under a sultry sun, the only signs of life a lone gate guardian and a glint of steel as a spearman walked the ramparts. Above it all the red dragon banner of Powys curled lazily in a breath of wind. Satisfied that all was quiet there Eofer put back his heels and eased his horse forward with a click of his tongue.

The Powys' herd had cleared the final loop of the brook, they were within a hundred yards of the old willow as he exited the tree cover and walked his mount to the mid point of the field. Free of the shade, Eofer felt the warmth of the sun on his back for the first time that day as he waited for the others to form up, fanning out into a skirmish line to either side as they looked for the signal. A quick glance ahead confirmed that the stable hands, intent on heading off the herd as they approached the turning point, were still unaware of the threat which had appeared to their rear. Eofer exchanged a smile with Ioan at his side, the excitement which lit the Welshman's face all the confirmation he needed that the plan was going well.

Eofer raised his spear and let out a cry, throwing back his heels as he drove his mount forward. A heartbeat later the cry resounded around the field as it was taken up all along the line, and a new storm thundered across the meadow as the line of horsemen increased their speed to a gallop.

Ahead, Eofer saw the moment when the first enemy rider became aware of the danger now rapidly closing from the south, and he laughed in triumph as the first faces turned their way and mouths gaped in shock and horror. To either side his men saw the consternation on Powys' faces and redoubled their efforts to unnerve the men ahead, their cries now a full-throated roar rolling along the valley floor in an unstoppable tide.

As he had expected the stable lads, faced by an onrushing wall of armoured killers abandoned their charges, turning the heads of their own mounts aside and scattering in all directions like a flock of panic stricken birds. The English gave full voice to their victory cry as the men of Powys fled and

Eofer hauled at his reins, turning his own mount aside as the men of his war troop gathered around him. Eofer peered back down the field, his eyes fixed on the twin stone towers, the massive gatehouse of Cair Luit Coyt and the dark shadowed rectangle which marked the position of the gateway itself. The guard had disappeared, but to his joy there was no sign of any other movement there.

Osbeorn came up alongside him and the duguth grinned. 'The guard's gone inside,' he beamed, 'you know what that means!'

Eofer laughed and pulled the head of his horse back to the north. 'He's gone inside to raise the alarm.' He clapped his man on the shoulder as the war party began to head back northwards. 'We have caught them napping. Come on,' he cried above the din, 'let's get these horses away.'

Ioan and his right hand man were at the rear of the herd, waving their tawny cloaks above their heads and whooping for joy as they drove the horses onwards. The rest of the Welshman's gang had moved forward, fanning out on either flank, the air bejewelled as they guided their prizes across the stream in an explosion of spray.

Intent on driving off their charges neither one of Ioan's men saw the attack until far too late, and Eofer opened his mouth to cry a warning as the pair, mounted warriors dressed for battle, seemed to appear from nowhere. Before Eofer could head them off steel flashed as the leading enemy rider brought his sword blade slashing down, and blood misted the air as Ioan's man flew backwards from his saddle and tumbled to the ground. The dead man's companion, faster or luckier than his friend threw himself aside, ducking away from the follow up strike as Eofer and his men put back their heels and raced to confront the attackers. Within moments Eofer's horse had reached the brook, and he shifted the weight of the spear in his hand as he sought the point of balance, drew back his arm and prepared to throw. The instant that the horse rose up above the lip of the bank Eofer's arm snapped forward, launching the dart towards the swordsman. Closer now the thegn blinked in surprise as he saw that the leading attacker was no more than a boy and, despite the fact that the lad had just taken the life of one of his companions he willed his spear to miss its target. Even in the heat of battle it would be an unworthy act, and he was thankful when the following rider urged his own mount forward to throw his shield into the path of the missile. An instant later the spear thudded into the lime-wood board, the force of the strike throwing the warrior's arm back and opening his own body up to a following strike.

Horses were scrambling up the bank now to either side of the eorle, and Eofer watched as a several spears converged on the enemy warrior as he twisted in desperation. The veteran began to recover, dragging his shield forward as the darts cleaved the air, but Eofer could see that it was too late and a heartbeat later the spearpoints thudded home.

The boy had reacted to the attack, hauling around the head of his own mount to face the threat. Eofer was the closest to him, and he took in the details of his opponent as Gleaming rasped from its scabbard. Maybe six winters in age, the boy's shoulder length flaxen hair indicated that was as a Saxon of high class, undoubtably the son of an important member of Cynlac Goch's army. A cream coloured sark edged with a wide golden band was split at the waist by the broad belt of a warrior, the silver studded leatherwork flashing in the morning sun. Raising his gaze Eofer's suspicion of his opponent's nationhood was confirmed as he saw that a green cloak was pinned at the shoulder by a circular brooch in the Saxon style.

Eofer was aware of his men crowding forward to finish off the first Saxon, and he saw the look of anguish which washed across the face of the youth replaced by a snarl as the boy gritted his teeth and urged his horse into the attack. His shield still strapped firmly to the saddle of his own mount, the Englishman sat tall as the Saxon approached, hoping that the boy's lack of experience would be his downfall. Eofer held Gleaming out wide as the horses raced head on, and his heart leapt as he saw that his opponent was taking the bait. As the boy brought his sword sweeping around, arcing in towards Eofer's unprotected midriff, the eorle calmed his breathing and concentrated on matching his own movements with those of his mount. As his opponent's blade slashed in an inch above the ears of his own horse, Eofer's arm shot vertically upwards. His judgement was perfect and within a heartbeat the steel strips of his vambrace had deflected the blow, the momentum flinging the Saxon's sword arm wide. Eofer just had time to see his opponent's look of triumph transform into one of horror as the horses sped past one another and Gleaming cut the air. Eofer felt a satisfying thud as the pommel of his sword connected with the shoulder of the lad, and he caught a momentary glimpse as he shot sideways through the air.

Turning back he could see that older Saxon was no longer a threat, his body chopped to a bloody wreck as he had struggled to defend his charge against overwhelming numbers. The boy lay motionless on the riverside several yards away, and Eofer gave Horsa a look of concern as the duguth peered down from the back of his horse at the apparently lifeless form on the grass beneath him.

'Is he dead?'

Osbeorn slid from his saddle, grasped a handful of hair and tugged the boy's head back. 'Not yet, lord,' he replied with an obvious air of disappointment. Drawing his knife with a flourish he held the blade to the boy's upturned throat, glancing back as he awaited the nod which would deprive the lad of his life.

'No,' Eofer said, 'he could come in useful. Tie him to his saddle, he comes with us.'

7

'Here it is, lord,' Ioan cried above the rhythmic clatter of horseshoes on stone. 'This is the place.' Up ahead twin pillars marked the crossing, the ancient stone bridge which carried the Roman Road northwards shimmering in the heat of the midday sun. 'The bridge carries the road across the River Mease,' he continued as the Englishman raised his chin to peer across. 'The track which I told you about runs alongside the river, straight through the woodland, pretty much as far as the Fosse Way.'

Eofer nodded. 'Get them across and heading south straightaway. The sooner I get off this road, the better I will feel.'

Ioan snorted a reply. 'You and me both, lord.'

Osbeorn had already led the advance party across in a storm of hoofbeats, and Eofer indicated that they move on with a wave of his arm as he waited for the rearguard to come up. His eyes moved among the leading group as they cantered along the far bank until he spotted the short figure of the Saxon boy among them. The lad was conscious now, sitting upright in his saddle again as he recovered from Eofer's blow and the fall which followed it. The thegn was pleased to see that he rode between Horsa and Finn, and as far from any of their new British friends as possible. The latest additions to the ranks of his duguth would guard him no less vigorously than the Saxon's previous guardian, although hopefully with a happier outcome if they were called upon to defend the boy. The hostility shown towards him by Ioan and his gang was understandable of course. The Saxon had cut down one of their own, and he could only imagine his own hard-heartedness and that of his men if the dead man had belonged to Eofer's hearth troop. But he knew that the boy could only be the son of a leading warrior in Cynas Goch's army, his fierceness, bearing, and the quality of his clothing made that plain to see, and Eofer knew that he had captured a prize potentially more important even than the fifty war horses which they were taking back to Leircestre.

Octa was leading the rearguard, Grimwulf, Anna, and the dark twins Crawa and Hræfen up the road towards him, and Eofer reflected as he sat and waited and the sun beat down on the changes which his hearth troop had undergone in the past few years. An involuntary smile came as he recalled his old duguth Imma Gold. The man had combined a heady mix of qualities and he missed him still. His handsome looks had been matched by the openness of his smile, he had been of the type that every man aspires to be and every woman wants to snare until a cowardly attack had laid him low beside a river in Juteland. The youth Oswin had fallen at his side, too soon to realise the full potential of his wordplay, although the memory of those verses which he had composed in life still brought a smile to the face of his lord on dark winter nights. Rand, stabbed in a moment of madness by his only shield-maiden, the Briton they had named Spearhafoc, the sparrow hawk. The girl had been a force of nature, as wild as a storm, gods-blessed he was sure. But the force and fury of their power had been too much for her, and he had banished her from his hearth after removing the fingers which she needed for her bow work. Now Thrush too was gone, he sighed, and although he knew that he had done right by his oldest friend, he knew too that he would miss his weorthman every waking moment.

To balance the losses Tiw had seen fit to guide men of worth his way. Horsa had shared his own captivity in Daneland, while Grimwulf had been rescued from the same fate in an earlier raid. Both men had added remarkable qualities to his war band, and he was proud of them both. The youth Anna had joined them after the war of fire and steel, following the death of his father during the battle at the ridge against Ubba silk beard and his men. The boy's smithing skills had been more useful than he could have ever imagined, and the small hand axes which were the lad's speciality, the franciscas that had given the Franks their name, had added a useful and deadly weapon to their arsenal.

The sound of approaching horses drew his attention back to the south, and he urged his own mount back onto the roadway with a squeeze of his knees. Octa came up, reining in and shooting his lord a grin. 'It's all clear as far as we can see, lord,' he cried as the others bunched in his wake. 'We spotted a small hillock off to one side of the road and watched from there. We could see a good mile or so back the way we came and there was no sign of any pursuit, there must have been even fewer men in the Cair than we thought. Maybe,' he added with a wicked smile, 'we should double back, chase away the garrison and round up the rest of the herd?'

'Or,' Eofer replied, 'we could not test the benevolence of

the gods, get off the road and rejoin the others before their friends return. Come on, let's get going. I have a feeling that this place is going to get a lot busier sooner rather than later.'

Octa fell in at his side as they passed the stone pillars which marked the entrance to the bridge itself and clattered across. Once they had gained the track Eofer dug in his heels and increased the pace to a gallop. Despite the lack of opposition to the raid from the men within the Cair, he was well aware that the valley of the Trenta contained an invading army. At any moment a column of *horswealas* could appear from any direction. If a strong force of horse Welsh did suddenly harden from the heat haze, the successes of the morning could easily turn into a disaster, not only for Eofer and his men, but also for the English settlements this side of the Fens. Shorn of its commander and a large part of its garrison Leircestre, a key fortress in the region, would lay at the mercy of Cynlas Goch and his rampaging army. Despite the telltale dust cloud which the increase in pace produced, Eofer was certain that it was a risk worth taking.

The tree line was within sight as the land rose gently away from the floodplain of the Trenta and they soon passed into its welcome embrace, the only evidence of their passage a brace of startled egrets, the white of their plumage stark against a sky of the bluest hue.

Back within the shadows the ground underfoot was still moist from the morning dew, and Eofer urged his horse on as the likelihood of pursuit receded a little with every step. Within a short while the tail end of the column came into view, and Eofer instinctively slowed his mount as he saw that they had come to an unexpected halt. Octa was an experienced duguth, a doughty warrior, the veteran of many shield walls, and he too had sensed that all was not well ahead, urging his horse alongside his lord as his hands moved instinctively to release the linen peace bands which held his sword secure within its scabbard. His reaction when it came was short and to the point, and Eofer felt a flutter of pride that his hearth man was as steadfast as the name of old king Offa's sword.

'Trouble?'

Eofer shrugged, twisting in his saddle to speak to the others. 'Something may be wrong up ahead, prepare your-selves.' As the youth donned their helms and hefted spears, Eofer turned back to Octa. 'Ready Oct'? Let's go and see what is holding them up.'

As they came up the looks which greeted them seemed to confirm the suspicion that the halt had been called to await their arrival, and the riders moved aside as best they could to enable the pair to squeeze past them between the narrow path and the riverbank. The captive horses were strung out in a line, each group of ten linked to the lead horse by a length of rope attached to a head collar. Ioan and his men had dismounted and the Welshman handed the rope to one of his men as he saw that Eofer had arrived. He came across and the Englishman saw the disquiet on his features.

'Smoke lord, up ahead,' he said, as Eofer swung himself down from the back of his own mount and joined him on the track.

Eofer raised his chin, drawing in the air like a hound seeking a scent. He shook his head slowly. 'I can't get it.' He glanced at Octa who shook his own head in reply.

Osbeorn and the others had ridden forward fifty yards as they used the added height to scan the way ahead for the source of the smoke, and the duguth slid from the saddle as he saw his lord approach and doubled back to join them. 'I thought that I caught a whiff a short while ago lord but I could not be sure. These boys seem pretty certain, though.'

Ioan nodded. 'We are. If Cynfelyn says that he smells smoke there is a fire nearby, you can be sure of it.'

'There is always the smell of woodsmoke hanging in the air, even in high summer. Could it just be a nearby hearth, or someone clearing land?' Eofer suggested. 'Or charcoal makers?'

Ioan spoke to Cynfelyn and beckoned him across. The Welshman hitched up his shirt, twisting around to reveal an angry puckered slash which cut across the skin of his back as Ioan spoke again. 'If anyone can tell the difference between an innocent hearth fire and burning wattle and thatch lord, it's Cynfelyn. This is from the falling beam which pinned him when his childhood home was fired by a Powys raiding party and saved his life.' Eofer looked askance and Ioan explained. 'His family were slaughtered, but the burning beam trapped him in the building until the end wall collapsed. It buried him but also put the flames out, and he was able to dig himself out when the raiders had left.'

The canopy above the track swayed gently as light airs plucked at the treetops, the breeze finally carrying the unmistakable smell of burning to the wider group. There was no longer any doubt, and Eofer hauled himself back into the saddle, donning his battle helm and hefting his spear. 'Bring the horses along slowly,' he said, 'while we spy out the road ahead.' The men of his hearth were copying their lord's action, urging their mounts into line as they waited for Eofer to make his way forward to lead them. He paused before he moved away as instincts honed to a keen edge across the battlefields of the northern world caused him to nail Ioan with a stare. As lovable a rogue as the man seemed, he was without doubt still a rogue. 'We will see you soon; remember that a few of my youth are still at the rear of the column. If we don't meet again very soon and this is a ruse to make off with the horses, if you somehow manage to drift away with my valuable prizes or my men come to any harm, no waste-land would be remote enough nor sea wide enough to keep you from tasting the edge of my sword.'

Eofer just caught the look of beatific innocence which crossed the Welshman's face at the suggestion that he could be planning to double-cross him, before he was past and skirting the flank of his own men. Osbeorn was waiting at the head of the column with Horsa, and Eofer was pleased to see that their expressions were stone-hard as they prepared to fall in behind him. 'Keep your wits about you lads,' he said as he reached the clear trackway ahead, 'there could be any number of men in the trees and we would never know until we heard the first arrow whistle past our ear.'

The waters of the river pressed in on the track as Eofer led them southwards, the air above hazed by cranefly as the sunlight slashed the shadows. Rounding a bend the smell of burning hung in the air like a pall, and Eofer could see up ahead that the path angled away from the course of the Mease, cutting across a small glade before finally breaking out into a clearing beyond a small stand of oak.

The first sounds began to reach them, course laughter, fearful screams, as the war band edged towards the final screen of trees. The noises were familiar to all warriors, and the men closed up, tightening straps and gripping weapons a little tighter as they prepared to face the mayhem which they knew would great them within a very few moments.

Eofer passed from light to shade as the tree line was reached but within the blink of an eye he was through, halting his mount as he waited for the others to fan out to either side. The scene which greeted him was much as he had expected. The roadway curved away to the south-east, its stony surface stark and grey against the richness of the summer grass. Beyond it a small farmstead was burning, the liquid flames licking the doorway, the roof thatch a torch.

The owners, a man and wife, their four sons, were already chained by the iron necklaces which denoted their new status in life, thræls, the lowest of the low. A spearman stood over the group as others made a heap of their belongings, and the thegn made out shields and spears among them. A quick glance at the war shirts worn by the man and his eldest son confirmed that they had been the owners of the weapons, and Eofer realised that the ceorls had put up a fight before they had been overwhelmed by numbers. Such men were the future of the nation, frontiersmen who would push the English border ever westwards, ploughing their holding with one ear cocked for the war horn that would send them racing to arm; they deserved better than a life of thræeldom.

As the Englishmen drew up into a line, Eofer's attention was drawn away to the north. At the edge of a field of barley, rich and green as it ripened under the hot sun, another of the slavers was striking an object on the ground, the man's staff rising and falling maniacally as he struck and struck again. The first cries of alarm carried to them as a man turned to point, and men scrambled for spear and shield as they came together to face the threat which had materialised suddenly from the trees.

Eofer and his men remained unmoving as the raiders shuffled together into a makeshift shield wall, dark faces topped by darker hair peering at them above their shield rims, and the eorle let the uncomfortable silence drag on as he sought to unnerve the slavers by his inaction. The madman at the edge of the field had finally noticed that they were no longer alone, and as he turned, Eofer saw for the first time the large wooden cross which hung at his neck. The Christ priest seemed to be the leader, and Eofer held his ground as the man stalked across to take up position at the head of his men. Planting his staff foursquare he hailed them in the Welsh tongue. 'Welcome friends, we are here with the blessings of Cynlan Goch,' he started, still unaware of the identity of the newcomers. 'We do God's work, scouring pagan filth from greater Powys so that His bounty may nourish the righteous.'

Beyond the priest the shield men were exchanging glances, unlike their leader still unsure as to whom they were facing, and Eofer decided that the time to reveal his identity had come. The English line kept pace with him as he moved slowly forward across the clearing with Finn as *Cumbolwiga*, and Eofer watched in amusement as the priest attempted to make out the design on the burning hart banner as it hung lifeless in the still airs and they drew closer.

The first doubts began to enter the mind of the man before him, and Eofer saw him take a pace back as his eyes narrowed and then widened again as he realised that these were no Christian men before him.

Eofer raised his chin, flicking out to left and right, and the Powys' line folded back on itself, moving into a crescent as the horsemen lowered the tips of their spears and walked forward to envelop them. To his surprise the priest grew even more emboldened as the hopelessness of his position became obvious, and the man strode free of the line as his face twisted into a snarl. 'Be gone from here,' he spat, flecks of spittle filling the air between them, 'these are Christian lands. God has sent a cleansing army to scour these valleys clean of idolators. Run east, back to your snake ships, before the Lord smites you for your wickedness.'

The mention of idolatry drew Eofer's attention back to the field edge and he slid from the saddle, barging the priest aside with the wide board of his shield as he walked across. It was how he had expected to find it, and Eofer's hand moved to the golden raven which shone from Gleaming's scabbard as he turned, his own face now a scowl of indignation. Pointing at the broken figure at his feet with the point of his spear, he struggled to contain his rage as he rounded on the Welshman. 'Do you know who this represents?'

Despite the evidence of his rage the priest shot back a reply, his voice heavy with pride. 'The devil which you call Thunor, pagan.' He raised his arms to the sky, turning in a circle as he called to the heavens. 'Great Thunor, send a fire bolt to strike me dead for my desecration. Show these people the power of your vengeance.' The man lowered his arms and turned back to face the Englishman. His features had softened, and he shook his head slowly as if talking to a child or a fool. 'You see pagan, your gods have no power here. These are Christian lands and we are his people. There is only one God and Iesus is his son. Come,' he said, painting his face with a smile as he gestured to the west. 'Follow me to the river, let me wash the sin from you in the cleansing waters. All heaven rejoices in the repentance of a sinner.'

Eofer could see the Welshmen shuffling their feet nervously as his eyes flicked across them and back to their leader, and he knew the thoughts which would be going through their minds. Any hope of an escape from the confrontation with their lives had probably disappeared the moment that the figure of the pagan deity had been destroyed. Now the fool had antagonised the leader of this war band further with his talk of baptism and redemption. They were dead men, only a miracle could save them now.

Eofer, struggling to contain his rage, tossed his spear and

shield aside as he untied the peace bands which held Gleaming secure in its scabbard. The sword flashed as he swept the blade clear, and he took a pace forward before the miracle which the slavers had prayed for arrived.

'Lord,' a voice cried, 'I ask for this man's life.' Eofer hesitated as he recognised the voice and looked to the west. Ioan spoke again, the anguish in his voice obvious to all. 'Lord, spare this man of God and I will forego my payment.'

Eofer looked about him as he realised that the rest of the column had gained the clearing while his mind had been fogged with rage. The realisation had a sobering effect. If his attention could be distracted to such an extent that three score horses could arrive without his knowledge by the ramblings of a fool he had lost his edge, the edge which had kept him alive in fights from Swedeland to the lands of the Franks and beyond. He hesitated, offering the cleric a withering glare as he came to his decision. 'Osbeorn, disarm these scavengers. If they offer any resistance kill them where they stand.' He shifted his gaze. 'Octa, remove the thræl collars from these folk and chain the slavers together.' He shot Ioan a shrug and a smile. 'If you are to give up your share of the horses, you will need to make a profit elsewhere. I am told that the girls at Tewdwr's place don't come cheap.'

He turned his gaze back on the slavers and nailed them with a stare. A heartbeat's hesitation and the first spear clattered to the hard ground as the men lowered their shields and chose a life of thrældom over a bloody and certain death.

Despite the fact that Ioan's intervention had saved his life, the barbarian before him had thrown his generous offer of salvation back in his face and the priest's eyes narrowed with hatred . 'Burn then!' he cried, his arms rising once again as he called down his God's judgement. 'Burn in hell.'

Eofer had heard enough. His patience tested to the limit

and beyond he strode forward, reversing Gleaming as he did so. As the churchman clasped the crucifix and mumbled a prayer for his own soul, Eofer's arm swept across. A moment later a meaty thud broke the silence which hung over the clearing as Gleaming's silver pommel made contact with the side of his skull, and a horrified gasp escaped the lips of the watching Britons as their God-man spun away.

His temper still barely under control the eorle followed up quickly, striding forward to prick the priest's throat with the point of his sword. 'Never,' he growled, 'confuse me with someone who will worship your God of weakness. My name is Eofer king's bane, all men of worth know my reputation. My place at the ale benches of Valhall is assured. Woden is my lord, I have no place in my heart for others.'

Osbeorn and the men of his troop were already moving among the others, releasing the ceorls and transferring the rough iron collars to the glum looking spearmen.

Ioan had appeared at his side, and the Briton placed his hand upon Eofer's sword arm as he spoke. 'That's enough lord,' he said. 'I ask as a favour, let him go...for me.'

Eofer's eyes moved from one to the other, and although the sincerity in Ioan's expression was genuine enough the hatred and contempt in the eyes of the priest remained.

Gleaming whipped up then, the wicked blade paring a flap of flesh from the man's cheek before he could raise a hand to defend himself. With a flick of his wrist Eofer severed the leather thong which suspended the crucifix at his neck, and as the pendant came away he gave the priest a hefty kick. 'Go on,' he said, 'be on your way. Remember this man in your prayers; he saved your miserable life here today.'

A growl of protest came from Ioan's men as the priest fell forward to sprawl in the dust but Eofer was past caring, and as the man scrambled to his feet and his hand moved up to push the bloody scrap of flesh back into place he shot the thegn a look of utter hatred. 'My name is Gildas,' he snarled. 'Remember *my* name Eofer king's bane, as I shall yours. The Lord will ensure that our paths cross again, and when they do I will watch you die.'

8

E ofer drew rein as the Fosse Way broke free from the confines of the trees, dipped and crossed the meadow to the age puckered walls of Leircestre. Osbeorn and Octa curbed their own mounts, fanning out protectively as the thegn indicated that the rest of the column move down into the vale. Even this close to the safety of the English town their eyes darted this way and that as they probed the shadows for any hint of a threat to their lord. He snorted softly to himself. With Hemming's departure he would need a new weorthman. It would seem that the contest for that exalted position within his hearth troop had already begun.

No small part of him felt relief as he saw that the white dragon still curled from the high point in the town, and he mentally shelved the excuses he had been forced to prepare for the loss of the settlement to the army of Powys while Icel had been in the north.

He had been right after all he mused as he watched the riders cross the water meadow and approach the great gate of the city, the gods had willed him westwards for a reason. That reason had not been the most obvious one, despite the fact that they were returning with a goodly number of war-bred horses and a bonus of thræl-men in the prime of life. The reward for their aggression had been a far greater one than even the greatest of Cynlas Goch's herds. New horses could be bred or bought but land was finite, and the presence of an English stronghold almost within sight of his base at Cair Luit Coyt would not only threaten his supplies and reinforcements but hopefully shake the confidence of his army. They would know now the mettle of the men who opposed them. If the woodlands beyond the Cair were as impenetrable as Ioan had assured him, any defeat now and their line of retreat was vulnerable to attack by this new force which had sprung up in their rear.

The British kingdom of The Peaks to the north was already hostile to the king of Powys, his meeting with their emissary Ceretic ap Cynfawr in Icel's hall had shown him that, there would be no escape route for a beaten army in that direction. No, Eofer reflected as he watched a haze of crows circle the distant town, Woden was fighting at their side, weaving his god-spells as he guided the English in the opening moves of the great war to come. The armies of Iesus would be thrown back to the valley of the Hafron. The weakness of the Christ priest Gildas had confirmed to him all that he had suspected, despite the hold which the God had over the people in the old lands of Rome. Christianity was a religion for weaklings and women, he himself had looked into the eye of the Allfather and seen the truth of it.

A pang of regret overcame his thoughts at his loss, a loss which he doubted he would ever fully recover from. Hemming had gone from his immediate circle, but his old friend had acted with speed as soon as his decision to become warlord of the Tamesætan had been taken. Within the hour, the timbers which the Tame Settlers had used to ring Tamworthy had been uprooted and the new fortification of Tamtun was already beginning to take shape. Helped by the brilliance of the moon men had laboured through the night, and as the washy light of the false dawn had crept into the eastern horizon the main bank and ditch had been completed and the first of the oak timbers of the palisade slotted into place.

It had been a wrench for both men when they had parted in the early morning. Hemming had been a youth in the hearth troop of Eofer's father, Wonred, they had been, in fact, friends for life rather than thegn and duguth. But if any man had earned the chance to win a reputation of his own it was his bluff companion, the man who had saved his life more times than he cared to admit. Despite the disorientating sense of loss, Eofer knew that he had done the right thing. Icel's embryonic kingdom on the Trenta needed men of Hemming's quality if it was to survive and grow.

Eofer came back from his thoughts. Osbeorn and Octa were still making a great show of checking the greenwood for imagined danger, and Eofer snorted again as he recognised their keenness to take up the mantle of senior duguth.

The thegn lifted his chin and ran his gaze across the valley. The column was nearing the gatehouse, and he allowed himself a smile of self-congratulation as figures appeared among the crenellations on the wall and the guards waved in welcome.

Among the glint of spear blades and helms a flash of blue showed where the smaller figure of Seaxwine bobbed among the riders, the captive dwarfed by the men surrounding him. The boy had opened up following Eofer's confrontation with the slavers and the Welsh churchman Gildas, and in return for his word that he would not try to escape, Eofer had allowed him to keep the small ring sword which hung in its baldric. He had inspected the weapon as he pondered the decision and saw just how finely crafted the thing was. For a boy of his age to own such a thing had confirmed his first impression that the boy's family must be of some importance. Slowly gaining the lad's trust, Eofer had discovered that there was no love lost between the Christian firebrand and Cynlas Goch's Saxon mercenaries who were still, despite the fact that most had been born and raised on the island of Britain, fervent in their devotions to the gods of their ancestors. As Eofer had suspected, the boy had turned out to be a son of the Saxon leader he now knew to be called Seaxwulf Strang, Seaxwulf the strong; he had been handed the key to unlocking the enemy, all that remained for him to do was to bring that key to the lock.

Ahead the tail-end of riders passed into the shadow of the great wall of Leircestre, and he pursed his lips and whistled, throwing his own guards a broad smile as they turned back his way. 'It will be a lot quieter without the big man,' he said as their faces brightened seeing their lord's good humour return. 'But at least there will be a lot more ale to go around.'

'WHERE IS HE?'

The warrior indicated Icel's hall with the point of his spear. 'We put him up in the ætheling's hall, lord,' the man replied. 'Nobody seemed to know exactly where you had gone, so we told him he had best stay put and await your return.'

'*Who* is he?'

'Say's his name is Einar Haraldson.'

Eofer's eyes narrowed in surprise. 'A Swede?'

The guard shrugged. 'He wouldn't say, lord. He said that his message was for your ears only.'

Eofer nodded as a groom came from the stables and led his mount away. Men were coming from all across the town as word spread that king's bane had plundered the king of Powys' fortress and made off with a number of his prized war horses, and the excitement writ large on their faces told of their pride that a blow had finally been landed on the invader. His own men were moving among them, spreading word that a new English burh had been thrown up near the headwaters of the Trenta itself. Fighting men were needed there, free land was available; every man who pledged to carry his spear to Tamtun was to assemble at the western gate at sunup the following day where silver, food and drink would be provided to see them on their way. The British had had things their own way for far too long but suddenly all could sense that the Powys' tide, seemingly unstoppable when they awoke that morning, was on the cusp of the turn.

'Right then,' he said, as Osbeorn and Octa began to push a path through the throng with the shafts of their spears, 'let's go and find this mystery man and discover what is so important.'

Men smiled and dipped their heads as Eofer passed, thankful that the fightback had begun. Ioan and his men were travelling in the opposite direction having already deposited the newly enslaved Powys' with an associate, and he shot the thegn a grin and gave the thumbs up, jangling a bulging bag of silver as he made his way towards The Tewdwr. Eofer snorted. Three days had passed since they had first met in the tavern but it felt like three weeks, and he suddenly felt weary as he made his way across the open space at the centre of the town.

A figure was striding towards him, and Eofer knew immediately that this was the man who had sought him out across the waves. Tall and slim, the warrior's weatherbeaten features showed the thankful if deadpan expression of a man who was nearing the end of a long journey. A simple woollen cap and a close cropped beard sat above hardy travelling clothes of the finest quality, and Eofer slowed his pace as the guard left them to return to his duties. Osbeorn walked ahead to ensure that the messenger was unarmed before admitting him to the presence of his lord. Eofer had killed a king of Swedes in battle and they would have as good a cause as any to want him dead. Satisfied that all was well, the duguth stood aside as the stranger dipped his head.

'Welcome to Leircestre, Einar Haraldson,' Eofer said with a smile. 'Congratulations, you have found me at last.'

The ghost of a smile played about the man's lips at the thegn's jaunty welcome, but he quickly suppressed it as he prepared to speak. Eofer knew the impatience he must be feeling to finally complete the task given him by his own lord. He was not so easy to find, having the tendency to take off at a moment's notice. It was a quality which his wife had found exciting in the early years, but one which had begun to come between them as they aged and their priorities in life had begun to drift ever wider apart. As the Geat prepared to speak Eofer realised with a start that it was the first time that he had thought of Astrid since he had watched Icel depart, that morning on the wall with Hemming, and he wondered at it. Einar spoke again drawing his attention back to the present, but not before the now familiar hollow feeling when he thought of his home life stole upon him. Suddenly he realised who the man standing before him must be; this was no Swede but a Geat, and an icy cold hand twisted his gut as he steeled himself and voiced his greatest fear. 'Weohstan?'

'Your son is well, lord,' Einar replied with a smile of reassurance.

As a sense of relief drove the chilling fear from him, Eofer saw the Geat flick at look at Osbeorn and Octa and moved to lay his concerns. 'These men are two of my duguth, doughty warriors who have my full confidence. Anything you have to say to me can be said in their presence.' He looked around to check that they were out of earshot of any passers by, but those in sight were giving the group a wide berth as they hurried down to discover the cause of the commotion at the stables. 'Deliver your message Einar, you'll be hard pressed to find a quieter place in a town the size of Leircestre.'

The Geat composed himself, drawing himself up to his full height as he finally spoke the words he had rehearsed in his mind throughout the long journey from his distant homeland:

'Heardred, King of Geats, lord of Wægmundings, bids his most honoured kinsman Eofer Wonreding health and joy. May he drive his enemies before him, crush their proud necks and take pleasure from the wailing of their women.

You will be aware of the situation here in Geatland. Ever since I offered my protection to the æthelings Eanmund and Eadgils, their uncle, King Onela has pressed for their return. However, powerful forces within Swedeland wished to avenge the death of the old king Othere and the æthelings, Othere's sons, naturally became the focus of their hopes. Already facing the enmity of king Onela's allies the Danes, I had little option but to offer Geatish aid to the rival faction.

It would seem that I was mistaken in doing so.

My borders are harried daily and a full invasion is expected before the barley ripens. When last we met you promised me your sword on a windswept Frisian strand. I take up that offer now. Gather a mighty host about you, sword-bold victory thegn. Come east across the prow-plain; let us fight again shoulder to shoulder, Engle and Geat, as did our own fathers before us.'

Eofer's heart sank as the Geat stood back, the relief at finally fulfilling his mission written on his face. Clearly the man was expecting him to jump for joy at the prospect of war, but Eofer knew that the news could scarcely have come at a worse time. His mind raced as it desperately scratched about, forming a reply to the messenger's expertly delivered communication which would enable him to delay his decision without appearing anything other than thrilled by the request.

Before him the Geat was smiling, but the smile was beginning to slowly seep away like ale from a cracked drinking horn as confusion at the thegn's lack of reaction showed in his eyes. 'That's excellent news!' he answered finally, reaching forward to grasp the messenger by the arms. The Geat's face creased into a smile as he got the reaction he had expected all along, and Eofer placed a friendly hand on his shoulder. 'It will take me a few days to make my plans, and then you can convey my reply back to my kinsman. I am sure that you could do with a celebratory drink now that you have fulfilled your task, this is Osbeorn,' he said, ushering the man forward. 'He will take you down to the best tavern in Leircestre where you can meet some of my lads.'

Einar made to reply, but Osbeorn had caught the look in his lord's eye and knew what was required: before a sound could leave his mouth the Geat was being led away. As the sound of his duguth describing the delights to be had at The Tewdwr became lost in the general hubbub of the burh, Eofer shared a look with Octa at his side. 'Shit!' he hissed. 'That is all we need.' He sighed and pursed his lips as his duguth waited to hear what was to happen next. Normally Hemming would have been on hand, offering good advice before he even had time to ask, but those days were gone. Until one of the duguth showed that he was the man for the job he would have to make do with a more general gathering when he needed advice, but at least he now knew the ideal place to go. 'Tell the duguth that we will meet at the mithraeum at sundown,' he said. 'Get yourself down to the Tewdwr and tell the man himself to have plenty of ale and mead there in good time and we will discuss what to do.'

Octa dipped his head and scurried away, but paused and turned back as Eofer called after him. 'And keep an eye on our young Saxon friend. Let him drink as much as he wants but don't let him go upstairs, especially if Horsa is up there. We don't want to frighten the lad!' They shared a laugh as Eofer, finally alone, let his eyes run across the town as he thought. It would be midsummer in three days and preparations for the festivities were already underway. With Icel still in the north he would normally have been expected to preside over the midsummer *Thing,* the great council of the leading men in the area, but the war had changed that. Now men were loathe to leave their steadings unguarded, and he had sent word that they should remain there until the situation improved. That at least had been a blessing of sorts, but it added yet another reason why it would be difficult for him to leave.

As for *gathering a mighty host,* he snorted at the thought. With Hemming now at Tamtun, it would take all the men that Eofer could scrape together just to give his old weorthman an even chance of surviving the storm which would soon break upon his wooden walls, much less assemble a ship army to fight overseas. He raised his eyes, gazing out across the wide expanse of the old Roman forum. Men were happy, a victory had been snatched from the jaws of the Powys wolf, and now this.

A harsh *prrrk* drew his eyes westward. Shielding them with the ledge of his hand, Eofer squinted into the glare and wondered at the sign he saw there. The raven called again, dipping a wing to beat its way northwards as the dragon flag of Anglia snapped at its tail.

9

A drawn-out belch echoed in the space as the others exchanged a grin. 'No,' Osbeorn continued before taking another slug of ale, 'don't laugh, I mean it. What word is most likely to be the last one you say before you croak?'

'Handfast.'

They all turned their faces towards Octa as Osbeorn screwed up his face. 'Handfast?'

Octa nodded as the laughter danced on in the eyes of his companions. Eofer was sat at the head of the chamber, and he chuckled to himself. The ale was weaving its spell. Soon the father of the gods would enter their minds and the giddiness would be upon them. Rank and seniority would be forgotten, and Eofer would discover the true feelings of his men. A pang of regret came again at the absence of Hemming, his right hand man in so many ways, but he was pleased and a little surprised to find that the feeling of loss was passing as he became more and more comfortable with the fact. On the long bench opposite Osbeorn was repeating his question as the others exchanged looks of amusement. 'Handfast? That doesn't make sense.'

'Sure it does,' Octa replied. 'You asked what's the last word you will say before you die. Just before I die, old and toothless, I am going to say but I didn't know she was handfast!'

As laughter thundered in the small space of the temple, Osbeorn frowned. 'No,' he said levelly, 'that's not what I asked.'

Eofer settled in at his place at the head of the room, watching the conversation with interest. He had removed himself from the group with this type of drink-fuelled confrontation in mind, and he watched keenly as Octa defended his reply. 'Yes you did. You said, what word is most likely to be the last one *you* say before you croak, and I said *handfast* and told you why.'

'But that's not what I meant.'

'Then you should have made yourself clearer.'

Hackles were beginning to rise, and Eofer recognised the moment when the smiles began to fade from the faces of his jovial band and the air in the small room began to crackle with menace.

Denied his favourite pickled eggs due to the fact that they were to spend the night cooped up like chucks in a hen house, Osbeorn had been in a sulk all afternoon. That was his own business, but he had brought the bad humour to the mithraeum and that was Eofer's. That there had been a reason for it, however trivial, was neither here nor there; it was his lord's request and he was obliged to put his own problems to one side. Eofer had heard it said that his duguth's farts were strong enough to let themselves out of the room more times than he cared to recall, but he had a serious problem to discuss and, short of a weorthman, he had sought their advice.

As the pair glared across the short divide, Horsa made his own contribution to the conversation.

'Ooh.'

All faces turned his way, and Osbeorn screwed up his face in question. 'Ooh?'

'Yes, ooh,' Horsa repeated. He reached forward, refilling Osbeorn and Octa's cups before topping up his own and explaining his remark. 'A few years ago, when Æmma had my oath, we were raiding down in Frankland.'

Eofer sat back, impressed by the way in which his new duguth had snuffed out the rising tension in the room. Humorous stories and tales of fighting were always guaranteed to capture a warrior's undivided attention, to combine the two had been a masterstroke. He settled back to enjoy the tale as the tension drained away and the anticipation of a good tale showed on men's faces. Most of Eofer's men had lived their entire adulthood in each others company, and the fact that Horsa had travelled widely as a member of Æmma's oath-sworn meant that suddenly there was a new stock of tales to be had as they sat at their cups.

'We had raided this settlement and were making our way back to the ships when the local lord turned up and blocked our path,' he began as a hush descended on the little room. 'Anyway to cut a long story short it came to push of shields, and I managed to skewer this Frank with my spear and he just went...*ooh.*'

There was a moment when the men in the room exchanged looks of wonder, before a thunderous laughter boomed in the space. Eofer found that he too was laughing uncontrollably at the absurdness of the tale as Octa, forgetting his spat with Osbeorn, added to the mirth. 'What,' he said, 'just...ooh?'

'Yeah,' Horsa replied as the laughter redoubled. 'Just...ooh...like that. But because of the way he said it, like I had just trod on his toe or something, without thinking I said sorry.'

As the men doubled up, Horsa managed to blurt out the remainder of his tale. 'Anyway,' he said, as the others wiped tears from their eyes, 'as he starts to go down we make eye contact, and I can see him thinking, "you see all that blue shit sliding down my legs? That's my guts you bastard, it's a bit fucking late for sorry!"'

Eofer flicked a look towards Osbeorn to catch his reaction to the story but, to his disappointment, he still appeared put out that his question had not been treated with the seriousness he thought it deserved. The duguth was sat with pinched lips as he glowered at the others, and Eofer watched with interest as he finally gave up any hope of having his original question answered to his satisfaction and supplied the answer himself: 'It's shit.'

The others were beginning to recover their composure after Horsa's tale, and they exchanged looks of bemusement as Octa looked across and narrowed his eyes. 'What is mate?'

'That's the word which most people say as they die: shit. Think about it,' he went on as the others began to snigger. 'Remember the time down in Frisia when that fool tried to oar walk in his mail shirt and he slipped after about three oars? What did he say before he disappeared beneath the surface?'

Octa nodded. 'It's true, he did say shit; just before he smacked his face on the wale.'

'And what did that Dane say back in Scania, when he realised that we had trapped them between Eadward's shield wall and our own, and Spearhafoc's arrows were whistling around his ears?'

'You are right, he said shit, too,' Octa admitted. 'Still,' he added with a smirk. 'It's not as funny as...*ooh*. Like ooh... you bugger, or ooh...you pinched my skin then!'

As the others began to laugh again, Osbeorn's expression began to cloud over. Eofer decided that he had seen enough. Leaning forward from the shadows, the eorle cut in before all of Horsa's good work was undone. 'That's enough oohing and buggering for now, you are all here to help me decide how we respond to King Heardred's call for help. I will tell you all I know, and if anyone has any thoughts on what we do next this would be a good time and place to share them, here, under the watchful eye of the Roman warrior-god.' Eofer glanced at the tablet inset into the wall at the head of the underground room to add emphasis to his words. Foreign or not a god was a god, and their own ancestors had not been so remote that they had been unaware of the might which had been the empire of Rome.

As the mirth subsided and men set their faces he addressed them again. 'As you will all know by now, Geatland is threatened with invasion by the Swedes, possibly in alliance with our old friends the Danes. King Heardred has asked for my help to face down these twin threats with what men I can attract to my banner, a thing which I am honour-bound to do not only through our ties of kinship, but to repay the help and succour which he showed to you lads when you turned up out of the blue in his kingdom with a small army of huscarls hot on your heels.'

The duguth gave a snort of irony as they thought back on the long chase through the backwoods of Scania. They owed the Geats their lives and were eager to help, but the timing was appalling as Eofer confirmed.

'Unfortunately this request could hardly have come at a worse time. Not only are our settlements here in the marches under attack, but we have Thrush and his lads at Tamtun depending on us for support.' He spread his hands. 'You all know the problems, what do you suggest that I do?'

'Hemming's big enough and ugly enough to take care of himself, lord,' Osbeorn volunteered. 'As to the settlements there,' he jerked his head northwards towards the distant valley of the River Trenta. 'The ætheling will be back soon enough, possibly bringing reinforcements in addition to more horses. If we make our preparations now, we can be ready to leave the moment that he gets back.'

Eofer nodded but kept his thoughts to himself, using the awkward silence to draw further comments from those before him. To his surprise Finn was next to voice an opinion, and the eorle encouraged the youngest and newest member of his duguth with a smile. 'You could leave me here, lord, with the youth,' he offered. 'Then you could leave Leircestre as soon as you are ready. We could ensure that Hemming is not forgotten and fight alongside the ætheling and his men if they need us.'

A murmur passed along the bench as the duguth discussed the merits of Finn's suggestion before Octa spoke up in support. 'It's worth considering, lord. We could send riders back to Anglia tomorrow, spreading the word and asking for men to muster at Snæpe. By the time we get there we could already have a ship-army set to sail.'

Eofer swept them all with a look. 'So, that's what you all think? We either split our force or go straight to Geatland? Either way you think that we should go?'

Horsa cleared his throat, waiting until he had attracted their attention before offering his own advice. 'I don't think that either of those options are wise, lord,' he said. 'I know that I have only been in your hearth troop for a short time, and I was not present when the Geatish thegn protected the boys from the Danes, but I think that we need to finish what we have started here before we take ourselves off across the German Sea.'

Eofer worried his beard as he replied. 'And abandon my kinsman, the brother of my wife, to his fate? And what of my son?'

'With all respect, Lord,' Horsa went on. 'If the Swedes and Danes are looking to attack the Geats in unison, there is not much that the number of warriors which you can attract to your banner in such a short time could do to change the inevitable outcome. The Geats lost a good part of their army down in Frisland. For King Heardred to offer sanctuary to the sons of Ohthere was unwise, to then extend that protection to King Hygelac's son was madness.'

As the others protested, Eofer's voice cut through the voices. 'So what do you suggest we should do?'

'Stay here, lord, with full force. Hemming needs us, Icel needs us and most of all the English settlers here need us. We know the lands to the west as well as anyone in the English army and we have the young Saxon too. Find out if he can be used to drive a wedge between the Saxons and Welsh and exploit it before the big battle which must surely come soon.' Horsa cleared his throat again as the men in the mithraeum pondered his words. 'I know that they saved you boys, and I understand the obligation which you are under, lord. But I heard your speech at the symbol, back in the old country, and I saw the effect that it had on the warriors there. You looked into the eye of Woden and what you saw there caused us to leave our motherland. The truth is,' he added apologetically. 'If his enemies do attack, King Heardred's best chance of seeing this Yule is to tread the exile's path.'

Eofer's spirits lifted as he saw that at least one of his duguth would agree with his actions so far. Unbeknown to them he had already set a play in motion. As the men refilled their cups and began to debate the choices, his mind was already elsewhere.

'So, you see,' Eofer said as his companions shifted uncomfortably on the benches and stared at the tabletop, 'I cannot come yet. I will come, and come with all force as soon as I am able. But the situation here precludes it.'

The young Geat blanched as he came to realise that the task he had been set by his king would go unfulfilled. 'We will get you a fresh horse,' Eofer was saying, 'and get you back to your ship as soon as possible.'

To everyone's surprise the Geat shook his head. 'No, lord,' he said, 'that's not possible.'

Eofer narrowed his eyes as the men of his troop stopped tracing patterns in the ale slops with their fingertips and looked up sharply. Einar went on. 'I was charged with carrying a message here by King Heardred and ensuring that you reach him wherever he may be.'

Eofer took a sip of ale. 'My shipmaster can find Geatwic or Miklaborg without any help. I would even wager good silver that he could navigate the skerries off Marstrand blindfold, Einar.'

The young Geat pulled himself up to his full height. 'With respect, lord, my duty is only half fulfilled. The king explicitly charged me with conveying you into the presence of his person.' He sat back and folded his arms as the Engles regarded him with looks of admiration. It took guts to stand up to the will of a man of reputation. 'The fault is mine,' he continued. 'I have neglected to make the situation in my homeland clear to you.'

Eofer recharged the lad's cup and nodded that he continue.

'It is unlikely that King Heardred or any other Geat bearing arms still resides in any of the places you mentioned. The countryside is overrun with Swedish war bands, the main towns would be little more than deathtraps if the king remained there. I was sent to you because I am regarded as the best scout in Geatland, if anyone can affect a meeting between you, I can.'

Eofer sighed as the severity of the situation in his kinsman's realm became plain. The weight of guilt hung about him like a wet winter cloak, and he was grateful when Horsa added his own thoughts to the conversation. 'So, it is as well that Eofer was away from home when you arrived.' Einar raised a brow in question, and the duguth explained. 'Because if he had been, his wife, King Heardred's sister, would have had us all in the *Skua* and sailing eastwards before the tang of sea salt had left your hair Einar. And where would that have got us?'

The Geat's nostrils flared at the tone in Horsa's reply, and he fixed the Englishman with a stare. 'I made my orders clear when I repeated the message from my lord to your own,' he snapped:

'Gather a mighty host about you, sword-bold victory thegn. Come east across the prow-plain; let us fight again shoulder to shoulder, Engle and Geat, as did our own fathers before us.'

'The clue,' he said icily, 'is at the beginning. The "gather a mighty host," part.'

As the men stared unblinking at one another, Osbeorn shifted to one side and squeezed out a fart. 'He's got a point, Horsa,' he sniffed, proud of his effort as snorts of amusement swept the group. 'Of course,' he added with a disarming smile. 'Me and Octa know that, Einar, because we were there when you delivered your message. If my friend Horsa had been there he would have understood too.' He pushed a bowl of pickled eggs across at the bemused Geat with his forefinger. 'Here,' he said, 'treat yourself. It will help get rid of some of that trapped wind we are having to listen to.'

Einar's eyes narrowed as his mind attempted to untangle the weave of the duguth's accent. Although the languages of Germania were as much cousins as the folk themselves, local variations in wordage and custom could sometimes cause confusion.

The men of the hearth troop smothered smiles as they watched the Geat's eyes narrow in suspicion. Einar was pretty sure that he was being insulted, but as yet his mind lacked the ability to cut through Osbeorn's heavily accented English to confirm the fact.

Eofer moved to nip the conflict in the bud. 'That's enough,' he said, 'you have had your fun. Einar here has travelled a long way to deliver an important message, a task which he has fulfilled faultlessly.' He turned to the Geat as the others, the entertainment over for now, exchanged looks of amusement and went back to their cups. 'Einar,' he said, 'I understand your dilemma, and I am sorry that the situation here keeps me from returning with you to your homeland at this time.' He spread his hands. 'You say that your instructions preclude you returning without me, so it looks as if you will be stuck here for a while at least. What would you like to do while you are here?'

Einar opened his mouth to speak, but a burst of light split the room as the door was thrown open and a cry went up from the table at the foot of the stairs. They all glanced across in time to see Ioan's leading man stomp into the room. He looked Eofer's way before throwing a smile towards his mates and tipping an imaginary cup to his lips. As the Welshmen called for more ale, Cynfelyn sauntered across. A look from Eofer, and the youth were pushing back the benches, walking across to the nearest tables and taking the seats there to ensure that their lord's conversation was out of earshot of any not sworn to be his man. 'Come on Seaxwine,' Grimwulf said. 'Let's try Tewdwr's pork.' Eofer gave his youth a nod of appreciation as they followed on. If this was the news that he was hoping for all well and good, if not they may have a problem on their hands.

Cynfelin slipped onto the bench and sank a mouthful from an abandoned cup.

Eofer waited until he had finished drinking and indicated the Geat at his side. 'This is Einar Haraldson, he may be joining us for a while. You can speak freely, he has my full confidence.'

The Briton exchanged a nod with the Geat and Eofer was pleased to see that his words had had the desired effect. Any tension which had bubbled over to reveal itself in the spat with Horsa seemed to have been quelled now that the man no longer felt an outsider in a foreign land. Osbeorn threw him a wink: 'eat your egg, it will do you good.'

The introduction made, Eofer spoke again. 'Where is Ioan?'

Cynfelyn grimaced and indicated Seaxwine with a jerk of his head. 'Your boy's da insisted that he remain a guest of the Saxons until this is all over. I am to act as a go-between until the deed is done.'

Eofer nodded, it was a sensible precaution. Hostage exchange was a common arrangement in such situations but the Welshman was a bit of a rogue, not bound by any code of honour or lordship, and the possibility of betrayal still haunted him. Cynfelyn shook his head as he correctly read the thegn's thoughts. 'You will have to learn to trust us one day, lord,' he said. 'We may not be oath sworn to you, but we are on your side.'

'You are right,' Eofer replied, shamefaced. 'I do trust you. So, the arrangements are made?'

Cynfeyn smiled and grabbed an egg. 'It's all set,' he said, taking a bite. 'We do the deed on Midsummer night.'

10

ofer guided his mount to one side as he neared the crest
of the hill. Horsa made to join him but the thegn indicated that he carry on with a gentle sweep of his head. The
sky above was as dark as it would get on this auspicious day,
as the light of the sun barely dipped below the western limits
of Middle-earth before it reappeared in the east. On the slopes
which climbed away from the eastern flank of Leircestre
flames flickered as the population lit the fires which would
help to strengthen the power of the sun as it began its long
descent into the darkness of winter.

Despite their Christianity, Eofer had been pleased to see
that the British inhabitants of the town were as keen to keep
up the old rituals as the Engles. The English might be setting
fires to honour Balder and the Welshmen the old god Bel, but
both were gods of light and the similarity between them was
helping to bind the two populations together as they shared
food, the ale loosened tongues and inhibitions, and differ-
ences were forgotten as they leapt the cleansing flames hand
in hand. Both gods would be reborn at the winter solstice,
and it did not take a leap of imagination to realise that,

although the names were different, they must be one and the same.

As usual, Eofer reflected with a sigh, the Christians had piggybacked the tale. A kindly old priest had patiently attempted to convince Eofer at the celebrations earlier that the Welsh now celebrated the day as *Gŵyl Ifan Ganol Haf*, which he had translated to the bemused Englishman as St John's of Midsummer, born six months before their own lord of light Iesus Christ had descended to earth; but it was as clear as the nose on his face that the man was putting on a brave face as his flock cavorted drunkenly among the Bel flames.

Cynfelyn came up, and Eofer tugged at the reins, turning the head of his mount back to the west as he fell in beside the Briton. They exchanged a smile, and Eofer was disappointed with himself as he realised that he still looked for reassurance in the man's every move and word, despite what he had said back at the tavern. If Ioan was playing one side against the other Cynfelyn would be the first to die, but he had seen the bond which existed between the two men with his own eyes. Eofer prided himself on his judgement and despite the fact that Ioan was undoubtably a rogue and a cutthroat, he was sure that he had detected a sense of honour in the Briton; he thought it unlikely that he would sacrifice his friend's life for silver. Nevertheless their lives and possibly the future of Leircestre burh itself were at stake, and he asked the man to go over the plan once again as they crested the rise and the flickering flames outside the town retreated into the paleness of midsummer night.

Cynfelyn's teeth flashed white as he smiled at the thegn. 'You are right to be cautious, lord,' he said, 'but I promise that you have no need to fear treachery. Not only do we have more reason to hate the men of Powys than you Engles, but we make more silver in Anglia than we could ever hope to make in the hills and valleys of the west. Ioan and the boys all agree, lord,' he said. 'The arrival of your prince and his warriors into the middle lands is the best thing that could have happened to the people there, English and Welsh. These lands have been fought over for generations,' he explained. 'The last Arthur and his horsemen and their incessant wars against the Lindisware, and now Cynlas Goch and his spearmen want to do the same. Don't forget, lord,' he said, 'we men of Gwent have been fighting against Powys what seems like forever. You English have only just discovered what bad neighbours they make.'

Eofer snorted. 'It's true, I sometimes forget that the enmity between the British kingdoms goes back further and deeper than any hostility felt towards the English.'

The column passed into the blackness of the woodland, and Cynfelyn turned to Eofer with a hint of mischief. 'So, now that we are all friends again. Which part do you wish me to go over again, lord?'

The English thegn chuckled softly as the horses walked on. He was pleased that Ioan had sent his amiable friend with the news that the meeting had been arranged. His mind was as sharp as a seax blade, he could see why they got along so well. Reassured, Eofer replied as his own mind began to tease apart the weft and weave of his plan once again. 'Tell me it all, we have all night.'

'Well,' the Briton began, 'just as the boys settled down at their favourite table to spend their ill-gotten gains from the raid on the Cair, Ioan pitches up and tells us to drink up, half of us are off again.' He threw Eofer a look, and the thegn chuckled as his mind's eye pictured the long faces. 'As you can imagine, that went down well with the unfortunates who were chosen, so it was just as well that Ioan told them that king's bane would have settled their tallies with Tewdwr by the time they got back.' Eofer gaped in surprise, but he chuckled when he saw the broad smile plastered across the Welshman's face. 'Maybe I will. It will be worth the price if this thing works.'

It was Cynfelyn's turn to look surprised at the English-man's response to his joke, and a look of reflection came to his face. 'Ioan could be right,' he said finally. 'The boys and I grew up hating all Germans; pagan wolves who stole our ancestral lands and drove us west we were always told. Our churchmen preach that God has sent you to punish us for our sins, but the British people are not the sinful ones. They ask only that they be allowed to live their lives free from injustice, to be left in peace to raise their families without fear. But we live in an age of tyrants, as those who already possess more gold and land than they could need for a hundred life-times fight over the scraps which remain. Ioan believes that the English here in the east and the Saxons in the south will sweep away these despots and I am coming to share that hope.'

Eofer peered up ahead at the tall figure of the Geat as the Briton spoke. Given the choice between rejoining his friends at the ship back in Snæpe and tagging along, Einar Haraldson had leapt at the chance to see new lands as any scout would. Eofer was glad to have him along: sharp eyes and a sharper sword were always welcome. Despite the gloom, he could just make out the Saxon boy in the midst of his duguth. He was, he was now certain, the key which would unlock this new order of which Cynfeyn spoke, at least in the lands surrounding the valley of the Trenta, and he felt a flicker of excitement as he recognised the work of the gods in it. It meant that his decision to plant Hemming and his colonists deep within British lands had been part of their scheming, and he was sure too that his decision to delay his journey to Geat-land was the correct one.

Cynfelyn was still speaking at his side, but he knew the tale now and, reassured that all would be well he only listened to the odd snippet as the horses plodded on. It was the first time that he had ridden north from the town, and he ran a practised eye across the land as a half moon rose in the east. The night was warm, the smoky air as thick as a winter stew as the horses hugged the eastern edge of the woodlands. Men sweated in mail, cloaks and helms and the moonlight made cat-tails of the channels of the River Leir as they snaked away and edged behind a small hill.

Eofer drew his mount aside as he took a last look at the valley before the trees closed in once again, indicating that the Briton continue with a jerk of his head. Cynfelyn had hardly moved a few paces before Einar, keen for local knowl-edge, pulled back to ride at his side, and Eofer sniggered to himself as he watched their animated antics as they struggled against the lilt and burr of their accents to converse in broken English.

If the track up ahead was as useful as Cynfelyn promised, Eofer had great plans forming in his own mind for its future use. As the young Geat was intent on staying on until the duty owed his king had been fulfilled, he could also be put to good use. Scouting was rarely taught, the best had it in their blood. Backwoodsmen, men who thought of the depths of the forest not as the haunt of wolf-heads, dark elves and orcs, but as a place which provided them with all that they required to live well enough; a year-long larder far from towns and settlements with their rules, taxes and obligations to king, thegn and ealdorman. Geats, Swedes and Finns were among the best to be found anywhere in the north, and Eofer was quietly thrilled by the unexpected addition of one of the highly prized men within the ranks of his troop.

Within the hour the pair were leading them away from the stone sets of the Roman way, forging onward as the path turned from dressed stone to dusty track and the outliers of the great woodland to the west stood out as dark as a line of bladderwrack on a sun bleached strand. They picked up the pace as the night wore on, skirting a small collection of huts whose occupants decided to ignore the warning yaps of their dogs, valuing safety above all else as a war band rode through the darkness of the witching hours in the troubled land.

Soon they were back among the trees, and the path narrowed as the shadows moved in to muffle the hoof fall of their mounts. By the time that the moon had reached its highest point in the sky to the south Cynfelyn was leading the party along a smaller path, and Eofer, despite the trust which he placed in his guide, eyed the shadows as the trees pressed in and the night sky became little more than a star speckled strip above them. If they were to come under surprise attack, this was as good a place as any, but the passage passed without incident and before another hour had passed they were through, pouring out onto a scrubby hillside and thankful to put the shadows behind them.

Ahead, Eofer saw the men of his duguth move their horses into a protective arc, slipping hands into shield grips and hefting spears as Horsa manoeuvred the hostage safely into the grip of the armoured fist and waited for his lord to come up.

Eofer drew rein, exchanging a look and a nod with his new weorthman. 'Ready?'

Horsa nodded grimly, and Eofer sought to lighten the mood as he recognised the tension which hung heavy in the air around him. 'You could be about to take the name of your sword.'

'Lord?'

Eofer smiled. 'Fame-Bright: Weorthman for a single day.' He shrugged. 'It's a fame of sorts.'

He glanced at Seaxwine. 'Are you ready?'

Without waiting for the answer, Eofer urged his horse forward with a squeeze of his knees. The eastern slope of the hill arced away to the north as the stallion followed the old track upwards towards the summit, the route before them hugging the contours as it snaked up to the ridge line and doglegged towards the gateway. He ran his eyes across the ancient work as the horse climbed, marvelling for the umpteenth time at the vigour of the Britons who had populated the land before the coming of the legions. Everywhere he had ridden throughout the island it seemed that isolated hills had been turned into strongholds, and he reflected again on the character of the men, past and present, who had built them. Tough, warlike and proud, the very qualities which made the men and women of Britain so distinctive had been turned inward by those who wished to control them for their own gain. Petty kingdoms had sprung up wherever tyrants could exchange gold and silver for spear men, while the populations sweated in the fields and lived in squalor to keep them in their finery.

The path had risen to skirt the lower ditch, and an image of the work gangs of men long since gone to their graves labouring to clear the site of the trees ghosted into his mind. It must have taken hundreds of men a full summer or more to sweep the slopes clear of the mighty trunks, as others bent their backs breaking the earth at the summit to construct the ditches and ramparts there. For centuries shepherds had watched over their flocks, the animals cropping the slopes to ensure that the guards walking the palisade which loomed above them could spot an enemy the moment that they exited the tree line. Raising his gaze as they climbed he found that he could see all the way past the silver ribbon of the River Trenta itself from his lofty perch, deep into the foothills of The Peaks.

The Englishman shook his head as the track steepened and approached the final turn. Should the Britons ever realise that their island contained more than enough wealth and goodness within its shores, if they ever decided to concentrate on the overwhelming traits and values which bound them together rather than allow their leaders to play on the trivialities which separated them, they would become unstoppable. There would be wealth enough for all and any invader, Roman, Engle, Saxon or others yet unknowable, would be thrown back from whence they came.

Eofer guided his mount to one side as Horsa led the duguth through towards the dark gap in the earthwork. Seaxwine stayed at his side as they fell in behind, the riders fanning out into a protective screen as they gained the interior of the hill fort. As Eofer watched, Horsa twisted in his saddle to beckon him on, and the eorle and his charge passed through the gateway, spilling out into a vast bowl of land which had once been the interior of the fort itself. Ringed by the ancient walls the moonlight painted the interior with a silvery sheen, and Eofer's eyes followed the course of the central roadway as he saw the Saxons for the first time, formed up in their own knot of steel a hundred yards ahead. His own duguth moved aside, their eyes darting this way and that as they searched the hilltop for any signs of treachery as Eofer led the young Saxon forward.

A pair of warriors detached themselves from the pack up ahead, and Eofer saw Seaxwine stiffen with pride as they walked their mounts towards them. Like his own men the Saxons carried their spears reversed, and a wash of lime shining white from the face of their shields confirmed the state of parley between them.

The surface of the fort was a pottage of darkness and light, the hummocky ground the only sign of the halls and huts which had once filled the space. The stump of a tree, a silver fang in the wan light, its significance to those long-dead lost in the mists of time, marked the centre of the old settlement, and Eofer brought his mount to a halt there and studied the Saxons as they grew nearer.

They were, he grudgingly admitted to himself, impressive. The man who must be Seaxwulf Strang looked fully seven feet tall and powerfully built. Even without a mail byrnie the Saxon shone like a beacon as the moonlight played upon a boar-helm, arm rings of silver and gold and a large circular brooch, chip carved in the Saxon style. He wore a white shirt beneath a blood red kirtle, the sleeves and collar where they showed gleaming like ice in the moonlight, and a wide belt studded with silver wyrms, the design echoed on the surface of the great buckle which fastened his belt. Blue breeks tightened at the calf by white winingas complemented a cloak, fur edged in the same hue. His companion was only marginally less impressive in size and splendour, the Saxon's frame bulked up by a cloak of bearskin despite the warmth of the night.

These would be difficult men to outshine Eofer knew, despite his reputation and the fineness of his own arms and clothing, so he changed tack on the spur of the moment, steering his ship onto a new course as he sought to keep the initiative. Unbuckling his grim-helm he prised it from his head, running his hand through his hair and throwing the Saxons a welcoming smile. To his amusement he saw that his unexpected show of openness had done the trick, the pair exchanging a look which destroyed their carefully assumed air of superiority and interrupted their steely gaze. As the Saxons glowered at allowing themselves to be outwitted, they brought their horses to a halt a dozen paces away.

Eofer hailed them: 'My name is Eofer Wonreding, some men call me king's bane.' He gave a self-depreciating shrug. 'Others, Danes mostly, know me as hall-burner, although the Jutes also have cause to remember me thus.' He twisted in his saddle, pointing back to his hearth troop with a jerk of his chin. 'My herebeacn, the burning hart. Hrothgar, King of Danes, had cause to rue the day he woke the English dragon.'

Seaxwulf cast a look of indifference over Eofer's shoulder and returned his gaze to the Engle, studiously avoiding his son who sat patiently at Horsa's side. 'You say that you did great things, but those things are in the past; what a man does today echoes in the halls of the gods. Now, it would seem, you are reduced to ransoming boys for silver.' The Saxon leaned sideways in his saddle and let a silvery ball of spittle fall from his lips to show his distaste.

Eofer responded with an exaggerated look of surprise. 'The only mention of ransom has come from yourself Seaxwulf. Reputation, not silver or gold is the wealth which I crave.' He gave an almost imperceptible movement of his head, fixing the Saxon leader with his eyes as Seaxwine's horse plodded across. A flicker of surprise showed on Seaxwulf's face, but he held his gaze on Eofer as the boy fell in behind him. 'That is half of the debt which you owe me repaid,' he said. 'You killed one of my men, a man dear to me. If you have come to return my son and offer weregild for my loss, you may pay me now and be on your way.'

'Unless the custom in Saxland differs from those throughout the north,' Eofer replied, 'brave men killed in open warfare require no compensation. In English lands a horn of mead in Valhall and a seat alongside his ancestors seem reward enough for men of spirit and valour.'

Seaxwulf exchanged a look with the man at his side and nodded. Passing his shield across he used his free hand to unfasten the ties and draw the helm from his head. 'So,' he replied, leaning forward in his saddle and fixing the Englishman with a stare. 'If you are not here for those things, tell me Engle. What do you really want?'

11

'**A**nd then you gave him back!'

Icel laughed as he shook his head slowly from side to side. 'I knew that you would have a go for the horses at Cair Luit Coyt but I never dreamed of this. And throwing up a burh overnight, almost within sight of Cynlas Goch's supply base. Now that,' he said as a look of admiration came into his eyes, 'is an act of brilliance. Bloody minded and deadly, just like your namesake Eofer, the wild boar!'

Eofer gave the ætheling a look of surprise. 'You knew that there were horses at the Cair?'

Icel threw a friendly arm around his thegn, leading him away from the others. 'Eofer,' he said with mock indignation. 'Do you really think that I would take myself off to visit the Lindisware without leaving people to keep an eye on things at home?'

'And you knew that I would mount a raid on Cair Luit Coyt,' Eofer protested, 'despite the fact that English warriors were thin on the ground in Leircestre?'

'I told you before I left, Eofer,' Icel replied. 'I have parties of men riding all over. Just because you did not see them does not mean that they were not there.' The ætheling raised a brow at the eorle's look of surprise. 'Do you really think that I expected Eofer hall-burner, the terror of the north, the same man who split the king of Swedes head like a nut, to sit supping ale in The Tewdwr like a dutiful thegn? Don't fret,' he laughed as he revelled in the look of shock painted on the face of his underling. 'I was not keeping an eye on you as such.' The ætheling laid a reassuring hand on Eofer's shoulder. 'You know that you have my complete trust king's bane, but I need to have eyes and ears everywhere. I am building a kingdom here,' he said, his voice lowering once again as a thræl woman moved past them with a pitcher of ale, 'not just defending a frontier. When you are playing for high stakes, the price for failure is usually sudden, sharp and bloody.'

Icel reached down and filled two cups with ale from a jug. Handing one across he waited until Eofer had supped before levelling his voice. 'You can't save Heardred you know, however honour bound you feel. Just wishing that things were better does not necessarily make them so.' Icel frowned. 'Our days of downy chinned invincibility are behind us my friend, we have both been warriors long enough now to know that I speak the truth. Things happen unexpectedly, for good or ill. Mighty hosts are led south to Frisland on great adventures by spear-bold kings, only to have the gods withdraw their favours at the very moment of their greatest vulnerability.'

He dropped his voice as Eofer sucked his teeth in thought. 'A little bird told me that King Hygelac owed the king helm to the Allfather himself.' It was the second time in the conversation that the ætheling had surprised the thegn with his knowledge, and Eofer snorted at Icel's triumphant expression. Heardred had told him of this father's pact with Woden on the beach, the day after he had rescued him and his ship's crew from a chasing pack of avenging Franks. They had been as alone as two men could be sharing a lonely strand with two ships' crews, and he was certain that they had been out of earshot of any of the men that morning. Not for the first time, Eofer found himself marvelling at the ability of his prince to harvest information about the most obscure and secretive subjects from all over. Icel saw his surprise and winked, the men laughing together as they both repeated the ætheling's conclusion from earlier in the conversation.

'When you are playing for high stakes, the price for failure is usually sudden, sharp and bloody.'

The laughter trailed away, and the frown returned to Icel's features as he drained the contents of his cup and poured a refill. 'Unless the followers of these Swedish æthelings are more powerful than my sources suggest, his best chance of surviving the summer is to make sure that he keeps a fast ship at hand. Even if you left Leircestre today, by the time that you assembled men from Anglia and gathered the ships to take them across the sea it would be too late.' Icel took another swig and pointed the cup at the eorle. 'Besides, what makes you think that the Danes are going to allow an English flotilla to sail past their lands unhindered, especially after the events of the last few years. Danish settlers are beginning to move into our old lands in Engeln. Dragon ships are already sailing out of Strand and the Jutes to the north have been brought under their sway. We may have given them both a bloody nose before we left, but they are tough foes, not easy to knock out completely.' He snorted. 'We all spring from the same line, the Engles, Danes and Jutes. The sons of Shæf never know when they are beaten.'

As Eofer pondered on his words, Icel drove the point home. 'How much gold and renown would King Hrothulf shower upon the man who brought him Eofer king's bane in chains do you think? The man who not only burned Heorot, but rescued the rightful heir to his own throne from under the noses of his huscarls and led them on a fruitless chase the length of Scania?' Icel pulled a grin as the twinkle came back into his eye. He gave the eorle a friendly shove, and Eofer had to echo the smile despite the gravity of the conversation. 'And what was happening in Daneland, while all this was going on?' he went on. 'Harrowed from coast to coast, its shiny new king left wondering where his best troops had disappeared to! Even when they returned,' he chuckled, 'that bloody king's bane killed his priest and skewered his leading huscarl at holmgang!'

They laughed again as the mood lightened, and Icel lowered himself to a bench. Eofer slid alongside as he watched the smoke curl up from the long hearth and thought on his lord's words. The ætheling pushed a plate of cold meats his way and reached across to top up the cups. Without looking back he spoke again. 'Have you heard from Astrid yet?'

Eofer speared a hunk of meat with his eating knife and sniffed. 'No, she doesn't know anything about the situation in her homeland yet.'

Icel cleared his throat and shifted awkwardly. 'She does. The ship from Geatland first put in at Yarnemutha. They were told that you were here at Leircestre and your friend Einar set off overland after paying his respects to my father the king. The ship picked up a pilot and travelled down to your hall at Snæpe with a message from King Heardred to his sister. She will have known all about the situation in her brother's kingdom for a week or so.'

Eofer's shoulders slumped. 'Shit!' he hissed. 'That is all that I need now.'

Icel pushed a piece of meat around the table with his knife as if reluctant to continue. Finally he speared the morsel and held it aloft, turning it this way and that as he spoke. 'Are things still…difficult between you and your wife?'

Eofer shook his head. 'No, not at all. She thinks that due to her newly elevated status as full sister to the king of Geats she deserves to be wed to an ealdorman at the very least, not a lowly thegn. I disagree, and the last time I looked I was the one with the cock, so no, there is nothing difficult about the situation at all.'

'You know that my father would make you an ealdorman in the blink of an eye Eofer, if that was your wish. The gods know,' Icel chuckled. 'He has asked you enough times. So what's the problem?'

'I don't want to spend my days tallying crops and sitting on my arse,' he replied irritably. 'There is plenty of time for that when I am older.'

Icel snorted again. 'Ah, no wonder she is so miserable. Women can't fight and win a reputation of their own, they have to snare a man who can do so on their behalf. You get your sense of worth from men retelling your deeds, she gets hers from bearing the hero's children and surrounding herself with servants and wealth. It's no fault of hers or your own, the world has always been that way. Why not become my ealdorman, here in Leircestre,' the ætheling suggested. 'Maybe that would placate you both. You would guard the marches and she could run the hall, this hall,' he said, sweeping his arm in an arc, 'ringed by walls of stone, the work of giants. She forgets,' he said as a flash of mischief lit his face. 'We have been to Geatland, there is nothing to compare there, nor will there ever be. You could be Ealdorman of Leircestre, lord of all the lands between the Trenta and Brunes Wald. I will confirm Hemming as a full thegn, the lord of the Tamesætan, and ensure that his lands are held directly from you.' He gave Eofer a nudge. 'It will almost be as if nothing had changed. You can still campaign together, Tamtun is well placed to raid the Hafron Valley and push down towards the southern hills once we rid ourselves of Cynlas Goch.'

Eofer glanced across. 'That would make me the most powerful man in the region.'

'In your wife's eyes, yes,' Icel replied. 'In reality you would still be my man, and I have a few more plans which I am confident will bear fruit given a bit more time. The visit to the Lindisware was a great success. Much to my surprise, the woman it appears that my father is keen to marry me off to is rather lovely in looks and charming and witty in conversation, which is fortunate for me because an alliance between ourselves and the men in Lindcylene makes perfect sense for both parties. Tell me, Eofer,' the ætheling said as the eorle reached for a pork rib and began to strip the meat from it with his teeth. 'What do you know of the Lindisware?'

Eofer nibbled to the end of the bone and tossed the remainder to a waiting hound. As the dog loped away with its prize, the thegn gave a shrug. 'Not very much, lord: to be frank I am not even sure if they are Britons or Engles. The furthest north that I have been on this island is...' he cast about and gave a shrug of his shoulders, 'not that much further than here.'

Icel leaned in, and Eofer saw the wolfish mien which he knew so well come to the ætheling's face. He too felt the thrill of the moment as it become clear that the talks which had just been concluded between the Engles of the east and the Lindisware had ranged far beyond a mere marriage arrangement.

Icel's eyes shone with barely suppressed excitement. 'I

want my leading men to know all there is to know about the wars which we have gone before us here. If we are to survive and flourish in these lands, we all need to understand the past alliances and animosities so that we can best judge who are most likely to be our friends and who will naturally feel inclined to oppose us in the present.'

Icel nodded towards his cup. 'It's a bit long-winded so I will need a refill. Make sure that you pay attention though,' he smiled. 'I shall be asking questions afterwards.'

The pair shared a grin as the ale flowed. Icel sank a draught, kicked back and began. 'During the time when my great grandfather back in Engeln was overcoming the Myrgings and bringing them under English sway, the first Arthur was attempting to do the same with the British kingdom of Lind Colun, what they now call Lindisware. Offa the Great defeated his enemies, and it looked for a time as if Arthur too would succeed, but the leaders of Lind Colun hearing of the power of the English king and the completeness of his victories, sent east for help in exchange for scot as the Romans had done before them. Offa sent a kinsman, Winta, with a war troop who arrived just in time to face the full might of Arthur's attack.'

Icel took another drink as Eofer sat enthralled at the tale. A day of introspection and awkward questions concerning his marriage had been replaced by tales of Offa and Arthur. He took the opportunity to guzzle from his cup as Icel continued. 'You remember the bard that accompanied Ceretic ap Cynfawr, the legate from The Peaks?'

Eofer nodded. 'The one who told the tale of Arthur's twelve great battles?'

'Well, half of those battles took place against the people we now call the Lindisware, five of which were battles against Winta and his men. The Engles held a ford on a river called the Dubglas which Arthur and his horse warriors had to take to advance on the capital at Cair Lind Colun, what they now call Lindcylene. In five great battles, the English had the victory, but the British king of Lind Colun fell there in the final attack. He died without leaving an heir, so the grateful citizens in Lindcylene raised Winta to the king helm and married women from the leading families to his war leaders. The children of these took English names and embraced our gods to honour their fathers, and within a generation it was becoming difficult to tell Briton and Engle apart.'

'So, if Winta was so successful,' Eofer asked with a frown. 'Why did he not pay scot to Offa, his kinsman and lord?'

Icel snorted. 'I think that he must have thought that the gods had a hand in his elevation. At the same time that Winta was winning his war against Arthur, Offa went to Valhall and was succeeded by my grandfather, Engeltheow. As you know both the Saxons in the south and the Jutes to the north took the opportunity to test the mettle of the new king and the first years of the reign were hectic to say the least. Winta and his men were forgotten, and they obviously decided that they liked it that way.' To Eofer's surprise the ætheling chuckled at the thought. 'Who can really blame them, Eofer? They had fought well and carved themselves a kingdom from the body of Britannia with sword and spear, defeating her greatest son along the way. Who has ever given up a king helm manfully earned, and volunteered to be an under-king?'

'But all that changed when King Eomær led the people here,' Eofer said as he began to understand. 'Suddenly there was a powerful English kingdom an hour's sailing from their coast and armies spilling out beyond the great marsh of The Fens.' He took a sip from his cup and raised a brow. 'Better by far to throw open your arms in welcome, offer your kin all the help that you can and apologise for the wrongheadedness of men long dead, than find a field of spears coming against you up Ermine Street or the Fosse Way.'

Icel clapped him on the shoulder. 'You see? You are already starting to think like an ealdorman.'

Eofer narrowed his eyes as a thought came to him. 'If I *was* Ealdorman of Leircestre, where would you be, lord?'

Icel laughed aloud. 'Don't worry, I am not about to go off campaigning without you. I intend to push our borders northwards from here, across the Trenta and into the southern part of The Peaks. King Sawyl has already agreed to cede part of the northern bank to us in return for our help against Cynlas Goch and his Powys'. I am thinking of naming our new lands along the Trenta, Mercia, the Marches, to reflect the old borderland along the River Egedore fixed by Offa the Great, back home in Engeln.'

'Not West Anglia then, lord?'

Icel shook his head. 'I want to push against all of our borders and see what gives. If we can move west into Powys all well and good. But the Lindisware already have Anglian settlers on the north bank of the River Humbre, we may be able to expand in that direction.' He pulled a grin. 'West Anglia would sound a bit daft then, wouldn't it? Mercia means the same, whichever way that border lies. Whatever the future holds for us Eofer, you can rest easy that it will have more than enough opportunities to build reputations. There is still plenty of fighting to come, enough even for you king's bane! Think my offer over,' he said, as he stood and placed a hand on Eofer's shoulder. 'Astrid will think herself lucky soon enough. Geatland is lost, all our futures lie here, on this side of the sea.'

Icel walked away to leave his thegn to mull over his words. Eofer let his eyes run around the great hall as he pondered the idea of ealdormanship. The hall which could be his own dwarfed that which he had had built back in Snæpe, and he gave a drink fuelled snigger as he realised that the building there could fit inside with room to spare. The long walls were built of Roman brick, lime plastered from wainscoting to ceiling. Painted upon these, life-sized figures enacted the tales familiar to all; gods fought giants, eorles fought foemen, slew dragons. Sturdy posts of seasoned oak marched away towards the far gable wall, the heroes and dragons carved upon them picked out in reds and blues and gold, mirroring those on the walls to either side. High above, the old fire-eaten rafters had been dragged down and replaced, the stout beams, honey gold in their newness, cradling a roof of russet thatch. Four stone-edged hearths ran down the centre, drawing his eye towards the only wall built by English hands. The gable wall here had long since fallen when the ætheling had arrived the previous summer. Now it had been replaced in northern fashion. A framework of oak posts and beams abutted the old Roman brickwork, the joints and scarfs carved into the heads of fantastic beasts to protect those inside from murderous trolls, night-gangers and the *spellweorc* of witches.

Eofer walked back to the northern end of the hall as the sound of laughter echoed in the great space. A platform had been raised there bearing two chairs. The higher one was sturdier, high backed between twin god-pillars, one carved in honour of Thunor the other Woden, the Allfather. This was the lord of the hall's gift-stool, the high seat of honour, and Eofer fingered the armrest as he imagined the space before him ablaze with life. Warriors cram benches, perched on the walls behind them their weapons: swords, axes and spears glow dully in the crimson light reflected from fire pits. Rushlights flare in sconces of horn and silver: lines of shields bearing the burning hart of their lord march away at their sides. He turns aside and Astrid beams with pleasure from the lady of the hall's chair as thræls scatter sweet smelling juniper along the walkways. All her hopes and dreams made real by four over-mighty walls.

'Ealdorman?'

The voice broke into his thoughts, and Eofer looked up as the dream faded. 'Icel?'

'Before you decide on the wall hangings,' the ætheling said with a smile, 'we have more work to do. While you have been annoying the enemy, I too have been busy. The final battle for control of the Trenta Valley is almost upon us, but before the armies come together I want you to harry them one last time.'

12

Eofer rested his back against the bole of the tree. Reaching out he snapped another strand of grass, stripped the outer sheath with his thumbnail and wedged it into the gap at the top of his front teeth.

'Very countryfied,' Octa said as he glanced across with a smile. 'We'll make a farmer of you yet, lord.'

Eofer put on a rustic accent as he replied, and the rest of the troop chuckled gently as Octa went back to checking the hooves of his horse for small stones and the like. 'Nowt wrong with turning sods, lad.'

Stretched out, relaxing in the warmth of a high summer's day, the others joined in as Octa ran the palm of his hand along the horse's hocks.

'Nor, mucking out pig shit. Nowt wrong with that.'

'Aye, nor breaking your back picking a field of peas.'

'And what about starving when the rains don't come, or come too late?'

'Aye, that be true. Or some bastard army waits until you have spent the year ploughing, sowing, weeding and harvesting. You have all of it safely stashed away and then they turn up and take turns with your wife and daughters before they carry the lot off, and you have to watch the bairns slowly starve to death over the course of the winter. That be good.'

The sound of hoofbeats carried to them in their restful glade, and the humour melted away like morning mist as the men jumped to their feet, all thoughts of the rigours and dangers which was the lot of humble ceorls everywhere driven from their minds.

The men relaxed a touch when they saw who the rider was, but Eofer was pleased to see that most were beginning to check their weapons nevertheless. The horseman came into the clearing, guiding the animal across to the place where Eofer was brushing twigs and earth from the seat of his breeks.

'There is one coming, lord.'

Eofer spat out the stalk and nodded. 'How far have they got?'

'They are just nearing the place where the river takes a wide sweep to the south,' Einar replied. 'At the speed they are rowing I would say that they will be at the bridge not long after we reach it ourselves.'

Eofer nodded his thanks, flashing them all a smile as he mounted his own steed. The young Geat had proven his worth over the past few weeks, a time spent raiding and harrying the Powys outliers and supply wagons as Eofer sought to snap at Cynlas Goch's heels until the English and their British allies could gather their own army and put the beast to the sword. A tug at the reins and Horsa appeared at his side.

'Let's go!'

Edging out from the tree cover, Eofer led the war troop across the meadow to the dusty track. The boat would need to negotiate a sharp bend before they came into view and the Engles would be gone long before that occurred. The track curved away to the east, before joining the main route which ran as close to the Trenta as the gentle hills allowed. The arc would lead them even further away from the searching eyes of the guards on the supply boat, closer still to their destination, and Eofer once again sent a word of thanks winging its way to the Welshman Ioan whose local knowledge had proven such a boon in his raiding of the past few weeks.

Within a half mile they were there and the thegn drew rein, slowing to a walk as the others came up. 'Remember,' he said as they left the track and walked their mounts onto the packed earth of the main highway. 'We are approaching from upriver so the men on guard should assume that we are Powys' until it is far too late. Whatever happens,' he added, 'none of them must escape to warn those at the fort. Should one of them escape and get through to his friends we will not only have wasted our time, but thrown away a fantastic opportunity to hit these bastards where it hurts and lay the groundwork for our ultimate victory. Keep your shields in their carrying pouches and spears slung.' He shot them all a grin. 'We *are* all friends after all!'

The gesture was returned as the men of Eofer's hearth troop rechecked straps and fittings. Happy that all was well, the thegn clicked his horse on as the men fell into line in his wake.

The day was warm but overcast, a typical British summer day Eofer thought as he rode steadily along. White puffy clouds rolled slowly across from the west with only the occasional gull grey erratic to spoil the purity of a sky scrubbed clean of colour. Near the river the first horseflies and midges of the year hazed the air, and the men watched in fascination as arrow winged swallows and martins swooped and banked only inches from the ground as they harvested the summer bounty.

Rounding a bend the bridge hove into view, and Eofer kept the pace at a steady canter as the faces of the guards turned their way. A man slid from the parapet with an obvious sense of reluctance, stretching and placing the palms of his hands against his lower back as his friends strolled across to retrieve their weapons from a spear rack. Eofer allowed himself a smile of self-congratulation. He had purposefully allowed this to become a backwater in the ongoing conflict between the Powys' and their foes, bypassing the area during his recent spate of attacks on the enemy's supply line and fort-lets with just this in mind. Lulled into a false sense of security the bridge should fall to them with barely a fight.

Raising his gaze, Eofer saw the heat-haze shimmering over the land beyond the bridge. The valley of the Trenta was wide here, the lush greens of the water meadow which flanked each bank rising gently until they met the darker greens and browns of the woodland fringe. The men before him were likely to be smallholders, flock-men and the like, the equivalent of the English freeman the ceorl. He looked back at the men on the bridge and saw the way that they were attempting to add a touch of the fighting man to their bearing and imagined their thoughts. Real warriors were approaching and they would do their best to appear worthy of the task which had been assigned to them, but both sides would know the truth; they were there because it was a duty owed their lord. A payment in return for a roof over their family's head, just another obligation like the rest: the first bag of flour from the new harvest, ploughing his lord's land before his own. These men were clearly what the British called the Militia, and a pang of regret that he was to be the cause of their death came over the Englishman as he watched the men put on a show, pulling themselves up proudly to welcome their betters.

The roadway divided before them and Eofer guided his

mount away from the main track, leading the troop along the steady curve which led to their goal. The sentinels were lined up beside the approach itself and Eofer raised a hand in greeting in a final act of deception as he saw the face of what must be the leader come clear of the line and turn his way. Within moments they were upon them, and the thegn reined in as his men clattered onto the bridge and formed a menacing half circle around the bemused Britons. Free of the need for further subterfuge spears came into English hands, and Eofer slipped from his saddle and stood before what he took to be the leader of the little group.

'Does anyone here speak English? Saxon? Any language of Germania?'

The men cast fearful glances, enough to tell the thegn that they were aware of the words English and Saxon, if not conversant in the languages themselves. He tried again in broken Welsh.

'Saesneg? Sacson? Unrhyw iaith Germania?'

One of the men piped up, putting on a brave face, but the quiver in his voice betrayed the fear there. 'I know some Saxon, lord,' he offered. 'Enough to get by.'

'Good,' Eofer replied. 'You are?'

'Cadog, lord.'

'Cadog, tell your friends what I have to say and you may get the chance to see your loved ones again.' He looked the Briton in the eye and could see that he understood completely, but he made the point again just to make sure that the man was well aware that he held the lives of them all, if not in his hand, certainly within the honesty of his words. Eofer added a splash of menace to his gaze as he spoke again. 'I know a fair smattering of Welsh, as do most of my men. I am sure that between us we could converse in your tongue, but as I am a thegn and my men are the ones pointing spears at *your* throats,' he smiled wolfishly, 'Saxon it is. Bear that in mind when you translate. Just answer my questions simply and accurately and there need be no bloodshed here.'

The Briton nodded enthusiastically as his friends' eyes danced from Eofer to the spearpoints and back again.

'Right,' he said, 'we still have a little time to kill, enough to allow us to become better acquainted. Tell me your usual trades or occupations, how you spend your days when not invading other folk's lands.'

The guard turned to the others and spoke a few words in Welsh. One by one the men reeled off their usual occupations as the Saxon speaker added the translation. It was as he had suspected. Before him stood two shepherds, a huntsman and a smallholder. The earlier jokey conversation about the lot of the common folk had touched a nerve and he would spare them if he could, but the time available for merciful acts was running out now: he would have to move quickly. The boat would be nearing the bend in the Trenta, once it had completed the turn the bridge would hove into view, especially from the raised platform where the steersman plotted the course ahead. They would need to be out of sight long before that happened, or risk the success of the entire enterprise.

The dark twins, Crawa and Hræfen, had been entrusted with caring for the horses, following along as stealthily as they could until the main attack was over and the time came for their hearth mates to make their escape. A quick glance upriver confirmed that there was as yet no sign of the enemy boat and Eofer reached a decision. 'Cadog, our new land of Mercia has use for shepherds, huntsmen and soil tillers and you will be welcome to stay once we have driven Cynlas Goch and his rag-tag army back beyond the forest of Canoc. But for now at least I realise that your loyalties must lie elsewhere, and I would expect you to carry word of our presence straight to our enemies. Tell your friends what I have said, and tell them to remove their clothes and boots as quickly as they can and I will let you live.'

The guard thought to argue, but a look from Eofer told him that that would be unwise. As he relayed the instruction to his companions, the men of Eofer's troop were dismounting, unstrapping helms and shields from the flanks of their horses as they prepared for the fighting to come.

The twins were already slipping a rope through the harnesses of each mount as they prepared to lead the horses back into cover as Eofer spoke again. 'Lads, bind them hand and foot and throw them across the backs of the horses. Make certain that we have been successful before you take off,' he said. 'We don't want to end up stranded here without our horses should anything go wrong.' He pulled a wry smile. 'I daresay that Cynlas Goch and his men would dearly love to come across us wandering about like Christian pilgrims, especially after the mayhem we have been causing over the last few weeks. Once we are on our way, take our friends here deep into the backwoods and cut the soles of their feet. Set them free there and follow on as we planned; if one of them is a huntsman as they say he should be able to lead them out.' He caught Hræfen's eye as the youth began sawing at a length of rope, preparing the bindings he would need. 'Make the cuts nice and deep, we don't want them to hobble out too fast. Oh,' he added as the youth moved towards the first of the prisoners. 'Leave them a couple of spears, just in case wolves pick up the smell of blood. They are having a bad enough day as it is.'

Horsa had already scooped up one of the Britons' leather headpieces, the small dome looking more like a monk's tonsure than a low class battle helm as it perched precariously on his head. The duguth had moved across to the western side of the bridge, and he stood staring at the distant bend where the boat must soon appear as the men he had replaced piled their clothing on the roadway behind him. Eofer laughed at the sight of the ridiculous headpiece despite the tension of the moment as he called across. 'Nothing?'

'Not yet, lord,' his weorthman replied. 'It will not be long now though.'

'I agree. Get yourself back and sit by the far parapet, four of the youth are to replace the guards. He looked Horsa up and down. 'The boatsman will be familiar with this stretch of water and he will be expecting to see the usual guards, or at least something similar lining the wall.' He snorted again. 'Not a hulking great barbarian with a pimple on his head! Get yourself over to the far side of the bridge and join the others.'

As he looked back, Eofer was pleased to see that Grimwulf and Anna had bound the naked men and were throwing the last of them across the horses. Einar crossed to join the duguth who were already in place, resting their backs against the stone parapet, fixing helms and drawing swords as they waited for the boat to arrive. Beornwulf, Porta and Bassa were already slipping into the guards' discarded tunics and leather caps as Crawa and Hræfen mounted up and began to lead their unusual cargo back towards the tree line to the south.

'This looks like it, lord,' Grimwulf called out from his position at the parapet.

Eofer looked. Half a mile or so distant, the raised prow of the supply ship was edging clear of the bank as it negotiated the last of the switchbacks before the Trenta straightened out and ran down to the crossing. A quick look around confirmed that the duguth were all in position, and the last of the four youths who would replace the guards were tugging their tunics into place as they made their way across. The horses had barely left the approach road as they made their way down to the distant tree line but there was little they could do about that, it had been a close run thing as it was, but he was pleased to see that the dark twins had thought to sling the Welshmen with their heads pointing downriver. At a distance the whites of their arses should resemble sacks or linen bound packages, especially seen through the shimmering air of the heat haze which cloaked the meadow. It was just the type of sight which those on the boat could expect to see, and Eofer felt a surge of confidence as he took his place alongside the duguth. A quick look to the north-west confirmed that the roadway there was clear of traffic, and the war band settled in for the wait, fastening belt straps and preparing weapons as a break in the clouds finally revealed the sun for the first time that day.

Eofer raised his head and spoke as the youth lolled about the roadway, keen to appear as bored with their duty as the real guards had been only a short time before. Grimwulf, his elbows resting nonchalantly on the top of the stonework, spoke in a low tone as Eofer drew Gleaming from its scabbard and twisted the blade back and forth, admiring the ancient sword smith's craft for the thousandth time as the sunlight played upon the silvery-grey swirls.

'They are about halfway to us,' he murmured, 'moving quicker than I expected. Be prepared to make your move as soon as I take up my spear lord, or you could be taking a dip!'

Eofer looked to either side, exchanging a smile with his duguth. 'Helms on I think lads,' he said. 'We will frighten them to death before they can even reach for their weapons. And be careful when you jump,' he added as he pushed himself up into a crouch. 'They will have to slow down to shoot the archway but you will disappear in an instant if you miss the boat, it would be a wretched way to die. With any luck we will have caused enough mayhem on board to take the way off the boat as it goes under the bridge. As soon as it reappears downstream, come and give us a hand.'

The group touched the tips of their weapons in the pre-battle act which the English called *bindung*, the binding, and a last look told the thegn that the roadway was still clear in both directions as he fingered the eye of Woden on his scabbard and sent a word of thanks to the god. The Allfather was sure to be watching, daring and cunning were two of his own traits after all, and Eofer resisted the urge to scan the tree line for a hooded traveller come to watch the show as he forced his attention back to the imminent attack.

It was not a moment too soon as Grimwulf snatched up his spear and leapt the parapet, cloak flailing as he disappeared from view. Within a heartbeat Eofer was moving, pushing himself up and forward as the remaining youth rushed across to follow in their wake. A moment's hesitation as his eyes searched the deck below for the best place to land, and he launched himself onward as open mouthed faces began to turn upwards.

A rush of air and he was on the deck, knees flexing as they cushioned the blow. Before him a Briton was snatching up a hand axe from its stowage amidships, and Eofer jabbed out with Gleaming as the hatchet came up. At full stretch the wicked point could do little more than prod the man off balance, but it was enough to wrest the advantage from his opponent. The Briton threw out a hand as he tottered, making a grab for one of ropes which secured the cargo as he twisted back with a snarl; but Eofer was faster, stepping in to close the gap between them as his sword arm came back. An instant later the scowl was driven from the crewman's face as Gleaming clove the air, Eofer's blade sweeping across in a rising blow to strike beneath his opponent's jaw, cutting up and through, crushing bone and paring flesh until it emerged above in a spray of blood. As the axe clattered to the deck at his feet and his victim's hands moved up to clasp his shattered face Eofer was pivoting, his sword sweeping in an arc before him as he braced to face the next attack.

A quick look told him that Grimwulf had speared another defender in the chest, the youth's features a twisted snarl as he hoist his yowling victim overboard like a haymaker at harvest time. The man disappeared with a muffled splash as the rest of Eofer's youth rained down around him from the bridge above, and the eorle raised his eyes to the steering platform of the boat for any signs of resistance as he prepared to fight again.

Beornwulf crashed onto the deck at his side, the youth's head spinning around as an arm shot out and his mouth opened to call a warning, but before Eofer could swivel to face the unseen threat white light flashed as a powerful blow struck the back of his helm. Knocked forward by the violence of the strike Eofer just had time to tighten his grip on Gleaming, cursing his slackness as his eyes began to lose their focus and he prepared for death.

13

'Morning precious, how's the bump?'

Eofer's eyes flickered and immediately clapped shut again as the light drove hot needles into his brain. He reached up, fumbling with the cords which tied his helm in place as he sought to prise it from his head.

'You'll be lucky, lord. It's jammed as tight as a rat up a pipe.'

Eofer forced himself upright, wincing again as the pain in his head redoubled.

'Keep yourself still, Eofer,' Horsa said. 'That was a nasty crack you took there.'

Eofer's weorthman reached up and readjusted the awning above him. Feeling the cooling shadow passing across his face, the thegn forced his eyes open a touch. 'Who killed him?'

Horsa's eyes narrowed in question, but a moment later his face lit up as he realised the meaning behind his lord's words. 'You think that you were attacked from behind!' Despite Eofer's discomfort the big duguth was unable to suppress a laugh. He shook his head and snorted. 'You took a crack to the back of your head when the boat went under the bridge, Eofer. The next time that someone points and shouts duck in the middle of a fight just do it, it would be a good bet that they are not pointing out the nearby waterfowl!'

Eofer sighed. 'I only had time to see his mouth open and, crunch. It all went dark.' He ran his gaze across the boat as the importance of the day came back to him. 'Where are we, why aren't we moving?'

'We have laid up for a bit so that we arrive at this fort at dusk. We will be on the move again soon, don't worry. Here,' he said, handing over a clutch of willow stalks. 'Chew on these, and make sure that you swallow the juice from the leaves. It will help to deaden the pain.'

Eofer took the willow and began to chew. Although it was not as sweet and pleasant tasting as the grass stalks from earlier that day, everyone knew that the sap from the goat willow had magical healing properties. It would help to deaden the pain at least, and, given a little time reduce the swelling which was fixing his battle helm firmly in place.

Horsa jerked his head. 'Our man at the helm over there had a pot of honey. I have got Grimwulf grinding some of the bark into a powder. I will have him mix it with the honey when he has enough.' He gave his lord a sympathetic smile. 'The bark is faster acting than the leaf and more powerful, but it makes a crab apple taste sweet. The honey will take the bitterness away, make it easier to swallow.'

Eofer looked across. Three Britons were sat by the steering oar, their faces betraying their unease at their situation. Eofer thought that they looked about as happy as three mice trapped in a roomful of cats. 'Can they be trusted?'

Horsa gave a shrug as he replied. 'I spoke to the owner, the one with the soppy red hat. I gave him the choice between helping us or having his throat cut.' He flashed a smile. 'He chose to help us. The other two,' he added, 'are his kin. The stocky one, the one who looks like him, is his son you will not be surprised to discover. The beanpole is a cousin or something, his sister's son I think he said. Two powerful reasons to behave yourself and do as you are told I would say.'

'Tell me all that I have missed,' Eofer said as he ran his eye across the crewmen, 'and what plans you have made.'

'Well,' Horsa began, 'you didn't miss the fight, that's for sure. There were only five on board, the three over there and a couple of guards who came down with the goods from Cair Luit Coyt. You and Grimwulf got the guards, you may or may not recall. When the boat finally reappeared on the far side of the bridge and the duguth leapt aboard it was all over. You were laying flat on your face, there was a body missing half of its head in the scuppers and the three lads over there were crowded in the stern seeing which one could hold their hands the highest.'

Eofer stripped the leaves from another twig, mumbling through the mush. 'The beanpole.'

'Lord?'

Eofer squeezed the juice from the leaves with his tongue and swallowed. Whatever wizardry the willow contained was already having an effect, and he pushed the soggy mash to one side of his mouth as he expanded on his previous reply. 'The beanpole. He reached the highest.'

'Yes, lord,' Horsa chuckled as he recognised the return of Eofer's usual good humour. 'He did.'

'So what happened next, and why did you spare the crew? We can handle a boat as well as any river trader.'

'That is pretty much what I asked our new friend Alyn. He spewed something in Welsh at me and I was about to spit him when he hurriedly made his point in good English.'

'Which was?'

'Not only are they personally well known to the other river traders who ply the Trenta, but everyone knows the boat too. If its seen with anyone else but Alyn at the helm folk will know that something is wrong, whether they are wearing a ridiculous hat or not.' Horsa lowered his voice and shot the Britons a look. 'He's no fool either, lord, he guessed what we are up to straight away. He says that he is expected and well known at the fort. If the boat appears and he's not on it they will clam up as tight as a shell, we will never get in.'

'So, why is he willing to help us. Apart from the obvious fact that he still has a son, nephew and a head on his shoulders?'

'He was in Lindcylene, the main settlement in the land of the Lindisware.'

'Where Icel went?'

Horsa nodded. 'Alyn was there at the same time, there is an old Roman canal which connects the city to the River Trenta. All the talk there is of the great victory which they are going to win against Cynlas Goch this summer in alliance with the men of Anglia. There is no love lost between Powys and the Lindisware, they have fought each other for control of the middle lands for generations. It would seem,' Horsa said, 'that our friend shares their optimism. He is a trader whose livelihood depends on the goodwill of the local lord. In short he expects us to win, and he wants to make sure that he grabs this chance to be on the winning side.'

'How is it coming along?'

Anna looked up from his work, squinting as the sun fell upon his face. 'Not bad, lord, I will soon have it looking presentable at least. I am using the rounded handle of my knife on the inside as a horn, you know the pointy sticky-out bit on an anvil, and a mallet which I found amidships to tap out the worst of it. My tools are still packed on the horse with the twins. When I get them back I will find a real anvil in one of the settlements and have it looking as good as new. You took a fair old whack from the stone face decorating the keystone and the nose made this big dent,' he said, running the pad of his finger along the pitted surface at the rear of the helm. His face creased into a smile. 'It must have been a bit of a shock to get a Gippeswic kiss out here in the middle of nowhere, lord.'

Eofer snorted at the youth's humour as a clatter of wings drew his gaze across to the reed bed lining the bank. As Anna bent back to his work, Eofer watched as the lanky form of an egret hauled itself into the sky, the white of its plumage flashing a golden bronze in the westering sun. The bird hung suspended as its wings beat the muggy air, and the Engle felt a kick of anxiety as he saw the Christ cross outlined in flames in its form. The egret twisted in the air as it fixed its course, and the luminescence was snuffed out in an instant as it hugged the reed tops and made its way south. The shadows were lengthening by the moment and, raising his eyes once again, he saw the first brand flare into life on the walls of the fort as he realised just how close they were to their goal.

'Clear this spur and we are into the run in, lord,' Horsa said as he appeared at his shoulder.

Eofer looked across. 'Did you see that bird?'

Horsa pulled a lupine smile, already anticipating the fight to come. 'Sod the birds, they are lighting the torches. A bit early if you ask me.' He sniffed. 'Jumpy lot.'

Eofer looked at him in surprise. 'Hemming used to say that. And that bird, it took the form of a burning cross.'

Horsa looked at his lord and laid a friendly hand on his

shoulder. 'Are you taking the auspices, Eofer? I never had you marked down as a rune shaker.'

'But the flaming cross. It must mean something.'

'Of course it does,' the duguth replied patiently. 'It means that a white bird took off and was lit up by the rays of the setting sun. As for me repeating Thrush's words, I spent just about every hour with the man for more than a year, it's hardly a surprise if I picked up a saying or two.'

Eofer was about to speak again but Horsa beat him to it.

'Don't worry,' he chuckled, 'there is no Christian *déofol* waiting for us in the fort, and even if there was the gods sent you a sign that you will burn him out. You have seen enough of their churches now, Eofer. How many of them had a wooden cross on the roof or over the door?'

Eofer brightened. 'All of them.'

Horsa patted him on the shoulder and threw him a wink of encouragement. 'There you go then.' He glanced across and the corner of his mouth curled into a cheeky smile. 'Just how hard did that bridge hit you?'

'You are right,' Eofer snorted. 'It's been a long and eventful day. Get the lads together and we will go through the plan one last time. Let's make sure that everyone knows what to expect.'

As his weorthman made his way back along the deck of the boat, Eofer ran his eyes across the dark outline of the Powys' stronghold a final time. He had seen the place before of course, from the shadow of the southern woodlands, two weeks hence. Then, the last of the sharpened logs which formed the palisade were being lowered into place along the tops of the bank and ditch of the main defences. The whole looked complete now and, although small, it was an ideal base from which to control the surrounding countryside.

A stand of alder lined the bank casting long shadows

across the walls of the fort, and Eofer saw that a start had been made to felling them. Soon the land would be cleared of anything which could interfere with the all-round view of the guards, and the place would become all but unassailable to anything but a powerful army. It had to fall now he knew, *déofol* or not, or by late summer the place would be impregnable.

His mind drifted away to another such place, an English burh built to perform much the same function, deep within the land which the enemy considered their own. Tamtun had become all that he hoped it would be when he made Thrush Hemming the lord there. Traders in Leircestre had reported that traffic on Watling Street had practically ceased as word spread that the area had become a focus of the wider struggle between the Engles and Powys. His own attacks on the supply columns passing between Cair Luit Coyt and the army of Cynlas Goch spread out along the course of the Trenta had caused the enemy to cut back on their forays along the valleys which led south, adding to the general feeling that the tide was turning and the fates were with the English. Now, with the destruction of a completed fortress, fully manned and supplied, he hoped to sow the seeds of doubt within the core of the army itself.

A muffled cough at his shoulder dragged him back, and Eofer turned to see that his war troop had assembled and were waiting to hear his words. He threw them a smile as Horsa took his place among them.

'Here we are,' he said, 'on the cusp of our attack at last.' He ran his hand over the back of his head and pulled a wry smile, 'and all in one piece.' Horsa's willow and honey mixture had done the trick and the pain which had blazed behind his eyes like a hearth fire at midwinter had finally all but left him. Woden was the god of witchery, and whatever

magic he had used to imbue the tree with its healing properties, he was not the first nor would he be the last to be
thankful for the powerful spell-work. Smiles flickered for a
heartbeat at their lord's quip, but fell quickly away as the men
prepared their minds for war.

'I want to hit this fort, and hit it hard. Anything less than
the complete destruction of its garrison and the wooden parts
of the structure itself will be considered a failure.' He flicked
a look up at Alyn and saw that he was lending his weight to
the steering oar. The Briton was guiding the boat into the
final turn before the fort itself came into plain view. He
would have to be brief, but they knew their business and he
could see that they brimmed with confidence to a man. 'You
have all heard how Alyn has described the interior of the fort,
but we will run through it now. Ask any questions that you
can think of, or put me right if you think that I have misun-
derstood anything myself.' He gave a self-depreciating shrug.
'It has been known.' His finger stabbed out as he asked the
first question of the men.

'Finn.'

'Yes, lord?' The new duguth beamed, proud to take the
honour of answering the first question.

'What will we see as we approach the fort from the
river?'

'The main walls come down to the riverbank and then
extend out into the river itself for several yards. The begin-
nings of a jetty has been constructed to enable boats to
unload, but this will almost certainly still be incomplete.'

'So?'

'So the area will be strewn with building materials and
the like, things to keep an eye out for if it's gloomy.'

Eofer nodded and moved his finger across to Anna, from
the newest duguth to the latest youth to join his troop. The

boy had lost his father, his only remaining family in the fighting at the ridge, back in Daneland during the war of fire and steel. Eofer had allowed him to tag along during the migration to the new land, but the lad had more than proved his worth in many ways and all had been delighted when he had sworn an oath to Eofer and joined their band.

'What else will we see there?'

'A wall, lord, twenty paces from the river's edge.'

'None of us have ever seen this wall, Anna. Describe it for us.'

The boy flushed as faces turned his way, but he cleared his throat and carried on. 'The wall is made of vertical timbers driven directly into the soil. This screen is about ten feet high, a good height to allow defenders stood on the interior fighting platform to stab down with spears at any attackers below them.'

'There is no earth bank?'

'No lord, neither inside nor out.'

'Porta. How do we get past this wall?'

'Through the gate, lord,' the youth grinned. 'Which they will leave open for us.'

Eofer snorted as gentle laughter rolled around the group. 'Let us hope so. But if they don't, you all know what to do and who your partner is?'

A sea of nodding heads accompanied guttural grunts as the men confirmed that they did.

'Has this wall a gatehouse?'

Porta shook his head. 'Only a covered section above the gate, there are no defensive features as such.'

'Grimwulf, what will we see when we enter the compound?'

'Four leather tents, lord. Two on our left to house the workmen who are building the fort, and two facing them across the way who belong to the warriors whose job it is to defend them. Eight men to a tent in the Roman fashion makes twenty warriors and a similar number of artisans.'

Smithing had given Anna a sharp mind, and he threw a questioning look at his fellow youth as he tallied up the numbers involved. Grimwulf delighted in explaining his number work to the amusement of the others. 'Each ten man group is assigned a tent, but a quarter of them are always on guard duty. So,' he smiled as he poked the boy with a finger, 'they only need room for eight men in a tent at any one time.'

Eofer bobbed his head in agreement. 'And?'

'And that's about it, lord,' he answered with a satisfied smile. 'They have been kept busy constructing the defences. The only building so far within the boundary of the fort is the church which stands near the main gate. The horses are picketed in the corner opposite.'

Eofer nodded with satisfaction as a sharp whistle came from the rear of the boat. Eofer looked across to see the steersman pointing forwards. The bows had cleared the final turn, and Alyn was centring the steering oar as he guided the craft the final hundred yards or so to the landing place. The crewmen were moving for'ard uncoiling the ropes which would tie the craft to her moorings, and Eofer gave his final instruction as the first challenge carried to them from the rampart.

'Einar.'

'Yes, lord?'

'You fight with the duguth. Grab your gear lads, and anything which might make you look like you are trying to be helpful. Once we are inside hit them like Thunor's hammer!'

Anna handed him his grim helm as he passed, and Eofer secured it to his belt as he retrieved his shield and spear from their stowage place amidships. Shouldering the great board he bent again to hoist a sack from the deck and waited for the boat to ground. His men were doing likewise as Alyn pushed the rudder away from his body and angled in towards the bank.

The sky was still an ochre wash to the west, but the waterfront was mostly in gloom, and despite the tension of the moment Eofer once again wondered at the fact that the British had left the stand of alder in place so close to the fort. It was slapdash, and he hoped the man in charge here was as slack in other areas of his defences. He could see now that the gateway into the fort was still open, two spearmen lounging there as they waited for the new arrivals, and he knew that Alyn had been truthful when he had told them that the sight of his distinctive red hat would quash any suspicion that the incoming boat could contain anything but friends.

The boat gave a shudder as the keel brushed the shelving river bottom, and Eofer looked on as the Welsh lads leapt ashore and made her fast to the mooring posts. Moments later he too was on the bank, and he moved aside as the others landed beside him with a crash of boots and a jangle of metalwork.

Alyn called out, and the guards at the gate exchanged a look before one of them reluctantly ambled down to the water's edge. Stepping from shadow into light, the man shielded his eyes as he called to the boatman in their native tongue. 'Who are your friends, Alyn?'

'*Sacsoniaid*,' he replied. 'I am taking them up to the big fort.' The boatman smiled. 'Some Engles rustled their horses at the Cair, so they hitched a lift with me.'

The guard flicked a look across to the place where Eofer and Horsa were waiting for the rest of the duguth. Saxons or not, the sheer size and the aura of belligerence coming from the men before him demanded that they afford the newcomers respect. Barbarians were unpredictable at the best of times, if they had had their horses stolen from under their noses their precious sense of honour would have been badly knocked; they would be itching to fight someone, anyone who gave them half an excuse, and he knew from experience that gabby Britons, allies or not, would do just fine.

Alyn had read the spearman's thoughts, and he called over again. 'It's alright, this lot are just off the boat. They can't understand a word of Welsh.'

Eofer caught the man rolling his eyes. Osbeorn had noticed it too, and Eofer had to stifle a laugh as he recognised the mischievous twinkle he knew so well come into the duguth's eyes. The guard sauntered across, motioning to Osbeorn as he came. 'Come on then, hurry up. Get that stuff inside and we can all eat.'

Osbeorn narrowed his eyes, his expression deadpan as he feigned incomprehension. As the guard let out a weary sigh, the big man offered up his sack of goods with an imbecilic smile.

'No I don't want it, take it that way,' the guard snapped, blind to the fact that the rest of the war band were moving past him towards his lone friend at the open gate. The Welshman tried again, raising his voice and slowing his speech in the manner of all Britons when faced with a foreigner unable to understand their tongue. Eofer, despite the tension of the moment had to turn his face aside, masking his laughter with a cough as he caught the exchange.

'Go…that…way.'

'Bitte?'

'Follow…your…mates…you…thick…Hermann.'

Eofer raised his gaze, his blood quickening as he saw that Horsa and the leading men were a dozen paces from the gaping entrance and its dozy guard. He shouldered his spear and followed on just as another figure appeared framed by the posts, silhouetted by the campfires within. Eofer narrowed his eyes as a spark of recognition kindled within him, but his stomach went into free fall as the figure took a pace forward into the last of the day's light, the horror on his face plain to see as English plans became dust.

14

As the double doors began to close, Eofer snapped into a run. The others had recognised the man too and Horsa threw himself forward, hoping to shoulder the doors wide before the locking bar could be dropped into place. Shouts were carrying to them from the compound, and they all knew that the chances of the attack being successful were sluicing away by the moment. Horsa crashed into the gate, the force of the strike causing a cloud of ochre dust to billow from the boards, but Eofer saw with consternation that the defences were solidly closed to them. Already the duguth were moving to the sides and Eofer cried out as he came on. 'Youth! Get those shields ready!'

The back-up plan quickly took shape, the youth fanning out to either side of the gateway as all need for pretence fell away. The duguth had turned back, taking the few paces necessary to make the leap, and Eofer felt satisfaction despite the ruination of his original plan that he was now best placed to lead the attack.

Anna and Bassa were the first to get into position and Eofer angled his run towards the pair as they gripped the shield tightly, flexing their knees as they made a platform between them. A heartbeat later and Eofer was leaping, right foot leading as he drove forward and up. His momentum slammed him into the palisade, the roughly hewn wood scouring his cheek as the youth lifted him with a grunt and he flew upwards. Lights flashed like suns before his eyes from the fires within the compound and he knew that he had cleared the top of the wall. Eofer's arm shot out to hook himself up and over; a moment's free-fall and his back crashed onto the fighting platform and he rolled, bracing himself as he tumbled down into the fort itself.

Back on the ground the eorle sprang to his feet, his spear coming around as a dip of the shoulder caused his shield to slide down on its carrying strap. The instant his fist closed around the handle the shield came up, and Eofer threw his shoulder behind the big board as he prepared to face the first of the defenders.

The guards had recovered quickly from their surprise and a spearman was almost upon him, but Eofer sprang forward yelling his war cry, driving the thrill of an easy victory from the attacker's expression in an instant. His aggressive reaction had drained some of Briton's confidence, but the man was committed to the attack and he pushed down his fears and came on. Eofer took the spear thrust on the face of his shield, deflecting the dart aside as he drove forward. Horribly exposed to a counter strike, the Briton twisted in desperation as he sought to open the distance between them, but Eofer stabbed downwards as his opponent spun away, the point of his spear sliding smoothly into the soft calf muscle of his trailing leg. As the spear came back Eofer twisted his grip, angling the spearpoint upwards and thrust again. It was an old trick, one which he had used a hundred times in battles and skirmishes, and it worked again. The Briton raised his shield in desperation as the blade came in, but blind now he did not even see the moment that the Engle dropped the spearpoint and thrust again. The scream of pain as the blade opened his groin told Eofer that the strike had been true, and as the first man to lead the counterattack fell away Eofer swung around to face the next threat.

Another Briton was following in, hefting his spear as his friend lay howling at the base of the palisade. Eofer braced again to receive the attack but the man suddenly slid to a halt, raising his eyes in horror before turning tail to run back towards the centre of the fort.

A quick look to left and right confirmed what he already suspected, and he sprinted towards the enemy campsite as his duguth rained down into the compound from the walkway above.

As his head snapped around he was already drawing back his arm, ready to let fly with his spear at the nearest Briton. The retreating guard was a dozen paces ahead of him, his panicked warning cries echoing in the space, and Eofer sighted and released as the camp began to come to life. The spear flew true, spinning the Briton around as it took him in the shoulder, and Eofer watched as the gore spattered point emerged from his chest as the man fell.

Eofer was still moving, his legs pumping like bellows as he leapt the prostrate figure. Beyond the fallen guard he saw for the first time that a start had been made to a watch tower at the centre of the compound, and his eyes darted to left and right as he searched for any other changes to the layout as he ran. The tents which he had expected to see now flanked the wooden structure, and he concentrated his gaze on the right-hand group as the men there began to rise from the fireside. The glint of firelight on steel confirmed Alyn's description of the campsite, here were the warriors, and he angled towards them as Gleaming slid from its scabbard.

He was still thirty paces away, the first men were rising to their feet and he pounded on, desperate to get among them before they recovered from their surprise.

Twenty paces, and the first Welshmen were snatching up spears from a rack.

Ten paces and the eorle threw his shoulder into his shield and braced for the crash. His world narrowed as he came on, the rasping of his breath the only sound to break the rhythmic pounding of his feet in the moments before contact, and then he was airborne, leaping the flames and yelling his war cry. An explosion of sound enveloped him as his great battle board hurled spearmen aside, and his sword arm swung as he landed among them. Men who only a short while earlier had been relaxing with friends, sharing meat, ale and laughter at the end of another easy day spent watching others toil under the hot sun were bowled aside as the English warlord cut a murderous path through their ranks. Gleaming swept in a bloody arc before him, men falling like barley before the harvest reaper as he cut a bloody swathe.

Taken by surprise, unarmed, the closest men scrambled away as best they could from the death dealing madman who had appeared in their midst, and Eofer yelled and attacked again, hacking at unprotected heads and shoulders as the terrified men scattered before him. A space opened up, and Eofer paused for a heartbeat as he searched out the most likely threat.

Near the cooking fires a small group, more finely dressed than most, had been the first to recover their wits, snatching up shields and weapons as they moved shoulder to shoulder and prepared to come against him. The man in the centre stood a head taller than any other, his mouth twisted into a snarl of hatred behind a close cropped beard as black as night. A linen tunic of brilliant white trimmed with copper-gold braiding at the hem, cuffs and neck was cut by a baldric of rufous leather, and Eofer watched as the man calmly drew his sword and hefted his shield. Here, he knew, was the leader of the warriors at the fort, and Eofer's mind raced as he saw that the man's stand of defiance, the calm eye at the centre of the storm which swirled around him, was drawing more men to his side with every passing moment.

The Englishman knew that he must keep up the attack or risk losing the initiative and his eyes slid downwards, seeking to wrest any advantage he could from the few feet which separated them as he grimly stood his ground and waited for help to arrive. A faggot nestled at the edge of the hearth, the flames licking hungrily at the ties which bound the bundle together, and Eofer's heart leapt as he saw the strand part and the individual sticks tumble in a blazing heap. Eofer seized the chance, springing forward like the maddened boar of his namesake as the Welsh battle lord dropped into a fighting crouch and prepared to receive the charge.

As Eofer leapt he trailed his right leg, dragging the toe of his boot through the powdery ash as he once again vaulted the flames. The moment that he felt his boot slide beneath the bundle his foot shot forward, scattering burning sticks in a comet tail of flame and sparks.

Taken by surprise the Britons instinctively flinched as the fiery brands rained upon them, snatching heads aside, taking a backwards step as Eofer leapt the gap to crash down among them. The flaming sticks had cleared a space for him, little more than the width of his shield in depth but it was enough, and Eofer stabbed out as a face appeared to his right. He was beginning to tire as the effects of the blow to the back of his head earlier that day came back to sap at his strength, but he knew full-well that the moment he let the intensity of his assault drop, even a little, the Welsh would rally and over-whelm him.

Within a heartbeat the counterattack he had feared arrived as the British chieftain recovered from his surprise, the big man driving his shield forward in a powerful punch as Eofer faltered. The domed metal of the boss crashed into the eorle before he could haul his own shield across to cover, and although the metal face plates of his grim helm saved him from suffering catastrophic damage, light flashed in his vision as the pain at the back of his skull returned with a vengeance. A wave of nausea swept over him, powerful and unstoppable like a tidal bore, and all Eofer could do as his legs threatened to collapse beneath him was hurl himself forward and hang on to the Briton as he prayed to the gods that help would arrive soon.

The Engle dug in with his feet as he felt the heat of the hearth scorching the back of his calves, flexing his legs to return the push, and as he began to recover he realised that his desperate action had brought him face to face with the brawny Welshman. Little more than a hand's width separated his own helmeted head from the black beard of the brute, and Eofer braced himself for the pain which would follow as he gritted his teeth and drew back his head. Helmet-less the Welshman was wide open to the attack, and Eofer felt and heard the crunch as his head came forward and his opponent's nose crumpled under the very first blow. The Briton wavered, taking a rearward step as Eofer drove his head forward again and again and the black beard reddened.

The step back reopened the gap between them but this time it was the Englishman who was on the attack and Eofer grabbed at the opportunity it presented to finish his opponent. Black beard was blinking away the blood from his eyes as

Eofer snatched his short seax from its scabbard, throwing his head forward a final time as the knife came free. Movement at the corner of his eyes caused him to stay the thrust as the Briton's cantrefs saw that their leader was losing the fight and moved to his aid, but a blur of colour and the crash of wood and metal told Eofer that his own men had finally arrived to support his attack. Blinded by the blood in his eyes, the Welsh leader never saw the flash of steel as Eofer twisted his wrist, angling the short blade to stab upwards. An explosive gasp washed over the eorle as the chieftain reeled under the attack and Eofer twisted the knife, sawing upwards to open the wound as he drew back his arm and stabbed again. He felt the Briton weakening a little more with each plunge of the short sword, and as the man began to totter he shoved him away.

The surrounding area was clear now as the duguth drove the Britons further into the fort, and Eofer dropped the seax as he prepared to finish the duel. Attached to his wrist by a short leather lanyard the handle of Gleaming was back in his hand in the blink of an eye, and the Engle swept the broad blade in a low scything cut as the man began to stagger. To his surprise and disappointment the Briton saw the strike before it connected with his knee, and Eofer tried to pull the stroke as his opponent dropped his shield to deflect the blow. As shield and sword were swept aside, Eofer's head shot forward a final time to hammer into the ruin of the chieftain's face. The man was blind now as blood sheeted from his temple, and Eofer moved in, sweeping Gleaming around as he renewed the thwarted attack. This time the strike got through, and the British war leader finally crumpled as Gleaming cut deep, smashing bone and severing tendons as Eofer slid the sword clear and hacked again. Already a bloody mess the follow-up blow cleaved the joint in two, and a look of disbelief crossed the Briton's face as he finally went down.

The immediate danger over Eofer took a dozen paces aside, wincing as the pain which had plagued him since the attack on the boat redoubled. He fished inside the pouch which hung at his belt for a finger full of the honey mixture, raising his eyes to scan the compound for the first time since he had made his one man attack.

Horsa was leading Octa, Osbeorn and Einar in a frenzied assault on the remainder of the British warriors, hacking and slashing at the unarmed men as they attempted to retrieve their weapons and organise a resistance. Moving fast, Eofer could see that the four were on the brink of victory as men fell left and right under the silvered arcs of their sword swings.

Eofer scooped another dollop of the honied willow as he watched, sucking at the mixture as another wave of nausea washed over him. The fight on the right seemed to be going well, and the thegn cast a look across to the opposite side of the compound to see the results there. Finn had been entrusted with leading the youth against the workmen gathered around their cooking pots, and the thegn looked on with satisfaction as he saw that there too the fiend were being put to flight.

Suddenly a bell began to toll, the sound slight and irregular at first as the ringer fought against the inertia of rope and pulley, but within moments the bell was pealing loud and clear over the fighting in the compound below and the wider environment of the riverside itself. Eofer knew instinctively that it must be a warning signal, and he left the bloodied wreck of the chieftain on the ground as he began to seek out the source. He raised his eyes to the walkway which girded the walls of the fort, but the guards there had gone and there was no sign of any signalling device. The watchtower was still little more than the height of two men, and his mind raced as the sound of the bell continued to fill the evening air. Then he had it, and he leapt the hearth once again as he set off towards the far end of the compound.

Skirting the place where the duguth were cutting down the last resistance, Eofer saw for the first time the telltale glint of silver as his suspicions were confirmed. The church was smaller than he had expected, but the wooden cross above the gable confirmed that it must be the place as he pounded on.

Two warriors were flanking the doorway and Eofer could see immediately that unlike the men who had only a few moments before been relaxing at their evening meal, these were armed and ready, tough looking in mail and helm. He knew they would be much harder to put to flight, but the clang of the bell drew him on, and he increased his speed as he heard an answering bell chiming somewhere in the distance.

The secret was out, the warning sent far and wide, and the thegn knew now that time was against them. Already he could imagine horse-welsh throwing themselves into their saddles and spurring through the gates of the fort at Hreopedun to come to their countrymen's aid. If mounted warriors were closer still Eofer and his men could be in even greater danger, and he prayed that the dark twins were nearby with the horses.

There was no time to take anything but the most direct route to the building, and the guards lowered their spears and brought their shields to bear as they prepared to defend the man inside. That man, Eofer knew, could only be the man he had seen at the river door, the churchman who had recognised him from the earlier attack at the farm, and Eofer cursed himself for listening to Ioan and his men and sparing the priest's life there.

A petal of flame caught his attention off to the left, and Eofer slid to a halt as he looked across. Porta was touching a burning brand to a pile of hay as Beornwulf heaved more of the horse fodder to the base of the parapet with the tip of his spear, and Eofer cupped a hand, calling out as the easiest way to flush the priest from his lair revealed itself to him. The youth looked up as they recognised their lord's voice, and they hurried across at his signal.

'It may be a bit too late now that the warning has been taken up elsewhere,' he smiled ruefully, 'but I want to silence the bell and kill that bloody priest if I can before we leave this place. Porta, work your way quickly around the building. Touch your brand to the thatch and get it roaring as soon as you can. Beornwulf,' he said, turning to the lad. 'Let's put your spear to better use. You can help me take on the guards.' Eofer fumbled inside his pouch as another bolt of pain shot through his head, scooping another finger of Horsa's painkilling mixture into his mouth as Porta bore away under a pall of smoke and flame.

He shot Beornwulf a look and a wink of reassurance that the pain in his head was bearable as he prepared to lead the charge, but the youth was indicating the church with a flick of his head as Eofer tightened the grip on his shield. The sound of steel on steel carried to him before his head had even halfway turned, and Eofer knew that the delay had thwarted his own attack. Horsa and the men had cleared the opposition and their momentum had carried them as far as the church, and he snorted as his suspicion was confirmed. 'Come on,' he said as the first flames began to eat at the eaves of the building. 'Let that be a lesson: never pause during an attack, once your momentum stalls you quickly lose control. Let's round up the horses, I am sure that Horsa and the duguth can take care of things there without our help.'

The garrison's horses were corralled in the opposite corner of the fort and the pair doubled across as the fires began to take hold all about them. With the ending of anything resembling organised resistance to their attack the youth had moved on to the next part of the plan, pairing up and moving through the compound, carrying the flames of destruction as they went. As smoke and embers drifted in the warm evening air Eofer saw that the horses were growing panicky, tossing their heads, nostrils flaring at the nearness of the thing which animals feared above all other. The last thing that he needed that day was a kick or blow from a fear crazed horse.

'Go and find Grimwulf,' he said, 'he grew up on a horse farm. Tell him that we need a man with his experience.'

The rhythmic tolling of the church bell faltered and then stopped completely, and Eofer glanced across in time to see the last of the guards there fall to Octa's sword. The roof of the building was ablaze from end to end, the flames roaring and leaping from a thatch which was tinder dry after the heat of the summer, but the duguth leapt the bodies of their foemen nevertheless, darting inside as Grimwulf appeared at his shoulder.'

Eofer looked at him in surprise. 'That was quick!'

The youth smiled. 'I was already on my way, lord. Horses hate fire, I knew that I would be needed. Beornwulf has already gone to open the gates,' he said with a flick of his head. 'I will handle this no problem, they are already tethered together I will have them good and safe in a trice.'

Free for the moment, Eofer looked back into the centre of the fort as the youth went about their tasks. The smaller gate, the one which had been slammed shut on them at the beginning of the attack, had been opened by the first men to follow him across the wall. Through it the youth had flooded in to wreak havoc among the workmen as they relaxed at the end of a long day, and Eofer felt a pang of pity at their plight. He would have spared them if he could, just as he had the men at the bridge, but they were the reason why the blow had fallen here. Deprived of the use of his skilled artisans and the means to finish his forts, Cynlas Goch and his army should delay their march until replacements could be brought east. He had bought his own prince and folk precious time. Bodies lay where they had fallen, pooling blood reflecting the flames which now surrounded them in a vision of the Christian hell.

A thought came to him then as he reflected on a fight now won, and he gathered up a small ale barrel and a pair of cups from its unseeing owner and walked back through the smoke. A flash, brighter, more intense than the rest caught his eye, and the English eorle raised his chin to watch as the flames consumed the red dragon flag of Powys.

The man was where he had left him of course, mortally wounded men usually are. Eofer set himself down onto a dead man's stool, filled two cups and handed one across to black beard as he waited for the signal that they were ready to leave.

15

They paused at the tree line and looked back. Even at a distance the heat from the flames brought a blush to their cheeks, and the men of Eofer's hearth troop stared in wonder at the destruction they had wrought. Horsa was the first to speak as the flames cast a glow over the darkening meadow and turned the river beyond to bronze. 'It's an amazing thing, fire,' he breathed, putting into words the thoughts of them all. 'It's almost as if it is alive.'

Eofer nodded in agreement as he watched the fort burn in silence. As dry as old bones after the summer heat, the wood had come ablaze as soon as the torches were brought near. The palisade which crowned the earthwork banks was already a perfect ring of fire, the flames, red, orange and yellow, leaping and curling in the soft evening airs. At the centre of the fort the flagpole was now a flaming wand, as movement across the river caused Eofer to raise his gaze and look to the north. He motioned with his head. 'A few more moths drawn to the flames.'

A mile or so from the northern bank of the Trenta, the age polished sets of Ryknield Street ran as straight as any spear shaft. It was the main route east for the army of Cynlas Goch, and a detachment of riders were walking their mounts down towards the river as they too became bewitched by the sight of the fort's fiery end.

'Well, that should help spread the news well enough,' Horsa replied, 'that and the bell.'

'And the smoke,' Eofer added as he switched his gaze skyward.

The pair watched as waves of smoke as black as night billowed and boiled above the dying fort before the higher winds teased it apart and carried it off to the east. 'That will be the supplies.'

Eofer smiled to himself and sucked his teeth at the thought of a job well done. They had made a pile of all the building materials and tools they could find. Most of the ironwork, hammers, saws and the like, had disappeared beneath the surface of the Trenta, but the larger items had joined the rest of the supplies; soaked in the pitch and tar of the woodworkers' trade, they had added to the roaring inferno as they led the last of the horses through the gate. If he had the right of it, Eofer had now denied the army of Powys not only their skilled artisans but the tools and supplies essential to their work. The next fort along the chain, the big one at Hreopedun, was little more than a shallow ditch and bank as the men there waited for the carpenters and smiths to complete their defences. With those skilled workers now gone, the fort would remain little more than a four cornered earthwork deep in enemy territory.

'It was a shame that he got away, though. Who would have thought that a church would have a rear door for the priest's personal use?'

Eofer looked at his weorthman. 'Gildas?' He raised his

chin towards the river. 'It would seem that he is a hard man to kill.'

Horsa let out a long, low whistle. 'The bastard has got more lives than a cat.'

Beyond the fort a familiar bedraggled figure was hauling itself up the far bank and waving frantically to the horsemen there.

The eorle shrugged. 'I have a feeling that our paths will cross again, I should have hit him harder that first time. Come on,' he said, as the riders on the far side grew nearer. 'We have given the hive a good shake, let's be on our way before the bees swarm. We have a far sadder duty before us.'

The pair hauled at the reins, turning the heads of their horses to the south. The others were waiting patiently for the senior men to lead them away from the scene of their triumph, and Horsa spoke to Osbeorn as the horse came up.

'We tried to tell you mate.'

Osbeorn returned a blank look. 'Tried to tell me what?'

'The guard, back there at the riverside. The one you stuck at the start of the attack.'

Osbeorn still looked nonplussed. 'What about him?'

'His last word was Hermann.'

DAWN'S golden light was washing the meadow as they broke free from the trees. The grey line of Watling Street crossed their path a mile ahead, and Eofer turned to the scout with a smile of gratitude. 'Well done, Einar,' he said. 'No hound dog could have found their way through the backwoods with a greater sense of direction.'

The Geat smiled his thanks as the others came up, the smile echoed on the grateful faces which clustered around them. 'The backland was my home as a boy. We have places which have yet to feel the press of a man's footfall in the forests of Geatland. That,' he said with a shrug, 'was an evening stroll.'

Free of the gloom at last, the war band tossed their torches aside as Eofer pointed the nose of his mount to the east. Gaining the roadway they made good time, and within the hour their destination hove into view on its mound. Eofer shielded his eyes against the glare as he took in the sight. Tamtun had grown, doubled in size it looked to him, in the first month of its existence. The rough palisade which girdled the crown had been strengthened by low watchtowers at each corner and a further wooden wall had been added, reaching down to gather in the track which meandered its way upwards from the riverside. A sturdy gatehouse guarded the entrance to this outer defence and Eofer could see the returning light glinting from the spearpoints of the sentinels on watch there. Haloed by the rising sun, the hall of the thegn of Tamtun rose high above it all, the golden thatch and painted beams bold in their newness.

The mournful note of a war horn sounded across the vale as they came into sight of the watch, and Eofer called across his shoulder as they plodded towards their destination. 'Grimwulf, hoist the herebeacn. Let them know who we are.' The war banner opened with a crack, and Eofer gave in to temptation, casting a backwards glance, thrilling to the sight as the burning hart caught the sun.

As he turned back Horsa was pointing ahead. 'Do you want me to take a couple of lads and see to our friends?'

Eofer lowered his gaze and scanned the road ahead for the first time. A small group of horsemen had gathered to one side of the path, the pale oval of their faces turned towards the newcomers, and he wondered that he had not noticed them before. Horsa read his mind and snorted. 'I only saw them when one of the horses shifted, lord. Tired eyes,' he said with a weary smile, 'that was a long night. Shall I go or not?'

Eofer could hear the reluctance in his weorthman's voice, so it was a relief to them both when the riders revealed their identity by their actions. Throwing themselves onto the backs of their horses, they put back their heels and raced away to the south. Eofer shook his head. 'Men of Powys, sent to keep an eye on our boys. Let them go, it can only help our cause if they report that the number of English warriors here have increased still further.'

'They knew our herebeacn straight away,' Horsa said with a look of pride. 'If they recognised us by our war flag, you know what that means, lord?'

The ends of Eofer's mouth curled into a smile as he realised what his duguth was getting at. 'They know our war banner either by sight or reputation and they don't fancy meeting us if they can help it.' A flash of wolfishness came into his eyes, despite his fatigue. It had been a full day since any of them had enjoyed a wink of sleep. The crack to his own skull at the bridge and during the fight with black beard at the fort had been draining enough, but the entirety of the night had been taken up peering into the murk as Einar had led them southwards by use of badger runs, deer tracks and the like. It had kept them safe from any pursuers bent on taking a blood price for the butchery at the fort, but a night spent under torchlight had taken its toll on tired eyes. 'You are right,' he replied. 'I doubt that tales of king slaying in far off Swedeland and hall burnings among the Danes and Jutes are a staple of Welsh bards. They know us and fear us by our deeds here, in Britain.'

The horn sounded from the ramparts again, and Eofer watched as a familiar figure appeared there. His heart leapt at the sight and he raised a hand in greeting as they left the

Roman hard way and took the path which arced northeast-wards. Thrush Hemming threw a wave in return before turning back and disappearing into the fortress.

In a short while they were there, and Eofer led the weary war party into the shadow of the great burh and through the lower gate. The guards beamed as they dismounted, stretching aching limbs and flexing joints as grooms hurried up, hauling saddles and tackle from the horses as they guided them towards the paddock.

'Youth,' he said sadly as the final horse was led through the gate. 'Stay with our friend until Hemming can provide something suitable to bring him up. Even in death he remains part of our brotherhood until the pyre consumes flesh and bones.'

They nodded their agreement as the spearmen at the gate came forward to mark the wounds on the fallen hero and hear the tale of his death, sharing ale and news with his friends as his erstwhile thegn led the duguth away.

Hemming stood hands on hips, silhouetted between the posts of the upper gatehouse as they shouldered shields and spears and climbed the path, the smile driven from his face as he too saw that one of his old friends had paid the ultimate price for his valour. A quick headcount told him that the duguth were all present at least, and the ghost of a welcoming smile returned as Eofer led them upwards. Hemming dipped his head to his lord as they drew near, but Eofer stepped in and drew him close and bade him hold his head high. They shared an embrace as both men's hearth warriors looked on proudly, and Eofer clapped his old weorthman on the shoulder as he ran his eyes over the defences which towered all around them. 'You have done a magnificent job here old friend, I can scarcely believe the change in the place.'

Hemming snorted. 'It's funny just how fast you can get

things done when you have powerful foemen a short ride away.' His demeanour soured as his eyes strayed to the compound at the foot of the hill and his voice dropped to a whisper. 'Who fell?'

'Anna.'

Hemming sighed. 'So young. He died well?'

Eofer nodded. 'Spear in hand, surrounded by enemies.'

'That's all that we can ask of the gods, lord. To give us an ending worthy of a man when the old girls hover over our life thread with their shears of woe. You boys look like you could use a place to sleep, I will have a pyre prepared while you take your rest.' He frowned. 'The bitches know that we have had enough practice this last month.'

EOFER TOOK another sip from the cup, licking the honeyed mead from his moustache as his eyes wandered over the plain below. 'This is good stuff, Thrush.'

'One thing we are not short of is beehives,' he replied, sweeping the area below them with an arm. 'The water meadows are full of wildflowers, all the way down to the road. I'd lay odds that the whole area is a carpet of buds in the spring.'

'Tamtun burh is impressive,' Eofer said proudly. 'Haystack is over the moon.' He shot his old duguth a smile. 'The ætheling said that he would make you a full thegn once we have thrown Cynlas Goch back beyond the forest of Canoc, and I am going to become your ealdorman, the Ealdorman of Leircestre.'

Hemming's brow crinkled in surprise. 'So you are settling down after all, lord? I know someone who will be happy with that.'

'I will keep the ship and hall at Snæpe.' He dug Hemming

in the ribs and shot him a smile. 'So we can still go raiding further up the coast or over in Frankland when the fancy takes us. Sæward and his lads can run the hall there on my behalf, collect the tolls at the river crossing and keep an eye on the Wulfings to the south.'

Eofer noticed Horsa hovering at the corner of his vision, and he glanced back in acknowledgement. 'It looks as if they are ready,' he sighed, the good mood broken. 'Let's go and send the lad onwards.'

Hemming nodded as they swung their legs back from the edge of the parapet. The shadows in the valley were easting as the long day came to a close, away to the west a small group of horsemen sat at a safe distance. 'It's time to move back anyway,' he said. 'Our friends arrive the same time every night, hoping to pick off a man or two from the ramparts. The hilltop remains in full sunlight for a time while the valley becomes cloaked in shadow.' He pursed his lips before continuing. 'They have excellent bowmen, we have already lost a couple of men to them, either at sundown when we can't see much westwards because of the setting sun or later if any guards are foolish enough to let themselves become backlit by the light of a torch.' He saw the look of surprise flash across Eofer's face at his apparent lack of aggression and gave a snort. 'Oh, we go out and strike back at them lord, make no mistake. There was one time,' he said with a wry smile, 'that Sigmund led a group out one night and spied on a couple of Powys' sat swapping yarns around a small campfire. With his knowledge of Welsh he can pick up useful tidbits of information like that before he polishes them off.'

Eofer's ears pricked up at the mention of the name. Sigmund had been a gift to Hemming's troop from the ætheling himself. 'How has your new weorthman been doing?'

'He's a good lad. Not as good as *your* old one, lord,' he said with a smile. 'But he knows his stuff. Thanks for sending him out with the recommendation.'

Eofer nodded. 'Thank Icel, he was one of his gesith after all.'

Hemming nodded earnestly. 'I will, Eofer. I appreciate all the help that the both of you have given me here. Men arrive nearly every day bringing news and adding spears to our defence. I can see the effect that it has on the men here, they know that they are valued and not forgotten.'

He fixed his old thegn with a look of gratitude. 'I wont forget it either, nor the honour which you have both shown me. I am strong enough here now to withstand all but a prolonged siege, and the men are confident that help will arrive from Leircestre or Grantebrycge long before they can starve us out. You can count on me, lord,' he said earnestly. 'We will carry the fight to our enemies before the new moon waxes.'

Eofer pulled a smile, a little embarrassed by his old weorthman's words. Somehow Hemming's earnestness made him uncomfortable; it was, he had discovered on his travels, a peculiarly English trait. To Eofer's relief Hemming remembered that he was halfway through a tale before the situation became too awkward, and he snorted with amusement as the man furrowed his brow.

'Where was I before I got sidetracked?'

'The two Britons were at the fireside.'

'Ah yes,' he chuckled as he took up the thread of the tale. 'Just as Sigmund decided that this pair were more interested in prattling on about the delights to be had from tumbling with sturdy women called Blodwyn and the like rather than their leader's glorious war of conquest, one of them decides that he needs to take a shit and disappears into the night. When he returns, what does he find, grinning at him from the fireside?'

'Sigmund?'

Hemming shook his head and chuckled with delight. 'No sign of our lads, they were already halfway back to the burh. All he saw was his friend's head fixed to a spearhead waiting for his return.' The pair laughed aloud as Hemming struggled to finish his tale. 'They even carried the rest of the body away to make it look spookier! All that the boys heard was a strangled yell and the sound of running. It wouldn't surprise me if he hasn't slowed down yet!'

Rounding the corner of the hall the mirth was driven away as the pyre came into view. Muffled conversations trailed away as the waiting men noticed their approach, and Eofer crossed to Finn who was waiting with the flaming brand. He was glad that the new duguth had taken responsibility for the duty. The pair had struck up a close friendship over the course of the year or so that Anna had been among Eofer's hearth troop and, despite the fact that Finn had lately been elevated into the ranks of the doughty ones, the bond had remained firm.

Eofer took the torch with a nod of thanks and turned to the waiting men. Despite the solemnity of the occasion he was glad to see that heads remained raised, the pride in the manner of their friend's death obvious in their bearing. He spoke the eulogy, praising the skill and humour of the young boy who had joined their troop on a dark hillside in Daneland and mourning his loss. Raising the brand aloft, Eofer called on the wælcyrge to gather his soul and hasten him to the hall of the slain, before he swept the torch in a fiery arc and thrust it deep within the timbers. Soaked in pitch and fats the pyre caught easily, and Eofer stood back as the lad's spear-brothers came forward one by one to share their own memories of Anna and his time among them. Mindful of Hemming's earlier warnings about the bowmen of Powys, Eofer ushered them away as Crawa finished his piece, and the group moved back to sit deep within the shadows at the lee of the hall as sparks twisted and danced in the darkening sky.

Einar was sat with them, and Eofer asked the Geat if he could entertain them with a story of his own as he had no memories of Anna to share. The idea was quickly taken up, and a cup of Hemming's finest mead was thrust his way as the scout cleared his throat and prepared to tell the story of King Hygelac's disastrous raid against the lands of the Frisians and Franks.

Einar drank deeply, cleared his throat and began as Anna's pyre began to settle. 'I led the scouting party who first discovered the army of the Frankish prince, Theudobert.' This was unexpected news, even to Eofer, and the men sat tall as they craned their necks to hear every detail of the tumultuous day. 'I was scouting along the Roman Road which ran south to Frankland with my kinsman Gunnar Gunnarson and two Englishmen Oslaf and Offa who had come along for the fun of being on campaign, when about ten miles south of Dorestada we trotted clear of a wood and came almost face-to-face with a dozen Frankish horsemen doing the same thing as us. Two of them took off before we could close on them, but the others stayed to fight.' Einar cleared his throat. 'My cousin Gunnar fell there, but the ten remaining Franks paid part blood-price for that loss, sore as it was to me.'

The Engles nodded earnestly as they recognised both the scale of their victory and the personal cost to their new friend.

'I was the best climber out of the three remaining, so I scurried up a tree and peered away to the south. What I saw nearly knocked me from my branch.' He pulled a wry smile as he sipped again from his cup. 'A mighty host was darkening the road.' He shook his head, obviously still awed by the sight which had greeted him that day. 'Ten, fifteen thousand strong,' he shrugged as the Engles shared looks of wonderment, 'coming on beneath their Iesus crosses and gaudy war banners; it seemed to be an army without end. We rode straight back and reported to the king. He took the news calmly,' he said with obvious pride. 'Despite the fact that the king's son Heardred, your own kinsman lord,' he said with a nod of recognition to Eofer, 'had already taken part of our army and all the ships to sea, ready to begin the journey home. The great rivers thereabouts, the Masa and the Rin, divide into many channels as they approach the sea and King Hygelac led those remaining with him onto a large island to deny the Frankish army passage. The bridge at Dorestada was the only one for miles in each direction so holding the Franks there would enable the bulk of the army to get back to the ships, but as we deployed word came of a second army moving up to our rear. Before they could close the trap, the king sent me to warn the fleet that the enemy were on the move.'

He grimaced before taking another pull from the mead cup. The Engles already knew the story from thereon, they had rescued Heardred from the Frankish fleet themselves and heard the tale firsthand. Einar shrugged. 'I know that you yourselves witnessed the end. I stole a skiff and managed to get picked up further along the coast. After a hard fight we managed to batter our way clear.' He spat. 'The sea lay dark under a press of Frankish sail, it was a grim day.' Einar lowered his gaze and spoke in a voice as thick as honey in winter. 'To think that I should live at such a time, to bear witness to the end days of my country.'

The tale had lowered spirits and Eofer reproached himself, but Hemming had listened in and the mood lifted again as a platter of freshly roasted deer meat was brought out and laid before them. The eorle nodded at his old weorthman in recognition of his foresight, kicking back on the bench as the men's spirits returned with their appetite and they tucked in.

Eofer examined the pits and scratches at the rear of his helm, running the pad of his thumb across the incomplete repair work as the pyre flared for a final time and collapsed in on itself. Anna had promised to hammer and polish them out once they had reached a smithy, but neither man then knew that it would be the hands of another smith who would complete the task. Eofer let out a snort of irony as the stack settled and the enemy shields that ringed it folded down into the white heat at its core. No man knew the length of his life thread, but despite the injustice often felt by those left to mourn all were thankful for it.

A roll of thunder sounded in the distance, and Eofer looked up from his cup as he recognised that Thunor was in the sky. Like most Engles Anna had always worn the hammer amulet of the god at his throat, and although he would have expected the smith god Wayland to welcome the boy's spirit to his forge, the thunder god seemed as good as any. The sound came again, different in tone this time, man-like, and he gave a knowing smile as the voice of another youth, a boy long dead, carried to him on the wind:

> *Then on the hill, a balefire was kindled.*
> *Wood-smoke billowed black over blaze,*
> *keen was the roar of flame,*
> *till the fire had burst the frame of bones,*
> *hot at the heart.*

16

A spearman crouched in the courtyard, bent over as he offered up the fire steel to the kindling. The sparks were bright in the dusk, and the Engles watched from cover as the first fronds of flame flickered and were fanned into life. The Briton's features were thrown into relief as the fire grew, pinched cheeks and a hooked nose, black bushy brows stark against a skin made sallow by weeks on campaign. Others came across as the flames were fed, and soon men were moving from thatch to thatch, touching brands to the eaves as an unseen woman wailed in pain and distress.

Half a dozen ceorls were standing in line, waiting sullen faced for their turn to have the wooden slave collars fitted to their necks, and an inhuman wail of pain and despair rose from the group as a bairn, too burdensome to bring along, was dashed to the ground and run through. As the ashen faced men and women were manhandled back into line and the wooden pegs which secured the collars worked roughly into place, the leader of the raiding party shook his head and kicked out a boot. 'Not that one, he will never keep up and I am not hanging around any longer than needs be.' The Briton hawked and sent a gobbet of phlegm spinning into the dust. 'We are not so far from that new barbarian fort, and I don't want to get into a fight just so that Cynlas Goch can top up his pile of silver. Anyways, nobody will get a full days work out of that old coot,' he sniffed and pointed to one of his men. 'Ifan, see him out.'

The English warriors watched with heavy hearts from the shadows as the chosen man exchanged looks of bewilderment with his family members and a middle aged woman plucked at his sleeve in fear and desperation. Ifan grabbed at his tunic, the old threadbare thing testament to the fact that the settlers had little to offer by way of plunder save a lifetime of work for their new owners, twisting the thing and giving it a sharp tug which sent the man staggering towards the nearby woodland.

The watching pair eased back into the shadows as the man shuffled across, instinctively narrowing their eyes as the spearman forced him to his knees little more than a dozen paces before them. Both men had been warriors long enough to know that the eyes were more than the windows to a man's soul, the whites of the eyes were the most visible thing as the light began to fade and the hours of darkness approached.

Backlit by the flames the pair, victim and executioner, were little more than silhouettes. The old man raised his chin, and a new-found defiance kindled within him as he came to accept that his time on Middle-earth was drawing to a close. The action had raised the level of his gaze to that of Hemming's own, and the big warrior's eyes flared with anxiety as he recognised the moment when the old man picked him out from the shadows.

Hemming moved a forefinger slowly across to rest against his lips as he held the elder's gaze in his own, and an understanding passed between them that the wrongs visited on the man's family would be avenged, even if he did not live long enough to witness the act. The ghost of a smile played about the ceorl's lips, and Hemming risked a gentle bob of his head in recognition of the old man's bravery as the first spear thrust threw him forward onto the grass. A moan drifted across from the captives as they watched their elder spasm in death, and Hemming froze as the spearman raised his gaze and looked his way. The Briton must have sensed the change in the old ceorl's demeanour in his final moments, and he made as if to approach the tree line as he tugged the spear clear and a frown came to his face.

'Ifan!'

The cry brought the man up short, and he turned back in question.

'Come on it is getting dark, and I want to get back at the camp while we can still see.'

The English pair watched as the Briton hesitated, and Hemming gripped his spear as he prepared to dart forward and run him through, but another summons followed and he shrugged his shoulders, flicked a final look at the tree line and loped back across the clearing to rejoin the others. The Welsh leader lost no time in hustling the captives out of the village, and Hemming and Hryp shared a look at the closeness of discovery as they shuffled away.

The huts were a fiery holocaust now, and Hemming gave the nightmare scene a last look as the pair shuffled back into the greenwood and melted away.

The shadows were merging together as the sun sank in the west, but Hemming had marked the path well and in a short while they were back where they had left their hearth mates. The pair slid down the bank as faces turned their way, and Hemming gave the thumbs up as excitement began to build within him. 'It's on lads!' he said happily. 'There are only six of them and they are going to do just what we hoped.'

The men exchanged grins as they began to haul themselves into the saddle. Hemming mounted and took the reins from a companion as the men fastened helm straps and fingered gods-luck charms for the umpteenth time. 'Right,' he said as they pointed their mounts to the north, 'Eadgar will lead: Hryp and Beonna are with me.' He ran his eyes around the group a final time before they left the shelter of the glade. 'Any last questions?' The riders shook their heads, flashing smiles of anticipation as they prepared to carry death to the men who had tormented their people all summer long. 'Good,' he said. 'Let us go and show these Powys that the land hereabouts is English land.'

Hemming led the riders down into a stream bed which skirted the clearing and guided his mount northwards. On his righthand side the land banked steeply upwards; knee deep in leaf mulch from the previous autumn's fall, the deadening effect was perfect cover for the war band as they hurried on, eager to get ahead of their foe. Half a mile on a small watercourse joined from the east, and Hemming led Hryp and Beonna along it as the others splashed away.

The murk was closing in around them as the horses walked on, but Hemming had led men out of the burh at every opportunity as soon as the defences were secure and well manned, and he now knew the lands which were promised to him intimately.

If a small part of the thegn felt guilt at the deaths back at the settlement, the experience gained over the years told him that they were unavoidable, that losing men was sometimes a necessary thing in war. He had learned his craft at the side of a master of warfare, the king's bane himself: he understood warfare and was certain in his own mind that he had left nothing to chance. They had watched the columns of smoke hazing the skyline, growing nearer and nearer each day as another English settlement burned and the Britons harried his lands. But he had bided his time, waited until the numbers were evenly matched before he had harvested the defences at Tamtun of some of the more promising and experienced men to accompany him on his counter raid, Spear-Engles, the best of the best. These Britons, killers of bairns and greybeards, were already as good as dead.

The final rise was ahead and Hemming slid from the saddle and hobbled his mount in its lee. As Hryp and Beonna mirrored his actions he retrieved the shield from its carrying place on the horse's crupper and shouldered his spear.

The pathway along which the enemy would be travelling was just beyond the hillock, and the trio skirted its base as the sounds of shuffling feet carried to them on the wind. The Britons and their captives were making better progress than he had anticipated, the lateness of the hour spurring them on, and he sent an invocation to the gods that the rest of his war band would be in place in time to spring the trap.

The place he had chosen was just ahead, and the three Engles quickly checked that the way was clear before Hemming's men left his side and doubled across to hide themselves in the shadows on the far side of the path. They reached cover just in time as the first of the British riders rounded the bend and came into view, and Hemming watched from his place of hiding as the sad party approached under the blows and curses of their captors. A quick glance across told him that the pair were in position, the silvery glint of their spearpoints just visible in the gloaming, and he followed their example, hoisting his own daroth as he waited for the column to reach them.

They were still moving faster than he had hoped but the

haste was making them careless, and the leading rider passed by without a glance to either side as the guards chivvied the captives along in his wake. The new-made thræls were abreast of him but no guards appeared alongside them, and Hemming gripped his throwing spear as he prepared to strike whether Eadgar and the others had reached the blocking position further ahead or not.

The light was failing as the first stars showed overhead, and Hemming willed his men to appear as he wrestled with the decision.

Suddenly the slaves shuffled to a halt as the guards at the head of the column pulled up abruptly, and Hemming prepared to attack as several guards ran past, the alarm writ large on their faces all the confirmation he needed that his men had finally arrived to bar the way forward. The slaves were craning their necks, looking ahead in an effort to make out what more the gods could possibly think to inflict on them before this day was over, and Hemming risked a peek to the south. Two guards remained at the rear, but the column was long and he was satisfied that they were too far back to intervene in the coming fight before the killing was done.

It was time, and Hemming stepped from cover, hurling his daroth with all his might as slack jawed faces turned his way in shock and surprise. Before the dart hit he was moving. A woman's scream cut the air but he was running freely now, the backs of the guards little more than a few feet before him as his hand moved across to draw his sword from its scabbard. Up ahead, out beyond the men who were about to fall beneath his blade he caught a scroll of smoke and flames, and he knew that the Eadgar and the others were blocking the path, brands held high as they held the attention of the enemy.

In the moment it had taken to glance away the daroth had found its mark, and the first Briton to fall spun around with the familiar look of horror and disbelief which the Englishman had seen on the faces of those who were about to die everywhere. His sword was already in his hand and he leapt into the air, sweeping the blade in a high arc as another daroth flew in from the side to bury its point in the small of the mounted leader's back. His next opponent began to turn as the danger to their rear became known, but Hemming's sword was cleaving the air and a heartbeat later the blade was slicing through muscle, smashing bone as it bit deeply into the Briton's shoulder.

Hemming's momentum carried him forward and he crashed into the backs of the guards, shouldering the dying man aside as his companions finally began to react to the death all around them. But the English were quicker, and before the Britons could bring their own weapons to bear Hryp and Beonna were among them, jabbing high and low with their gar, the stout shafted stabbing spears a blur of motion as they peppered the fiend.

The men at the head of the column were down in the dust and Hemming swung around to face the pair at the rear as the sound of hoofbeats told him that the others were riding down to help finish the job. The light was failing fast, but he caught the flash of movement as the last of the Britons saw the fight was over and plunged into the greenwood in a desperate effort to save their skins.

The riders came up as the last traces of life were being extinguished from the remaining Powys', and Hemming turned to the captives as the horsemen urged their mounts forward and shouldered their way into the tree line in pursuit of the two escapers. 'Who leads here? Who is the headman?'

A ceorl stepped forward, the light of deliverance shining from his features as he realised that his family may yet have a future together despite the horrors of the day. The man bobbed his head and tried to say his thanks, but emotion got the better of him and all that came was a half stifled sob. Hemming placed a hand on the man's shoulder, drawing in a breath as the madness of battle began to drain from him. 'Do you have a place to go,' he asked gently. 'You cannot go back to your homes until the Powys' have been chased from our land.'

The headman shook his head sadly. 'No, lord. All that we have, all that we have worked for has been taken from us in a day.'

Hemming pursed his lips. 'I understand, but you cannot return. If the Powys' discover what has happened here they may well return with more spears. We are growing stronger by the day and we will win this war, but for now if you have no place else to go which offers a degree of safety you must go to Leircestre.' The man still looked hesitant, bemused by the horror of the last hours, and Hemming cast a look at those still standing in line to his rear as he waited for the man to gather his wits. His men were moving among them, removing the pins which held their slave collars in place and sharing the contents of their drinking skins.

Above them the sky was darkening quickly, the stars which had seemed little more than a haze of light at the start of the attack now sword-blade bright. He had to get moving if he was to regain the safety of Tamtun burh this night. They had already been away for two full days as they hunted the small bands of Britons who were creating mayhem throughout the land. If he was to be thegn to these folk it was his duty to protect them in time of war and he was doing his best. But however hard he strived on their behalf the issue would be decided elsewhere, and soon; he would have to hope that victory in the east would spell the final death for Powys' ambitions in the lands around Tamtun. Eofer had told him of their plans, that night as they shared mead on the rampart and his men had prepared Anna's pyre. Win the battle at Hreopedun and they would chase the enemy out of Cair Luit Coyt and back beyond the forest of Canoc.

He led the ceorl aside, away from the ears of others as he began to lose patience. The man was clearly distressed at the events of the day, but he would have to grow a thicker skin if he was to survive and prosper on the frontier. 'Look,' he said, as he pinned the ceorl with a look. 'This is not a request. You will lead these people to Leircestre or I will see to it that your village will be under the authority of a new head man. Take this,' he said, fishing a handful of silver coins from the purse which hung at his waist. 'Leircestre is overcrowded with folk fleeing the Powys' at the moment but this will at least get you and your people food, even if you have to sleep in the open. It's not so bad,' he added as he attempted to soften his orders with a smile of reassurance, 'warriors do it all the time, and not always in weather as balmy as this.'

The sound of returning horses drew his eyes back to the woodland, and whoops of joy came from the ceorls at the sight of the bloody spear points as they were held aloft in triumph. Hemming turned back to the headman. 'That's the last of them, get yourself moving. I can't spare any spearmen to escort you, but feel free to take what weapons you need from the dead men here. Go back to your village, bury any valuables which they may have missed and take as much food as you will need. Travel the back roads as well as you are able and you should reach safety within four or five days.'

THE HORSEMEN SAT at the edge of the woodland and scanned the clearing. Ahead of them the track which led to the burh showed grey in the moonlight and Hemming sucked his teeth

in thought. Hryp was at his side, and the warrior whispered a
question as nervous men swept the meadow with their gaze.
'Let me and Beonna ride at your flanks lord. If an arrow does
come from the gloom it will keep you safe.'

Hemming snorted softly and turned aside to murmur a
remark of his own. 'Do you hear that Beonna? Hryp has
volunteered you to take an arrow on my behalf.'

'That's because he owes me silver, lord,' the reply came
from the darkness. 'Never place your trust in a man who
owns his own dice!'

Hemming raised his shield and glanced about him as the
men chuckled softly. It was only a short ride to the gatehouse
but they would be in full view the whole way. Suddenly the
effort they had made clearing away the trees and bushes from
the land surrounding the hill fort seemed like it may have
been a mistake. He shook his head as he thought back on the
example set by his own lord. Eofer always led from the front,
whatever the danger: he would do no less.

He raised his voice so that all could hear. 'We will go
straight in. I shall ride at the head of the column and we
should be inside before any bowmen can draw a lead on us. If
I am wrong,' he shrugged and threw them all a smile, 'if
nothing else I have taught you how to build a fine pyre over
the last few months!'

A last glance about him and Hemming kicked back his
heels, hunkering down behind his shield as the horse left the
safety of the trees and made for Tamtun. Listening hard he
strained to make out the telltale whicker which would tell him
that arrows were cutting the air about him but he heard none,
and he hoped that they would come through unscathed.

The gates rose before him, and Hemming drew rein as a
demand that they identify themselves came from the wall
above. He cupped a hand to his mouth and made the reply.

'Heorot!'

The doors were swinging inward almost before the word was out, and Hemming urged his horse forward to lead his men into the courtyard before they came together again. Slipping from his saddle he exchanged a tired smile with the guard as his men dismounted around him. They had been out for days deep within the lands threatened by their foemen and not lost a man. It was, Hemming knew, the type of thing which would build his reputation and attract good spearmen to his hearth.

'Welcome home, lord,' the guard was saying as a groom came across to lead his horse away. But the tone betrayed that there was more to follow, and Hemming sighed in his weariness and raised a brow as he waited for the axe to fall.

'One of the patrols came in today, lord,' the guard continued apologetically as he recognised the look. 'They are with Sigmund, in the hall.'

17

'Well, I don't know,' the ætheling said with a frown. 'Maybe if we asked everyone to breathe out at the same time we could squeeze a few more in?'

Eofer chuckled under his breath as the steward went back to his duty, calling out his orders as his underlings scurried away to do his bidding. With a soft whistle and a shake of the head, the thegn looked out across the packed space of the old forum. Horses and men jostled each other in a chaotic scrum, whirling about like freshly stirred soup as the stewards attempted to create order from chaos. Icel came across and the pair shared a look, the ætheling casting his cares aside to snort at the amusement he saw reflected there. 'This should be your responsibility ealdorman. Maybe if Thrush Hemming would stop sending every waif and stray to us here with a purse full of silver we could find a place to put everyone. Why do you think that I was so keen to get shot of the place?'

'I am not ealdorman yet, lord,' Eofer replied. 'And Thrush is doing a fine job out west. Harrying, tying down men who could otherwise be here harrowing the heartlands.'

'Don't be so defensive Eofer,' Icel snapped back. 'Hemming is big enough to fight his own battles. If I were not sure of that fact he would still be your weorthman.' It was about as close to a rebuke that the eorle had ever received from his lord and it confirmed his fears that the constant strain was taking its toll on the man. The prince pulled a wry smile as he realised the same. He made a fist and lightly punched Eofer on the chest by way of apology. 'Hemming is doing well,' he sighed as he returned his gaze to the multitude below. 'I just wish that he would send a few folk down to Grantebrycge for a change! Still,' he said as he forced his natural sense of optimism back to the surface, 'I shan't fret, they will be gone within the week and I shall be leading the first settlers across the Trenta in the spring. You heard the words of the guda, Woden wills it. Old one-eye himself is spoiling for the fight.'

'Be that as it may,' Eofer replied. 'Woden's presence doesn't ensure that we will have the victory. Whatever the priests say the old goat does enjoy chaos, and an English defeat will certainly hand him that.'

'We sacrificed a white bull, a fine war stallion and a highborn Briton to the Allfather,' Icel said. 'If that's not good enough for him, he can kiss my arse.'

Eofer shook his head and sighed. The ætheling had never been the most reverent of men where the gods were concerned; he hoped that his lord's easygoing attitude towards them amused Woden, Thunor and Tiw as much as it did the ætheling himself or a kiss would be the last thing they could expect. He had already been bitten on the arse once that year and it was not something which he planned to experience again in a hurry.

Despite his cares and worries, Icel's eyes sparkled with pride as he scanned the open space below. Men had been arriving for the best part of a week in response to his summons, and now the old walls of the town were full to near bursting point as they left the taverns and buildings. Bidding their farewells to wives and whores alike, the men were lifting their chins as they attempted to pick out the war banners of their own leader from the mass of boars, wolves and bears, crowding forward towards the northern gate as the shadows lengthened around them.

'Come on, lord,' Eofer said, plucking at Icel's sleeve. 'Let's get down there. Fighting men were never meant to live in towns. Once the army is on the move you will feel better.'

Eofer cast a look towards the west as the pair paced the steps which led down from the walkway, high on the walls of Leircestre burh. The sun was all but spent for the day, the treetops rimmed with gold as the late summer night came upon them.

'Are you sure that your man will be able to find this place? It will be as black as pitch once we enter the forest, Barley-moon or not,' Icel was asking.

Eofer cast a glance to the east. Rime-mane the sky horse was already pulling the great white orb into the heavens, the huge bowl casting its steely glow across the hilltops as Icel chattered on. The eorle's mind drifted away as he looked, back across the sea to the wolds of his birth land. The harvests had been even better in Anglia and he was confident that Gefion, the giver, had accompanied her worshippers despite the distance involved. *Halig monaþ*, holy-month, was upon them, and it spoke volumes for the loyalty of the populace to the ætheling that men had left the land at such a time to fight for their lord at the very moment that every pair of hands were needed to gather the crops. His mind came back, and he flushed as he saw the questioning look on Icel's face as he awaited the answer to his question. 'Einar is a Geatish scout lord,' he offered in reply, 'he could smell his way there if needs be.'

The ætheling laughed for the first time that day, and Eofer returned a smile of his own. 'You see,' he said. 'We are only a dozen paces into our journey and your cares are sluicing away.'

Icel returned the smile. 'You were right, Eofer. I needed to *do* something, rather than keep turning over problems in my mind. You are closer to the gods than I, give me some advice from old one-eye.'

Eofer thought for a moment as they walked. 'How about:

> *'The foolish man lies awake all night and*
> *worries about things;*
> *he's tired out when morning comes and*
> *everything is just as bad as it was.'*

Icel looked across, the surprise written on his face. 'Woden said that?'

'So they say lord.'

'That's pretty good.'

Eofer shrugged. 'He *is* the god of knowledge.'

'Really?'

'He had to sacrifice an eye to drink from Mimir's well to gain it.'

'I did always wonder.'

Horsa and Einar Haraldson were waiting at the foot of the staircase, and Eofer gave his weorthman a friendly clap on the shoulder as he came up. 'Einar here will guide us and I shall be riding at the head of the column with the ætheling. Once the army begins to sort itself out, take my hearth troop and fall in immediately to the rear of Icel's gesith.' The pair exchanged smiles at the honour being shown by the prince to their little band before turning to force a way through the throng.

Icel spoke as he watched them go. 'You have sent men to chase the Powys' horsemen away?'

Eofer raised a brow and sighed before he replied. It would seem that his friend was just not the gods-fearing type. 'Yes, lord. Just like I have the past few days. And I have remembered to send out extra riders to confiscate any horses and asses from the settlements which line our route.'

'And told the owners that the animals will be returned to them once victory is ours?'

Eofer cleared his throat as he remembered Cynfelyn's quip about paying off the debts at The Tewdwr. 'Yes lord, of course. I took the liberty of adding the promise of a silver coin from your own purse for their trouble when they pitch up at Leircestre to reclaim them.'

It was Icel's turn to look surprised, but like Eofer before him he saw the sense in it and flashed a grin. 'The promise of a profit to go along with the removal of a hostile army from their backyards should keep even the most devout Christian at home, particularly as he would have to walk through the night to warn Cynlas Goch that we were on our way. What do they get if we lose?'

'If we lose I shan't care, because I will drinking alongside my kinsmen in Valhall.'

'That's the spirit!' Icel replied gleefully. 'You will make a fine ealdorman.'

Spearmen were going on ahead of the pair, forcing a path through the press, and in no time they had reached the great gates which barred entry to the fortress. Their mounts were already in place and the pair exchanged a look which confirmed that they were both well aware of the importance of the moment. Eofer took the reins, leading the horse aside as he read the ætheling's intention in his expression. As the black raven war banner of the prince was hoist aloft, Icel took two paces and hurled himself up over the rump of the beast. Clearing the horn with ease, the fully armoured warrior settled into the saddle as a roar of acclamation rose into the darkening sky. With a deft flick of his wrist, Icel wheeled the horse about, facing the mass of soldiery as his banner man hastened to his side.

Flanked by his own raven and the white dragon of Anglia, the warrior-prince waited for the clamour to lessen before walking the horse towards them with a squeeze of his knees. As the noise fell away, a voice hailed him from deep within the multitude:

'Give us a speech, Haystack!'

Despite the solemnity of the moment, laughter echoed back from the old walls of Leircestre as the ætheling met the shout with a laugh of his own and a broad smile. At his side Eofer too beamed at the cry and his lord's happy reaction to it. It confirmed that his earlier advice had been sound, once on the move the ætheling was back to his old self. Icel was best known among the ceorls and freedmen by the nickname on account of his straw blond hair. Unusually among the warrior class he had a habit of clipping it short, and its waywardness and resemblance to the sheaves of barley and rye which dotted the countryside at this time of year had led the people to attach the affectionate eke-name to their popular prince.

Icel waited for the mirth to subside, sweeping the multitude with his gaze as men quietened and faces turned upwards in expectation of the words to come. 'Country-men…' he began, as the crowd formed an arc and the expectant buzz fell to a whisper. 'Brothers.'

Eofer dropped his gaze, aware that the great attack could

yet be stillborn if an assassin lurked among the throng, but Icel's gesith were there, sharp-eyed, ready to honour the oath they had sworn to exchange their own lives for that of their prince, and he allowed himself to relax as Icel spoke.

'In a short while those gates behind me will swing open and we will march through to keep our date with destiny. Fight well and we will remove the threat of Powys from these lands forever, an age-old scourge driven from the lands bordering the Trenta. You men,' he said as his arm swept in an arc before him, 'have been chosen by whichever god you hold close to your heart to be the spearpoint which will drive these beasts away. I know,' he said, his voice taking on a steely edge, 'what ravages and woes you have suffered at the hands of these men from the west this summer past. Men, women and bairns alike killed out of hand, their holy shrines desecrated, the farms and settlements hacked from the unforgiving woodland which surrounded them made cinder and ash.'

Eofer realised what Icel was about to do, and he watched as his eyes ran across the sea of heads before him, congratulating himself as he picked out the swarthy man who would be singled out by the ætheling even before his searching gaze reached him and his hand stabbed out.

'What is your name, friend?'

The man blanched as all faces turned his way, but his companions voiced their support and he cleared his throat and replied. 'Gwynfor, lord.'

'Gwynfor?' Icel repeated as the man shifted uncomfortably. 'A Welshman then, and glad I am to have your spear. And what is the name of the man at your side?'

'Wihta, lord.' He reached across and ruffled the hair of a lad at his friend's side. 'And this young 'un is his son, Swinna. He may look sweet but his spear has already tasted

Powys' blood, back in the spring when they tried to kill his father, whore his mother and enslave his brother and sister.'

Icel unfastened the scabbard containing the knife at his belt and tossed the blade across. As the boy snatched it from the air the ætheling spoke again. 'Then you have done more for Mercia than your prince Swinna, though I aim to right that wrong in the coming days.' As the boy stared wide-eyed at his gift and men crowded around to gawp, Icel continued. 'Your friend was well named Gwynfor, Wihta the white.' The crowd chuckled at the comment. The man was taller and slimmer than the Briton with a shock of hair paler even than the ætheling's own, his son already a fair copy. Icel raised a brow as he continued to question the man. 'Neighbours?'

Gwynfor grinned happily. 'More than neighbours, lord. Shared owners of a fine ox!' The fyrdmen; smallholders, drovers, shepherds, men of the fields and woodlands roared their approval, and Icel waited for calm before he drove home the point he had been waiting to make.

'Well, Gwynfor the black, Wihta the white and Swinna the brave, you leave this place as Briton and Engle, Christian and *pagani*, but when you return through those doors behind me three days' hence you will be men of Mercia. For that is the prize I seek, why I have asked you to put aside your scythes at this busy time, take up your spears and don the trappings of war. Once we have chased this army of cutthroats back beyond the western forests, one law shall apply to all, good law which recognises only a man's worth, not the accident of his birthplace but the right of his claim. Lend me your spears for a day and I will hand you that future and more. Fight shoulder to shoulder with me and I will make you this promise. You need never fear the depredations of a raiding army again.'

Icel paused as the buzz of expectation returned, and Eofer

could see that his friend's words had lit a fire within men's hearts which would take more than a rampaging army to extinguish. An idea had been born in the shadow of Leircestre's great walls, a dream which all free men whatever their background could share. Like all births the act would likely be long drawn out, painful and bloody, and the child would need to be nurtured as it grew in strength. But with the first great victory the seed would take root, the idea that Briton and Engle could share the island as equals, build a future together, and Eofer watched in admiration as Icel leaned forward in the saddle and threw them his most charismatic smile. 'What do you say,' he said. 'Shall we go and make our dream reality?'

ICEL PURSED his lips as he shared a look of concern with his thegn. 'You can see for miles!'

Eofer puffed out his cheeks as his eyes scanned the road and fields ahead. The wide vale which carried the River Leir northwards to its junction with the Trenta was awash with life despite the lateness of the hour. The Barley-moon cast a silver sheen over the land, turning night to day; the ancient stonework of the Fosse Way to a rod of iron before them as they led the first Mercian army towards its day of destiny. 'At least we can see that the outriders are doing their job,' he volunteered. 'If anyone does try to alert Cynlas Goch to the danger, our lads will see them before they can get very far.'

At any other time the strange herds, horses of all sizes, asses and mules which had passed them periodically on their way back to Leircestre would have been the source of hilarity within the ranks of the army but not here, not this night. Nerves which had already been stretched as taut as bowstrings were straining against the nocks as the valley widened and the terraces of the hinterland came into view. The first Engles to arrive here back in the days of Offa and Engeltheow had cleared this land, cutting back the forest to work the clayey soil with the heavy ploughs which they had brought from the unforgiving soils of Engeln. Almost a century on, the terraces were awash with settlements and outlying farms, and the army cast anxious looks in their direction as they marched north in silence.

'They should all be English,' Eofer offered helpfully. 'I daresay that most of the people there have fathers, sons or brothers in the army.'

'Still,' Icel sniffed. 'It would only take one man, woman or child willing to sell out his people for a fistful of silver and things could go very badly for us. Or a Briton,' he added with a worried frown, 'or we could be spotted by a Powys' patrol that evades our scouts.' Icel made to add another possible calamity to the list but Eofer cut him short.

'Lord, what's wrong? You may be able to fool others but you cannot fool me. You know that we need the light of the Harvest-moon if we are to use the cover of the night to gain the hill fort. A thousand men can't move through the land in daylight without someone noticing. The men of Powys know that the battle must come soon. Think how they must be feeling. Miles from home, all their carefully laid plans to sit out the winter and harry the lands hereabouts made ash by the actions of king's bane and Thrush Hemming.' His grin flashed white in the moonlight. 'Who would you rather be at this moment? Icel Eomæring or Cynlas Goch?'

Icel pulled a thin smile. 'You are right.' He craned his neck and squinted at the moon. Rime-mane had hauled the brilliant ball high above the southern hills, making spectres of the harvesters thronging the fields. Women paused at their work, stretching aching backs, their expressions a curious mask of pride and dread as their menfolk marched to war. Children, shoeless in the stubble-field moved behind the lines of reapers; scooping up armfuls of the precious stalks and binding them into sheaves, stealing excited glances as they dreamt of the day they too would carry spear and shield against hate-filled foemen.

He was about to say more when the rumble of wheels on stone drew their heads back to the road, and the pair smiled despite their cares as they recognised who the wagon contained. Eofer leaned in. 'Before you ask lord, I told the men to allow the ceorls to keep any animals needed for reli- gious reasons, it being harvest time.' He shrugged. 'I thought that it was a risk worth taking, and I doubt that a traitor would choose an ox to sneak past our scouts. It wouldn't do to anger the gods, not tonight of all nights.'

Icel raised a hand, halting the onward march of the soldiery as the ox driver came to a halt before them. 'Greet- ings, lords,' the man said, whipping his leather cap from his head and clutching it to his chest. 'A nice night for a walk.'

Icel and Eofer exchanged a smile as a rumble of laughter came from those members of the gesith who rode within earshot. The man was obviously the worse for drink and, raising his chin to look at the passengers, Eofer could see that he was not alone. Men and women were picking themselves up from the floor of the cart where the sudden stop had proven too much for their ragged sense of balance. One figure however was standing tall, and Eofer ran his eyes over the *hærfest-cwen,* as her attendants checked that all was well. The figure of Gefion the harvest queen was, he had to admit, a pretty fine effort considering the drunkenness of the party. Seven feet tall, the barley figure was crowned by a ring of wildflowers and dressed in the finest of garments. A blue kirtle was worn beneath a blood red mantle, pinned at the shoulders by twin disc brooches of inlaid sliver. The double loops of a honey-amber necklace were draped across her chest, while a sheaf of barley was cradled before her above a hand scythe which gleamed white in the moonlight.

Icel bowed to the goddess and the man beamed with pleasure. Tall and ruddy, the ox driver looked every inch the countryman, from his wild ginger mop to his dust streaked boots. He held out a jug and the pair smiled as they saw that his shovel-like hands almost enclosed the thing. 'Cider, lord?' he offered. 'It's the first scratting of the year.' The ceorl's belly swelled as he stifled a belch, but a loud hiccough cut the night air anyway. He puffed out his cheeks and held his nose before deciding that it was too much effort. He would live with the hiccoughs. 'Elves are about, shooting their bolts. Sneaky buggers.' He hiccoughed again before he recalled his offer and pulled himself up straight, raising his chin as his face broke into a soppy smile. 'Would you care to drink to the harvest queen lords?' he asked with studied formality. 'It's made from early windfalls. A bit raw still, but it's a proper drop of jollop.'

A warm laugh rolled from the ætheling, lifting the spirits of Eofer and the nearest gesith as they saw the cares of the day roll away from their lord. Icel leaned down from the saddle as the wagoners sang and cavorted, oblivious to the presence of their prince and his army. 'I would be honoured,' he said, 'to drink to the lady.' The man handed the container over, looking on gleefully as Icel raised the jug to the night sky and hailed the barley figure and her attendants:

'Wæs hæl!'

Despite their fuddled minds, the occupants of the wagon had been well rehearsed in their duties for the night, and the answering cry came back in a full throated roar:

'Drinc hæl!'

Icel sank a mouthful and gave a shudder, the cider maker looking on proudly as he handed it across to his thegn. Eofer took a draught before passing the vessel back to the delighted gesith behind him.

'You are a bit early to gather the harvest,' the ætheling was saying to ginger. 'Tonight is only the first night of the Barley-moon. You have the best part of a week before the dark nights return.'

The man shook his head. 'I wish that were true, lord,' he replied as he struggled against the effects of the drink to set his face in a frown. 'A storm is coming and it could be a big 'un, just look at yonder moon. See that halo around it? A sure sign that is. And the birds are quiet.'

Icel laughed. 'It's nighttime man, of course the birds are quiet.'

'Not like this,' the ox driver replied. 'They were roosting long before dark, that's a sure sign. Just take a deep breath,' he said, drawing the warm night air in through the flare of his nostrils. 'Smell that, lord? The plants and trees always smell stronger before a storm, that's why we are out here tonight, breaking our backs to gather the barley before it hits.' He giggled as a fruity rasp carried from the revellers listening in. 'Well, some of our folk are breaking their backs. Nearly done though,' he said with a smile. 'Then we can have a proper drink.'

'We had all best be getting on then, friend,' Icel replied. He slipped a silver band from his arm and tossed it across to the moon-faced ceorl. 'Here,' he said, 'plant a few more apple trees in the spring and when they crop, wassail our victory.'

Icel clicked on his mount, chuckling as he drew abreast the wagon and its charges. The driver was waiting patiently for the return of his jug as it made its way back through the army, turning to call out before they got out of earshot. 'Don't forget, lord. You mark my words, there will be titty clouds in the morning.' He made cups of his hands as his ætheling looked back. 'Great big round ones, like this. When you see them growing darker, Thunor and his goats will be close behind.'

18

The gesith broke free from the trees and put back their heels, thundering away as Icel and Eofer followed them out onto the moonlit hillside. The pair drew their mounts aside, watching as the army tramped from the shadows, weary smiles lighting the faces of the footsore warriors as the end of their journey hove into plain sight. Einar had been good to his word and led them here with the accuracy of a sight hound, and the thegn gave a snort of amusement as he saw the Geat scout waiting for the others to come up with the air of the dog who had got the bone.

Eofer caught his lord staring at the sky now that they were clear of the woodland path, and he urged his horse across with a squeeze of his knee. 'No titties yet, lord?'

Icel snorted. 'No, but the wind is beginning to worry the treetops.' He pulled a face. 'Maybe old red nose knew what he was about after all?'

Eofer raised his eyes and saw that the ætheling was right. The sky was still clear for now, the moon as bright as a newly struck coin, hanging in the air away to the south. But a breeze had got up, not so much as to cause a remark in normal times, but the days ahead would be anything but normal, whatever the outcome. They were close now to the unfinished fort that contained Cynlas Goch and his cantrefs of household troops, so close that Eofer was sure that he could feel the tension crackling in the air as the army of Mercia gathered at the foot of the incline.

'You never told me the name of this place?' Icel asked suddenly. 'I can't call it the hill fort forever.'

'Bruidon, lord,' Eofer replied.

Icel raised his eyes from the treetops and studied the dykes and ditches ringing the hilltop. 'Don is the English word for a long hill,' he said, 'I take it that the first part is Welsh. Any idea what it means?'

Eofer smiled as the army spread out in their wake. 'That means hill too.'

Icel snorted. 'So you have led the army upon which all our hopes depend to a place called hill-hill?' He shook his head. 'First the cider king and now this. This night is becoming madder by the hour.'

'Another in need of a name change then?' Eofer suggested.

'No, leave it. Bruidon, I like the sound and anyway,' he added. 'If we are to make a kingdom here for Engles and Britons together it is a good name.'

Eofer's own hearth troop had edged closer and Horsa caught his eye. Eofer smiled and gestured across with a jerk of his head, the smile repeated on the face of his weorthman as he received permission to approach the leaders of the army.

'Did you get any of the cider?' Icel asked as the duguth approached.

'Just a mouthful, lord. I made sure that the rest of the lads only had that much too. If we are to be busy soon I didn't want the men worried about their own dodgy guts when they should be thinking about gutting the enemy.' He ran his tongue across the front of his teeth as he came to a halt before them. 'Rougher than a fishwife's tongue,' he joked. 'Keep guzzling that stuff and they would have melted!'

They shared a laugh as Icel returned his gaze to the hilltop, watching as the men of his own gesith neared the summit. 'Will the Lindisware be there yet, lord?'

Eofer shook his head. 'No, they are not due here until the second night of the Barley-moon. Horses are difficult to hide at the best of times and they take a lot of feeding. We cannot let them graze the hillside in plain sight, so we would have needed to bring sacks of oats along with us. Not only are we moving too fast for wagons, but likely as not they would have got stuck on the forest path. It's best that they arrive as close to the attack as possible.'

Eofer had turned to Icel for confirmation that he had understood the planned meeting correctly when he saw the ætheling stiffen. The riders who had gone on ahead where milling about as they decided how to respond to something unexpected, and they watched as half a dozen riders broke away and urged their mounts inside the fortress. The remainder of Icel's gesith carried on as planned, crossing the ridge line as quickly as possible to minimise the chance of being caught silhouetted against the skyline in the milky light, before becoming lost from sight as they moved down to the woodlands beyond to look for any sign of the enemy.

Horsa was the first to speak as the last of the army clattered from the tree line behind them. 'Well, if they are not too worried, neither am I.' The pair threw him a questioning look, and the duguth explained. 'If the army of Powys was waiting for us behind those walls, our lads would either be already dead or haring back to us. As it is, they feel safe enough to leave whatever they saw to a small group and carry on with the job which you gave them, lord.'

Eofer and Icel exchanged a look, and the ætheling blew out through his lips. 'Let us hope that you are right. The thought of the fiend cascading down the hill towards us as we are, disorganised and with our backs to the wood, fills me with dread. I was a fool,' he admonished himself. 'I should have sent men on ahead to check that all was clear, before we exited the forest. That is what scouts are for, not to hold your hand in the dark. I was so busy turning over the problems that a bloody thunderstorm would pose to our attack that it slipped my mind.'

'Let's get up there,' Eofer said as he attempted to lighten the mood. 'I am as much to blame as you are. A fine ealdorman I would be if I let my lord blunder about the countryside without offering him my advice. As Horsa says, if your own gesith are happy that there is no threat there to yourself and the army then there is none.'

Horsa had picked up on Eofer's comment, and he put in with a remark of his own. 'I'd best pack my things when we return if we are moving from Snæpe then lord.'

Eofer grimaced as Icel looked on in amusement. 'Forget that I said that for now, becoming ealdorman is one possibility. Another is that we shall all be lying as cold as stones on the banks of the Trenta soon and Leircestre will revert to its British name, so keep it to yourself for now. Come on,' he said. 'the sooner we get the men inside those earthen banks, the sooner they can rest.' He flicked a look at Icel, and the ætheling nodded his agreement. 'Eofer is right, what is done is done. The men need food and a place to lay their heads. Let us complete our journey for this night,' he said, 'hill-hill beckons.' He hauled at his reins, urging his horse into a canter as the army began to follow on, men forcing tired legs into a last effort as they sweated the final rise of the day.

Eofer followed on as Horsa doubled back to lead the rest of his hearth troop the final few yards. The banks shone white in the raking light of the moon, a circlet of steel to safeguard them for the coming day. As soon as the horse warriors from the Lindisware arrived they would scout the enemy and plan the attack. Eofer caught up with his prince as he reached the gaping entrance to the hill fort, and he was relieved to see that Horsa's suspicions had been confirmed. Two of Icel's gesith were there to report their findings to him, and Eofer was glad to see that the warriors' swords and shields had been returned to scabbard and crupper as he too reached the gateway.

'It seems that we were not the first to arrive after all,' Icel called as he came up. 'A pair of Hemming's men are already here. Come,' he said, the concern showing through the weariness on his features. 'Let us discover what good tidings brings them all this way.'

They passed through into the body of the fort itself, and Eofer searched out the familiar hummocks and pathways for the men in question. The remainder of Icel's men had gathered at the centre of the clearing, around the stump he had thought a silver fang at his previous meeting here with the Saxon leader Seaxwulf Strang, and he recognised the men from Tamtun as they moved forward from the group at their approach. Eofer and Icel slid from their saddles as the men bobbed their heads, and Eofer introduced them to the ætheling as they awaited permission to speak. 'These men are Hryp and Beonna, lord,' Eofer said. 'We met at Tamtun.'

Eofer saw pride shine in the warriors eyes that a man of reputation had recalled their names, despite the briefness of their earlier meeting. It was a thing which he had needed to work at in earlier years, but his father had always impressed on him the importance of committing men's names to memory, however lowly their station in life, and it had become easier over time. The ghost of a smile caused the corners of the messengers' mouths to curl upward for a heart-beat, before their discipline reasserted itself and they switched their gaze back to the prince.

'Well, Hryp and Beonna,' Icel said as the pair straight-ened their backs. 'You don't have the look of men coming to report a great victory. It's been a long night, don't bother with all the "Hemming sends his good wishes and trusts that this message finds me well," nonsense at the beginning, go for the throat lads, spit out your news and we will see what needs to be done.'

Hryp was the senior of the two, and he cleared his throat and began his report. 'The British have been reinforced, lord. A few days ago a hundred mounted warriors passed north of Cair Luit Coyt and took Ryknield Street north-eastwards. A pair of our lads tailed them until they crossed the Trenta and carried on to the east. With darkness coming on the boys were worried that they would fall into a trap, so as soon as they felt sure of their destination they hurried back to Tamtun to report their findings.' Hryp cast a glance at his companion. 'We had just returned to Tamtun from a raid ourselves, but Hemming told us to get back in the saddle and get down here as fast as we could.' He shrugged. 'He guessed that you would tread this path to Hreopedun, so we did as ordered and here we are lord.'

Icel gave a grim laugh, despite the bad news. 'Well, I did ask you to cut out the nonsense. If nothing else that was short and to the point Hryp, I appreciate it.'

Behind him the men of the fyrd had finally reached the hill fort, and their footfalls and the jangle of metal echoed back from the walls as Icel nodded that he understood the importance of the news. 'If that is all lads,' he said finally, 'you have my thanks. There will only be cold food tonight but you are welcome to it before you head back.' Hryp made to protest but the ætheling cut him short. 'I know that you would rather stay and fight alongside us now that you are here, but I want you to return. Hemming will need to know that you got through and reported the situation to me, and I wish to tell him what I intend to do in response so that he may act accordingly.' He slipped two silver arm rings from his forearm and handed them across. 'Finding your way here, through what we must consider hostile territory was no mean feat. Accept these as a mark of my gratitude and respect and wait to carry my reply back to Tamtun.'

The pair's eyes widened in surprise and gratitude at the gift, and Icel indicated to Eofer that he walk with him with a flick of his head. As Hryp and Beonna proudly slipped the rings onto their own forearms, ætheling and thegn sought out the shadows, each man alone with his thoughts. Away to the south the army of Mercia had gained the fortress now, the last of the weary spearmen tramping into the great hilltop oval and seeking out a place to spend the night. Eofer had already reached his own conclusion as to the best course of action to take, but he kept his council and allowed his lord to be the first to speak his mind.

They passed by the horse lines, the men there too busy removing saddles, checking hooves and a dozen other chores which would need to be done before they looked to their own bellies to notice that a prince and eorle were passing by. Finally they reached a place which was raised up higher than most, a perfect circle which both men knew marked the outline of a former hut. Icel indicated that they sit, and both men lowered themselves to the grassy ridge and stared away towards the encampment. The first clouds were starting to appear, high up, dappled silver by the moonlight, and Icel stared hard at them and nodded as if receiving a message from the gods.

'Mackerel sky, mackerel sky, never long wet, never long dry.'

Eofer crinkled his brow. 'Lord?'

'It's a saying,' he explained. 'One which my old wet nurse used to say. The silvery scales of the clouds there resemble the flanks of the fish. When you see them it often means that a short, sharp storm is approaching.'

'A cunning woman was she, lord?'

Icel flashed a smile. 'No, as daft as a brush. What is cunning about letting another woman's brat suck on your tit all day.'

They laughed together before Icel went on. 'But she did know her weather. It looks as though Gefion's ox driver may have had the right of it.' Icel turned to his thegn, and Eofer was surprised to see that his lord's worries seemed to have lifted. 'I may have been a bit tetchy today and I apologise, Eofer.' The ætheling held up a hand to cut short any protest from his eorle before continuing. 'Something was picking at my mind even before we left Leircestre, and I couldn't put my finger on it until now. I thought that the gods were telling me not to continue with the attack but now I am not so sure. Think on it,' he said. 'Cider kings leading god-wagons tell me that there is a great storm coming. We get here and Thrush's men are waiting for us to let us know that a hundred of Powys' finest horse Welsh have bolstered their defences. Not only that,' he added with a look. 'They went to great pains to try and sneak in without our knowledge, leaving Watling Street and picking their way through the forest of Canuc on order to give Thrush and his men a wide berth.' He turned his face to Eofer, and the thegn could see to his delight that the confidence which always seemed to infuse his lord's every undertaking had rushed back like a tidal bore. 'They are not setting a trap for us, Eofer,' he said. 'They are preparing to launch their own assault on Leircestre. What with your own attacks up and down the valley of the Trenta, and now Hemming threatening Cair Luit Coyt and Watling Street from the burh at Tamtun, they cannot afford to sit tight and wait until the campaigning season starts again next spring. They need to decide the matter, now, this year. Take Leircestre and Mercia is stillborn. Sawyl Penuchel in The Peaks will come to terms with his fellow Briton and the Lindisware will retreat back behind the marshes and rivers which have served them so well in the past. I thought that the gods were telling me to delay the attack until all of my forces came together but something irked me, something that I could not understand or explain and it tormented me all day. And then I realised that they were not warning that I was courting disaster, they were telling me to attack quickly, before the enemy marched.' He sat back and smiled. 'And now,' he said. 'You are going to do the duty of a folctoga like your father did for my own, a leader of the king's armies. Whatever your own personal feelings, whatever you would order yourself in my place. Tell me why I am wrong.'

Eofer gaped like a fish out of water. He had reached the same conclusion for very much the same reasons, but he understood the sense in the ætheling's request and he racked his mind to provide reasons why they should delay. He looked back to the south, and his mouth made a line as the most obvious reason lay sprawled all about the clearing.

'The men are too tired, lord. The warriors are fine of course, not only did they ride here but they are trained and bred for fighting, inured to fatigue once war horns sound and the banners unfurl. But the fyrdmen,' he said with a shake of his head, 'they are all in. They have been eating the dust thrown up by our horses' hooves all day long, with only the thought of a meal and a good sleep to drag them up the final hillside. Now you want them to carry on through the night and fight against a powerful foe in the morning.' He looked at Icel who sat there fingering his beard as his mind sifted the advice. 'Even if we can bring them to face the enemy before we are intercepted, they may well break if they come under sustained pressure.'

Icel nodded as he watched the clouds gather. 'Another.'

'We need to wait until the Lindisware horsemen arrive. Cynlas Goch has been reinforced by horse-welsh, a hundred or so. Even acting alone they could cause mayhem if they discover us before we are in a strong defensive position. Together with the mounted troops already in the fort they pose a formidable threat, not only to our battle line, but to the whole army if the ceorls do break. It will be a slaughter fit to keep Welsh bards in silver for generations, barely a man will escape. Mercia will die on the banks of the River Trenta.'

'Another.'

Eofer followed the ætheling's gaze, looking up to study the clouds. They were clustering, moving on at a pace. 'The storm,' he finally said. 'It's moving in from the west as most storms do, in all likelihood straight into the faces of our men. If it is as severe as the cider man and your old friend saggy tits seem to think, we shall have to fight almost blind while the Welsh will have their backs to the worst of it.'

Icel snorted at the description, flashing the eorle a smile before going back to worry the strands of his beard. 'Another,' he said. 'And don't be so disrespectful to my poor old nurse.'

'Return to Leircestre and gather in the people from the surrounding settlements and their supplies. Before Cynlas

Goch arrives, send to Anglia for a relief army. They should arrive long before Yule, and whether our allies stand firm or seek to make a separate peace, we shall emerge from our fortress and crush the Powys' between ourselves and King Eomær's *here.*'

Icel raised a brow and turned his face to the eorle. 'That is a very good idea, Eofer,' he mused. 'Excellent in fact.'

Eofer chuckled at his side. 'But still not good enough, lord,' he said. 'Because you have already decided to march tonight and bring the enemy to battle in the storm filled morning, missing allies, a stronger than expected fiend, footsore fyrdmen or not.'

19

He walked the line of dozing men as the duguth and gesith moved among them, tapping thighs and arms with the heels of their spears. 'Come on lads,' he said. 'We have a date with hel!' The men of the fyrd groaned, exchanging looks of disbelief as the thegn walked on. 'Come on boys, on your feet,' he urged. 'She's not the type of girl who likes to be kept waiting.' The more awake were tugging at their friend's sleeves, dragging the unwilling men back from what was, Eofer had to admit, a well earned rest.

The decision made that the attack would take place the following day it was imperative that they push on as soon as possible, despite the weariness which filled the camp. The odd fyrdman here and there grumbled at the interruption, but one look from the warriors was enough to still them.

'What's up lord?' a man asked as he struggled to his feet. 'We thought that this was it for the night.' Eofer stopped and gave him a smile of sympathy. 'We need to push on as quickly as possible.' He went to move away but paused as he decided that the man deserved more than an instruction. No doubt he would rather be laying beside his wife now, or drinking to Gefion and giving thanks for a successful harvest, but he had foregone these pleasures to carry his spear against his lord's enemies. Eofer raised his voice a notch so that all those close by would hear as he spoke again. 'Where are you from?'

The ceorl was stuffing the few belongings he had brought along with him back inside a woollen sack and his eyes widened in surprise that such an exalted figure as the king's bane should engage him in conversation, but he raised his chin proudly and answered as his friends looked on. 'It doesn't really have a name, lord,' he shrugged, 'not yet at least. It's not much more than a couple of huts and a barn, half a dozen miles south of Leircestre.'

'Well,' Eofer smiled, 'unknown man from an unnamed place. The Britons have been strengthened and the ætheling thinks that they are preparing to attack the settlements around Leircestre, maybe even the city itself. We think that Cynlas Goch and his Powys are looking to destroy all our settlements in the Leir Valley, maybe even as far as Brunes Wald, before the winter sets in. The gods have seen fit to place an English army here, now, at the right place and time to put a stop to their schemes.' Eofer paused and looked about him. All the men within earshot were climbing to their feet, moving his way as they listened to what they now knew would be a pre battle speech. He reached out, taking the man's outstretched hand in his own and hauled him upright. 'What is your name, friend?'

'Swithin, lord,' the ceorl answered proudly.

'And you honour the gods, Swithin?'

'Yes, lord. I am a smallholder, farming is my lot in life, Thunor my god. We sacrifice the odd lamb to old copper knob each spring and he sends us rains and sun in the right amount to grow our crops.' He pulled a crooked smile and cast a look around him. 'Ain't that right lads?' A chorus of voices assured him that, not only was he far from alone in his devotion, they all shared his high opinion of the thunderer.

Eofer smiled, relieved at the good humour on display. Despite their tiredness it seemed that there was still plenty of fight left in the men. 'Well,' he said, sweeping them all with a look. 'Picture your lands, your families. Foreign men think to take those lands and call them their own. Enslave those families, yours and mine.' He shot them a grin. 'Let us send them home to think again.'

Eofer was pleased to hear his speech greeted, not by acclamation, but by murmurs of agreement and a steely resolve. It was just the response he had hoped to hear when he began to address them, and he clapped Swithin on the shoulder and wished him gods-luck as he moved on.

All about the moon-washed bowl men were climbing to their feet, gathering up weapons and shouldering shields as movement at the gate drew Eofer's attention. Horsemen were entering Bruidon, and Eofer walked across as Icel's gesith returned from their sweep to the north.

Haystack was moving across to hear their report before breaking the unwelcome news that they were about to go out again, despite the fact that they had already been in the saddle since sundown the day before. Eofer was pleased to see that Icel was not beyond carrying food and ale to the men, men who would have little enough time to take it before they rode to war.

The leading rider slipped from his saddle, and Eofer was about to move on when he noticed that the man was pointing his way. Icel turned and beckoned the thegn across with a sweep of his hand, and Eofer was almost up with the group when he saw the reason for the summons. The relief on Cynfelyn's face was obvious when the Briton saw him coming through the crowd, and Eofer exchanged a brief nod of recognition as he turned to Icel. 'I can vouch for him, this is Ioan's man, Cynfelyn,' he explained. 'The man who led us to Bruidon the first time.'

'We found him on the road, lord,' the gesith explained. 'He said that he was taking important news to you at Leircestre so I brought him here to find out the truth of it.' The gesith looked at Icel, and Eofer saw the ætheling give a nod that all was well. 'Here,' he said, handing across a bag of bread and bacon to the horseman. 'Share these out and I will be along in a moment to tell you about the change in our plans.'

Eofer could see that Cynfelyn was itching to speak. Looking back Icel noticed too, and he offered the Welshman a drink from his own ale skin as he nodded that he should begin. Cynfelyn took a quick swig and launched into the reason for his sudden appearance. 'Cynlas Goch's army has been strengthened in the last few days,' he said. 'Ninety warriors arrived yesterday, and there is a rumour that more will be arriving soon.' The Briton took another swig of ale and handed the skin back with a grateful nod. His eyes flicked from thegn to ætheling and back again as he waited for his sensational news to draw a comment from the Englishmen. When neither man reacted as he had expected, Cynfelyn tried again. 'Ioan discovered that they are building up their forces in order to launch an attack on Leircestre very soon. He sent me to warn you so that you would not be surprised by their numbers if you still intended to make an attack of your own.'

'We heard that it was a hundred,'

'Lord?'

'We heard that a hundred fresh riders arrived at the fort,' Icel repeated.

Cynfelyn looked bemused. 'Where did you hear that lord?'

The English leaders shared a smile. 'We have our own eyes and ears along the valley of the Trenta and elsewhere. However,' the ætheling added, 'your coming here with that information does reinforce Eofer's opinion that you are trustworthy, that you would risk your lives to bring us warning. Where is Ioan now?'

'Heading west, lord, with the rest of the boys. If he had gone east he would have aroused suspicion, so he going to double back when he reaches the River Mease and meet me back in The Tewdwr.'

Eofer noticed Icel's brows knit together at the mention of the unfamiliar name and supplied the answer. 'It's that ramshackle drinking and whoring den, lord. Down by the eastern gate.'

Icel cocked his head. 'They went west, but you were able to amble over this way without attracting attention?'

Cynfelyn pulled a roguish smile. 'I have been leaving at sunset off and on for a week or so,' he said. 'I told the guards that I have a woman further up the valley. Ioan and I have been supplying them with ale to turn a blind eye. After a while it just became normal to them and I came and went as I pleased.'

Icel nodded, obviously impressed at their forethought. 'So,' he said, 'you know the area well. We are attacking the fort from the south, coming down the valley of the watercourse that my men call Hreopedun Brook. How long would you say it will take an army on foot to get there?'

The Welshman looked horrified at the suggestion. 'You can't go that way, lord,' he blurted. 'Even if there are no night riders out, the guards on the walls will see you coming a mile away on a night like this.'

They all glanced up instinctively. The clouds were thickening. Lower clouds, more rounded than the fish scales high above were rolling in from the west, their bulbous faces shining white in the moonlight like the shields of an advancing army.

'If that is so, where would you suggest that we attack?'

Eofer was struggling to keep a straight face as the ætheling probed and questioned. They had discussed the path which the army would take as it approached the Powys' fort at the place the English settlers had named Hreopedun, Hreopa's farm, days before, in council back at Leircestre. Local men who had fled the depredations of the Britons had told them of another way, a small track, overgrown from lack of use, known only to those with need to penetrate the deeper parts of the woodland. Like as not it was still unknown to Cynlas Goch's men at the fort, but even if they had stumbled upon or discovered its existence some other way, it would seem unthinkable that an army should force its way through when there were faster and easier routes on at least three sides. Eofer's mind came back from his thoughts, and he listened in as Cynfelyn unwittingly confirmed his trustworthiness and possibly kept his head upon his shoulders with a simple statement.

'There is a pathway which leads north from here, lord,' he was saying. 'It's only three miles or so in length and it brings you out by the road which follows the southern bank of the Trenta. It's a bit small, but I have travelled the length of it and an army like yours, unencumbered by wagons and the like will force a way through, no problem.'

Icel nodded. 'Will you show us the way?'

'Yes, lord.' He pulled a face and a smile finally crept onto Eofer's face as he realised what was coming next. 'I am not a fighting man though,' Cynfelyn was saying. 'I can scout and drive horses but a spearman I am not.'

'Don't forget your spear, Cynfelyn.'

The little group shared a chuckle as Beornwulf's smile widened. 'Remember,' he added. 'The pointy bit really hurts, so keep it facing towards the enemy.'

Cynfelyn clucked his tongue, and Eofer shared a look of mirth with Einar as they watched the tough Welshman wrestle with his rising temper. His aversion to spear work was through choice the English thegn was sure, not lack of practice or ability. Unlike most men, blinded by tales of honour and the slim chance of making more wealth in a day than they could wrest from the ground in a lifetime of hard work, the Briton had long ago realised that he would live longer and better using his wits than as part of the herd. He intervened before either man could say another word.

'How far is it from here?'

Cynfelyn shot the youth a sour look before softening his features as he turned. 'Half a mile lord, I don't want to risk the horses any closer than this, they are liable to whinny at any time, especially if they get wind of the horses at the fort. It will be the ideal place to picket them when the rest of the army arrive too.' He ran his finger along the wooded outlier ahead. 'The trees there will hide the horses and deaden any sound that they make before the attack if the ætheling still intends to surprise them. There is a small bridge across the brook up ahead. It's usually left unguarded as close as it is to the encampment, but I noticed spearmen there when I left earlier.' He shrugged. 'I guess with all the preparations for their own attack, they are not taking any chances.'

'Right,' Eofer said. 'The quicker that we can spy out the

way ahead, the quicker we can get the army back on the move.' He looked at the youth. 'Beornwulf.'

'Yes, lord?'

'We will be back as soon as we can. The night is drawing on and the ætheling wants us to be in position before sunup.' He pinned the lad with a stare to emphasise the words which followed. 'If you hear lots of noise coming from the west, you know what to do.'

Beornwulf nodded. 'Yes, lord. Leave you to your fate and warn Haystack that you have been discovered.'

'Whatever you do, don't be tempted to come to our aid. If we fall, we fall. If the army is discovered before they are in a position to defend themselves the whole of Mercia falls.'

The youth nodded again, grim faced. 'I understand, lord. You can count on me.'

Eofer smiled and clapped the boy on the shoulder. 'I know that I can, otherwise you would not be here. Keep alert and we will be back before you know it.'

Cynfelin and Einar had already moved off and were waiting for Eofer in the shadow of the tree line. He jogged across and joined them as Beornwulf attempted to melt into the background as well as a man and four war horses could. Eofer flashed them a grin. 'Let's get going.'

The three men set off at a steady pace, skirting the edge of the woodland as it curved to the north, mirroring a great meander in the river's course. Eofer glanced upwards as they walked. The moon was still visible, a silver nail head driven into the blackness of the night sky, but the mackerel sky of earlier had all but cleared away to the north-east and the billowing mass of greyness was almost upon them. He inhaled as he moved, gulping down the damp air of the water meadow as his mind sifted the smells. Old ginger had been right he decided, the smells of woodland and pasture did become stronger as a storm front approached, and he wondered at the fact that he had never noticed before.

'Your boy is a laugh,' Cynfelyn whispered.

Eofer shook his head in reply. 'He is still young, a wound or two will drive the mirth from him.'

'It could be arranged. I thought for a moment he was going to start the old, "there was an Englishman, a Welshman and a Geat," joke.'

Eofer narrowed his eyes, and the Briton snorted softly. 'It's a type of joke we have at home. Remind me later and will tell you a few.' Eofer made to question him again, but froze as Einar halted suddenly and held out a hand. The eorle stood stock-still, quartering the shadows as the Geat began to tease the nearest branches apart. Finally he turned back and indicated that they take to the trees with a movement of his head. In a heartbeat he had been swallowed by the darkness, and moments later Eofer had followed Cynfelyn in. The light from above was just enough to allow the thegn to make out that Einar's fieldcraft had uncovered a path made by an animal of some sort, a badger or fox it looked like, and the rounded tunnel although low to the ground, offered ideal cover and a more direct route to Hreopedun itself. Eofer ran on, doubled up as he attempted to keep the shaft of his spear free from the branches and trunks which pressed about on all sides.

The Romans of course would have driven the main road straight through the trees, clearing a pathway without a moment's hesitation. But the track which hugged the southern bank was British, no doubt ancient when the legions first arrived, almost as much a part of the land as the people were themselves. Eofer reflected on the difference as he ran. It was such a small thing, the course of a road, but the contrast which it showed in the mindset of the two people was stark.

Up ahead his companions had reached the far side of the woodland spur and the trio crouched low, fanning out as they inched carefully forward. Eofer ran his eyes across the ground before him and, satisfied that he was still within the deep dark of the woodland interior, he raised his gaze to look across the site of Hreopedun for the first time.

The fort itself was little more than four walls of banked earth with a shallow ditch before them. As he had hoped and expected no wooden palisade lined the crests and no central tower rose into the air, and he allowed himself a feeling of pride as he saw just how successful his earlier attack on the fort-let upriver had been. Unworked logs were stacked to one side, awaiting the attention of the woodworkers' axe, adze and draw-knife, but the men themselves lay in their graves little more than three miles distant, the tools of their trade either thrown into the waters of the Trenta or twisted and bent by the heat of the fires they had set as they left.

Between their own position and the fort, Hreopedun Brook came down from the southern valley, wound its way across the floodplain and became lost from sight in a fringe of reeds. Halfway between the the Trenta and the woodland edge to the south, the track followed a terrace of higher ground before dipping down to cross the brook by way of the bridge which Cynfelyn had mentioned back at the horses. The original plan had called for him to ride ahead of the army, storm the bridge, and deny passage to the Powys' until Icel could bring up the army and deploy it for the fight. Now that he was here in person he could tell at a glance that Cynfelyn had been right: the banks either side were little more than gentle slopes, minor obstacles to men on foot. Horses would barely break their stride as they swept around either side to engulf the plucky band on the bridge long before any help could arrive.

A small brazier burned on the western bank, and Eofer watched a pair of warriors saunter to and fro as they wished away their watch. The thegn quickly ran his eyes along the skyline to the south. Twin hills bestrode the brook, both heavily wooded, and switching his gaze back to the west he noticed to his disappointment that despite the dryness of the previous month the grassland there looked bare, pitted and rutted by the passage of Cynlas Goch's horsemen. The clouds above had grown darker still in the time it had taken them to reach the fort, the dove grey wall now a duskier hue marbled white as old red beard approached, and he sent a small invocation to the god that he rein in his goats, slow the approach of his sky cart until the armies came to grips.

Cynfelyn sidled across and touched his sleeve. 'Seen enough, lord?'

Eofer nodded. 'Yes, let's get back.'

20

Het þa hyssa hwæne hors forlætan, feor afysan
and forð gangan-

He then bade each of the warriors to let go of
his horse, to drive it far off and march
forwards-

The words of the poem flitted through his mind like a bat in the night and were gone.

'Quiet now,' Eofer breathed. 'Hold your line.'

The pre dawn darkness would help to hide them from Powys' eyes, but it did little for formation keeping. Men looked to left and right, searching out the faintest glimmer as they pivoted about Icel's position at the centre of the road. Somewhere far away in the great woodlands to the south a wolf's doleful cry haunted the night air.

Eofer cast a look to his left. The crown of the first hill rose above the valley floor, the great humped back of an ocean-going whale breaking the surface before it plunged back to the depths. Any moment now the line would come to a halt at the pinch point where the lower slopes petered out a quarter of a mile short of the Trenta.

Above them boiled a witches brew, the earlier moonlight a memory as the rising wind drove the clouds eastwards.

Osbeorn at his side was munching on something, the sound loud in the oppressive silence which hung over the valley. Eofer shot him a look, but the beatific smile which greeted what he had intended to be an admonishing stare drove it away, and he flashed his teeth in a grin at the happy face of his long-time friend and companion. Horsa was tucked in on his right hand side where any weorthman should be, and he took comfort from the press of the man's great shoulders against his own as they walked towards the enemy.

The men in the front rank came to a halt as the stop point was reached, the English line ebbing and flowing, forwards and backwards like a silvery tide on the cusp of the turn as men adjusted their position in the gloom.

Eofer allowed himself a brief flicker of joy that they had reached the place of battle undetected. Not too far ahead he knew that the first of many men to die that day had already made their way to their Christian God, to sit at His feet and bask in His glory, and he wondered again that tough fighting men should seek such an eternity. The bodies of the men guarding the bridge would already be growing cold as Icel's men wiped the blood from their blades, and he shook his head again at the absurdity of this place called Heaven. Even a single day there would seem as a lifetime to a man of war.

'Right,' he breathed, as men stared at the earthen walls opposite. 'Helms on.'

Unhooking his own battle helm from its carrying hook, Eofer took a final look at the piece, running a finger through the road dust on the plates as his men hoist their own. Four panels set into cross bands of iron, the whole given a sheen of silver by smith-cunning: Weyland's work back in Engeln. The full faceplate a mass of writhing wyrms, a wild boar standing silent guard over each eye. The walu, the great domed crest which ran from front to back to protect his head from sword swing or the frenzied hack of an axe, a zigzag pattern of dark and light bands running down to the head of the dragon itself and the red garnet eyes gleaming between his own.

A metallic jangle came from either side as the men of the Mercian army heft their own helms. It was time, but the thegn took a moment to brush the smut from the dome as Horsa rolled his shoulders, warming blood and muscle for the hard work to come in the dawn. A final look around the plates as he did so, King Ongentheow falling to his old blade, Blood-Worm. He cast a thought back to a mist-filled morning back in the old country. He had left the blade there in the grave of his grandfather, as that man's son had handed Gleaming to his own son and they had prepared to move west across the sea. Now Wonred too lay dead there; he hoped that the incoming Danes had given the old man a send-off fit for a worthy enemy. Woden riding down a fiend: the wolf-warrior dancers. He wiped the dust from his hand as he raised the battle helm, fumbling with the ties beneath his chin as the familiar weight pressed down upon his head.

A twist to the rear. The storm front had not yet reached the horizon there, and the first glimmer was coming into the sky off to the east. Grimwulf was backing him up, and he exchanged a smile and threw a heartening wink as spears were hefted all along the line. The timing was perfect, and he turned his head back to the west and looked for a reaction. The gloom was drawing back like a receding tide as the day approached. More and more of the treelined slopes were hardening from the murk, inky black as the vale grew brighter despite the blackness of the clouds above. Shining Mane the sky-horse was approaching fast, hauling the sun back into the welkin as men shifted, chewed at lips and stared ahead.

Horsa murmured at his side. 'They must be blind, lord.'

Eofer flicked a look back along the front rank. English spears were being raised, a thousand points of light flickering as they caught the first rays of the sun. He snorted. 'Someone is about to get a nasty surprise, that's for sure.'

Suddenly it came, and the English line shivered in anticipation of the fight to come as the first flame winked into life on the rampart opposite.

The need for concealment finally gone, Eofer raised his voice a touch so that the men of his troop could clearly hear. 'Remember,' he said, 'no chants or war cries yet. Hold your position and keep your spear raised.' He looked back across his shoulder and threw the youth a smile. 'There are half-asleep men over there trying to work out why the eastern brookside has suddenly sprouted a sea of lights. Let them think that they are looking at will-o'-the-wisp awhile longer. There will be plenty of time for shitty breeks when they realise the truth of it.'

Back on the ramparts more lights were appearing, the dancing flames moving backwards and forwards as their owners exchanged what little they knew about this phenomenon that had appeared in the dawn. A smaller flame detached itself from one of the brands, and the Engles watched as the point of light which marked the path of the fire arrow arced through the air towards them, and the first rumble of laughter came from the English ranks as they watched it plummet to earth fifty yards from their front ranks.

Osbeorn spat in disgust. 'As if we would stand in bowshot. It looks like today is going to be a pushover.'

'More likely I will looking for another duguth before the day's out,' Eofer growled in reply. 'If you underestimate your enemy, the chances are that you will end the day being scooped up by a battle-maiden and taken up to Valhall. You should know that well enough Ozzy,' he said testily. 'Every army contains its fair share of fools.'

A blush of pink lit the men lining the earthen bank of Hreopedun fort, helms became gold, spearpoints flames, and Eofer knew that the sun had finally topped the trees of the spur behind him.

In full view now, the English army came alive as the low mournful howl of a battle horn sounded from the centre of the ranks, and men laughed for the release as the answering war cry thundered out into the crisp morning air and the tensions of the night fled tight chests and fear twisted guts.

Eofer turned back, shooting Grimwulf a grin as spears jabbed the air and men roared and hollered like madmen.

'Harefoot.'

'Yes, lord?'

'Hoist the burning hart. Let them know how much trouble they are in!'

'Yes, lord!'

As the herebeacn caught the dayspring Eofer glanced to left and right, watching as the *cumbolwiga* of his fellow warlords followed suit, the standard bearers raising their own lord's colours: reds, blues and golds gleaming in the dawn as they wooded the air.

The strident blare of horns carried to them from the Welsh encampment, and the men on the earthen wall there could be seen scurrying to-and-fro as the scale of the threat which had materialised suddenly in the dawn became obvious. This was the full scale attack which both armies knew must come, neither side could dare to hunker down into halls and farms for the coming winter in the knowledge that their greatest enemy lay in strength less than a day's ride from their hearth.

They had thought to be the ones to strike, but Icel had stolen a march: the fate of Mercia now lay in the hands of the gods.

As if to confirm the fact the first peel of thunder rolled across the valley of the Trenta, and the sunlight was extinguished as the clouds veiled the sky to the east. Hands were clasping gods-luck charms up and down the battle line as several guda led a struggling captive down the slope, but Eofer had seen it all before and he raised his eyes as he waited for the first enemy warriors to appear. A hush descended on the Engles as their priests forced the man to his knees and raised their faces to the sky, but Eofer kept his gaze fixed on the walls of the fort as the first signs of organised movement appeared there. The cries of the sacrifice ended abruptly, and Horsa noticed his lord's disinterest in the proclamation and mumbled at his side: 'Are you not interested in the god-signs, lord?'

Eofer snorted, flicking a look down as the chief priest flourished a long curved blade and bent to open the victim's chest. 'How many fights have you been in?'

Horsa puffed out his cheeks as he thought. 'Countless small ones, but only four that you would call pitched battles.'

Eofer was already looking back as the first British horsemen came from the fort, but he could hear the unspoken question in the tone of his man's reply. 'And how many times have the guda sacrificed to the gods between the armies and foretold the outcome in the poor sod's innards?'

'Half a dozen?' Horsa replied with a shrug.

'And of that half a dozen or so times, how many times have the priests told you to throw down your shield and save yourself while you still could?'

Horsa's laughter sounded unnaturally loud in the silence which had fallen on the field, and Eofer could sense rather than see faces turning their way in admiration and disbelief that they could joke at such a time. The thegn put their worries out of his mind; he knew that only fools cowered before the gods, and he watched dispassionately as the priest thrust his hand deep into the gore that had been a man.

'My father once told me that the gods are powerful but fickle. Show them respect but place your trust in your own sword arm. It is good advice,' he said nonchalantly. 'It will serve you well if you live by it.'

Horsa's reaction was drowned out by a powerful wave of noise, and Eofer watched in amusement as the guda announced that the omens were favourable. The army of Powys was beginning to stream through the unfinished gates of the fort, and Eofer gave a grunt of satisfaction as he saw how disorganised they were. Men were still struggling into cloaks and war sarks, cramming helms upon their heads as they sought out their friends and headed across to gather beneath their lord's banner.

The first flash came as lightning arced, and Eofer counted in his mind as they waited for the thunder which would follow. It came soon, and he gave a snort of amusement as voices all around him confirmed his own count: Thunor's cart was rumbling along only five miles distant and closing fast.

The guda was facing them now, holding aloft what looked like a bloody heart, but all heads were turning to look away towards the river as the ætheling appeared there on horse-back. The thunder was building as the storm approached, but Icel seemed oblivious to its violence as he hauled the reins and guided the majestic beast along the front of the shield hedge. The army quietened as the prince passed them, and Eofer studied the animal as it approached. The fine chestnut was a full stallion; he knew for sure because he had taken the horse from outside Cair Luit Coyt himself. Now its flanks shone in the gloomy surroundings, the high fronted saddle ablaze with gold and silver as it proudly paced the ground before them.

Icel ran his gaze across the assembled men of Mercia, and the ghost of a smile came to him as he began to speak:

'Well,' he cried, 'here we are, on the verge of our first great victory.' He looked about him and pulled a face. 'How do I know we will be victorious I hear you say?' Icel cast a look across to the guda and back again. 'Because the gods say so?' He shrugged. 'It can only help.'

Eofer saw that men were beginning to exchange worried glances. This was not the type of pre battle speech they were expecting: fire and *brynstān*, an exhortation to grasp a chance for glory. The silence seemed to stretch forever as the ætheling's horse walked on.

'My work is already done,' the man said finally. 'The reason that you are here on this stormy morning made plain by better folk than I. Cast your mind back to the sights that we all witnessed in the valley of the Leir, and you will see the reason that you will win this day fixed in your memory. Grey-beards, too old now to take up a war spear but not so feeble that they cannot help to put food into the bellies of their grandbairns this winter. Lines of women and children, bare-foot in the stubble: Gefion and her maids, the old cider lord, King Gut-Rot himself! Now imagine that place if we fail here today. You have all heard the tales from the west, how English settlements have been singled out for destruction, their people enslaved or killed out of hand. I have been there, as have other men here, and we can tell you that those tales are true. The gods have handed us this chance to put an end to that war of annihilation, to send this Cynlas Goch to his God, where the Christian priests assure me he will answer for his sins. One of those futures will become a reality, on this day, in this place. It is in our hands. Let us make the best choice.'

The sound of a war horn drew Eofer's attention and when he looked back he saw to his surprise that Icel had dismounted. No cry of acclamation had greeted the conclusion of the ætheling's speech, no baritus, the great war cry of northern folk had risen like an ocean roller to crash down onto the heads of the enemy, and Eofer feared that he had misjudged the mood. Icel retrieved his shield and spear from their carrying straps as a priest came to lead the horse away, the ætheling crossing to the men in the front rank of the English line to offer words of advice and encouragement.

Hundreds of the enemy had left the fort in the time that it had taken him to make his short speech and the first horsemen were making their way towards the little bridge, but a slow drumming sound began to rise from the English shield wall, and Eofer felt a tingle of excitement as the steady thrum of ash shaft on lime wood board rose into the morning air. The beat pulsed with a terrible intensity and a look at the faces of the men holding the English shields told the thegn that his lord had pitched the battle speech just right. Outnumbered, the Engles and their British allies would need to fight a defensive battle until the horsemen from Lindcylene arrived to snap the trap shut on Cynlas Goch and his Powys'. A rousing speech was fine to whip up excitement in men prior to a headlong charge, to send fire coursing through their veins, but Icel's words had produced the steadfastness, a grim determination in the thin line to hold on as they imagined the faces of loved ones back home who were depending on them to prevail. The upcoming fate of Icel's horse would act to reinforce their resolve: their prince would stand alongside them, shoulder to shoulder: celebrate the victory with them or end the day bloodied on the turf.

The horse had been hobbled and forced to its knees by the priests and the men looked on as the chief guda, his white robes already blood spattered from the earlier sacrifice, came forward to bring the blade of an axe crashing down upon its skull. As the horse collapsed and shook in its death throes, others were already opening the belly, scooping out great ropes of blue-grey gut as they thrust a hand inside to remove the liver. The crash of spear shaft on shield had become a deafening wall of sound, drowning out the ominous rumblings from the clouds overhead, and Eofer laughed despite the nearness of battle as Horsa leaned in and shouted above the din. 'If I was a betting man, lord, I would lay good odds that these auspices will be taken very quickly.'

British horsemen were across the bridge and beginning to angle upslope towards the place where the sacrifices had taken place, and Eofer smiled as the guda indicated that the signs were good, picked up the hems of their long robes and sprinted up the rise to safety. He flicked a look at Horsa. 'They obviously opened the liver, poked about or whatever it is they do and decided that the gods were telling them, *throw them a quick thumbs up and scarper!*'

The horse Welsh kicked in, their torsos already arching back as they prepared to throw the first darts of the day. English shields came together with a clatter as the horsemen approached in file before turning to canter along the length of the wall, and Eofer was pleased to see the men keep their discipline as the Welshmen released one after another. Despite the slope, the effects of height and speed would give the horsemen a far greater reach; that even the lowliest ceorl had seemed to understand the fact and resisted the urge for retaliation bode well for the day ahead. As the spears thunked into boards up and down the line, Eofer risked a look towards the bridge. The army of Powys was streaming across now, their leaders urging the men forward as they sought to make full use of the horsemen's covering attack, and he gave a snort of irony as he saw the enemy doing exactly what they had hoped. If this was to be the battle to decide which nation ruled the valley of the Trenta nothing short of total victory would do. Already the red dragon battle flag showed where the tyrant himself had crossed to close with the English and, raising his gaze, Eofer felt a stab of hope as a lightning flash illuminated the bearskin clad figure of Seaxwulf Strang beneath his own war banner. The Saxon leader must have persuaded his paymasters that he would be best used as a reserve, and Eofer watched as he led his war band across to take up a position on the far bank of the brook.

Made overconfident by their superiority in numbers, the army of Cynlas Goch had thrown caution to the wind in their excitement and desire to come to grips with the enemy. Despite its shallowness Hreopedun Brook was enough of an obstacle to deny a retreating army, its formation already shattered, any hope of maintaining a cohesive defence as it was chased from the field.

Icel had instructed Thrush Hemming's men, Hryp and Beonna, to wait at Bruidon until the men from Lindcylene arrived that morning before returning to Tamtun. Told of the new battle plan and their part in it, the mounted warriors of their allies would be perfectly placed to deliver the killing blow to Cynlas Goch's hopes of victory. When the Lindisware did thunder along Hreopedun Brook later that morning, the British would be trapped in the field before him, unable to regain the relative safety of the fort and massacred to a man.

Of course, Eofer reminded himself, if their allies were delayed or failed to arrive Cynlas Goch's confidence could yet be well-found. If that was the case he could very well be looking out across his own resting place.

21

'This is more like it,' Osbeorn murmured at his side. 'I have heard enough blather from these boys to last a lifetime.'

Eofer watched as the *bera serc* strode free from the English line and planted his feet foursquare. The priests of both armies had seen him too, and Eofer snorted as he recognised the look of gratitude pass across the faces of both sets of men as they realised that their part in the day's events were drawing to a close. It was an interesting thing, he decided as the bear shirt raised his shield and shook his spear in the first act of the challenge. Despite their hostility and bitter hatred of one another, it would seem that the holy men of both sides had more in common than they realised. Both were clearly running out of ideas and ways in which to enthuse their own worshippers, and the longer the confrontation had dragged on, the more desperate both sets of men looked for a sign that their spells were having some effect.

The storm which had broken over them a short while before had initially been seized on as proof of the divine power of their respective gods but the men of both armies had suffered equally, sheltering beneath the boards of their shields as raindrops and large and heavy as berries had pummelled them. To the amusement of both shield walls the priests had had the worst of it, and their bedraggled appearance as the rain front passed and men reappeared from cover had caused a ripple of laughter to run through the men at both ends of the field.

Clearly, the appearance of the champion could not have come at a better time for them, and the Christian priests thrust their crosses into the air, throwing a final curse in the direction of the accursed pagans at the top of the rise as the guda of Woden and Thunor mirrored their actions, raising rune-cut staves to hurl their own parting curses down the hillside. The stag priest of the English was last to leave the field, the horns and deer pelt shimmering in their dampness as he clouded the air with a handful of dust, cast a parting hex at the Christian fiend at the foot of the slope and followed his acolytes.

The English champion was already calling his own invocation to the gods as the priest moved back past him with a final blessing, and a steady thrum got up as the Engles beat spear on shield:

one…one-two…one,
one…one-two…one…

The Britons at the foot of the slope were catcalling, gesticulating as the warrior jumped and danced, calling down the spirits from the smoke black sky, and Eofer studied the man at the centre of the storm. He had always thought Feóndulf a braggart and a bully like all of his kind, and he was keen to see if his deeds would match up to his boasts. Hanging about King Eomær's hall back in Theodford like a bad smell or off causing trouble for decent hard-working folk, the king's bear shirts lived outside of what men considered normal society. They neither married nor worked, farmed, collected scot owed to their king or any other duty: they were kept for war, mad dogs ready to be unleashed on the king's enemies, and this was their day.

Feóndulf was striding the slope beneath the snarling head of a bear, the headdress and pelt which hung at his back teased out in the freshening wind. His face and bare body were a mass of runic spells, and Eofer saw for the first time that the markings were dedicated not to the Allfather as he had expected but to the warrior god of their ancestors, Tiw. Woden the Allfather had been the first to learn the secrets of runes following his self-sacrifice on the windy tree, but Tiw was the old god of war and bunching his personal rune in groups of three was powerful magic.

The baritus got up then, the warriors in the front three ranks of the English shield wall swinging the great boards before them as the sound began to build. A low hum at first, the sound soon rose to fill the hillside as the men called on the gods to bear witness to their bravery in the coming battle. Each sound change in the war cry was accompanied by a movement: left foot forward...*unsh!* right foot...*aah!* before the shield came up to catch the final cry, amplifying and deepening the shout as it boomed and rolled around the valley: *ooosh!*

The baritus came again: *Unsh...aah"...ooosh!* as the English champion spun and cavorted before them. Still no challenger came from the ranks of the men opposite, and the thrill of the fight to come began to course through the eorle as the men all along the line began to beat their spears upon their shields and cry the age old English war cry:

Ut!...Ut!...Ut!

Out!...Out!...Out!

The rolling wall of noise was suddenly interrupted as Feóndulf, now a frenzied slathering madman, tired of waiting for an opponent and launched himself downslope. The English line roared as their hero drew back his arm and sent his spear sailing over the British, and he drew his sword as the ritual dedication to the Allfather arced down to bury itself within the ranks of the enemy near the red dragon banner of Cynlas Goch himself. Eofer watched in admiration as Feóndulf gathered speed on the slope, his legs moving smoothly as they delivered him to his death.

At the top of the rise the whole of the army of Mercia was craning forward, eager to witness the moment of impact as the bear man aimed for the centre of the Welsh line. A heartbeat before the man hit a shiver of fear ran through the men facing him, as they came to know that it was they who would have to stop this mad charge or pay for the failure with their lives. The eyes of every man on the field were concentrated at the point of contact, and the very air seemed to still, time itself stand frozen in anticipation as Feóndulf reached the foot of the slope and powered on. The crash as the men met came a moment later, Eofer crying out as loud as any as the first men were bowled aside by the Engle's momentum. The wan light of that storm-darkened morning shone dully on the blade of the bear-man as he hacked and hacked again at the heads of the men before him; scything a path through the front ranks to scatter those at the rear, where the battle-shirkers shrank before him and melted away like ice in the sun.

Eofer looked away as the Britons began fold around the hero, exchanging knowing looks with the other thegns and leaders of the army lined up to either side. The attack had done its work, the English fighters were ready for battle and filled with confidence despite their lack of numbers, and

Eofer stood proud of the battle line as the noise began to trail away. He knew that Feóndulf had been overwhelmed without the need to look; at this very moment he was going down under a blizzard of spear and sword blades as he paid the price for his bravery, and Eofer hoped the gods had witnessed the man's end, despite his earlier feelings towards him.

A howl of outrage came from the front ranks, but Eofer and the other leaders were already in place, ready to reimpose the discipline which each of them knew would be the differ-ence between victory and death that day as the jeers from the foot of the slope came again. As the line steadied, Eofer took a look back to the west. The men of Powys had obviously expected the lone attacker to be little more than a battering ram, opening up a gap in their defences through which the men at the top of the hill would sweep down and through. The relief that that had not been the case was evident now in their voices. Already Cynlas Goch had sent the Welsh leading men moving through their ranks, shoving men into position as they began to prepare for an advance of their own.

A line of golden light cut the meadow, and Eofer glanced up in surprise. A tear in the cloud cover had allowed the early morning sunlight to sweep the field for a heartbeat before the rent had closed again. The glow had lingered on the small troop gathered in their war glory beneath the red and gold banner of the Saxon giant. Seaxwulf was clearly visible, and the eorle gave a snort as he recognised the bearskin clad figure to his right, his weorthman from the first meeting still in place like any good right-hand-man should be.

The boy Seaxwine was there, the group staring his way as they picked out the burning hart from among the war banners on the hill, and he fought against the desire to raise a hand in acknowledgement as the light faded again. Another band of blackness was sweeping in, darker this time than the one which had gone before, and Eofer wondered who would benefit the most when the inevitable rain followed. The earlier rainstorm had been blinding for the men on the hill, but the slope before them had taken a pounding from the horsemen as the Welsh rushed across the bridge and deployed at the start of the day and the rains had only added to the mess.

Not knowing the English battle plan the horse-welsh had been sent to cover the deployment of the spearmen as they streamed across the only bridge to take up their position at the foot of the slope. They were not to know of course that the English had had no desire to take the fight to them while they were still divided and disorganised, but if the rains were about to return just as it seemed that the Britons were about to mount their own first attack of the day, the slope could quickly become a quagmire.

As war horns sounded at the foot of the hill Eofer took a last look around him. The place of slaughter had been chosen on his recommendation and he felt the weight of expectation despite the fact that the final decision had been Icel's. Away to his left the battle line was firmly anchored to the spur of land which came down from the hillside. Heavily wooded, the rising land beyond would be impassable for horsemen and heavy going for all but disorganised groups of spearmen. To his right, the place where the shield wall ended had largely chosen itself. There the land fell away as water meadow became marshy riverside, impassable to horsemen and spearmen alike. They had taken and now held the highest point on the valley floor, despite the rigours of the night march down from the old hill fort and the tense transit of the ancient trackway.

Icel had set his banners on a knob of land to the rear, his own personal herebeacn of the black raven alongside the white dragon of Anglia, and Eofer regarded the figure of his lord with pride as he picked out the blond mop of hair surrounded by his gesith. Ready to rush to the aid of any point in the line which came under intolerable pressure or exploit a weakness in the enemy, Haystack's personal guard were some of the toughest and most experienced warriors on the field.

He had done all that he could to give the army of Mercia, the very first *here* to bear that name, a fighting chance. His confidence boosted by what he saw Eofer turned his face towards the enemy. If they could just hold out until the Lindisware arrived to roll up the Britons from the rear he felt certain that the day would be theirs.

High above, thunder rolled as the first drops of rain began to spatter the ground around them. The wind had dropped to little more than a breath, the wind-driven chaos which had thrown the earlier droplets like slingshot forgotten as the Welsh crashed their shields together, let cry a roar of defiance and came to claim their victory.

Eofer's mind recalled previous fights as he watched the slow ascent. When the scops and bards weave their tales and drink befuddled men toast their victories as the wind howls about the eves, lines of heroes come on undaunted, facing down the arrow-storm in their desperation to come to grips with the enemy. No man was afraid, there were no battle-shy dragging their feet as they attempted to filter to the rear of the line. It was never like that in reality he knew, as fear twisted guts and turned the contents of bowels to water. But there was one thing that the poets did get right, every time: each man, be he a king's gesith, thegn or herdsman, a warrior for the day, *was* a hero. If he survived the fight he became one of the few, the men who would in later life roll back his sleeve as wide-eyed children gawped at his scars and tell them that he got them fighting for king and folk at such a place, on such a day as this.

The men of Powys had come to a halt, shuffling back into line as the dips and hollows of the slope worked to tease it apart. The leading men were bawling commands as they prepared to come forward again, and Eofer raised his gaze to sweep the vale one last time before the rain blotted out the view. The Saxons were still on their terrace, ready to move forward when summoned by their paymasters. At the foot of the hill the Welsh leader and his hearth troops, the men they called cantrefs, were facing upslope, ready to carry the red dragon banner forward as soon as the English line broke under the coming onslaught. The pieces of the game were perfectly placed, and his thoughts melted away as a cheer rent the English line.

'This should thin them out,' Osbeorn was saying.

Eofer looked and saw that the remaining bear shirts were coming out to do battle with the fiend, and he watched as the giant men took up position a dozen paces from the English spear hedge. A wild-eyed warrior, bare chested, his arms ringed with gold jogged up, bared his teeth in a wolf-like snarl and turned to face downhill.

'What is his name, Ozzy?'

'Blódulf, Blood-wolf, lord.'

'Any good?'

'He thinks he is, he is a bear shirt after all.' He sniffed. 'A nuisance most of the time, but if he is anything like his mate Feóndulf it may have been worth putting up with their antics all these years. Despite the fact that they are bear shirts they call themselves the wolf brothers. Each of them has replaced his birth name with a wolfish name, Feóndulf we have already seen, Blódulf there and his mate Hæþstapa, heath-stepper, beyond him.' Osbeorn lifted his chin as he leaned forward from the line. 'That looks like Mearcweard, border-watcher, beyond them.' He hesitated, narrowing his eyes as he looked along the face of the war hedge. Finally he shook his head. 'Sorry, I can't tell the others apart from here.'

'No matter, the scops will recall them when they weave their verses. The boys have balls,' Horsa said, 'even if that is unlikely to last. Six men against how many?'

Eofer had quartered the enemy as they formed up and had the figure to hand. 'Just shy of two thousand,' he answered confidently. 'If you don't include the cantrefs and Seaxwulf's Saxons.'

'So that's…?' Osbeorn murmured as he attempted to work the odds.

'About three hundred each,' Eofer replied with a grin. 'So don't begin tucking in to your breakfast just yet, we still have work to do.'

The Engles were yelling their war cries and beating their shields as the Welshmen dressed their lines, threw their shoulders into their war boards and came on. They were close now, so close that even the most reluctant spear man had accepted that the only way to escape was through the ranks of those at the lip of the rise, so they gathered their courage, put their faith in God and climbed. The bear shirts were filling the vale with their own battle songs, the notes rising and falling in time with their movements as they crouched and flexed, springing this way and that as they clove the air with their wide blades. The stygian gloom which had descended on the vale was suddenly lit by a flash as great as any which had gone before: lightning wove wild patterns in the sky and a curtain of rain swept down to veil the scene.

Thunder boomed, and as if waiting for the sign the bear shirts launched themselves down the slope.

The men of Mercia howled and yelled encouragement as

their countrymen hacked and slashed only yards away, and great bites were torn from the battle line opposite as the Powys' shrank back before the onslaught. Eofer blinked the rain from his eyes and checked to left and right. The wolf-men were cutting deep swathes through the British ranks, hewing to left and right as the enemy recoiled before them, but the thegn knew that the fight could only last a short while before they were enveloped and cut down. He turned his head, calling instructions to the men of his hearth troop as the first of the Britons began to break through. 'Ready lads, here they come. Mark your man and make every thrust count.'

Instinctively his left foot slid forward, just a touch, readying himself to spring forward as he listened for the signal. Drawing confidence from the press of friendly bodies all around him, Eofer glared above the rim of his shield as he watched the first of the attackers push their way past the place where Blódulf was still dealing out death all around.

The Britons attempted to close up as they poured through the gap and Eofer fought down the overwhelming desire to attack while the men before him were disorganised and at his mercy. The Welshmen knew how vulnerable they were at that moment, and Eofer took delight from their fearful glances as he willed the war horn to sound. Suddenly it came, the haunting wail repeated up and down the line as other horns blared. With a cloud ripping roar the English line moved forward as one, a shimmering wave of steel and leather which swept into the disorganised men before them, crashing through their makeshift defence before it had the chance to reform.

A man had turned to flee but there was no way back through the crush of bodies and Eofer drove his spear into his spine, twisted it clear and took a step forward. Another Welshman had kept his wits as panic began to grip his countrymen and Eofer watched as he threw his shoulder into the back of his shield and came on screeching like a gull, desperate to break through into the clear spaces beyond. The Engle braced and a heartbeat later the air was driven from his lungs as the big boards came together with a thunderous crash. His opponent was powerful, short and stocky, a difficult man to unbalance. Eofer felt his body tipping forward as his feet struggled for grip on the rain sodden grass, but his duguth were there and the pair took a pace to left and right, wedging him with their shoulders until his feet gained a purchase.

It was his opponent's turn to feel terror's icy grip now as the momentum went out of his attack, and he twisted in desperation as Osbeorn and Horsa took it in turns to stab at his unprotected sides. The man went down with a final snarl of defiance, and Eofer ground his boot into the spearman's face as he stepped forward, thrust his spear into the back of another panic-stricken Briton, released the bloody shaft and drew Gleaming from its scabbard in one fluid movement.

The attack was faltering, and Eofer risked a look towards the river as a space cleared before him. English banners were moving forward all along the line as the fiend were forced backwards by the ferocity of their counterattack and, looking back to the front, Eofer was shocked to see the bare chested figure of Blódulf emerge from the crush. Still wary of his slashing blade despite their desire to be away from the place of slaughter, Welshmen were channelling around him as they fled down the slope.

The English battle line moved forward far enough to gather in the wolf brothers who had survived the brawl, fighting alone like rocks in midstream as the enemy flowed all around them. Even the Engles were careful to give the madmen a wide berth until they were sure that the fury had left them, and Eofer exchanged a look of surprise with Horsa as he saw that the skies were clearing. The eorle closed one eye, squinting up at the patch of blue as the men around him jeered at the backs of the enemy. 'That's your mackerel sky for you,' he said. 'Never long wet, never long dry.'

22

'They don't look so cocky this time.'

Eofer looked back down the slope to the Welsh positions. It was true, they had underestimated the will of the English war host and he had been surprised by it. The leaders of Britain might be their own worst enemy, too busy fighting among themselves to unite and drive the real enemies from their island, but nonetheless they were not complete fools.

He ran the events of the morning through his mind yet again as the spearmen of Powys shuffled into line. Three times they had come, and three times English steel had sent them scurrying back to the foot of the rise. They seemed determined to end it as quickly as possible: did they know about the Lindisware? Was there a traitor among the Britons in the Mercian army? At the back of his mind Eofer knew that his greatest worry was that Ioan and his men had betrayed them to Cynlas Goch, but Cynfelyn had satisfied Icel of his loyalty back at the hill fort and Haystack was nobodies fool. Besides, if that had been the case they would have been intercepted long before they appeared before the walls of Hreopedun, there were more than enough places where they could have been annihilated on the march. What if they had pitched up at Bruidon and the hill fort had been filled with the enemy? It was obvious that the Britons had not the slightest inkling that the army of Mercia was about to appear before them from their reaction that dawn: so what was unsettling his mind, being a bloody nuisance, digging and poking about in there like a boy with a stick?

Eofer became aware of a figure standing before him, and he blinked away his surprise as he recognised that it was the priest who had been administering prayers to the Christians in the army. As many as one in ten of the men who had left their ploughs and scythes to follow the ætheling to the banks of the Trenta were British Christians, the descendants of the folk who had lived hereabouts when the legions of Rome were little more than a rumour of terrible deeds done in far off Gaul. The man chuckled as he recognised the bemusement on the Engle's face. 'Can I offer to say a prayer for your soul, lord?' he chirped happily. 'And those of your men who will allow it?'

Eofer's hand went to his throat as he instinctively reached for his gods-luck charm before he remembered that he had gifted it to an ex thræl, back in Engeln. He had been part of a party who had attempted to block their path on the way to the ship, but they had parted on good terms nonetheless and Eofer snorted as the big man's parting words came to him on the wind and wondered for a moment how he fared: *I am Wulf shield breaker of the Long Beards, a free man.*

The Christ priest held his smile as Horsa laid a hand on his shoulder and leaned in, licking his fingertip and running it along the blood smeared blade of his spear. 'Only if you want me to make you another arsehole,' he said with a sneer. He jerked his head. 'Go on piss off, while I am in a good mood.'

The priest looked at Eofer for confirmation, and the thegn

rolled his eyes. 'I would do as he says if I were you,' he said. 'I have seen him gut a priest before, it looked painful.'

A war horn blared at the foot of the field, and Eofer clapped him on the shoulder. 'I should go and see to your own flock. It looks as though they will be busy again soon.' The Christian smiled happily as he moved away. 'Don't forget, lord,' he threw across in parting. 'If you call me, I will come.'

Horsa brandished his spear and made a point of twisting the blade to catch the sun. The priest was unconcerned, and he gave a parting wave as he called back. 'You are welcome too, my son. There is a place for all in God's kingdom, even for priests with two arseholes!' The duguth shook his head and grimaced. 'What is it with these people? Always happy, always smiling. They just never give up.'

'You would be happy too if you lived off of other folk's hard work.'

'What do you mean?'

'The tithe of course,' Eofer said.

Horsa gave him a blank look and Eofer explained. 'The tithe is the payment that all Christians make to free the priests from doing actual work to support themselves, so that they can go off preaching what they call the *gōspell,* the good news, the glad tidings.'

Horsa pulled a face. 'So, every Christian hands over a tenth of everything they produce, as well as the scot owed to their lord? You are right, no wonder that they are always so cheerful, if he stops again next time he comes past he is definitely getting a second arsehole!'

The horn sounded again and the Engles bent to pick up their shields. Slipping weary hands into handles they hefted the great boards and stared down the slope. Most men were on their second shield by now, the first little more than an

iron boss with a fringe of shattered wood, littering the grass
to the rear of the spear hedge like a field of fallen stars.
Moving fast and without wagons, the spearmen had had to
carry the heavy boards slung over each shoulder all the way
from Leircestre to the battlefield. It had been hard going, but
only a fool or a man who had yet to feel the very air move as
a spear blade whistled past his cheek begrudged carrying as
many of the linden boards as he was able.

Eofer watched as British heads came forward, the sign
that they were leaning in as they felt the ground rise beneath
their feet, and he gave the cutting edge of his spear blade a
final sweep for luck with the sharpening stone before popping
it into the purse at his side.

The chant got up from the English ranks again as their
foemen approached, *Ut...Ut...Ut...,* and Eofer clashed the heel
of his own ash shaft onto the lime-wood boards as he thrilled
again to the moment.

The Welshmen had learned their lesson after the first
attack in the rain-lashed daybreak, and despite the fact that
the bear shirts were a spent force, they knew now the quality
of the host arrayed along the lip of the rise and they took their
time, girding their courage as they prepared for another hard
fight. The wolf brother, Blódulf, had been the only one of his
kind to survive the first fight; the others had been either killed
outright in the fighting or succumbed soon after to their
wounds and were already sinking ale and mead with Woden
beneath his roof of golden shields in Valhall, regaling their
own ancestors and all that would listen to the tale of their
death-fight.

Miraculously Blódulf has survived the fight without a
scratch, and Icel had recognised the hand of Tiw the war god
in it and drawn the man back to recover from his exertions.
The bear shirt had been a weakling for most of the morning,

like all of his kind as helpless as a bairn once the fury had left him, and Icel had left him in the care of the stag priest as the shield wall had thrown back attack after attack. Under the guda's care his strength had slowly returned, and the ætheling had honoured him with the position of ordman in his own personal gesith, the very point of the boar snout which would sweep down and smash their way through the ranks of Welsh-men, beat the red dragon banner of Powys down into the dust and snatch the victory when the moment came.

The attacks had left the grass before the English shield wall strewn with bodies, the full horror of what the scops and bards variously called the press of shields, the dance of spears: *wæpenþracu* the weapon-storm.

It was already mid morning, the stormy skies a memory as the sun shone steadily to the south: surely the Lindisware must be past the hill fort by now?

The rhythmic chanting trailed away as men concentrated all their energies on survival and Eofer knew that the Welsh were near. He looked up. A line of boards before him, steel helms glinting in the light, spears held ready to stab down into heads and necks: banners streaming, the light airs mewing through the gaping mouth of the red dragon men called *draco*. He shifted his feet and raised his own gar, moving his grip along the shaft of the heavy spear until he found the point of perfect balance and looked ahead. His opponent was obvious now, snake-eyes glaring over the rim of his board, and Eofer willed the final yards away as the Britons tramped on.

Ready!

A moment later the lines crashed together, men howling, grunting with effort as they threw their shoulders into their boards and spear shafts crisscrossed the air above.

Snake-eyes was pushing for all his worth, but Eofer was

no downy chinned boy and he knew this work as well as any man alive. He gave ground, an inch, maybe two, but he knew that it would be enough to send the thrill of success coursing through his opponent, and he readied his counterstrike for the moment which he knew was a whisker away.

There!

The pressure came off for a heartbeat as the Welshman adjusted his footing, ready to drive forward again and punch through the English line. He would be the first to break out into the clear space behind the enemy shield wall after a day of toil and bloodshed, in his mind the voices of the bards were already singing his praises when the first stab came. Another, then another, and the Briton's mind screamed in disbelief as the strength deserted the limb and he began to fall. His face was in the mud, the grass before his eyes a woodland as cold steel worked its way between helm and mail, and an image of Rhodri came as he waited for the end. The boy was stood atop the barn, waving proudly as his da went to drive the Saesneg back into the sea, and he felt the pain of their parting more than Beornwulf's downward spear thrust which sent his soul to Christ.

Eofer stepped across the prone figure of snake-eyes and jabbed his gar low. The Briton there still had the look of surprise painted on his face as he came to realise that the man before him had fallen, and he desperately attempted to alter his stance before the killers facing him could strike him down. He saw the stab and instinct took over. His shield dropped, and he dragged his spear down to deflect the blow as he sought to steady the line, but Eofer's spear thrust had been a feint, and the eorle twisted aside as eager hands reached past to drag him into their ranks. Before the Briton could react his shield had been forced aside, and the first blade plunged into his guts as the Engles in the rear tossed the lad between them, baying with joy as they tore him apart like a fox caught by hounds.

Another face reared up, a red beard and the gap-toothed rictus of a snarl, and Eofer shouldered him back, watching dispassionately as his gar slid into the white of the Briton's throat. Suddenly the pressure eased as the Welsh took a pace back, and both lines instinctively dressed themselves, clattering shields together as they gulped down air and blinked the sweat from their eyes. Engle and Briton alike panted like dogs in the hot sun until without any visible signal they crashed forward again, stabbing and shoving across the blood-slick grass.

The Welsh began to give: Eofer felt a quiver pass along the enemy line as the heart went out from the push, and he stabbed his gar into the shoulder of a man and left it hanging there as his hand moved across the draw Gleaming. The Britons too sensed that the attack had failed, and they began to hang back and glance rearwards as swords hissed from scabbards all along the English line.

Eofer drove forward, Gleaming chopping down at heads and necks as Horsa and Osbeorn held their places at his side. He saw the look of indecision on the face of the man nearest to him as the Briton frantically sought a way out from the carnage, but there was no way forward and the way to the rear was blocked by men as desperate as he. Osbeorn's blade cut the air, and Eofer felt his first moment of pity that day as he watched the man scream and twist away.

The spearmen of Powys were beaten again, and Eofer pulled up at the lip of the slope and cried out above the battle-din.

Hold!

The men of his hearth troop clustered about their eorle as Grimwulf brought the burning hart banner and planted it at his side. Earlier in the day when the enemy had been driven away in disorder, the slope had resounded to the thunderous roar of a victorious war host but those joyous moments were in the past. Men looked on hollow cheeked, their eyes red rimmed and sunken as the Welsh streamed away.

A boy appeared at his elbow, and Eofer indicated that he first take the water skins to his youth with a smile and a pat as any good leader would. His eyes ran across the slope before him as he waited for the others to slake their thirst. His duguth were still at his side, Horsa, Osbeorn, Octa and Finn and he took comfort in their presence as they watched the Welsh leaders rant and rave at their oft defeated host. The numbers at the foot of the hill were visibly fewer than they had been at the start of the day and, although the enemy still had numbers on their side, Eofer felt confident now that the Mercians had the beating of them. Hundreds of Powys' lay like bloody rags across the face of the hill, the sad bundles growing steadily in number until they fetched up as a grim tideline just feet away from the place where the English still stood shoulder to shoulder.

The skins reached the frontline and eager hands reached out to take them. Eofer tipped back his head, sighing with pleasure as the lukewarm liquid made his senses come alive. Osbeorn was the first to quench his thirst, and the others shared a smile and a laugh as he put their feelings into words. 'You know,' he sniffed, as the boy collected the empty canteens and scurried away to refill them at the river. 'As much as I like ale and mead, you can't beat a mouthful of water when you are *really* thirsty.'

As the harsh laughter died away, Horsa's anguished gasp caused Eofer's heart to come into his mouth. The big man was as steady as an oak, but the despair in his voice was clear and Eofer followed his gaze with trepidation as he turned back to the east. A column of heavily armoured horsemen were thundering along the woodland fringe, heading straight for the place where the ætheling's war banner snapped in the breeze. All along the English line fear-filled faces betrayed the same thought. While they had been fighting here, a second British force had either returned from raiding English lands or had been sent downriver with orders to attack their rear. In short they had been outflanked: despite their bravery the day was lost.

Horsa was already bellowing commands at the youth, turning them to face rearwards as others did likewise up and down the line. 'Remember,' he was saying, as the shields came together with a crack, 'we have faced down horsemen already today. We shall do so again.'

His weorthman's quick thinking had freed him from the responsibility of organising the defence, and Eofer used the opportunity to look towards Icel and his gesith on their grassy mound. The concern which he saw there was real, but there was something else, something which he could not yet grasp. And then he had it, the gesith were still facing his way, and although worry was etched onto the ætheling's features it was clear that the approaching horsemen were known to him. As he watched the leading rider raised a hand to slow the group a hundred paces from Icel and Eofer called out to the men within earshot; 'turn back to face downhill lads, they are on our side. Haystack will send word if there is anything we need to know.'

As men began to lower their shields all along the rear, Eofer checked the enemy for any sign of a reaction to this new development. The Powys' leaders were attempting to marshal their spearmen for another attack but it was obvious that their war-lust was beginning to wane, and men were making their feelings known as they saw the enemy strengthen.

'I can imagine how they feel,' Octa spoke at his side. 'The attacks have hardly been battle-cunning. Trudge up the slope and batter at the shield wall until the horsemen can sweep through any gaps and claim the victory.'

Eofer looked again. Men were pointing their spears at the reserve, still in place on the knoll beneath their war banner, and he wondered if he may yet have to fight the giant Saxon. They were one of the strongest groups on the field, and he could imagine the anger of the men of Powys that their leaders were attempting to purchase the victory with their lives while the barbarians supped ale and enjoyed the show.

Horsa touched his arm and indicated to the rear with a flick of his head. A boy was hastening across from Icel's position, heading straight for his troop, and Eofer bent to wrest his spear from the back of its last victim. 'Here,' he said, handing the gar across to the youth Crawa. 'Clean this up and restore the edge while I am with the ætheling.' Crawa took the spear as Eofer made his way back through the ranks of his men, and he was ready and waiting when the lad arrived. Now that the fury of the fighting had abated he realised just how uncomfortably hot the day had become as the sun rose higher, and he raised his chin to loosen the ties which were beginning to chafe at his neck. Prising his grim-helm from his head, he ran a hand through the sweatiness in his hair as the boy padded up.

'Icel Ætheling asks that you attend him, lord.'

He nodded as the messenger hurried off to summon the other thegns, nestling the helm into the crook of his arm as he made his way across. The horsemen had dismounted, the stallions pulling at the lush grass near the tree line as their leader conversed with Icel. Eofer could see that his lord was teasing his beard into a knot as he approached the pair. It was as sure a sign as any that he was thinking deeply on a problem, and he increased his pace despite his weariness following the night march and heavy fighting that morning.

The ætheling glanced up as he arrived before them, pulling a weary smile as he made the introductions. 'Cueldgils, this is Eofer Wonreding, king's bane. Cueldgils is the son of the Lindisware ruler Creoda, Eofer,' he explained. 'Come to bring us weighty news.'

Cueldgils gave Eofer a curt nod. 'We are not so isolated that we have not heard of the exploits of Eofer, king's bane,' he said. 'It will be an honour to fight at your side.'

Eofer looked from one to the other. 'We were expecting more of you, Cueldgils.'

'Sawyl Penuchel of The Peaks has broken our agreement,' Icel interrupted with a frown. 'As an ally I Informed him of our plans to attack, but he has taken the opportunity to make a grab for the lands of the Lindisware. Luckily he misjudged the timing of his stab in the back, and Creoda's horsemen had yet to leave to link up with us. Cueldgils has brought fifty of the best, but that is all that can be spared for now. We shall have to make do.'

Eofer nodded. It had not escaped his notice that Icel had spoken over Cueldgils as the Lindisware had made to reply to his direct question. If the son of the leader, whether Creoda styled himself a king or not, obviously deferred to Icel who was merely an ætheling after all, it was true what Haystack had said to Eofer back in Leircestre. Eofer decided that he would not call the man lord after all: after an absence of almost a century, it seemed that the Engles of Lindcylene really were back in the fold.

The other thegns were coming up from their positions in the shield wall in answer to Icel's summons, and Eofer turned to cast his eyes over the enemy as he saw for the first time the commanding view of the battlefield from the knoll. It appeared that the enemy spearmen had been persuaded to mount another attempt on the Engles after all. Seaxwulf still held his position on the mound opposite, but the horse Welsh were back in their saddles, walking the war horses towards the southern flank where the wooded spur jutted into the field.

Lost in his thoughts Eofer jumped as Cueldgils spoke at his shoulder, and the pair shared a laugh as Icel greeted the others. 'You have had a busy morning, Eofer,' the man said.

Eofer's mind went back to other fights, battles in foreign lands: Frankish meadow, Danish Ridgeline, Jutish river crossing: Ravenswood where he had earned his eke-name, king's bane. 'I have been busier,' he replied with a shrug.

'Well, take refreshment while you can my friend,' Cueldgils replied with a look. 'I already know what Icel has in mind. You are about to get busier still.'

23

———

E ofer's eyes darted from left to right as he drained the ale skin and held out his hand for another. He had always hated being away from the front ranks in any fight and he pulled the stopper with his teeth as he watched a lattice-work of spear shafts jab above the heads before him. He felt a dig in the ribs and turned to find Osbeorn's grinning face inches from his own. 'Gissa slurp.'

The thegn returned the smile as he handed the skin across. 'Pass it around, Ozzy,' he said. 'Before I drain the lot and find that I need to piss at just the wrong moment.'

The duguth took a swig and passed it back to eager hands. 'That's better,' he sighed. 'I can't wait to get hold of some of that Welsh ale though, lord.' He winked. 'It won't be long now.'

The short conversation had taken his mind off the wait-ing, and Eofer dipped his head at his duguth in acknowledge-ment of his thoughtfulness. The Christian priest from earlier hurried past, his arms red to the elbows, and he saw the tired-ness in his eyes as they exchanged a look and felt a newfound respect for the man. Tithe or not, he was doing the work of

God and man alike as he tended the injured irrespective of whether they bent their knee at a Iesus altar or wooded grove. He had seen him around Leircestre and Eofer decided to seek him out when he became ealdorman and find him a suitable place to tend his flock.

The sky above was clear now, all the god-driven frenzy in the dawn driven beyond the horizon. The treetops swayed in gentle autumnal airs, and he took a deep breath and sucked his teeth as the sounds of fighting began to trail away. The men were beginning to fidget behind him as the time approached, nervous laughter rolling around the group as Osbeorn farted and grabbed a last chance to piss into the grass.

Better out than in boys!

A stamp of his feet and a flex of his toes to get the blood moving again and Eofer reached forward, placed a hand on Grimwulf's shoulder and gave a squeeze. 'Ready?' The youth nodded without looking back as the latest Welsh attack began to falter. 'Right, get back behind me with your mates. Keep that banner high, let them know how much trouble they are in.'

A quick look to his left to check that all was well and Icel caught his eye and flashed him a grin and the thumbs up. Eofer laughed and shook his head in wonder at his lord's mettle as he ran his eyes across the ætheling's formation for what seemed like the hundredth time. Blódulf, the last bear shirt still standing was there in the place of honour, ordman, snorting like a bull at the very point of the boar snout. Icel's gesith, his own household warriors, the best of the best, were arrayed in wedge formation behind the mad giant with the ætheling himself standing proudly beneath his own black raven war banner and the white dragon of Anglia. Behind them Cueldgils and his men were standing alongside their horses, holding the reins as they prepared for the moment they would leap into the saddle and play their part in the counterattack.

The men of Eofer's war band were set in their own wedge, arrowing back in his wake as he prepared for the signal. Despite the fact that he knew that it was coming Eofer still jumped when it did, and the English ranks began to draw aside before him as the double note shrilled from the prince's hunting horn to fill the vale.

The moment the gap in the wall appeared Eofer broke into a run, shield held before him ready to batter his way through the retreating fiend. A wave of noise engulfed him, *Ut…Ut…Ut…,* and he was through, leaping war's grim tideline and angling off across the slope. The first of the beaten army were before him, jogging back to the foot of the rise as they had so many times that morning, but the first faces began to turn towards him in shock as he raised Gleaming and pounded across.

A tall man in a brightly patterned cloak was the first to fall, Gleaming sweeping in to take the top of his head clean off as he turned to face the threat. A man was bent double, struggling to help a bloodied friend back to safety, but Eofer's sword took his head before he was even aware of the new threat. Knots of Britons were beginning to rally, turning back to face the danger as Eofer led his hearth troop on, but they were too slow, caught in two minds between flight and fight as the English eorle put his shoulder into the back of his shield and smashed into them. Welshmen were sent flying, and Eofer drove forward as he sought to keep the momentum of the charge from faltering. Raising his gaze for a heartbeat he snatched a look towards the earthen walls which were his goal and was disappointed to see men beginning to appear there. He had hoped that the fort had been left empty but few plans, however well thought out, survived contact with the enemy and he lowered his head once again and powered on.

The men ahead of him were wavering and Eofer raised Gleaming once more, hacking at heads and shoulders again and again as he sought to drive them from the field. A spear darted in from the right but Horsa was there, and the spearman reeled away as the weorthman's own sword bit deeply into his shoulder. A face appeared above a shield but Eofer was faster, and he watched as the point of his blade jabbed forward to shatter teeth and bones as the man was driven back.

A space opened up before him and Eofer ran on as the rush lined banks of Hreopedun Brook came close. The lack of opposition gave him the chance to flick a look to the left, and his heart leapt as he saw that Icel's attack was sweeping all before it. The raven banner was cascading down the slope, the gesith a silver dagger aimed straight at the blood red Draco of Powys as war horns blared all along the English line and the rest of the army swept down in their wake. Beyond them Cueldgils and his Lindisware were holding Cynlas Goch's horse Welsh at bay as they fought to come to the aid of their leader, and a quick look across the brook told him that Seaxwulf, the Saxon warlord, had been true to his oath. The summer had passed since their first meeting beside the old tree at the hill fort, and although the Briton, Ioan, had carried messages back and forth between them, it was only really at this moment, seeing the war host standing fast on the hill as the battle hung in the balance that he could be sure that he had turned the man.

Their headlong drive had carried them to the lip of the brook, and Eofer splashed into the shallows in an arc of spray as all opposition melted away before them. This was the moment he had been dreading, ever since the plan had been outlined to him by Icel. The earlier storm had visibly added to the volume of water making its way down to the Trenta from the hills to the south, and he sent a prayer to the gods that the waters were not too deep to cross. Weighed down by his mail and impeded by his weapons anything but a quick and trouble free fording of the brook would cost him his life, either through drowning or at the point of a well aimed arrow or spear.

The water rose past his waist, and Eofer raised his shield and sword high as he forged ahead. Osbeorn and Octa moved forward to his left, shielding the thegn from the worst of the current, and he searched the far bank as his feet began to trend upwards out of the slime. The brookside was clear of spearmen but he fought down the disappointment as he saw that a line of shields, garishly quartered behind rims and bosses of cold harsh steel, now lined the wall of the fort with a war hedge of spearpoints glimmering like hoar frost on hawthorn above them.

Eofer emerged from the brook and climbed the bank, stamping the water from trews and boots as his hearth men scrambled up behind him. He walked forward a half dozen paces as his eyes scanned the defences ahead, searching for the place to strike. Despite the fact that the earthen wall had been faced with turf, the earlier rainstorm seemed to have found a weak point and a small dip had formed immediately opposite where he had emerged from the waters. The enemy had seen the weakness too, doubling up the numbers there the moment that they realised that they were about to come under attack, and Eofer moved forward to seize the opportunity it presented.

Horsa and Osbeorn were back at each shoulder, and Eofer knew that they had to move fast if they were to stand any chance of taking the wall in the first rush. If Cynlas Goch and his Powys' could regain the safety of the fort, they would very likely hold the English at bay for as long as it took for the reinforcements that Cynfelyn had mentioned back at Bruidon to arrive. Their horsemen still controlled the lands about Ryknield Street, and now the attack by the men of The Peaks on the Lindisware had opened up the real possibility that they had thrown in their lot with Powys after all. If that had occurred the Mercians were facing a powerful coalition, so they had to strike the head from the beast now, while the ruler of Powys was under their swords.

The glint of silver told him that more men were arriving to bolster the defenders by the moment: he would have to go now. A roar, *ready!* and he bounded forward before the reply had thundered around him. A last look up and he hissed with pleasure as he saw that the Welshmen were responding as he had hoped, rushing in to throw a knot of shields and spears at the weakest point. At the last moment, as the enemy warriors threw their shoulders into their shields and prepared to beat back the charge he changed tack, confident that the men of his troop would blindly follow where he led. The earthwork had meant to be topped by a timber palisade, but the men who were to build it had been put to the sword a while back when Eofer and his men had destroyed the fort-let, and the eorle took the dozen feet of earth bank in a few great strides as he angled away from the main concentration of defenders. He snatched a glimpse over the rim of his shield the moment before he hit and was disappointed to see that men were appearing there in numbers, but he threw his shoulder into the boards and braced in the moment before contact and came on.

The shields met with a crash of wood and steel and Eofer was thrown back onto his heels, but a heartbeat later Horsa and Osbeorn smashed into his back and he felt himself moving forward again as the men behind grunted with effort, dug in their heels and drove upwards. Another heave and he realised that he stood on level ground as he reached the lip of the bank, and Eofer raised his eyes above the rim of his shield as he sought an opponent. An old greybeard, his face grizzled and timeworn by summer sun and winter chill was there, open mouthed in horror at the sight of the barbarian warlord who had appeared before him, and Eofer stayed his sword thrust, barging the man aside out of pity as he swept on. A quick look ahead and Eofer saw that the wall on the inner side of the fort was steeper than outside. Planed timbers projected near the top, the supports for the walkway which would have encircled the finished defences, and he took one of them at a run and launched himself into space.

A pair of defenders rushed towards him as he landed, spears raised, their expressions betraying their glee. Eofer was off balance and vulnerable, but the eorle saw the looks change to fear as heavy boots began to crash to the ground all around him. Before the Britons could recover he was up and moving. Gleaming scythed across to take the nearest spearman in the hip, and he barged him aside knowing that his men would finish the job as he ran on.

The interior of Hreopedun fort was a mass of leather tents, but a central path led from the main gate in the south to the River Trenta on its northern perimeter, and Eofer skipped the guy ropes as he rushed towards it. Pounded by a rainstorm and thousands of booted feet the central pathway was a quagmire, and Eofer hopped from one grassy patch to the next as he rushed towards the gates. Men were coming through in dribs and drabs as the army of Powys was driven back across the brook by the ferocity of the English attack, but most were turning to the right, rushing to reinforce the walls as they looked to hold the rampant Engles at bay. Not a man among them expected the enemy to be already within those walls, and Eofer increased his pace as he saw that the way ahead was open.

His eyes played across the men before him as he ran, searching out the one who would be the first to feel Gleaming's bite. Within a moment he had him. A brute of a Welshman as wide as he was tall was standing in the main doorway, ushering men through into the interior and pointing out which parts of the wall needed reinforcing. Clad in mail, a fine blue cloak and a magnificently plumed war helm he was clearly a man of importance, and Eofer readied his sword as he finally broke free from the tent line.

Men began to notice him for the first time, to turn his way with surprise writ large on their faces, and he grunted with effort as he forced tired legs to put on a final spurt of speed. Eofer watched the warlord begin to turn as voices called a warning, but he had already closed the gap and he wound his body as Gleaming clove the air. A moment of resistance from the polished steel and the blade was through, and Eofer keened his war cry as he felt and heard the Welshman's skull shatter beneath the power of the blow. Gleaming came clear as men began to react to the fury of his attack, and he dodged aside as a spear thrust clipped his own mail shirt a glancing blow. Before him the British leader staggered and fell, and Eofer whipped his head this way and that as he searched for the next opponent. A spearman darted forward from the pack and his sword swept around in reply, but the blade whistled through air as his opponent saw his leader fall, his valour deserting him as he scrambled beyond reach.

A spear length had opened up between them and Eofer leapt the body of the British leader, planted his feet at the centre of the gateway and dropped into a crouch, ready to fend off the next attack. All about him the Britons were drawing back, covering each other with their shields as they abandoned the gateway to the enemy, and within a moment the reason for their fear became plain as the duguth began to appear at his side.

As his doughty men formed a ring of steel about their lord, Eofer felt able to raise his gaze for the first time, and his spirit soared at the sight which greeted his eyes. Icel's raven herebeacn was closing in on the far side of the little bridge as Cynlas Goch and his loyal cantrefs fought their way back to what they still believed to be the safety of the fortress. Only the width of Hreopedun Brook separated the white dragon of Anglia from the red of Powys, the short bridge sparkling like ice as sunlight played on steel and men struggled and died.

The mass of Britons had waded the waters of the brook itself and were lined up four or five deep on the near bank, stabbing and hacking at the Engles who were desperately trying to fight clear of the waters. It was the first time that morning that the men of Powys had held the advantage of higher ground and they were taking full advantage as they took their vengeance for their earlier suffering. Eofer watched as spears stabbed and swords rose and fell all along the line, but he knew what would give the Englishmen there fresh heart and he called out as the youth arrived to block the gateway completely.

'Grimwulf!'

'Yes lord?'

'Get yourself forward and make the signal.'

A pair of Britons, too caught up in the misery of their own suffering to notice that the way forward was blocked by a wall of shields and spears were approaching them, and Eofer laughed aloud at the sight of their faces as his herebeacn was carried past them and raised aloft. A cheer rent the vale as the banner was seen, and faces were raised their way as the white dragon of Anglia dipped in acknowledgement and surged forward again.

Others had seen the banner, and despite the strength of their position the first Britons began to detach themselves from the battle line, slinking away in ones and twos towards the nearby trees and safety as they saw the enemy to their rear. Their fighting qualities would be little missed he knew, men who ran from a fight were little more than *nithings,* but the sight would add steel to the attackers and bolster their courage as they hacked their way clear from the bloody ditch.

As if to confirm that the decisive moment in the battle had arrived a war horn blew on the far side of the field, and the Saxon war banner was raised aloft as Seaxwulf led his men forward. The fighting itself seemed to pause for an instant as the men of both armies watched them come, and Eofer sent a plea to the war god Tiw that his trust had not been misplaced. Seaxwulf broke into a run, the Saxons streaming down the hill beneath the wolf head banner of their leader, and Eofer felt the thrill of certain victory as he watched them slam into the knot of Powys' defending the bridge. A haunting wail rose into the morning air as the Britons came to recognise that the day was lost, and a shudder seemed to roll along the enemy line as the Saxons punched through the rearmost troops and kept on going, sweeping along the nearside bank as Welshmen scattered like startled deer.

Suddenly the British battle line broke and men began streaming away, discarding weapons and armour in their panicked efforts to escape the spears and blades of their foemen. The fyrdmen of Mercia struggled up the near bank as the opposition panicked and ran, levering themselves onto dry land and watching them go. If the exhaustion caused by their exertions had robbed them of their breath it was as nothing to their sense of wonder at having survived, and they let the fiend go as they dared to believe for the first time in days that they might yet live to see their families again.

An exhausted cheer rolled around the meadow and Eofer looked across just in time to see the red draco of Powys beaten down. Victory belonged to the army of Mercia, he was sure now the very first of many, and Eofer grabbed Grimwulf as the mounted warriors from Lindcylene thundered by, chopping down at heads and shoulders as they chased the beaten army from the field. 'Come on,' he said, the light of the triumph shining on his face. 'We have one last thing to do.'

As Horsa stepped in to take his place, Eofer led the youth back through Hreopedun fort. The Britons on the wall had witnessed the debacle at the brook and were streaming away. Aware that the English held the main gate they were making for the river, and Eofer ignored them as they made sure to give him a wide berth. 'Get that rag down,' he said as they came to the place. 'You know what to do.'

The youth hauled at the rope as Eofer slipped his own banner free. Within moments the flags had been swapped, and the pair stepped back and watched with pride as the burning hart snapped taut in a sudden gust. The Britons were splashing into the river, and Eofer looked across as he saw movement on the far bank. A large group of horsemen were there, their glum expressions betraying their allegiance. He knew that they were probably men of Powys, perhaps even the expected reinforcements a half day too late, but he hoped that they belonged to The Peaks.

24

'Just keep the best stuff. Swords, mail and helms. Spearheads and shield bosses can be lopped off and carried in baskets.' Eofer cocked a brow and a look of amusement came to his face. 'It is not like we are doing the carrying after all.' The men went away happy now that someone had made the decision for them. If it was the wrong one the finger of blame would not be pointing their way. A dragon's hoard of wealth lay strewn across Hreopedun meadow, and the beaten rump of the army of Powys were busy gathering them in, heaping them into piles as more of their kind loaded the weapons and armour onto carts and wagons. Others had the grim task of piling the bodies of their countrymen while yet more dug the great ditch which was to be the last resting place of their hacked and broken bodies.

'It doesn't seem right,' Horsa said. 'Leaving flesh and bones to moulder underground like that, you need a good blaze to release a man's soul from his body.'

Eofer shrugged as another party of Britons struggled past with their grim cargo. 'It's their way, custom rules in every land. They are fortunate that they are being taken care of at all. If we were not going to complete the burh here and occupy it ourselves they would have been left where they were as a warning to others not to carry spear and sword to Mercian lands. Anyway you forget,' he said, 'that my own ancestors still lay beneath the soil of Engeln even though the barrows have been ploughed out. One day the same fate awaits my own bones. Icel was going to build a pyre for the dead here but the Christian churchmen begged him not to. Apparently they need to be buried whole so that they can rise again at something called the day of judgement.'

Horsa looked horrified at his reply. 'So they lay in the ground until the end of the world and then get judged, all mouldy and grotty?' He shook his head in wonderment. 'And the priests expect people to give up the old gods for that?'

'Well, I am no expert but that is how I understand it. Why don't you go and ask old smiler, the Christian priest? Make sure that you have plenty of time on your hands though, once they get a sniff of a convert they never let go.'

'Christ-guda I can handle, lord. It's these wolves that turn my guts inside out.'

Eofer looked and saw that a party of slave traders were moving among the beaten men, eyeing up the day's haul as they tallied the lowest price they might get away with paying for their cargo of misery. In appearance each and every one could have been taken for an ætheling had it not been for their dark curly hair and swarthy looks. Fine woollen cloaks, edged with marten fur, were pinned at the shoulders by delicately worked brooches inlaid with garnet and glass. Embroidered tunics and strange baggy breeks of eastern silk: gold, silver and amber on arms and necks. A solitary knife hung at each man's belt, the hulking guards who accompanied them all the protection they would need. The Engles sneered with distaste as the slavers passed them by, babbling among themselves as they reckoned the profit they could wring from other men's bravery.

Eofer was about to make a reply when one of the traders broke off from his conversation and turned back sharply. A guard hastened to his side as the slaver walked across and began to run his hand along the shoulders and arms of a young Briton. The other prisoners paused at their work and looked on in disgust as the slave trader continued to run his hands over the young lad who had stiffened and flushed with shame. All those watching, Briton and Engle, realised the significance at the same moment, and a growl arose from them as the trader looked around in surprise. His guard caught the tension in the air and moved to draw his sword, but English spears were raised in a heartbeat and Eofer was relieved to see that the man was wise enough to stay his hand. As his colleagues returned with their own guards in tow, the southerner felt emboldened enough to turn a smile of amusement upon Eofer and his weorthman. 'This young man is beautiful,' he trilled. 'So fair and lithe.' A flash of mischief crossed his face as he continued. 'You northerners are so priggish. This one will warm my bed and then do the same for a man in the south, where the summers are hot and the winters are not so cold that they chill your bones. He will have a far better life than the rest, would you seek to deny him that?'

Eofer opened his mouth to reply but Horsa beat him to it. Pinning the southerner with a glare he spoke levelly in a voice dripping with menace. 'This one already belongs to us.'

The slaver gave a superior chuckle and made a dismissive gesture. 'Your prince has already sold them all to us, just the price is left to be agreed.'

With the man's casual reference to Icel the duguth knew

that he was out of his depth, and he looked to Eofer for help. He was not to be disappointed.

'He is a bowman. I need a bowman. He is mine.'

The slave trader looked from Eofer to Horsa and back again. Suddenly he laughed and shook his head. 'You men from the north. You have a certain magnificence but no sense of civilisation. Very well,' he said. 'Keep him, there are plenty of others.' He wafted across to rejoin his companions as the bodyguard edged away. Eofer made a point of running his eyes over the contrast between his own clothing and that of the guard as he went. The warmth of the day was beginning to dry Eofer's breeks and the lower half of his shirt where he had waded the brook, but his boots were thick with mud and a winingas had simply disappeared leaving one leg of his trews flapping in the breeze. A gash showed where a spear thrust had opened up several links in his mail byrnie, and his sword arm and hand were darkened by the blood of his foemen. He looked back through eyes haloed by weariness, sneering with contempt at the big swordsman as he contrasted the immaculate dress of the man with the war-weary state of his own. 'You are keeping your master waiting, pretty boy.'

The men of Eofer's band grinned at the man's discomfort as he lowered his eyes in shame and slunk away, and the Powys' joined in with the laughter as men there translated the words for their friends.

As the tension lessened and the prisoners got back to work Horsa began speaking to the boy. Eofer heard his own name mentioned, but his Welsh was either too poor to follow the conversation or the dialect new to him. Finally Horsa explained as Grimwulf came across to lead the unexpected addition to their numbers away. 'His name is Emyr, lord. He came east with his father and uncle but both were killed, his father earlier in the year and his uncle today.'

'So he is alone?'

'Just his ma and sister back west on the farm.'

Eofer nodded. 'What did you tell him about me?'

'I told him the truth, that you were a good lord, brave and just. He could tag along with us for now if he gave us his word that he would act like any other of your oath sworn, and place your wellbeing above his own. If he wanted to stay he would have to learn English and show his worth. If not he could return home and be the man of the family once things have settled down.'

'A HUNDRED SUNS…'

Eofer screwed up his face and looked at the man who had become his thegn, the first of his ealdormanship. They had been drinking for days, ever since they had returned from Hreopedun, and he was beginning to worry that the *giddig-ness* was permanent. Could a man drink so much that he remained sozzled for all time? He shrugged and chuckled at the wanderings of his own mind: it was worth a try! He took another sip and attempted to recall why he was looking at his man. Then he had it, and he forced his eyes to focus on the bearded face he had known since childhood as he asked the question. 'Who would want a hundred sons? The last dozen wouldn't need to be born, they could just walk out!' Hemming threw him a quizzical look before the beard was split by a smile. 'No, not sons,' he laughed. 'Suns, you know…like the one in the sky!'

Eofer giggled and took another sip. 'What in Thunor's hairy arse are you on about, Thrush?'

'Over there.' Thrush Hemming pointed at the pile of

booty taken from the army of Powys. 'The firelight reflecting on the steel: it looks like a hundred suns.'

Eofer looked and saw that it was true. Among them all, where the pile of metal curved away, a cooler glint was akin to a scattering of stars. The whole of the western wall of the hall, the hall which was soon to become his own, had been cleared of benches and tables the moment that they had returned to Leircestre. Cart after cart had returned from Hreopedun piled high with the spoils from the beaten army, helms, mail shirts, spears and swords of every type and quality. Strewn about the floor were the banners and flags of the invader, dirtied and torn by the passage of muddy boots. Above them all, pinned to the gable wall by dozens of spear points, was the red draco which had meant to fly over the conquered burh; now upended in dishonour, its long tail hanging limp with shame.

Leircestre itself was full fit to burst with men, as the fyrdmen celebrated their own survival and their newfound wealth for as long as they could before taking the long walk home, back to a life of responsibility and sobriety.

Cueldgils had already left for home, a small herd of fine war horses the reward for his part in the battle and the steadfastness shown by the Lindisware in their rediscovered loyalty to the line of Offa. Word had already come that the army of The Peaks had been thrown back with contemptuous ease by the Anglo-British nation, but he had taken a hundred of Icel's finest Sword-Engles with him in the unlikely event that they return before the weather broke and winter lay its white hand upon the land. The same messenger who had carried the word of victory to Leircestre had told them that it had been Gildas, the firebrand priest who had been under Eofer's sword twice that summer, who had been the driving force behind the treacherous attack. Harangued for days on end and threatened with something called excommunication by the holy man, Sawyl Penuchel had favoured the fate of his soul above his word of honour as a king; discussions were already taking place in English halls about how the army of Mercia could help him fulfil his wish for martyrdom sooner rather than later. Gildas already carried a scar from their first meeting, and Eofer made himself a promise that the next time their paths crossed he would finish the job once and for all.

A thræl woman bent to replace the jug on the table before them, her charms as full and inviting as low slung apples at hærfest month, and Eofer exchanged a look with Hemming as she flashed them a coy smile and made a great play at wiping up a spillage. 'Come on Thrush,' he said, pushing himself up with unsteady legs. 'Let's walk. My eyes are already jiggling enough.'

The long fire pits were blazing merrily, casting a glow over booty and drinkers alike. High above, up beneath the eaves, the wind holes had been shuttered for the first time as the first frosts that winter painted the town with its whiteness and the air inside was muggy with heat and smoke. Eofer took another pull from his ale horn as they walked. 'When are you heading back?'

Hemming pulled a face. 'In the morning, lord: Welshmen will not chase themselves away. Truth be told,' he added. 'As much as it gladdens my heart to see you and the rest of the boys I just don't feel part of the gang anymore.'

Eofer laid a hand on his old weorthman's shoulder and gave him a look of pride. 'That only goes to show me that making you my first thegn was the right decision. How long has it been since that night and day, desperately throwing up defences around the hill at Tamtun before the Britons at Cair Luit Coyt sallied and used our sorry hides for spear practice? Two...three months?'

Hemming nodded. 'Just over three months lord: just before the solstice.'

'Now you have a weorthman of your own and men like Hryp and Beonna, warriors who have your full confidence, enough that you will trust them to find their way to Bruidon and warn the ætheling and the army of Mercia that they may be walking into a trap.' Eofer clapped Hemming on the shoulder. 'Now you have proven to Icel that you can lead, as I always knew that you would, I could not think of a better man to entrust the safety of my lands and family to when I am over the sea.'

Hemming wrinkled his nose. 'I do envy you in that though lord, if the truth be told. It would be good to see the old lands again, just one last time. There is something…' He paused as he searched for the right words. 'Something…well…ruddy? about the old lands Eofer,' he said finally. 'I know that this land is tamer, softer, but I lie awake at night sometimes and worry that the sea is three days' ride away. I miss the salty tang on the breeze, the screech of gulls, rocky inlets and sandy dunes: racks of herring stretching away as the wind dries them on the strand. Shit,' he laughed as he realised how melancholy his words sounded. 'I even miss having the Jutes nearby to harry for fun!'

The hall echoed to the sound of their laughter and the warriors at the benches looked up from their ale at the sound, smiles breaking out all along the tables as they saw their leaders in such fine fettle. Eofer and Hemming moved aside as a scop strode the aisle, the sound of the lyre rising above the hubbub in the great space as the poet belted out a verse to their victory. 'I will be back by midsummer,' Eofer said. 'Once the Swedes relearn the fact that any enemy of the Geats is also the enemy of the Engles, King Heardred can reign in peace. The German Sea is not so wide that one cannot come to the aid of the other, and it will do my son Weohstan good to witness the force of English arms, before he forgets his race!' The new ealdorman glanced at his thegn, and Hemming recognised the look from old as the countenance of a wolf flashed across his features. 'This winter cannot pass soon enough, Thrush. Next year English arms crush the Swedes in Geatland and cross the Trenta to repay Sawyl Penuchel for his treachery. The gods love us old friend, who can stop us?'

'THIS IS AS FAR as I go,' Icel said as the horses entered the glade. 'Do you think that you can find your own way from here?'

'If I don't now, I soon will lord,' Eofer replied. 'This is the road which connects my lands after all. After this Swedish war is won I shall be back this way with more cartloads of booty.'

'You are keeping the lands around Snæpe then?'

Eofer nodded. 'I love it there Icel. Your father has already given me permission to throw up a barrow on the ridge when the time comes. When my spirit walks on stormy nights I can gaze out across the estuary and watch the waves crashing ashore on the spit there.'

Icel laughed. 'If you ever decide to hang up your sword Eofer, you can always become a scop!'

'I am not settling down just yet,' Eofer added defensively. 'Sæward will be acting as my reeve there and keeping the ships ready for when I need them. I may bring my scegth up to Leircestre, but I am having the same shipwright build me a snaca at his yard up at Yarnemutha which I will keep in a fine new boat shed on the banks of the Aldu, a big fifty oar snake ship fit for a sea-ealdorman.'

The pair dismounted and Eofer stretched tired limbs. The ætheling was still spritely, annoyingly so after a week on the ale, and Eofer reflected on his decision to scale back on his raiding...just a bit. Astrid had been right after all, even if for the wrong reasons, the time *had* come to take up the king's offer of ealdormanship. His own days of constant raiding and fighting were drawing to a close, but he knew that he gave down sound judgements from his gift-stool and he had two sons already with hopefully more to follow. Little Ælfgar had yet to wrap his hand around the handle of a sword, but Weohstan would soon return from foster and Eofer's heart sang at the thought of them fighting shoulder to shoulder against English enemies.

An old elm had succumbed to winter blow, and they let themselves down onto a sturdy bough as the men collected wood to cook the midday meal. Icel flashed his newest ealdorman a grin as he recalled the events of that summer. 'What a year it has been, Eofer. You should be proud of the part that you played in our great victory, not just with your sword arm, but with your scheming. If you had obeyed my orders and squatted in Leircestre like an obedient thegn when I went off to Lindcylene it might have cost us everything. Capturing the young Saxon and having the wits to use the boy to turn his father was a masterstroke, it's what separates great leaders from those who are merely great warriors. Discovering that Seaxwulf's oath of service ran out when the Barley-moon appeared was the key to everything. Mind you,' he laughed, 'I still had my heart in my mouth when they came roaring down from that hillock at the end of the battle. If they had played one against the other and renewed their deal with Cynlas Goch we could have been in deep trouble. It would have been unlikely that we could have got the army back up into the higher land, and even if we had I doubt that we would have had the numbers left to hold our old battle line. So thank the gods for your intuition and the loyalty of your Welsh friend.'

'What are you going to do with the Saxon now?' Eofer asked.

Icel shrugged. 'There are always plenty of uses for a war band of that quality. I may add them to the men crossing the Trenta this winter to teach Sawyl Penuchel a lesson, but their knowledge of the western lands will be invaluable in the future. Most of them were born there, although they still consider themselves as Saxon as any man born across the sea in Saxland itself.'

The pair smiled together as a robin landed on a nearby branch, cocked its head and regarded Eofer with interest. The red chested bird always seemed to appear when changes to his life thread occurred, and Eofer had wondered that the little bird was actually his fetch. The physical embodiment of a man's spirit often took the form of an animal or bird and were always close by, but rarely glimpsed unless they presaged great change. Icel carried on as the bird fluttered off and became lost from sight.

'What about Ioan and his band of rascals. Have you rewarded them yet?'

Eofer nodded as the first smells of cooking wafted across on the breeze. 'I gave them a hall in the town and bought Ioan a half share in The Tewdwr.'

'What, that old fleapit you described that night in Bruidon, the one by the eastern gate?'

'I had to bend the owner's arm a bit,' Eofer smiled, 'but it's always good business to keep in with the new ealdorman. Old Tewdwr said that Ioan and his boys probably owed him and the girls that much anyway, it was almost like asking him to give half of his place away for free!'

Squeals drew their eyes back across to the roadway, and the pair chuckled at the sight which met them. Several carts had drawn up, the people keen to trade news and food with warriors of their nation. Already several of the children were being tossed aloft and caught as the fighting men softened in their company, their elder sisters mooning and whispering among themselves as they watched. Safe now and with the harvest gathered in, new settlers were pouring into the lands despite the lateness in the year. The winter months would see new halls thrown up in Mercian lands, woodland cleared and the fertile ground made ready to receive their first ever seeding in the spring. Ceorls, free men: by old law each would carry a spear and shield as a mark of that freedom and at the rate which they were arriving, within the year the numbers available to man the Mercian fyrd could double. They chuckled again as a barrel was produced from some-where, the settlers laughing with delight as Osbeorn led them all in apple bobbing.

'How are your preparations going?'

'For the trip to Geatland? Well, lord,' Eofer answered. 'The king has allowed me to send the war sword throughout Anglia, and Sæward has sent word that the Wulfings wish to add men to the ship army. They are not without grievances of their own where the Swedes and Danes are concerned.'

Icel nodded. 'It is as you say, I only hope that you are not too late. Still,' he said, 'a war in the backwoods of Geatland.' He blew out and the mischievous look with Eofer knew of old washed across the prince's face. 'That sounds like fun. I wish that I could have come too but I could not strip men from the frontier, not after all the sacrifices which the people have made to win this land. I cannot even spare Hemming from Tamtun, it is vital that we consolidate the new march.' Icel smiled, and Eofer saw a flash of excitement cross his lord's features. 'In my lifetime I hope to carry the borders of Mercia across the valley of the Hafron, all the way to the western mountains and northwards up into the hills of The Peaks. Deal with Heardred's foemen and then bring your family out west Eofer, take up your ealdormanship. We have busy years ahead of us, we two. Along with my father's lands in Anglia, the Lindisware and the Wulfing lands, the English will soon be the most powerful people in Britain.'

25

As the horses wend their way through the final valley from home, Eofer felt his heart lighten at the closeness of it. A full summer had passed since he had last laid his eyes upon the centre of his world, the place where mead and ale flowed like water and he sat in judgement on his gift-stool. Astrid was there, and a smile came to his face as he imagined the delight with which she would receive his news. A full ealdorman, the lord of a Roman town encircled by walls of stone, ruled from a hall even larger than the hall of her brother King Heardred, back in Geatland. He felt at his side, snorting as he imagined the pride with which she would receive the gift. Icel had shown his generosity once again before they parted at the clearing by presenting Eofer with a golden set of girdle-hangers, the key-like pendants which hung from the belt of all married women and symbolised her rule over the hall of her lord and *bonda*.

Horsa had noticed Eofer's movement and had guessed his thoughts, and his mouth drew a smile as the horses began to climb the incline. 'Do you think that it will be enough, lord?'

Eofer looked at him and arched a brow in question.

Horsa nodded down at the purse which hung at Eofer's waist. 'The keys to the hall and the *ealdormanscip* which goes with it. A lord of Mercia,' he said with a sigh. 'And to think how close we came to ending our days winding our guts around wooden stakes.'

It was true. If it had not been for Thrush Hemming and the boys they would both have ended their days in a grove on the outskirts of Hleidre. That had been during the time of the war of fire and steel, but another great battle had just ended, the first battle in a war which he knew he would not live to see brought to its conclusion. The Britons were simply too strong to be swept away, the island too vast, but they had beaten back the best that Powys could throw against them and would do so again. Already the scops were moving from hall to hall in English lands, reciting the tale of the war-summer which men had come to call the *Scippan*, the Scathing. Life was good: tonight he would celebrate his homecoming with beef and ale before sharing the joys of the marital bed with a wife whose every ambition must now be fulfilled.

A lightness up ahead drew his mind back to the road before him, and Eofer took the final rise at a canter as they broke free of the trees. Half a mile ahead the sallow thatch which he knew so well hove into view, and he let out a yell of joy at the sight. The road levelled out, straightening as it followed a ridge line as straight as a spear-shaft the final few miles to Alduburh, and he snorted again as he thought of the grand sounding place. Glad to be home after the tempestuous events of the summer, Eofer reined in and cast a fond gaze across his lands as an autumn blow drove a scattering of tawny leaves across the heath.

In reality Alduburh was a collection of ramshackle huts, the home to a motley collection of fishermen and their families. A long shingle beach curved away there in a great arc to the south, running parallel to the coast for a mile before ending in a hook of land. The Romans had constructed a fort of sorts to guard against the raids made by his ancestors, but they had been overwhelmed by Engle spears and all that remained in his own time was a tumbledown watchtower, a tall warning beacon and the name which the invaders had bestowed upon it. This was the place where the Aldu emptied itself into the sea, and although the kink in its course added an extra half an hour of rowing to the journey home he had always thought it a boon.

The mere which backed the spit contained his salt pans. The long lead-lined basins were not his own introduction of course, sea water had been boiled here to extract the salt it contained further back in time than any man could recall, but they paid their dues to him like any other tenant. It was a good source of income.

Further inland the river was thick with fish traps, the posts and wattle screens known as sails and rods arrowing down to the long wattle sock which snared the fish themselves. Bass, flounder, eels and mullet were caught here by the barrel load, the hearty flesh gracing not only the long table in his own hall, but those for miles around.

With the tolls due to him from the crossing place into the lands of the Wulfings to the south and the sceatt paid to him by his tenants, Snæpe was, he knew, as fine a place for a hall as he had seen on either side of the German Sea.

Eofer made to haul at his reins, guiding his mount back to the roadway, when Horsa spoke at his side. 'It looks like we have visitors, lord. They have not spared the sail cloth to get here either,' he added ominously, 'looking at the state of their hull.'

Eofer dropped his gaze, running his eyes across the river-bank where his own ship, the little scegth *Skua*, was already snug in her boat shed for the winter. Alongside the coils of rope and pitch blackened detritus which littered shipyards throughout Middle-earth a pair of larger ships, thirty-five, forty oared dragons, were resting their wide keels on the grass. Looking closer the thegn could see that the strakes of the larger vessel were heavily salt-streaked, always the sign of a hull driven hard. Eofer called across his shoulder and Einar broke off from his conversation with Octa, hurrying forward as the others saw the ships for the first time and instinctively fingered their weapons. 'Lord?'

'I assume that one of those ships carried you across from Geatland. Do you recognise the other?'

The Aldu was sparkling like ice in the weak autumnal sunshine, and Einar shaded his eyes against the glare as he studied the hulls. Finally he shook his head. 'The ship on the right, the smaller hull, is the *Wave Dancer*, the ship which as you guessed brought me here this summer past. The other ship I have never seen before.' He shrugged. 'It could be one of ours, but at least we know that they came with peaceful intent.'

Eofer crinkled his brow and the Geat explained. 'Raiders don't tend to unship their mast and neatly stack their oars before plundering a hall, they want to be in and out like a fiðeler's elbow.'

Despite the uncertainties of the moment the Englishmen laughed at their new-found friend's description. After yule an English war host would gather, taking ship in the rivers and inlets as they carried spear, sword and shield to Heardred's beleaguered kingdom, and the amiable young Geat would finally fulfil the duty set by his lord. Until then it would seem that Eofer had guests for the winter, and plenty of them. Reassured by Einar's words, Eofer called across his shoulder. 'Smarten yourselves up boys! Grimwulf?'

'Yes, lord?'

'Hold that burning hart high.' He shot a mischievous glance at the young Geat still at his side. 'We have country cousins paying us a visit. Let us show them what a fame-bright English hearth troop looks like.'

He was about to urge his mount forward when a slight movement caught his eye, the dark shape silhouetted against the skyline as it stared his way. Horsa had been about to follow his lord's lead, and he curbed his horse with difficulty as the pause took him by surprise. 'What is it?'

Eofer indicated the distant hillock with a jerk of his head. 'It's lucky that Thrush is safely tucked away in Tamtun,' he replied with a chuckle. 'The old fool would be quaking in his boots if he saw that.'

'Lord?'

'Old Snarly yowl come to welcome us home,' he grinned. 'The year is almost up, it looks like he missed his chance to get us after all.'

Horsa looked across, squinting as he ran his gaze over the heathland. 'Whereabouts?'

Eofer looked again but the horizon was empty, and he shook his head at his own foolishness. 'I am seeing things now,' he snorted. 'Ignore me, we have been on the road too long. Come on,' he said as he put back his heels, 'let's kick our boots off and wash the dust from our throats!'

The horse moved forward into a steady trot as the rest of the troop fell in behind. Ahead, figures were appearing at the entrance to the courtyard beneath the high gable, and he watched as a man saw the banner and took off to report that the lord of Snæpe was home from war.

Almost before the horses had gathered speed they were following the spur which led to the hall, and Eofer hauled at his reins, angling them to one side of the compound as he led the war troop in a wide circuit. Whooping and bellowing their hearth-joy they thundered across the heath as men tumbled from hall and outbuildings to point and stare.

The loop completed Eofer guided them back to the path, curbing his mount with a flourish as he came into the yard. The others were arriving behind him in a brawl of clattering hooves and laughter, and Eofer slid to the ground at the very moment that Astrid came through the hall door. The horse snickered playfully in his ear, the animal looking forward to a night under cover and a bellyful of food as much as any, and Eofer pushed its muzzle away with a snigger before turning back to greet his wife.

Caught up in the thrill of the ride and his own homecoming, Eofer sensed for the first time that the smiles and merriment in the yard were not being echoed in the faces before him. Men were shifting uncomfortably, many looking at their feet, some even glaring at him with thinly disguised hostility, and the first feeling of unease crept upon him as the numbers of Geats in the yard increased by the moment. Two ships' crews, one a big dragon at that, could deliver a small army of warriors, and a quick tally told him that there were likely to be at least seventy fully armed foreign men hereabouts.

He switched his gaze away from the sour faced Geats back to the figure striding towards him as he began to get an inkling of what tidings these men had strained their sail to deliver. Astrid was marching across the space, her mood obvious in her purposeful movement and thunderous expression, her old thyften Editha bustling along in her wake. It became plain that the handmaid was pleading with her mistress as they came on, and the mask of joy which had painted Eofer's face began to drain away like ale from a badly tapped barrel as she got closer, his world narrowing as he wondered what words were about tumble from her mouth.

Astrid reached him, and Eofer was shocked to see that her eyes were as hard and cold as any stone. He pulled himself upright, conscious that whatever was about to happen would do so in full view, not only of the men sworn to him, but warriors from a foreign nation. His mouth opened to speak as he sought to impose himself on the situation, but it spiralled out of control before he could utter a word. Astrid's arm drew back and he watched unable to move for the shock of it, transfixed as if in a nightmare, as his wife's hand swept through the air to strike his cheek with a noise which resounded around the courtyard like thunder. Eofer took a pace back in shock and surprise as the horrified gasps of scores of men seemed to suck the very air from the place. Editha staggered back from her mistress' side, clasping a hand across her mouth as her eyes betrayed her fear for the woman she had served since she was a child. Astrid locked eyes with him, and Eofer's very soul seemed to recoil from the anger displayed there as she hissed the reason for her action. 'You are too late, hero. My brother is already dead.'

His wits were recovering from the shock of it all as his hand went to the handle of Gleaming, but the self-control which had served him well in battles across the northlands reasserted itself before the sword was drawn more than a hand's width from its scabbard. She looked down, and a sneer crossed her face as she saw that he had stayed his retaliation. Lifting her chin once again Astrid opened her mouth to spit another insult, but her vitriolic look turned to one of shock as steel flashed and a spear blade shot past the eorle to drive the air from her lungs in an explosive gasp. Eofer instinctively took a step aside, swinging around to face the killer as the ash shaft was drawn back to stab again. As Editha's screams echoed around the courtyard and Astrid's slender body began to crumple under the force of the strike, Eofer prepared to attack. Somehow Gleaming was already drawn, ready to strike, but he hesitated as he saw that it was his own youth Beornwulf who stood before him, the point of his spear slick with gore.

Beornwulf let the spearhead drop, holding his arms out wide to open himself up for the killing strike. Eofer looked at his youth, aghast at the speed with which his world had been turned on its head. The Geats were beginning to recover, and cries of outrage at the act resounded from the walls of the hall as the men of Eofer's own troop sensed the danger and scrambled to retrieve shields and weapons from their mounts. Eofer and Beornwulf locked eyes and the eorle saw the fear there, but the youth puffed up his chest with pride at the act and spoke in a voice wavering with emotion. 'I have remained true to my oath. None shall lay a hand on the person of my ring-giver, the man whose life I love more than my own. Don't think,' he said as tears rimmed his eyes. 'Strike me down quickly lord and put an end to the bloodshed.'

Eofer's eyes swam from Beornwulf to the angry Geats and down to the bloodied figure at his feet. Editha was on her knees, cradling her mistress' head, the very same one which had suckled at her breast all those years before, and Eofer willed his arms to act despite the reluctance of his conscious mind to order them. His thoughts were beginning to unscramble themselves after the shock of the last few moments, and he began to move his sword arm as he saw the sense in the youth's words. The Geats were taking their first steps forward as the blood of their princess pooled in the gaps between the cobbles, and Eofer jerked his head back instinctively as he heard the familiar swoosh of a sword blade cutting the air. Before he could think he was back on his heels, sloping a shoulder as he dropped into a fighting stance. Gleaming came around, slicing across to parry the attacker's blade, but a dark shape bowled through the air instead as steel flashed again.

The angry growls now came from English throats, and Eofer raised his eyes as Beornwulf's headless body sank to the earth to see that Einar had been the swordsman. The young Geat scout raised his voice so that all in the courtyard could hear as his countrymen hesitated, unsure how to react to the killings.

'I am Einar son of Harald, son of Thorbjorn, a Geat from the forests west of Edet. I give notice that I lawfully slew this man before witnesses, that I took the weregild owed to my folk for the slaying of Astrid Hygelacsdottir.'

Eofer looked beyond the young Geat to the men of his troop as the situation balanced on a knife edge. Several of the youth were recovering from the shock of their friend's death, raising spears, twisting their features into a snarl of hatred as they looked to avenge the death of their hearth mate and he barked an order at them to stay their hands, sheath their weapons now that the death had been avenged, the blood-price paid. Their tails were up, but he recognised the moment when the discipline which he and his duguth had drummed into them overcame the lust for revenge and the madness began to flicker and die in their eyes.

Only one there could not speak a word of any language of Germania, could not understand his plea nor the intricacies of the warrior code of honour, and Eofer looked on in helpless horror as Emyr snatched up a spear and prepared to fulfil the oath he had made on the field of death outside Hreopedun burh.

Eofer's mouth opened to call a warning, but before a sound could escape steel stabbed out again as the spear darted forward to bury itself in the young scout's back.

Eofer looked at the faces of his duguth as Einar sank to

his knees and saw his own growing realisation reflected there. The gods were having their last entertainment from this war band and moving on. Their wyrd was upon them.

A roar of Geatish outrage enveloped the courtyard again and Eofer whirled around, Gleaming raised and ready to parry. But his vision was already filled with mail and helms, angry snarls within bearded faces, and he gasped in shock and disbelief as the first spear blade slammed into his gut. As he doubled over another caught his shoulder a glancing blow, spinning him around as he fought to retain his balance despite the agony. The eorle staggered and a foot slid forward to recover, but the next seaman opened his thigh with a back-handed sweep as he passed and Eofer felt the strength leave the limb as it buckled beneath him. Salt stained boots filled his vision as he attempted to rise again and the clamour of fighting filled the yard, but the pain caused him to swoon as an invisible hand gripped his innards and held tight. Eofer fell back, his mind swirling with the horror of it as he turned his head towards the sound of steel striking steel.

Crawa was standing over the body of his brother, Hræfen the first to fall, and he felt pride despite it all as Horsa, true to the oath he had sworn in a distant mithraeum, gathered Osbe-orn, Octa, Finn and Sæward, Eofer's doughty men, to him. The leading Geats wavered as a thunderous English roar resounded around the little courtyard, taking a backwards step as the boar-snout came together in a crash of shields. Hurling themselves forward the fame-bright war troop cut a bloody swathe as they drove across to make their last stand around the fallen body of their lord.

Astrid lay at his side, and a whimper escaped her lips as the furore which had enveloped them all dragged her back from her own private hell. Her breathing was shallow, the blood at her mouth a scarlet spume as she fought for breath, and Eofer knew that Beornwulf's spear thrust had pierced a lung. He had seen it many times, they all had: his wife was slowly drowning in her own blood.

Astrid's eyes had clouded once again as her mind retreated into a world of pain, alone with her fears as all the children of Ash and Elm must be when the norns whet their shears and fix them with their steely gaze.

He reached across, brushing back her hair as he turned his face to hers. The last flicker of life which followed his touch caused the woman to bark up blood, and Eofer closed his eyes in grief as he felt the hotness spatter his face. When he opened them again he was surprised to find that her eyes had cleared.

'So,' she whispered, her voice a tortured rasp. 'Now you have killed me.'

Eofer's own breathing grew shallow, and he blinked in surprise at the vague realisation that the pain which had him pinned was ebbing away. For a moment Astrid's face filled his vision, but something else swam into view as the shadows began to gather and his eyesight lost its sharpness. Doors grinding open beneath a roof of golden shields: half-remembered faces look up from their cups and break into smiles.

'No Astrid,' he said. 'You killed us all.'

26

'I am bouncing all over the place on the back of this bloody ass, my helm has fallen over my eyes and I can't even see where we are going. I try to say something and all that I can get out is *I — I — I — I*. Every time I try to say more the bloody thing's back comes up to smack me into the air, and Eofer says, "we haven't got time for singing you arse, we are in the shit!"'

The men in the shelter laughed as Hemming bent his back to scoop a refill from the barrel. The mead was good, there was plenty of it, and he took a deep draught from the horn as he pushed back against the side strakes of the little *Skua* and glanced away to the east. A thin band of grey showed on the horizon, dull, shot through with darker strands like the edge of a newly hammered blade and he sighed. 'It looks as if the dawn is almost upon us: our time here is nearly spent.' As if in confirmation the baleful wail of a war horn drifted across to them from the encampment, and the men in the grave exchanged a look and hauled themselves to their feet.

Icel knelt and laid a hand upon the bearskin which covered the body of his man, flashing a smile as he worked a ring from his finger. 'Here old friend,' he said, 'a treasure fit for an eorle. Show this to your ancestors; be sure to tell them that it is a gift from an ætheling to a hero.' Icel lingered a moment as he ran his eyes across the face of his greatest warlord, the familiar features now sallow and drawn in death.

Two full months had passed since word had reached the king in Theodford of the fate of Eofer and his hearth troop. Drawn by the smear of smoke, the first ceorls to discover the scene of carnage had carried the bodies of their thegn and his warriors to the moot hall. As men mounted a watch over the noble remains, the hundred had echoed to the wail of war horns as fyrdmen snatched up spear and shield and rushed to the muster. The sight of the flames on the skyline had drawn the local thegn and his war band from across the river, but the ships had gone from their berth before the Wulfings could gather to give battle, and although they gave chase as best they could the raiders were already hull down on the horizon by the time they drew rein on the seashore. It was the first time that Engle and Wulfing had united to face a common threat, and although the killers had escaped it bode well for the future.

Nobody seemed to know who had done the killings, although the Danes were suspected and they would have good reason. The body of little Ælfgar had been discovered alongside that of his thyften, a single sword stroke to the back of the lad's head had sent him to Hel's cold hall. His mother Astrid had simply disappeared, some thought back to Geatland but news had come of that nation's fall and it seemed unlikely.

Coelwulf stepped forward as the ætheling rose to go. Eofer's neighbour from back in Engeln laid a small vessel of blue glass into the crook of his old friend's arm, and then it was Hemming's turn to say his parting words. As Eofer's first weorthman walked the deck planks of the little scegth he thought back on past voyages they had taken together. The sea spray would never again burst over its bows nor the wind sing in its rigging: manhandled the half mile from the little River Aldu, up onto the ridge near the charred remains of his hall, the *Skua* would soon be conveying Eofer's soul to a far loftier place. Hemming fished inside the purse which hung from his belt and leaned in. 'Do you remember this, lord?' he said. 'It's the comb which we fought over as lads.' He reached forward and gently teased the hairs of Eofer's beard before placing the comb with the other things. 'Take it with you,' he whispered as he choked down the tears. 'An eorle should look his best when he pitches up at Woden's hall. And save me a place,' he added sadly. 'We both met Snarly yowl out there on the Sandlings, and I have no family to die before me.'

Wulf was the last, as was right. Eofer's brother stepped forward and bent low. He spoke at length, and although the words were too softly formed to carry, the others knew what they would be. Kinsmen needed avenging, another, Eofer's son Weohstan was missing. The king had provided a ship and crew, given his gesith leave and a war band to accompany him. Their bow would be breasting the waves before the first snows whitened the land. Wulf finished saying his piece, pulling the bearskin up to cover his brother's face before joining them at the stern.

Hemming took a last look at the things which would accompany his lord into the next world as they lingered, loathe to leave the presence of the man they had loved in life.

Eofer himself lay amidships. At the head of the burial chamber the eorle's shield rested against the far wall, the nicks and slashes in the leather facing telling the tale of their last fight together. A handful of spears lay alongside Gleaming: the stout gar which had stabbed out across shield rims into the faces of hated foemen the length and breadth of the north and a few daroth, the slender darts which would be thrown to pierce the heads and chests of battle dodgers in the rear. At his side his grim helm, a folded mail shirt, drinking horns, a lyre: gaming pieces. At his feet two wolfhounds and his favourite gyrfalcon, a gift from Astrid's father Hygelac, King of Geats; closer still to the mourners the war horse of Cynlas Goch himself. The stallion had been sacrificed at dusk the night before, the limbs and head removed and carefully arranged so that they could cram the great body inside the dart like hull of the scegth.

A group were hovering at a respectful distance, their eyes cast downward as they leaned on their tools, dun coloured clothing and close-cropped hair marking their lowly status. Icel raised his chin, looking out beyond the thræls at the grey line which was widening by the moment. Overhead the stars were paling, with just the brilliance of the morning star left to outshine the returning sun. 'Come,' he said. 'It's time.'

There was still a final act for them to perform before the orb edged the earth's rim, and they crossed to their horses as the slaves crept across to heap soil over the tomb. The stallions waited at the road, each mount decked out in its war splendour, and the warriors donned their helms and took up their spears as they hauled themselves into the saddle.

As flaming brands were handed to each rider, a woman's voice floated across the heath, a mournful keening as she bemoaned the loss of an eorle, a hero of his people. Wailing, she tore at her clothes and hair, rubbed grey ash into the wounds in grief. Beyond her, prow on to the bank, snake ships rode at anchor, *Hwælspere: Hildstapa: Grægwulf,* as their scipthegns mourned the loss of a friend.

Hemming saw that the leaders were almost upon them

and his heart sang with pride that such men could gather to honour his lord. Eomær King of the Engles: Wehha lord of Wulfings: Cueldgils son of Creoda: Cynric ap Cerdic of the folk who now called themselves the Westseaxna: Hrothmund Hrothgarson, Prince of Danes.

Icel raised the brand and put back his heels as a flicker of light showed to the east. Chanting dirges of loss he led the riders around the Howe under a wolf grey sky:

> rídend swefað,
> hæleð in hoðman…

> *the rider sleeps,*
> *the hero in his grave…*

A HEARTBEAT later they were all steering their horses around the barrow, the dawn resounding to the thunder of hoofbeats as the warriors shook their spears at the heavens beneath a dragon tail of smoke. The laments drifted across the heath, came to the ears of the leaders there, and King Eomær's chest swelled with pride as the deeds of his greatest thegn were made known to all.

Soon the thing was done, torches tossed aside as Shining Mane dragged the sun back into the sky. Kings and princes were crossing the moor, showing the riders honour as they served those closest to the eorle southern wine, and Hemming smiled a greeting as Cynric approached. Icel was at Hemming's side, an ætheling dressed for war, and the Engles dipped their head in thanks as gold chased goblets were passed around.

The sun lay upon the horizon now, the pale ball gilding the crests of distant waves as the day began. Gulls were in the sky, their raw piercing cries matching the mood, and Hemming let out a mournful sigh as the vessels came together. 'Who would have thought that it would end like this?'

The æthelings, Engle and Seaxna shared a look, and Hemming's mouth curled into a smile as Icel replied for them both. 'No, old friend, this is not the end. This is just the beginning.'

AFTERWORD

'Between the end of Roman government in Britain and the emergence of the earliest English kingdoms there stretches a long period of which the history cannot be written. The men who played their parts in this obscurity are forgotten, or are little more than names with which the imagination of later centuries has dealt with at will.'

Those are not my words but the opening lines of the very first chapter of Anglo-Saxon England, the second book in The Oxford History of England series, Sir Frank Stenton's classic overview of the age, and I had to smile as I read them again whilst researching for this book. The first half of the sixth century in Britain is the very darkest period of the so-called 'Dark Ages'. Even the scribes who scratched the entries onto the vellum of the Anglo-Saxon chronicle are silent about events which occurred during what was even to them ancient history. Largely the product of the later West Saxon kingdom, little of historical note is mentioned outside that area in the chronicle for the entire sixth century save for the odd report that the kingship of Northumbria had changed hands.

Any 'history' for the lands which would constitute the Anglo-Saxon kingdom of Mercia that we can piece together at this distance in time centres mostly around a people known as the Iclingas, the people of Icel. Certainly the later kings lists which began to be recorded in the seventh century refer to this shadowy character as the founder of the dynasty and mention that he was the son of Eomær, the last king to rule continental Engeln. Unfortunately the routes which gave relatively easy access to the area at this time, the rivers Trent, Nene and Welland among others, also provided the same for the people who later moved into their old lands in Engeln, the Danes. It is probably safe to assume that every written record for the early Mercian kingdom was destroyed along with the monasteries which housed them in the later viking wars of the ninth and tenth centuries.

That the heartland of the later kingdom was in the area around the headwaters of the Trent Valley is widely accepted. There is a heavy concentration of early style place names in the area around Tamworth, Repton and Lichfield based on personal names, but also those relating to heathendom, always a reliable sign of pre seventh century settlement in England. Wednesbury (Woden's burh): Tysoe (Tiw's hoh, or hill spur) was named after an ancient red horse which was carved into the hillside there and is thought to have been dedicated to the war god: Weeford (holy ford), very close to Cair Luit Coyt itself are only a few examples. In the spirit of a picture being worth a thousand words, I have tried to illustrate the extent of the forests and marshlands which drove the early settlers so far inland and the rivers along which they travelled on the map at the front of this book.

Modern studies are also reaching the conclusion that the early English kingdoms were far more Anglo-British than traditionally thought. In the first book in the series, Fire &

Steel, I had Eofer aiding Cerdic and Cynric to regain the lands in what was to become Wessex in a British civil war. Cerdic, Cynric and indeed the majority of their sixth century descendants had thoroughly British names so it made sense to do so. Mercia often allied itself with British kingdoms, especially Gwynedd, in the later centuries against their common Anglian enemy in Northumbria and it would be far from surprising if this kingdom was also in fact a mix of British and English inhabitants ruled by the old Anglian elite.

Lindsey is similar in many ways. The people who are here called the Lindisware, later the Kingdom of Lindsey, perhaps best illustrate the racial fusion hinted at in Wessex and Mercia. Its location, on a ridge of land surrounded by marsh, rivers and sea, lent it a special isolation which was ideal for takeover by invading people. The Angles of the fifth century seem to have arrived first as laeti, armed war bands, in the employ of the post Roman territory of Cair Lind Colum. That they later took over by whatever means is entirely plausible, it would certainly mirror developments on continental Europe at the same time. Perhaps the crisis did come as a result of the attacks by an Arthur?

The problem of Arthur's existence and his battle list has kept the printing presses in business for decades. I chose to overcome the arguments for and against various historical figures by making the name Arthur, Celtic Artos-Viros, Bear-Man, a title rather than the name of an individual. Straightaway the problems of time and distance were overcome. Suddenly it made no difference whether Arthur lived in the south-west, English midlands or even present day Scotland. Time and location restraints disappeared, and I could concentrate on the storyline. The first five of the twelve battles of Arthur which were listed in the eighth century History of the

Britons by the Welsh historian Nennius are usually linked to the area of present day Lincolnshire, and it is entirely possible that any overlord uniting the British kingdoms against barbarian incursions would choose to repeatedly attack the hybrid state developing there.

Another Welsh source, Gildas, is one of the most famous sources for our period. His work, On the Ruin and Conquest of Britain, is thought to have been written in the 540's so it should have been an important contemporary account at a time when the heathen Angles and Saxons were still awaiting conversion to Christianity and the literacy which accompanied it. Unfortunately Gildas does have an unfortunate tendency to rant rather than inform. The aim of his work seems to have been to castigate the British leaders of his time who are, through their own lasciviousness and debauchery, bringing down the wrath of God on their people in the form of pagan barbarian invasions. That the man had a real hatred of the Germanic incomers leaps from just about every page, and as a later day Englishman I enjoyed introducing him to my tale and having Eofer give him good reason.

Cynlas Goch, the villain in our tale, may very well be the Cuneglasus denounced by Gildas as one of the Five Warlords of his day. In fact he goes so far as to accuse him of not only being 'one who raises war against men, indeed against his own countrymen, as well as against God,' but in another passage denounces him as 'You bear, you rider and ruler of many, and guider of the chariot which is the receptacle of the bear.' Arthur of course was the Bear Man, and this war 'against his own countrymen' ties in nicely to our tale. Sawyl Penuchel, Sawyl the Arrogant, King of The Peaks was also a contemporary, and if little more is known about him perhaps his title might be another good indication of the type of men who were able to gain power as the province of Britannia began to fragment in the Roman twilight.

A further problem which the later viking invasions and raids illustrate is the need for speed and mobility. On land this essentially meant the availability of horses for the attacking force up until late in the twentieth century. Even Hitler's invasion of Soviet Russia in the second world war relied upon horsepower more than the offensive power of the panzer divisions. Eighty percent of the supply echelon, that's over one million horses on any given day, were used by the German Army in that great conflict, so the pressing need for horses by Icel and his Engels would have been a crucial requirement to any campaign at this time.

Eofer's barrow at Snape again is a historical reality. Dated to the mid sixth century, earlier than the burial field at Sutton Hoo ten miles to the south, the mounds were excavated in the nineteenth century. One barrow contained a ship burial, smaller than the famous one at Sutton Hoo, but containing the bones of a man with a sword, glass claw beaker and a magnificent gold ring. Known simply as the Snape Ring and now kept at the British Museum, I made sure to include it in my tale as a gift from Icel to Eofer in the final scene alongside the glass beaker from his old friend and neighbour, Coelwulf.

Old Shuck, Blæcce shucca or Snarly yowl is a hell-hound, one of many such demons found in local folklore all over Britain. Many of you will recall the death of the British sea wolf in book three of my earlier Sword of Woden series and his curse on the Engles at his sacrifice and burial on the Haigh, present day Sutton Hoo. Their appearance is said to presage death and destruction and I thought that it would add not only a local flavour to the tale, but aid the continuity between the series'.

Cliff May
East Anglia
June 2017

CHARACTERS

Ælfgar Eofering - Eofer's second son.

Alyn - A British boatman on the Trenta.

Anna - A youth.

Astrid Hygelacsdottir - Wife of Eofer, sister to Heardred king of Geats.

Bassa - A youth.

Beonna - A member of Hemming's hearth troop.

Beornwulf - A youth.

Blódulf - Blood-Wolf, the surviving bear shirt at the battle of Hreopedun.

Ceretic ap Cynfawr - Legate of Sawyl Penuchel, king of The Peaks.

Crawa - A youth, one of the dark twins.

Cueldgils - Son of Creoda, king of the Lindisware.

Cynfelyn - A British rustler, Ioan's trusted right-hand-man.

Cynlas Goch - Cynlas the Red - King of the British kingdom of Powys.

Editha - Astrid's *thyften*, her hand maid.

Einar Haraldson - A Geatish scout attached to Eofer's war band.

Eofer Wonreding - king's bane.

Eomær Engeltheowing - King of the English.

Feóndulf - Fiend-Wolf - A bear shirt killed at the battle of Hreopedun.

Finn - Eofer's youth, raised to the position of duguth following Hemming's departure.

Gildas - A British churchman. Later to become famous as the author of De Excidio et Conquestu Britanniae (The Ruin of Britain), one of the few contemporary accounts of events during the late fifth and early sixth centuries in Britain.

Grimwulf - A youth.

Gwynfor - A British spearman, friend and neighbour of Wihta.

Heardred Hygelacson - King of Geatland, Astrid's brother.

Horsa - A duguth. Succeeds Hemming as Eofer's weorthman following his departure.

Hræfen - A youth, one of the dark twins.

Hrothmund Hrothgarson - A Danish ætheling, in exile in Britain.

Hryp - A member of Hemming's hearth troop.

Icel Eomæring - Son of King Eomær of the Engles. The leader of the Iclings, the people who are fighting to establish the kingdom of Mercia.

Ioan - Leader of the British rustlers.

Octa - Eofer's duguth.

Osbeorn - Eofer's duguth.

Porta - A youth.

Sæward - Eofer's duguth and shipmaster.

Sawyl Penuchel - Sawyl the Arrogant - King of the British kingdom of The Peaks.

Seaxwine - Son of Seaxwulf Strang, captured at Cair Luit Coyt.

Seaxwulf Strang - Seaxwulf the Strong - Leader of the Saxon federates.

Sigmund - Hemming's weorthman.

Swinna - son of Wihta. Gifted Icel's knife before the army leave Leircestre for Hreopedun.

Tewdwr - Owner of the taverna which bears his name in Leircestre.

Thrush Hemming - Eofer's first weorthman. Later raised by

Icel to a thegn controlling the lands around Tamtun.

Weohstan Eofering - Son of Eofer. In Geatland at foster with his uncle, King Heardred.

Wealhtheow - Widow of King Hrothgar of Daneland and mother of Hrothmund.

Wihta - An Engle spearman. Father of Swinna, the best friend of his British neighbour, Gwynfor.

Wulf Wonreding - Eofer's brother, a member of King Eomær's personal guard, the gesith.

PLACES/LOCATIONS

Aldu - River Alde.

Alduburh - Aldeburgh, Suffolk.

Brunes Wald - Bromswold forest.

Bruidon - Breedon-on-the-Hill (Hill Hill-on-the-Hill!),
Leicestershire.

Cair Luit Coyt - Wall, Staffordshire.

Canoc - Cannock Chase.

Colnecestre - Colchester, Essex.

Fleama - Fleam Dyke, Cambridgeshire.

Grantebrycge - Cambridge, Cambridgeshire.

Hafron - River Severn.

Hreopedun - Repton, Derbyshire.

Isca - Exeter, Devon.

Leir - River Soar.

Leircestre /Ratae - Leicester, Leicestershire.

Lindcylene - Lincoln, Lincolnshire.

Pencric - Penkridge.

Snæpe - Snape, Suffolk.

Snotingaham/Tigguocobauc - Nottingham, Nottinghamshire.

Tamesas - River Thames.

Tamtun - Now part of Tamworth, Staffordshire.

Tamworthy - Tamworth, Staffordshire.

Trenta - River Trent.

ABOUT THE AUTHOR

I am writer of historical fiction, working primarily in the early Middle Ages. I have always had a love of history which led to an early career in conservation work. Using the knowledge and expertise gained we later moved as a family through a succession of dilapidated houses which I single-handedly renovated. These ranged from a Victorian townhouse to a Fourteenth Century hall, and I added childcare to my knowledge of medieval oak frame repair, wattle and daub and lime plastering. I have crewed the replica of Captain Cook's ship, Endeavour, sleeping in a hammock and sweating in the sails and travelled the world, visiting such historic sites as the Little Big Horn, Leif Eriksson's Icelandic birthplace and the bullet scarred walls of Berlin's Reichstag.

Now I write, only a stone's throw from the Anglian ship burial site at Sutton Hoo in East Anglia.

ALSO BY C.R.MAY

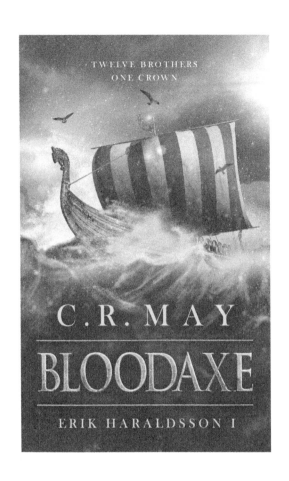

BLOODAXE

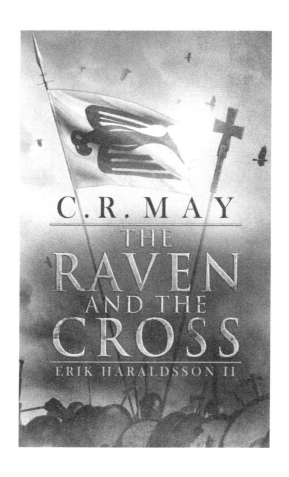

THE RAVEN AND THE CROSS

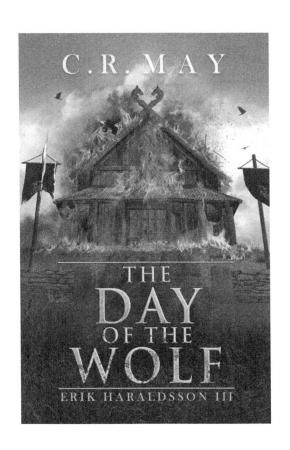

THE DAY OF THE WOLF

SPEAR HAVOC

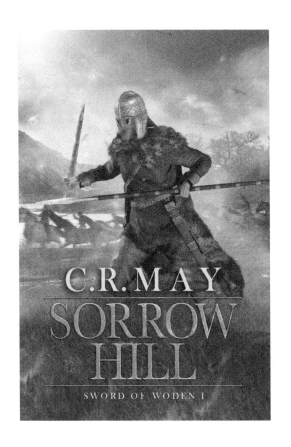

SORROW HILL

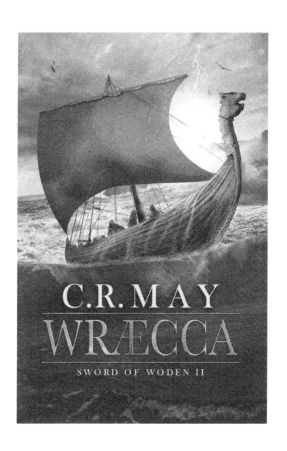

WRÆCCA

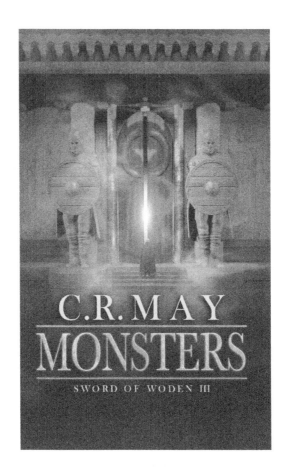

C.R. MAY

MONSTERS

SWORD OF WODEN III

MONSTERS

DAYRAVEN

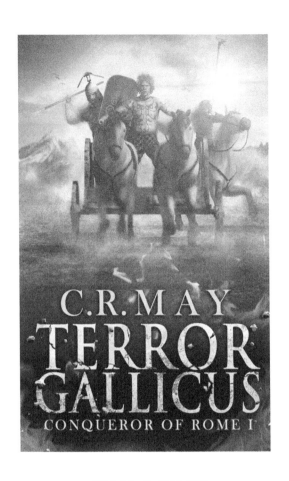

TERROR GALLICUS

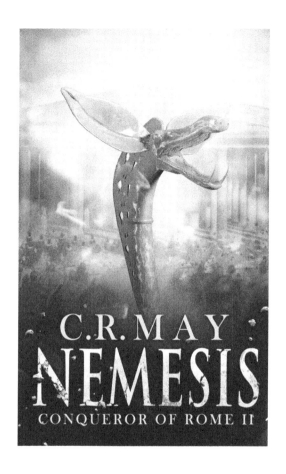

NEMESIS

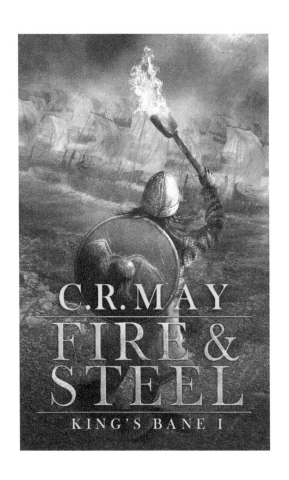

FIRE & STEEL

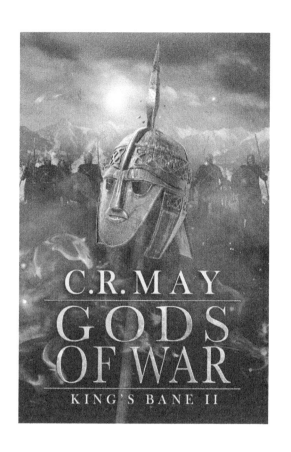

GODS OF WAR

Made in the USA
Monee, IL
04 May 2021

67586170R00198